Children
of Hachiman

Lynn Guest

THE BODLEY HEAD
LONDON SYDNEY
TORONTO

For my mother and my father

British Library Cataloguing
in Publication Data
Guest, Lynn
Children of Hachiman
1. Title
823'.9'IF PR6057.U4
ISBN 0–370–30311–3

© Lynn Guest 1980
Printed in Great Britain for
The Bodley Head Ltd
9 Bow Street London WC2E 7AL
by Redwood Burn Ltd
Trowbridge & Esher
set in Monophoto Imprint
by Keyspools Ltd, Golborne, Lancs
First published 1980

CONTENTS

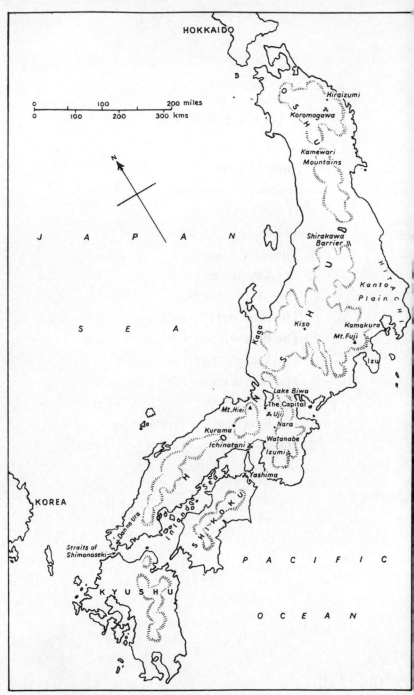

Medieval Japan

Author's Note

Medieval Japan resembled medieval Europe in that agriculture was the common way of life and land was the basis of the economy, owned by the Court, the Buddhist church and the great samurai lords. The soil was farmed by peasants, who paid rent in produce and labour, or by warrior-farmers who paid in produce and military service. Merchants, who would become so important to Japan later, lived in the few towns, despised by nobility and peasants alike as vulgar money-grabbers. Trade with China and Korea was controlled by a few enterprising samurai who did not mind dirtying their fingers on commerce for a good profit. The Buddhist monasteries were important centres of administration and culture but by the twelfth century they had become rich, corrupt and very warlike. The monks were the only group who never hesitated to take up arms against the government to get what they wanted. Shinto, the indigenous animist religion, existed alongside Buddhism, occasionally mingling with it. However, the Shinto shrines, with one or two exceptions, were rarely great landowners or politically active.

Until the twelfth century the country was amazingly stable and peaceful, governed by regents appointed from the wealthy and powerful Fujiwara family, ruling in the name of the Emperor, who was usually a child and always weak, a sacred figurehead believed to be descended in an unbroken line from the Sun Goddess. The Court resided in the capital, first Nara but from the eighth century onward, Kyoto. The Court and the Capital were the emotional heart of the country, so much so that the concept of rebellion against the Emperor was repugnant to most Japanese.

The Court hierarchy and procedure, based like so many Japanese things on a Chinese model carried to a static

extreme, ignored the production of wealth and local and national administration, regarding them as mundane matters best left to clerks. But food, dress, scent, painting, calligraphy, music, dance, poetry and love, the important things, were governed by formal and irrevocable rules, innovation and originality being firmly dampened. It was a world that was 'civilised' in both the best and worst senses of the word, a world totally isolated from the rest of the country. It was this that caused the downfall of the Fujiwara.

Each Emperor abdicated as a youth and was replaced by an infant; the former Emperor then took holy orders and retired to a separate palace thereafter referred to as the Cloister Court. By the twelfth century several of these retired Imperial monks chose not to withdraw from political life but, indeed, to take a more active part. Because these Cloistered Emperors were intelligent and ambitious the Cloister Court became the centre of intrigue against the established order – the Fujiwara regents. These sacred politicians did not want progress or change, only a share of the power. But the split caused in the Imperial Court left an opening for men who did want change – the powerful warrior class that was to dominate Japanese history for eight hundred years – the samurai.

The two major samurai clans, the Taira and the Minamoto, were descended originally from earlier Emperors; disinherited princes who had become provincial landowners and warlords attracting local men to their service as farmer-warriors, to fight, in the name of the Emperor, against the aboriginal tribes. When these tribes were driven north the clans took to fighting among themselves, acquiring considerable wealth in the process. One cadet branch of the Fujiwara family turned samurai and set up a marcher domain called Oshu to defend the north of Honshu against the aborigines. Far from the Capital, protected by high mountains and magnificent rivers, laced with gold mines, Oshu, under its samurai ruler, Fujiwara Hidehira, had a short fling as an independent kingdom.

The Taira held vast estates on the west coast and

controlled the profitable trade with China and Korea, while the Minamoto were centred on the rich farm land of the Kanto plain. The family 'seats' were usually no more than a fortress or a fortified village, and eventually the more successful and ambitious chieftains were attracted to life in the Capital, a few even serving as Court ministers. But the strength of the two clans remained in their provincial roots and it was because their authority covered the whole country that they became the real power in Japan. Although the samurai were regarded by the exquisite courtiers as crude and uncultured (most were), by 1160 the Fujiwara regent had formed an uneasy alliance with the Minamoto chieftain, Yoshitomo, against the Cloistered Emperor, Go-Shirakawa, who turned to Taira Kiyomori for assistance.

The wars that followed were very like Europe's medieval wars: ambitious, capable warriors each fought to establish their own dynasty as the single power behind a revered but weak throne, a throne that these unscrupulous men were prepared to manipulate for their own benefit. The church stood by, a powerful potential ally willing to be wooed on to one side or the other if the rewards were enticing enough. The peasants, unconsulted, endured and survived.

This colourful, romantic period of history has always attracted Japanese chroniclers, poets, playwrights and artists. We know that the Imperial family and the important samurai certainly existed, but their exploits and personalities have been so embellished by legend and chronicle, so operatically distorted by Kabuki and Noh drama that, except for the few facts about their accomplishments and their deaths, they have become men of glamour and mystery. As for the many subsidiary characters, we do not know whether they were real or the products of creative imagination. One can visit Benkei's tomb in the ruins of Hiraizumi but does the great monk really lie there? No one knows.

Important Characters

THE IMPERIAL FAMILY:

Go-Shirakawa, d. 1192 – the Cloistered Emperor
Emperor Takakura, d. 1181 – son of Go-Shirakawa
Emperor Antoku, d. 1185 – son of Takakura and Taira Tokuko

THE MINAMOTO FAMILY:

Yoshitomo, d. 1160 – chieftain of the Minamoto clan
Tomonaga, d. 1160 – Yoshitomo's son
Yoritomo, d. 1199 – Yoshitomo's son –
later chieftain of the clan
Noriyori, d. 1193 – Yoshitomo's son
Yoshitsuné, d. 1189 – Yoshitomo's son
Yorimasa, d. 1180 – Yoshitomo's uncle
Yukiiye, d. 1186 – Yoshitomo's brother
Yoshinaka, called Kiso, d. 1184 –
nephew of Yoshitomo and Yukiiye

THE TAIRA FAMILY:

Kiyomori, d. 1181 – chieftain of the clan
Munemori, d. 1185 – Kiyomori's son
Tomomori, d. 1185 – Kiyomori's son
Shigehira, d. 1185 – Kiyomori's son
Lady Nii, d. 1185 – Kiyomori's wife
Empress Tokuko, d. 1213 – Kiyomori's
daughter and Takakura's wife

THE OSHU FUJIWARA:

Fujiwara Hidehira, d. 1189 – chieftain of the clan
Yasuhira, d. 1189 – his son, later chieftain of the clan
Tadahira, d. 1189 – Hidehira's son

WARLORDS:

Lord Wada – a Minamoto
Lord Miura – a Taira who joined the Minamoto
Lord Kajiwara Kagetoki – a Taira who joined the Minamoto
Hojo Tokimasa – a Taira who joined the Minamoto

YOSHITSUNÉ'S RETAINERS:

Benkei – a monk
Hori Yataro – a samurai
Kisanda – a groom
Masachika, also known as Shomon, the Holy Man

THE WOMEN

Tokiwa – Yoshitomo's mistress and
mother of Yoshitsuné
Shizuka – a shrine dancer
Taira Tamako – Yoshitsuné's wife
Hojo Masako, d. 1225 – daughter of
Hojo Tokimasa and wife of Yoritomo

OTHERS

Oni-ichi Hogen – a Yin and Yang master
Asuka – his daughter
Imai – a retainer of Kiso's

1. The Sons

The youth lay sprawled on his back in the crisp snow; his oval face, furrowed with pain, faded to an ugly creamy colour accentuated by the pure white bed of snow. The lids and hollows of his closed eyes were the same dull grey as the winter sky. Only shuddering breaths proved that he still lived.

Around him stood three figures, two men and a young boy wrapped in bulky fur cloaks, each carrying a sword and a bow; quivers, spiky with arrows, hung on their backs. Their square powerful forms could only partially protect the dying boy from the wind and swirling snow and even as they watched, flakes began to settle over him like a premature shroud.

The youth's eyelids twitched. His lips moved stiffly in a painful attempt at speech, making a sound so faint that the elder of the men had to kneel, leaning over to make out what he was trying to say. Then the samurai rose, his coarse, heavily bearded face impassive.

'He wants me to kill him now, here. He is right. It is the only way.'

'How far until we reach Oi? Couldn't we carry him?' asked the second man, looking at his master, his deep-set eyes rimmed crimson with fatigue.

'It is impossible to say, especially in this snow. In any case, the Taira won't be far behind us now. You know as well as I do, Masachika, that we cannot afford to slow down. Not now.' His voice was gruff for he too was exhausted.

Masachika spoke again, deference and concern in his voice, 'Shall I do it, my lord?'

But Yoshitomo was already unsheathing his sword. 'No, it is my duty. I am his father.' He turned to the boy standing beside him. 'Yoritomo, go on to Kamakura before

this storm gets worse. Start now. Move as fast as you can.'
He looked into the boy's narrow eyes, experienced and cold
beyond their thirteen years. 'You are young but you fought
like a true samurai. Get to Kamakura and raise troops in
my name. If any of my sons survive, it will be you.' He
motioned to the boy lying in the snow. 'Bid him farewell
and a good journey to the Western Paradise.'

Only a slight hoarseness betrayed any emotion over the
task before him. Minamoto Yoshitomo had other sons –
infants – useless. But these two, Tomonaga and Yoritomo,
had fought bravely by his side for the last month, sharing
the elation of believing victory was theirs followed by
the dour knowledge of defeat. If Yoshitomo had been a
reflective man, he would not have hurled his family and his
clan into political intrigues he did not understand, but the
tutelary deity of the Minamoto was Hachiman, the God of
War, and Yoshitomo served him enthusiastically, without
too much thought. He had been called upon to fight his
enemies and that he had done valiantly. However, he did
not hide from himself that his rebellion had failed, that he
would be unlikely to invade the Capital again, that his
bitter rival, Taira Kiyomori, would pursue and punish his
family. Tomonaga, wounded in the attack on Kiyomori's
Rokuhara Palace, would be the first of his sons to die a
violent death. Yoshitomo did not believe he would be the
last.

Yoritomo prayed briefly over his elder brother and then
strode off, head down, into the snow. Patches of feverish
scarlet were beginning to blotch Tomonaga's face; his hard
young body, toughened by a soldier's life, quivered. The
manservant, Masachika, knelt and pulled out a rosary of
large wooden beads. Without emotion he recited the
formula to carry the boy to the Western Paradise as his
master, sword in hand, stood ready. With one swift
downward stroke Yoshitomo pierced his son's heart;
another clean blow severed Tomonaga's head. They threw
it into a ravine to save it from exhibition on top of a Taira
pike. Snow was already covering the headless corpse as the
two men pushed on to the east.

The district was hilly and heavily forested; snow, lying deep over thickets and gullies, made riding impossible and walking treacherous; it was not the ideal route for a speedy retreat, but there were many members of the Minamoto clan scattered about, mostly small landowners with at least a few samurai in their service, and the hope of gathering these men into a new army forced Yoshitomo to take this tortuous mountain road to his stronghold at Kamakura on the eastern plains.

Among these local Minamoto was Osada Tadamune, Yoshitomo's one time father-in-law, whose daughter, long forgotten, had died in childbirth years ago. After battling against a blinding snowstorm in the hills for several days Yoshitomo and Masachika finally made their way to Osada's fortified house, on a bluff protected by deep moats and palisades, over which flew the white banner of the Minamoto. Their welcome was cordial, indeed they seemed almost to be expected. Osada knew about the rebellion and the fighting in the Capital and he fulminated against the outrageous tyranny in which Taira Kiyomori held the Imperial Court. As he led the exhausted men to their quarters he promised twenty armed and mounted samurai to accompany them to Kamakura the next day – a rather generous promise, Yoshitomo thought, from a man noted for his avarice.

When Osada suggested a bath, Yoshitomo needed no further urging. His large frame ached with fatigue, old wounds and improperly cared-for new ones, and although he had had only two baths in his life, he remembered the comfort of the hot water and the pleasant rasping of the cleansing ash rubbed into his calloused hide.

Followed by Masachika he strode across the snow to the bath house, a small thatched hut with two tiny rooms: one, a fire-room where the water was heated, and the other, a bath-room with a huge wooden tub set squarely on the dirt floor. Blazing hot water poured through bamboo pipes from the fire-room cauldron to the bath. Groping blindly through the steam, Masachika unstrapped the sections of

his master's corselet and pulled off the thick bearskin boots. The Hachiman sword, a family heirloom of great value, lay on a sword rack in Yoshitomo's quarters, but he had worn his short sword and dirk to the bath house. These were put aside along with several cotton padded under-kimono, padded trousers and an over-jacket of stiffly embroidered brocade, soiled and torn from long wear and hard fighting. Yoshitomo had no intention, however, of bathing naked, a repulsive custom better left to the lower orders. Wearing a light cotton kimono, he eased himself gingerly into the tub as Masachika peered through the steam in fascination. Only the massive shoulders and the heavy dark head of his master remained above water level. Yoshitomo closed his eyes and relaxed.

There was no fine ash for washing. Masachika left the hut and hurried to the house to fetch it, returning a few minutes later with a box. His master still sat in the tub, but his head now lolled back against the rim. He did not greet the servant. As Masachika placed the box next to the tub he glanced at the silent man. Yoshitomo stared back. Masachika lowered his eyes. Blood poured from a wide gash in Yoshitomo's thick throat, staining the white kimono. Through the steam, the servant could see the bath water turning slowly to deep crimson.

The door to the fire-room gaped open on broken hinges.

*

Taira Kiyomori regarded Yoshitomo's concubine, kneeling before him, with the interest of a man who loves women and with the cold amusement of a victor. Lady Tokiwa had to endure his impertinent scrutiny for, as a prisoner of war, she was not allowed the normal feminine privilege of withdrawal behind concealing curtains. Considering what a crude soldier Yoshitomo had been, thought Kiyomori, she was surprisingly appealing – small and delicately boned, a tiny figure nearly overwhelmed by her many kimono puffing out about her and by the long, glossy sheet of black hair, gathered simply by a ribbon at the nape of her neck. Lady Tokiwa's features were perfect: chalky white

powder offset brown almond eyes and full red lips. Feathery eyebrows had been skilfully drawn in high on her forehead. The make-up concealed any visible traces of the weeks of anguish, confusion and physical terror that she must have suffered and this Kiyomori admired, hoping his own women would do as well in similar circumstances.

Curiosity satisfied, he allowed the customary screens draped with heavy silk gauze to be placed around her, accepting her modestly murmured gratitude with a curt nod. He stroked his long moustaches with a well-cared-for hand and said, 'Well, madam. You have eluded us since Yoshitomo's death but now you come to plead for the life of your mother and your infant son. Is that right?'

Lady Tokiwa replied in a low voice, 'I have returned to the Capital to place myself at your mercy, Lord Kiyomori. My mother is being held by a Taira samurai. She is an old woman, of no danger to anyone. I beg you to release her.'

'And where have you been – you and Yoshitomo's sons? My men have been searching for you for several weeks. It is only now that you make yourself and the brats available.'

The soft voice came slightly muffled from behind the screen, 'My lord, when Taira soldiers fired Yoshitomo's house I managed to escape with my own infant and with my step-son, a boy of five. His mother was a courtesan, now dead. We fled to the hills east of the Capital and took refuge in a convent.' She hesitated. 'It was not until Masachika, his servant, brought news of my husband's death and my mother's imprisonment that I realised you were searching for me. I came to you freely in the Rokuhara Palace with these innocent children.'

Tomomori, the second son of Kiyomori, said quickly, 'And this Masachika. We want him. Where is he?'

There was a distinct pause before the quiet voice behind the curtains continued, 'He accompanied me to the Capital and then disappeared. I do not know where he is but I believe he intends to take Holy Orders.'

'How convenient,' remarked Tomomori. Kiyomori looked at his son quizzically; he could not quite place the name Masachika, but he knew he should be able to.

5

Kiyomori, his two sons and Lady Tokiwa sat in the centre of a vast floor of shining polished boards. The men, cross-legged on reed mats, were arranged in a semi-circle facing the screen of curtains around their prisoner; their bright robes and Tomomori's steel corselet, lacquered in brilliant colours, glowed against the severity of the plain wooden walls and the dull brown and black kimono of the samurai, lesser members of the clan, who stood silently watching the interrogation. A lacquer vase holding a spray of late camellia broke the military formality of the room.

Munemori, Kiyomori's eldest son, sat on his father's right. He was an indecisive fool and looked it. His hands twisted nervously in his lap. He possessed an infuriating tendency always to agree with the last speaker, eyes flickering from face to face as he struggled through wafting clouds of confusion to come to a clear decision. It often depressed Kiyomori that after all his work to build and enrich the Taira clan his successor might be this wittering son. Even Tomomori, unsubtle and unimaginative as he was, would be far preferable.

Tomomori, a brusque, ruddy samurai who, despising the silk robes of his brother and father, wore a corselet and leggings everywhere but the Court, was bored by this interview and tapped his fingers on his iron fan to show it. Ridiculous to bother with the woman. Kill her and drown the brats and be done with it – she could tell them nothing, neither could the baby nor the five-year-old. But Yoritomo, the eldest surviving son of the defeated Yoshitomo, was another matter. Although only thirteen years old, he had fought in the rebellion and had been in his father's confidence. He had been captured near Kamakura by a zealous Taira retainer and had been brought to the Capital. Now he languished in a fortified room here in the Rokuhara Palace. Tomomori thought he should be tortured to extract information and then beheaded. He had said so but the others hesitated; Kiyomori because he did not want to appear too bloodthirsty in the Court's eyes and Munemori because Kiyomori had had the last word – so far. Tomomori respected his father's ability but sometimes

wished he was more of a samurai and less of a politician; for Kiyomori military details were not as interesting as manipulating Court ministers, and it was typical that although he had been told about Masachika's escape several times he had forgotten who the man was. Now Tomomori repeated the information impatiently.

'Masachika was in the fortress when Osada killed Yoshitomo in the bath house. He managed to escape with Yoshitomo's head and his sword, the Hachiman sword. Osada, because of his stupidity, received considerably less silver than he expected for his treachery,' Tomomori added drily. 'Naturally we want to find the servant and the sword, especially the sword as it is important to the Minamoto. Can we not dispense with this woman and question Yoritomo, who will at least be of some use to us? There are many rebels still to locate and destroy.'

Kiyomori nodded at the screen of curtains. 'What do you propose we do with her and the children?'

'My father, it is obvious,' barked Tomomori in exasperation. 'Even if we don't kill her, certainly the three boys must die. Yoshitomo would approve. He became chieftain of the Minamoto by murdering all the opposition in the clan. He had only one brother and one uncle left: one too stupid, the other too clever to bother him. He saved us a great deal of work but it is up to us to kill the rest.'

Kiyomori winced. Lady Tokiwa was a woman and her death was unimportant but he was becoming sick of slaughter. Why should she die? She was young and lovely, a loyal daughter and mother. Being the mistress of Yoshitomo, a coarse, bearded brute, could not have been pleasant for such a gentle creature. He stroked his carefully trimmed moustache thoughtfully and considered how pointless her death would be. The Court regarded political murder as barbaric and vulgar and although the courtiers were usually political fops in Kiyomori's opinion, the idea of Lady Tokiwa's murder did indeed seem distasteful.

Munemori piped up nervously, 'Yes, Tomomori is right. Yoshitomo killed all his Minamoto rivals. It is the judicial and accepted thing to do.'

Kiyomori shot him an irritated glance. 'The Taira and the Minamoto are both samurai clans who, despite being descendants of Emperors and designated to protect Emperors, are looked upon as savages by the courtiers. Perhaps we now have a chance to prove we are civilised.'

'Yes. Yes, quite. Spare the woman and the babies,' muttered Munemori.

'Just the woman,' growled Tomomori, 'not the sons.'

Kiyomori stared at the curtains. He thought he heard a stifled sob. 'The Taira do not want the same reputation for bloodshed as the Minamoto. The infants can be placed in temples. No one need know who they are – foundlings to be reared as monks.'

'And Yoritomo, the eldest son?' asked Tomomori sharply. 'The countryside is crawling with samurai loyal to the Minamoto. He is thirteen and an experienced soldier, probably the new chieftain of his clan.'

'Must the Taira execute thirteen-year-olds to remain in power?' rebuked Kiyomori, closing his eyes.

'Thirteen-year-olds grow up to be thirty-year-olds,' muttered Tomomori.

Munemori nodded in vacuous agreement, ignored by both men.

Kiyomori said, 'There is always exile. It is the traditional way of dealing with rebels. There has been too much bloodshed – far too much. Bloodshed causes more bloodshed and what do we gain?' Kiyomori summoned one of his warriors with a gesture. 'Take Lady Tokiwa to her son and step-son. Release her mother. Yoritomo is to be kept under strict guard until I have decided.' He turned to his sons. 'The Cloistered Emperor must be consulted, if only for appearances' sake, and he will no doubt prefer exile as a solution. I don't say he is right but we must consider all sides of the matter – political as well as military.'

He watched Lady Tokiwa's tiny figure shuffle out of the room between two tall samurai. How could such a delicate creature have tolerated Yoshitomo's vulgarities? Once again he caressed his neat moustache.

Tomomori ground his teeth in ill-concealed irritation. He knew Yoritomo would live.

*

Kiyomori struggled out of his palanquin and slid across the polished veranda of the Hojoji Palace, his bare feet entirely covered by long voluminous trousers of deep blue brocade that trailed out behind him. Full Court dress was one of his vanities and he paused to check that everything was perfect. He was particularly proud of this kimono, a magnificent violet silk heavily embroidered with silver and crimson camellias. His manservant deftly adjusted the stiff headdress and the ceremonial quiver of silver and black lacquer, both knocked askew in the cramped palanquin.

It was bitterly cold. In the bleak gardens, the ponds were frozen grey and the blossom scattered over the graceful bare boughs of a plum tree by the veranda were white and chill as death. Kiyomori shivered. This audience would not be pleasant.

The Imperial Guards made only cursory bows to the samurai as he swept into the wide empty hall.

Kiyomori arrived at the Hojoji Palace just as Go-Shirakawa, the Cloistered Emperor, had finished the afternoon recitation of the sutras. Religious duties sat light as swansdown on his plump shoulders and there was little that was ascetic about the appearance and surroundings of the Imperial monk. A sleek man with a smooth round face, small shrewd eyes and a wide sensual mouth, the former Emperor wore beautiful robes of plum and rose, falling open over his rotundity to display exquisite combinations of shade, pattern and texture painstakingly chosen. He sat on a cushion in a large, gracious room warmed by many bronze braziers. The fierce Capital winter was blocked out by superb screens painted in the Chinese style and heavy silk tapestries from Korea. By his side there was a gold and lacquer tray with wine and sweetmeats to refresh himself throughout his religious ordeal.

Kiyomori was kept waiting nearly an hour. He might be the most powerful man in the land in reality, but in ancient

Court procedure and to Go-Shirakawa he was still only a samurai. When the Taira chieftain was finally admitted, he knelt with bitter humbleness, touching his forehead to the floor.

'Lord Kiyomori, we greet you. What brings you to the Imperial Enclosure in such weather?' Go-Shirakawa sipped his warm saké.

Kiyomori, not invited to relax, head still down, spoke in a voice muffled by his violet silk sleeves. 'I hope the Sacred Highness is well and that the cold weather does not inconvenience him.'

'We are indeed well but it is not concern for our health that brings you here. Are there new developments?'

'Your Highness, Minamoto Yoritomo and the two infant sons of Lord Yoshitomo have been found and are now in the Rokuhara. We also have Lady Tokiwa.'

'Ah, the Lady Tokiwa. A most charming woman, extremely beautiful. What do you plan to do with her? Take her as a concubine? Spoils of war?' Go-Shirakawa smiled rather cruelly at the bowed head before him.

Kiyomori fumed against his sleeves. 'Your Highness, I came to consult with you before taking any action against the prisoners. The Taira are but your servants.'

'Quite,' rejoined Go-Shirakawa, lifting the delicate celadon cup. 'Our feeling is that we have had enough unpleasantness, but naturally you of the samurai have your own ways of dealing with things. The Taira and the Minamoto have been murdering each other for decades. No doubt you intend to continue.'

Kiyomori said icily, 'The Minamoto are provincial barbarians who slaughter for power. The Taira do not. I do not wish any more bloodshed than necessary. Perhaps Lady Tokiwa and her young sons could be sent to a convent.'

'Sit up, Kiyomori! It is impossible to hear you clearly. You are mumbling into your sleeves. A warrior can hardly need so many kimono and so much padding. We frail monks living an ascetic life must have protection from the Capital winter, but a hardy soldier like you! You pamper

yourself.' The Cloistered Emperor sipped more saké.

Kiyomori sat back on his heels but kept his eyes on the floor until his temper was totally under control. Go-Shirakawa continued sweetly, 'A religious life could be the answer for the two younger sons, but what a pity to incarcerate such a lovely creature as Tokiwa in a nunnery with a shaved head and drab robes.' The Imperial monk's plump face reflected genuine regret at such a fate. 'By all means send the boys to Kurama as pages for the religious life but we are sure you can think of a better use for Lady Tokiwa. No doubt she will be most grateful to see her lover's children spared. The problem would seem to be the eldest surviving son.'

'Yes, Your Highness. Yoritomo is thirteen and well trained in martial skills. He fought with his father in the attack on the Rokuhara.'

'And, therefore, he should die?'

Kiyomori replied firmly, 'Death is not always the samurai way but it cannot be denied that his presence in the Capital is dangerous ... Perhaps exile, the traditional punishment?'

'It was certainly the punishment in more traditional times,' said Go-Shirakawa drily. 'Then exile shall be the solution. Some grim isolated spot far from the Capital.' He gracefully stifled a yawn. 'Or behead him. Really, I leave the choice to you.'

'There have been enough deaths. Perhaps Your Highness has a guardian in mind for the boy?' Kiyomori was willing to let his sleek opponent have his way in that.

Go-Shirakawa tipped his round head on one side, his eyes narrowed to mere slits as he pondered. 'There is the Hojo family in Izu. Hojo Tokimasa fought with us against the Minamoto and will want some recognition for his services. Besides, he is a member of your clan.'

A particularly ambitious and unreliable member, thought Kiyomori, but he replied, 'A highly capable man and an excellent choice, Your Highness. I shall arrange it. The young children will be sent to temples in Kurama.'

'And Lady Tokiwa?'

'She shall remain in my household where she can be watched.' Kiyomori started to stroke his moustaches but remembered where he was and stayed his hand.

Go-Shirakawa smiled his sweet, not very pleasant smile. 'What an original solution. As for the rest of the clan, Minamoto Yorimasa, Yoshitomo's uncle, will continue at the Court. He remained loyal during the rebellion and he is old. The rest of the immediate family are dead, we believe, except for Yoshitomo's foolish brother, Yukiiye, who has fled?'

Kiyomori bowed in assent.

'Later we shall discuss your own rewards. You will wish, perhaps, to augment your lands in the west, on the Inland Sea, since the trade with the Chinese seems so profitable. And a title as well. Lord Chancellor? But now, before your return do take a little saké.' He turned to the servant in the shadows behind him. 'Tametoki, bring a cup for our samurai friend.'

After Kiyomori's departure Go-Shirakawa called Tametoki again. The servant approached from the gloom where he waited in constant attendance, a respectful distance from the pleasant warmth of the braziers.

'A message is to be sent to Hojo Tokimasa in Izu. Remind him that he is the servant of the Cloister Court before all else. He will bear in mind that he, and his new ward, may be called upon to serve the Cloistered Emperor at some later date. No one is to hear the message but Tokimasa himself. Go.'

Go-Shirakawa settled himself comfortably on his cushion and popped a sweetmeat into his mouth.

*

In the early spring two parties of Taira soldiers set out from the Rokuhara Palace. One group travelled eastwards to the rugged Izu peninsula where the thirteen-year-old Yoritomo was delivered into the care of Hojo Tokimasa with instructions forbidding the boy martial training and any contact with Minamoto partisans. Yoritomo, sullen and uncooperative, refused to eat or speak.

The second party left the Capital and rode westward to the Kurama Mountains, the site of several large monasteries where Yoshitomo's two youngest sons were deposited. Five-year-old Noriyori was presented as a novice to a large temple in the foothills. His half-brother, Yoshitsuné, a baby of less than a year, was carried up to Kurama Temple to become a page.

His mother, the Lady Tokiwa, moved into the women's quarters of the Rokuhara Palace. Within a year she had borne Kiyomori a daughter.

2. The Holy Man

Yoshitsuné strutted down the steep path between the sutra hall and the armoury, one hand proudly resting on the hilt of his new wooden sword. It was too long for him, just as his leather corselet was a little too large and needed a thickly padded underjacket to keep it from chafing. Behind the armoury was a flat dusty space dotted with large bales of hay; monks, their saffron robes bound up for easy movement, jabbed and thrust at these bales with halberds. Yoshitsuné strode into the centre of the practice yard and stood, spread-legged, his small head cocked in an arrogant pose. One of the monks, scarred and gnarled, caught sight of the boy and stopped, wiping the sweat from his pitted face with a knotted, dirty forearm.

'Here, look at this!' He tugged the deep yellow robe of his neighbour. 'What have we here?' Several of the monks stopped to look at the child, decked out in his leather armour. One wandered over to examine him. 'Where did you get that?'

The boy answered in a high firm voice, 'It was a presentation from the Abbot. I am ten today and it is time I had a sword and a corselet if I am to be a fighting monk of Kurama!'

'I thought a fighting anything was the last thing he was supposed to be,' muttered the gnarled monk to his friend, a wiry youth who leaned on his halberd and gazed raptly at the boy. 'The Abbot heard me telling him stories about Hachiman Taro and gave me a tongue-lashing for filling his head with samurai lore.'

'But look at him! A little samurai if ever there was one. The Abbot knows he'll never make a monk of him. Not now that we're forbidden to fight.' He banged his halberd in the dust and laughed.

'I just don't understand. The Abbot defies Kiyomori,

14

head of the Taira clan, and gives the child a wooden sword. But he forbids us to tackle those bastards at the Mount Hiei monasteries or let us march on the Capital to demand our rights.'

'If we attack Mount Hiei we'd have to fight the Taira as well as the monks. It's too much to take on. The Abbot knows it and so does Kiyomori. Anyway, the sword is only a toy and Kiyomori will never find out.' He called over to the boy, 'Show us your marvellous new weapon.'

Kurama was a monastery noted for its bellicose monks – only Mount Hiei had a fiercer reputation. Kiyomori's most popular political move had been to confront these fearsome warriors of Buddha and force them into an uneasy peace with one another, but the bonzes kept their weapons sharp and growled challenges regularly at their old enemies.

Yoshitsuné preened and strutted, his child's top-knot gleaming in the sun and his smooth cheeks glowing with excitement and pride. He had only come, he claimed, to find Kenzo who was to be his teacher, but he was obviously enjoying himself. The monks laughed and teased him – few believed that their small charge would take religious vows, despite Taira orders.

Kenzo, young and moon-faced with a well developed right arm, began to show the boy some essential sword strokes while the others drifted back to their practice. Yoshitsuné, eyes sparkling, clutched the hilt with small hands and swung his sword in an arc over his head. Kenzo made him repeat the exercise again and again, but the boy never tired and each time he tried to increase the arc.

A man walked around the corner of the sutra hall and stood watching the scene. Although very thin, he was tall and broad-shouldered. A clean, faded robe hung loosely on his gaunt frame. His face was shaded by a large sedge-reed hat and he carried a begging bowl and a staff. Slowly he removed the hat to reveal a long, lean face, dominated by a pair of deep-set intense eyes. After watching a few minutes he walked over to Kenzo and Yoshitsuné.

'Well, my son. This is a change from Chinese classics

and flute practice. I trust you said your prayers this morning?'

Yositsuné bowed. 'Yes, Shomon, I said my prayers and read some of the Lotus Sutra and practised my calligraphy and the flute. But swordsmanship is important for a man; the Abbot agrees and has given me this himself.' He held out the beautifully carved sword.

Shomon nodded gravely. 'The body must be trained as well as the mind and the soul.' He turned to Kenzo. 'His swing seems promising – train him carefully.' His powerful gaze fixed on Kenzo's round face; the monk stared back in fascination until Shomon turned and disappeared down the path to the main temple compound.

Kenzo beamed at Yoshitsuné. 'You made a ·good impression on the Holy Man of Shijo, so now get back to work so that we can impress him even more.'

The scarred monk muttered to his neighbour, 'Doesn't it strike you as odd that a holy man like Shomon would encourage the boy? You would think he'd want him to fast and pray. The child is intelligent and well-born, a potential abbot at least.'

'There's more in it than just that. If Yoshitsuné is a Minamoto as it is rumoured, why isn't he in a minor house instead of a big monastery with a military reputation?'

'Easier to watch?' The other shrugged. 'Anyway, Kiyomori thinks he has pulled our teeth. We are supposed just to pray and pay our rice taxes.'

*

Shomon visited Kurama regularly. Nothing was known about him except that he lived a simple, ascetic life, using the Shijo Temple in the Capital as a base for his wanderings around the countryside. Welcomed by various abbots who respected his fervour and piety, he was regarded as a good influence on their unruly congregations. His interest in Yoshitsuné was considerable, not only in his spiritual training but in his intellectual and physical development, and the boy admired the Holy Man,

although he was a little awe-struck by his commanding eyes and gentle but stern manners.

One day soon after Yoshitsuné's twelfth birthday Shomon arrived at Kurama with a begging bowl and a rosary as usual but also with a mysterious long bundle wrapped in faded crimson silk. That evening after prayers Shomon went to Yoshitsuné's room, a tiny cell-like enclosure separated from the others by a thin partition, barely more than a screen. The two sat on the wooden floor with the silk-wrapped bundle between them. Shomon studied the boy's face, an oval with childish but perfect small features, the same face as Tomonaga, who had died in the snow at his father's hand, and Yoritomo, exiled to the lands of Hojo Tokimasa.

'Who are you, boy, do you know?' demanded the monk suddenly.

'Yoshitsuné, the son of Yoshitomo, and the ward of Kurama Temple.'

'Why are you here in Kurama? Where is your father, your family?'

'My father is dead. I am told he was a rebel, that he plotted against the Imperial family. As for my family, I do not know. Perhaps they are all dead. So the Abbot says. Why do you suddenly ask me all these questions, Shomon? What does a holy man have to do with such things?'

Shomon smiled and shook his bald head. 'It is time you learned something of your past and your future, Yoshitsuné. My name before I took holy vows was Masachika. Your father was Minamoto Yoshitomo, chieftain of the Minamoto clan, and I was your father's manservant, the man who helped him put on his armour for his first battle and his last, and it was I who found him dead, murdered by a traitor.' His voice became hard. 'I took his head and his sword to preserve them from indignity at Taira hands and escaped through the mountains. The head I buried deep in the snow – it never stood on a pike at the Rokuhara Palace. The sword I kept with me.' He indicated the bundle. 'It is here. You will carry it from now on to avenge Yoshitomo's death.'

Yoshitsuné stared at the man and then at the bundle. Shomon's eyes glowed fiercely back at him. The gentle mouth so accustomed to holy sutras was a thin firm line.

'Revenge? Against who?' the boy asked eagerly.

'Against the tyrant Kiyomori and his clan, the Taira.'

'Kiyomori is the Lord Chancellor and the servant of the Emperor. It would be like striking a blow at the Sun Goddess herself,' said the young student of Buddha primly.

Shomon snorted. 'Ha! You've been well taught. The Abbot is a weak but pious man. He thought he had to rear you on lies to save your skin. He wishes to deny you your samurai blood.

'Kiyomori is no one's servant. Oh, he pretends to obey the will of the Cloistered Emperor who pretends to advise his son, the Emperor Takakura, but in fact Kiyomori is the ruler of the land. Go-Shirakawa is only a cypher for this ambitious Lord Chancellor. Already there are many Taira in high positions in the Court and the Emperor Takakura has taken Kiyomori's daughter as his consort. A samurai Empress! The clan control everything from the ministers of the Court to the thugs of the Special Guard who prowl the streets of the Capital. The chieftain of the Taira makes himself and his clan rich on wealth wrung from the people while they starve. Even the great temples at Mount Hiei and here at Kurama swallow his authority and pay great rice taxes.' Shomon flicked the thin wall of the cell with contemptuous fingers but his voice was low enough to escape eavesdroppers. 'One man tried to thwart this Taira ambition. Your father. Yoshitomo fought the Taira with the approval of the Court and, indeed, of the late Emperor, but the Cloister Court under Go-Shirakawa supported Kiyomori and tricked your father. He died and the Minamoto clan plunged into disgrace.' Shomon leaned closer to the boy. 'But this won't last. As Shomon the Holy Man, I travel the whole country searching out members of the clan who survive in poverty: the poor samurai struggling on his plot of land and the ruined warlords, they want to talk to me. The Minamoto have often quarrelled

among themselves but now all desire the same thing. They are waiting!' he finished with a flourish of triumph.

'For what are they waiting?' Yoshitsuné asked softly.

'For a new chieftain.'

'And will he be me?' The boy's eyes were wide with the anticipation of glory.

'It is unlikely. You may have great gifts but you also have a cousin and two brothers who are older and more than competent.' Shomon ignored his disappointment and asked, 'Tell me, Yoshitsuné, do you know who Hachiman Taro was?'

'Oh, yes! He was a samurai but he was the greatest warrior that ever lived – the most wonderful swordsman, the most brilliant general. Why, he could fly through the air! Wait!' He stared at Shomon. 'I remember now. The people gave him the name Hachiman Taro – the first born of the War God – because he served Hachiman so well, but I remember now that his real name was Minamoto Yoshiie! Oh, Shomon, he was one of *us*!' His black eyes sparkled.

'He was your ancestor, your great, great-grandfather and, although I doubt he did actually fly through the air, he was indeed a very fine warrior.'

'Oh,' breathed Yoshitsuné. 'My great-grandfather! Wait until the monks know of this! They are always telling me stories of him.'

'Do they tell you about his sword?'

'It was the most magnificent sword ever forged. Some say Lord Hachiman forged it himself. Was it a real sword?'

Shomon looked down at the long slim bundle wrapped in red silk lying between them.

'That? Is that it?'

'That is it. It was passed through the family to your father. I rescued it from the Taira when Yoshitomo was murdered and have kept it safe for twelve years. Now it is time to pass it on. Lord Yorimasa, the old uncle of your father, and I have discussed it at length and we think it should go to you. You may be a great warrior some day, as great as your ancestor.'

Yoshitsuné looked at the bundle again. To own such a sword would be more than consolation for not being chieftain, but he was puzzled. If he were not to be chieftain, why should he have the sword?

Shomon answered the unspoken question. 'I have seen both your eldest brother, Yoritomo, in Izu, and Noriyori, your other brother who is only a few miles from here at another temple. I have even managed to find your cousin who was believed dead.' Shomon did not add, believed murdered by Yoshitomo. 'He lives in the mountain village of Kiso from which he takes his name. Despite Kiyomori's orders all three have been secretly taught the martial arts and all three are proficient. Several times a year I check their progress as I have checked yours. It is strange – although you look smaller and weaker you have shown greater promise as a swordsman.' Yoshitsuné's eyes shone with excitement as Shomon continued, 'Your brother, Yoritomo, and your cousin, Kiso, are grown men in their twenties and Noriyori is seventeen – they are good swordsmen but I have no doubt you will be better; that with luck and good training you may make an extraordinary swordsman. It is for that reason that I am passing the sword of Hachiman to you to use in the service of your clan.'

Mollified, for after all to be a famous warrior is an honour perhaps even greater than that of being chieftain of your clan, Yoshitsuné begged to see the sword. Reverently Shomon unwrapped the layers of faded silk, so old that parts of it crumbled in his hands. Suddenly chill steel flashed through the dusty crimson folds. The sword lay between them, gleaming in the lantern light. Shomon lifted it and held it out for inspection, the point resting flat on his sleeve.

The hilt was disappointingly ordinary, wood bound in sharkskin, rather worn and stained with sweat; the iron guard was inlaid with a simple design. But the blade – the blade was truly fit for a war god. As long as a man's arm and subtly curved, it was of the finest steel, perfectly welded to a tough iron core with a cutting edge tempered to razor

20

sharpness. On one side the Chinese characters for Hachiman, the Great Bodhisattva, were engraved; on the other, near the guard, there were eight tiny ideographs. Yoshitsuné peered closer. Each exquisitely carved ideograph represented one of the eight virtues: correct views, correct thinking, correct speech, correct activity, correct life, correct devotion, correct conception and the correct way. The ideal message for an instrument of death.

'May I take it?' He reached out a hand towards the hilt, stained with the sweat of his ancestors. Shomon nodded and the boy seized the sword and stood with it. The balance was perfect. He could feel the tense steel vibrating from the blade through the hilt to his hand. The sword seemed to become part of him, an extension of his being.

Shomon watched him gravely. 'Yes,' he said quietly, 'it was right to save the Hachiman sword for you. The others never held it as you do. Their faces never looked as yours does now.'

'I shall avenge my father's death immediately with the sword of my ancestors!' cried the boy.

'No, you are not yet ready for retribution. The sword must be wrapped again and put in a safe place until you are worthy of it.' He held out his hand.

For a few seconds Yoshitsuné obstinately grasped the sword. 'It is mine, the gift of Hachiman to the descendants of an Emperor.'

'It belongs to the Minamoto, of which you are the youngest child.' Shomon snapped his fingers. Reluctantly Yoshitsuné placed the sword in his hands and sat down cross-legged.

As he wrapped the weapon in its crimson protection Shomon spoke to the boy in a low firm tone, revealing plans and dreams that were too important to be endangered by an arrogant, untried boy.

'Most of the clan is scattered, living in obscurity, but there is one, Lord Yorimasa, your father's uncle, who is a respected member of the Court and a famous poet and it is he who leads us. Because he had never shown an interest in military affairs and because he is a learned gentleman the

Taira made no move to destroy him after the rebellion.' Shomon's attitude was respectful but cool. 'But he is proving to be a true samurai despite the life he leads. For years he has plotted quietly to restore the Minamoto as the supreme samurai family. He is old, so I am his arms and legs. I report to him on each of his young relatives but of course he will decide finally whether Kiso or Yoritomo will be chieftain and whether you will keep the sword.' Shomon's fierce eyes blazed at the boy and after a few seconds Yoshitsuné was forced to look away. Shomon continued calmly, 'If we do not have the blessing of the Imperial family to drive out the Taira we will be no more than outlaws. Only Yorimasa, on good terms with the Cloister Court, can win us that blessing. We have reason to believe the Cloistered Emperor wishes to be rid of his Taira "advisers".'

Yoshitsuné shifted restlessly, too young to understand or care about old poets and Imperial whims. Accepting this, Shomon switched to more pertinent matters. 'You, boy, have much to learn. You will stay here and continue your studies; we shall make you into a fine swordsman. Kenzo has taught you well but now others, monks of Kurama, as skilful as anyone in the land, will be your teachers. When we are ready you will be summoned.'

'How long? How long must I wait?'

Shomon sighed. 'I am afraid that you may have to wait years: the clan must be reorganised and we should win some other support – that of the great Lord Fujiwara Hidehira in Oshu, for example. But you must not become discouraged. Our enemy, Taira Kiyomori, is old, but Yoshitomo's sons are young and these things cannot be done quickly.

'I must return to my quarters now. Keep the sword in a safe place. It binds you to your ancestors.'

Shomon's instructions were followed closely. Every night Yoshitsuné slipped away to his professors, tough, cold-eyed monks who loved sharp steel far more than the smooth beads of a rosary. They taught Yoshitsuné the names of the Taira family, and he would slash with his

sword at bushes and trees named Munemori, Tomomori and Kiyomori, his skill growing each month until even his teachers were awed.

The Abbot watched sadly as the child turned into a youth. There was no question now of his taking holy vows, and as he became increasingly enthralled with his sword and its mastery, his conviction of his own future as a great warrior strengthened. The old man knew it was only a matter of time before Yoshitsuné left the temple for ever.

*

In Izu, the banished Yoritomo developed from a taciturn, watchful boy into a young man, suspicious, independent and highly intelligent. He met with Shomon regularly, devouring information about the Court and the Taira organisation at the Rokuhara Palace. But he kept his own counsel; Shomon found him inaccesssible although he respected his quick mind and ready grasp of any situation. Yoritomo begged practice in the martial arts from various sympathetic samurai in the service of his guardian, Hojo Tokimasa, and Tokimasa turned a blind eye to these lessons, obeying the implied wishes of the Cloistered Emperor, Go-Shirakawa. The youth was a competent swordsman and an excellent horseman but Shomon was sure that his skills were chiefly intellectual.

The only person to whom Yoritomo had shown affection was Lady Masako, the astute daughter of his guardian. She had been promised to an important Taira landowner, a good marriage to reward the Hojo commitment to the Rokuhara. The night before she was to go to the mansion of her betrothed she disappeared from the women's quarters; Yoritomo was also discovered missing. Hojo Tokimasa gave noisy but ineffectual chase; but when the lovers returned to the fortress they were accepted as husband and wife. The Rokuhara complained; Hojo Tokimasa made apologies; Go-Shirakawa smirked in the Hojoji Palace. In fact, Hojo Tokimasa was not at all displeased with his new son-in-law, whom he found impressively intelligent. Besides, he bore the Minamoto clan no grudge and was

irritated by his own slow advancement under Kiyomori and the Taira. He treated his rebel ward as a son, knowing this would please Go-Shirakawa.

In the foothills of Kurama, Noriyori, the remaining brother, also trained secretly. He was an amiable, generous man, much liked by the monks. Shomon found him not unintelligent but rather lazy and far too good-natured to be ambitious. Any spare time was spent in the local tea houses and saké shops, surrounded by country prostitutes and ageing courtesans who had retired from life in the Capital.

On his eighteenth birthday a party of Taira samurai came from the Rokuhara Palace with orders for Noriyori to shave his head and take his vows as a monk immediately. That night he disappeared. Eighteen much-enjoyed months later he turned up quietly at Izu to join his older brother at the fortress of Hojo Tokimasa.

3. The Capital

A pathetic group of hovels lay directly in front of the West Gate of the city; Yoshitsuné picked his way around stinking heaps of rubbish, avoiding a yellow dog that was too hot and emaciated to growl, and passed through the dilapidated gate. There was no guardhouse and no guards, nor would they have served any purpose – a child could have climbed over the collapsing walls of the Imperial Capital. The youth took off his sedge hat and wiped his face on his sleeve. Before him stretched a wide, straight avenue, rutted and choked with weeds; to his left and right ran another street, but stone and debris from the useless wall blocked it in both directions. The scent of fox came strong and acrid. He began to walk down the avenue, which was lined by more tumbled walls.

Heat lay over the city like a gauze veil, even the children and animals lay smothered and lifeless in whatever shade could be found. The willows drooped, wilting in the merciless glare. But Yoshitsuné kept moving, driven by a terrible thirst from the dry, dusty roads he had travelled that day. In a deserted courtyard he saw a well, but a quick sniff told him something putrefied in its depths. Ragged washing hung over the railing of a teetering veranda but when he approached the house a large dog ran out, grimacing with the ferocity of its greeting. Yoshitsuné sighed and went on his way. A canal bisected the avenue; the water was foul but he walked along it towards a stream. In the hills the streams bubbled even in the summer but here in the valley they became pathetic trickles. He scooped just enough to wash the coating of dust off his tongue and his throat and then he sank down under a listless willow to rest. The cicadas drummed steadily. He was too dejected to doze, too depressed by the unexpected squalor of the fabled Imperial Capital. What a city for the

descendants of the Sun Goddess!

Conscious of being watched, he glanced up. A girl stood in front of him, dressed in a greasy cotton kimono only loosely sashed at the waist and hanging open to reveal her breasts. Yoshitsuné, accustomed only to country women or the occasional aristocratic pilgrim, found this coyly immodest behaviour shocking. The girl squatted down and slowly lifted her thick hair to dab at her grubby neck with a piece of paper. 'It's hot!' she said abruptly. Her face was round and so were her eyes, she had neither blacked her teeth nor plucked her eyebrows away. A very cheap whore, he realised with sudden insight.

'We don't see your kind around here too often. Is that a sword in your sash? Are you a samurai?' She guffawed at the idea, much to Yoshitsuné's annoyance.

He looked at her coldly. 'It is a sword and I am a samurai. I have come to the Capital to serve . . .' He halted. Pride had almost made him give himself away. 'I'm thirsty. Where can I find something to drink?'

She watched him shrewdly, studying the smooth oval of his face, the wide, black eyes and the well-shaped mouth. His hair was tied up in a top-knot under a black cap and that to her meant a gentleman with cash. But his age she could not decide – his body would have been boyish, if it weren't for the powerful shoulders and calloused hands. Still, she thought, he was worth a try. Business was slow in this heat.

'What a broad pair of shoulders! Got any money?' She poked him with her finger and smiled. 'I could give you a good time, samurai or no.'

Yoshitsuné struggled to his feet, suddenly aware of his young body and his plain unmarked kimono. Perhaps he didn't really look like a samurai yet, but a whore was not going to laugh at Minamoto Yoshitsuné. He kicked out at her with his sandal. Surprised, she landed flat on her bottom, her mouth agape.

Yoshitsuné straightened his shoulders and barked, 'Now, tell me where I can find something to eat and drink in this place.'

26

The girl pulled her kimono together and scrambled up. Backing away she pointed along to the avenue. 'There are some stalls down there, but they're poor things. You won't find anything to suit you until you get to the eastern half.' She turned and scurried away along the canal bank.

Refreshed by his success, Yoshitsuné strode along the avenue until he found a noodle stall under a chestnut tree. A dirty canopy stretched over a few jugs of saké and a brazier for the cooking pot. The proprietor crouched down in the shade, ignoring the youth. With his new-found confidence, Yoshitsuné loudly commanded noodles and watched with pleasure as the proprietor leapt to his feet, bowed, hitched up his loin cloth and quickly filled a thick pottery bowl with cold noodles and soup. Yoshitsuné gulped down three bowls full, threw a string of cash to the man and said imperiously, 'Direct me to the Shijo Temple.'

The proprietor bowed again. 'That's easy, my lord. It's in the eastern part of the city. If you walk north on the boulevard you will see the walls of the Imperial Enclosure before you. Turn left on Shijo Avenue just before the main gates and follow it until you come to the temple.'

The Imperial Enclosure! As he hurried eastward the houses looked richer, long and low and set in gardens. There were more people on the street, languid in the heat, but clean and dressed in neat kimono. He passed through a market place; only a few stalls for cold noodles, bamboo fans or caged cicadas attracted business while the rest of the merchants dozed over their wares. Idlers drowsed under trees waiting for the sun to set and bring some slight relief.

Suddenly the avenue debouched into a broad boulevard, as broad as three avenues, lined by canals over which dangled tall willows, superb even in the heat. Behind them stood freshly plastered walls broken here and there by the red lacquered gates of mansions. Towering over the walls, paulownia and cedar trees shaded gracefully dipping tile roofs from the late sun. A few strollers and horsemen moved along the great highway. A palanquin hurried past, carried by sweating, grunting bearers; Yoshitsuné caught a

glimpse of shimmering silk through the lowered blind.

The Imperial Enclosure blocked the north end of the boulevard. Yoshitsuné stood and stared at the sun glittering on the red and gilt gates and on the spears of the Imperial Guard, his new sense of authority vanishing in the awed wonder of a newcomer from the country. Clattering hooves brought him back to reality and he jumped clear of a group of horsemen trotting down the middle of the street. Each man had a red band on his head and a red cloak with the Taira crest. The last man sneered down at the startled youth, 'Get out of the way!' and slashed at him with his iron fan.

Yoshitsuné felt a sharp elbow in his ribs. He had fallen back against a pedlar of crickets who was pushing him away so that he could gather up the tiny bamboo cages jarred off his cart. The pedlar glared at Yoshitsuné and then spat fiercely after the samurai. 'Taira bastards!'

Yoshitsuné stared at the horsemen trotting through the gates of the Imperial Enclosure. His only contact with the Taira had been pot-bellied agents calling at Kurama – bureaucrats, hardly men at all. But these were Taira samurai, killers. He shivered in the heat.

The Capital was a grid. Streets and canals ran north to south, east to west; the Imperial Enclosure dominated the northern quarter; the Rashomon Gate, even though dilapidated, still commanded the south. The north-east, crammed with temples and palaces, was prosperous and safe but the rest of the city had fallen with the times into ruin – what the Taira could not use they ignored.

The Shijo Temple was easy to find but Yoshitsuné walked past it, down to the Kamo River flowing sluggishly from the hills lined by broad beaches and spanned by graceful wooden bridges. Children played in the reedy shallows, their cries of pleasure dulled in the hot, still air. Yoshitsuné closed his dust-rimmed eyes to remember the rivers he had left behind in Kurama, cool and splashing and refreshing. The stink and noise of the town blanketed him. It had been a long day and the most difficult part was still to come. He wiped his face and went back to the temple.

28

At the gates a monk directed him through the complex of buildings, past the Buddha hall, gold gleaming silently from its dim interior, and past a delicate pagoda of wood and gilt, the first he had seen, to a small hut under an aged ginko tree – the cell of the Holy Man of Shijo.

Yoshitsuné called softly, 'Shomon, are you there?'

The door of the hut slid back and the Holy Man peered out. He nodded. 'Yoshitsuné. Welcome to the Capital. Come inside so that we can talk.'

Nonplussed by the matter-of-fact greeting, Yoshitsuné removed his sandals and stepped into the stifling single room furnished only with a leather chest, a shelf with a couple of bowls and a small closed altar on the wall. He bowed respectfully to the Holy Man. Shomon settled himself on the bare floor and gestured for the boy to do the same.

'I ran away,' blurted Yoshitsuné. 'The pressure to take vows was too great. The Taira would have turned on the Abbot soon so I left. Noriyori has been in Izu with Yoritomo for a long time. Now that I'm seventeen I think I should be there too, with my brothers. I only came to tell you that I'm on my way.' He bowed again, nervously.

'You are no such thing,' said Shomon sharply. 'Since you're here you'll be far more useful in the Capital.' He ignored Yoshitsuné's grimace. 'Noriyori and Yoritomo are just waiting, getting bad-tempered, hoping for some excuse to fight. Kiyomori and the Taira are arrogant and unpopular, but they are also careful. No false steps. No action. Yet.'

'What can I do here?' Yoshitsuné thought that if he had known Shomon would try to keep him, he wouldn't have come to the Capital to report his plans.

Shomon's face crinkled in a rare smile. 'Don't be absurd. You can meet Yorimasa, your father's uncle, tomorrow. Now you must be tired and thirsty. It's a long walk and hotter here in the valley than it is in the hills, as you have no doubt found out. Go to the dormitory and ask for food and a place to sleep. But one important point – so simple that you might forget – no one must learn your

name or your clan. The Taira will know you have left the monastery, and they will be looking for you. Give a false name if asked and say you are a foundling. After all, in a way you are.' He smiled again and slid the door open. 'And never carry that sword. It might be recognised. I'll see you in the morning.'

*

Early the next morning Yoshitsuné presented himself somewhat apprehensively at Yorimasa's mansion, a large compound surrounded by well-kept walls over which foamed morning glory and sweet-smelling honeysuckle. Servants bustled cheerfully about the main courtyard and the only armed guards he could see were by the carmine painted gate.

Yoshitsuné had always lived at the mountain temple of Kurama and temple life was all that was familiar to him – vast gloomy halls with pillars of whole cedars that he could not encircle with his arms; curved roofs of thatch over ornately decorated eaves; wide courtyards of raked sand under a sun filtered through pines. He had never been inside a private house and he followed the servant, gazing about him with unconcealed fascination. The offices where Yorimasa's clerks dealt with the affairs of his country estates looked similar to the temple's but the gardens – graceful miniature landscapes of trees, rocks and water – were tiny, tame copies of the uncontrolled nature he had grown up in. Instead of dormitories or sombre halls there were spacious pavilions with verandas of polished wood and linked by covered corridors. Several of the rooms were open, shutters pushed back and bamboo blinds rolled up, so that he could see the cool green reflections of the gardens dappled over the interiors. Menservants moved about discreetly, bowing as they passed, very unlike the chattering, quarrelling, jostling monks of Kurama.

Yorimasa sat erect on a straw mat in the centre of a small severe room opening on to a garden of evergreen shrubs. Sparse white hair was just visible under a stiff cap and his face and hands showed signs of great age; yet, he did not seem at all frail to Yoshitsuné. The bright black eyes

30

studying him were alert and his hands, though wrinkled, were still.

'You are the page from Kurama sent by Shomon of Shijo.' It was not a question but Yoshitsuné, kneeling, murmured respectfully that he was.

'Then come a little closer, young man. Here, on my left side. I no longer hear very well on my right.' Yorimasa lowered his voice slightly. Yoshitsuné slid nearer. The poet smelled of roses and old age. 'My hearing is adequate. So is my sight. Most of the servants can be trusted, but of course one cannot always be sure.' He smiled at his great-nephew. 'You are smaller than I had thought Yoshitomo's son would be, but there is a strong look of your father, and your shoulders and hands are those of a swordsman, just as Shomon said. Have you brought the blade?'

Shomon had permitted him to wear the sword this morning, knowing Yorimasa would want to see it. 'Yes, my lord.' He was impressed by his elderly kinsman; the old man's dignity and self-assurance slightly unnerved one whose pride stemmed from youth and beauty rather than experience. Gingerly he pulled the sword from his sash and placed it in front of Yorimasa, who drew it from the scabbard with his pale, creased hands. He nodded.

'Yes, this is the sword of Hachiman Taro. The tempering of the steel and balance are perfect. The work of the greatest swordsmith. Ah, and the engraving.' He turned the sword, resting the point on his sleeve, careful not to let moisture from his skin touch the blade. 'The Eight Correct Virtues – the message from Lord Hachiman, our family's deity. One could ask for no greater master, a native god who serves the Lord Buddha.' He looked directly into the boy's eyes. 'Lord Hachiman will not desert his loyal clan. He shall see that their pride is restored.'

Yoshitsuné said eagerly, 'My Lord Yorimasa, it is for that reason that I place myself at your service. What is it you wish me to do? I am capable with a sword. May I not lie in ambush for our Taira enemies and cut them down? I would die happy if I could take Kiyomori and his sons with me to hell.'

Yorimasa laughed, a strong, vigorous laugh. 'Shomon said you were young and naive. No, my boy, we will not cut Kiyomori down. We shall move against the tyrant only when the Emperor wishes us to destroy him and we have a strong enough faction to crush the Taira clan.' He snapped his fan open. 'They have had their chance. Kiyomori had genuine ability, which is why I supported him against your father, who was a rather brutal, muddled man. Loyalty to the Emperor precedes loyalty to one's clan and Kiyomori was the better man. But he has not looked beyond the interests of his clan. The Taira grow rich, but the countryside is disorganised. Bandits! Pirates! Only Taira ships and lands are safe – or those of Fujiwara Hidehira, the strong man of Oshu who bows to no one, certainly not to Kiyomori and the Taira. No, Kiyomori has made himself hated and he is blamed by the common people for every disaster, even natural ones.'

The old man smiled a smile of perfect malice. 'All of which is excellent for us, the Minamoto. We need only Go-Shirakawa, the Cloistered Emperor, to decide the Minamoto would make him better protectors than the Taira and then we can strike in his name, not as rebels against the Sacred Throne but as its saviours.'

Yoshitsuné sat enthralled. At Kurama he had felt rather than understood the atmosphere of irritation and frustration that often accompanied any mention of Kiyomori. Taira agents had been received with un-enthusiastic caution, their orders reluctantly obeyed or tacitly ignored, the rice taxes paid with sullen promptness.

Yorimasa clapped his hands. A servant shuffled in, carrying a tray with two black lacquered goblets piled with icy sherbert, glistening in the heat. Amused at the boy's astonishment at this unseasonal accomplishment, Yorimasa explained that ice was brought from the mountains in winter and stored in deep underground cellars to provide refreshment for the hot months. When the servant had bowed and vanished down the open corridor Yorimasa resumed.

'Now for the part you and your brothers are to play. I

hope to command the first attack but perhaps even that . . .' He brushed his yellow cheeks with his fan. 'As you can see, I am old. Your uncle, Yukiiye, your father's brother, is an utter fool, so Yoritomo or your cousin Kiso will lead the clan. Kiso is dour, a clever soldier and a leader, while Yoritomo is secretive, less attractive and yet, a man of considerable intelligence.' He fanned himself slowly, forgetting the boy's presence. 'Shomon has told me of some of Yoritomo's ideas for the future if the Minamoto succeed. It seems he would virtually abandon the Capital, leaving only a few trusted councillors in the Rokuhara Palace. He would set up a samurai government at the Minamoto stronghold in Kamakura, away from the Court and its attractions – a very interesting concept. Yoritomo thinks Kiyomori has failed to use the full possibilities of the samurai class. Extraordinary criticism from one so young, and yet he is right. Kiyomori has forgotten that he himself is a samurai, a warrior. So, nearly, have I,' he added thoughtfully.

Yoshitsuné was puzzled by such talk. Yorimasa saw this bewilderment and briskly changed the subject.

'Well, Kiso or Yoritomo will lead the clan. It is not yet decided. Your brother, Noriyori, and you will no doubt serve as commanders, but that is in the future. It is the present that interests you most, I believe.' Yoshitsuné nodded avidly, forgetting his manners.

'First we must make a samurai out of you. Shomon may be a holy man but he is still a samurai at heart. He is also a fanatic. Years of repeating the Lotus Sutra have done little to leaven his pride and his passion for revenge. Honour, loyalty, duty, courage – these are the greatest samurai virtues, the virtues that give our class its strength. But in the hands of a fanatic . . .' He paused and looked at the boy.

'You do not understand – perhaps some day you will. I am old and have spent many years in the Court. Shomon is too respectful to say that this has softened me, but he thinks it, just as he despises me for choosing the Taira side in the civil war. Masachika, the servant, held nothing, not even

the Sacred Throne, more honoured than his master. Shomon, the Holy Man, has not changed much, although perhaps Lord Buddha now just equals Yoshitomo, his old master.' His voice faded away.

Yoshitsuné's head was beginning to ache. Cicadas pounded in the garden; the suffocating heat had settled on the city again. His great-uncle was beginning to seem ponderous and confusing. Why wouldn't the old man get on instead of slowly fanning himself? After an interminable silence Yorimasa abruptly resumed, 'You will try to effect entry into the house of Oni-ichi Hogen.'

Yoshitsuné blinked. Had he been dozing? He concentrated fiercely on what Yorimasa was saying.

'Oni-ichi Hogen is a diviner, a master of Yin and Yang and the military tactician for the Taira. Kiyomori is not a great general and although Tomomori, his son, is certainly able, the Taira owe their military victories to Hogen. You, Yoshitsuné, are to investigate his records.' He paused for his kinsman to take this in.

'What must I do?' the boy asked helplessly.

'Enter the household however you can, but if you become his retainer your loyalty must stay with him. Remember that! A retainer must never betray his master. That is how samurai differ from others. Find out where Hogen's military texts are kept – the Taira battle plans and armament lists, maps and details of their fortifications.' He shot a sharp look at Yoshitsuné. 'You can guess how important those could be.' The boy nodded; he could only imagine their importance but he felt, suddenly, as though he had become a samurai, entitled to discuss tactics and strategy. Yorimasa continued, 'Take some time to find your way around the city and keep your eyes and ears open. No one knows you and that is an invaluable asset in this little world, so you will serve us not just in Hogen's household but in the streets as well. You will be a spy!' Yorimasa chuckled at the melodrama of his words. 'You can lodge at the Shijo, but see Shomon as little as possible. Never come here.'

Yoshitsuné made a brief, curt bow, partly to ack-

nowledge that he understood, partly to conceal his excitement.

Yorimasa closed his eyes. 'What else? Ah, yes. Become a true samurai.' The narrow black eyes opened and focused sharply on the boy. 'What does that mean? What is a "samurai"? Hachiman Taro, Kiyomori, myself, those brutes wearing Taira red in the streets, a warlord in the provinces with his corps of peasant soldiers or an independent lord like Fujiwara Hidehira with his thousands of men. All samurai. Different clans, different lives. There are Taira and Minamoto women living at Court, chosen for their beauty and wit. Kiyomori's daughter is Empress, and there are girls working in humble farmhouses. All samurai women. Some of us cultured and comfortable at Court, most of us illiterate oafs sprawled in our own dirt. Why are we all samurai?' He peered at Yoshitsuné.

Puzzled, Yoshitsuné offered an answer hesitantly. 'Many generations ago we descended from the Emperor – two clans, Minamoto and Taira, to serve as warriors.'

'Hmmm. To serve as warriors. It sounds so simple – and it should be – to protect our Emperor, heir to the Sun Goddess. But it is not simple any more. There are two emperors: one on the throne and one in his cloister. When they disagree ...' Yorimasa shrugged. 'Service, honour, loyalty; difficult virtues to practise in a confused world.'

'But honour,' said Yoshitsuné eagerly, 'to die an honourable death ...'

'Your death is determined by your karma. I hope yours – and mine – will be honourable ones.'

'I wish to be a great warrior, glorious in battle, to serve the Emperor and my chieftain.'

Yorimasa laughed. 'Let us hope, Yoshitsuné, you know to *which* Emperor and to *which* chieftain you should devote your loyalty and glorious deeds.' Yoshitsuné stared at the floor, resenting the laughter and yet suspecting he deserved it. Yorimasa sighed. 'Excuse me, my son. I am an old man grown cynical after years of pretending to be what I am not. While I sit on soft cushions and smile and seem to

enjoy the order of things half my mind is plotting against the people at whom I smile.' His face became, for an instant, very old and very grim. 'I wish to use the Emperor to restore my clan to power.' In a softer voice, he added, 'Are those virtues, honour and loyalty, really possible or only a dream? So few of us really seem to believe in them. Do I?'

The room was very quiet and very hot. Even the insects paused to consider Yorimasa's question.

Finally Yorimasa looked at Yoshitsuné and smiled. 'You wish to be a hero, like Hachiman Taro; to cover yourself with glory. Perhaps it is your karma. I hope so. But if it is your karma, remember, Yoshitsuné, the words of an old man who knows life is an illusion. Glory is a potent drug, dangerous and unpredictable.' He closed his eyes. 'Life is a mere feather floating in the breeze. Honourable death is freedom and must be assiduously sought.' He sighed again and opened his eyes.

Yoshitsuné leant forward. There was one thing he had to know and he wished to be told by a kinsman. The old man was tired but this might be his only chance. 'May I ask you one more question, my lord?'

'Yes, if it is a short one.'

'It is my mother. Who is she and where is she now? No one has ever mentioned her.'

Yorimasa replied gently, 'She is dead and as she was only a woman it does not really matter. Lady Tokiwa did what she thought was best – some say she brought disgrace to your father's memory. Perhaps. But she also preserved the lives of you and your brothers to avenge that memory. In any case she expiated her shame with the keen edge of a dagger. It took her some years to find the courage but eventually she put the blade to her throat. An honourable death for a samurai woman.

'Respect her spirit and pray for her. She was only a woman, but you are a man and must behave like one. Go now and put your youth and skill to work for your clan . . . and your Emperor.'

*

36

The small pavilion designated for royal births was isolated from the main complex of Imperial buildings. Thick rhododendrons surrounded it to prevent female contamination from seeping out to the rest of the enclosure and, despite the heat, the wooden shutters were firmly closed. A narrow door slid open and snapped shut to admit the steady stream of Court ladies and holy men assisting the Empress Tokuko, Kiyomori's daughter, through her labour. The monks remained in a small ante-chamber, rolling their rosaries through soft fingers and endlessly reciting prayers and incantations for the safe birth of a future Emperor.

The women crowded into the stifling inner room which stank of blood, sweat and incense. Most of them just watched, but occasionally one would kneel to dip a folded wad of paper into a bronze bowl of water and mop Tokuko's brow as she writhed on her white pallet. The continuous prayers of the monks struggled and clashed against the shrieks of agony wrenched from the young Empress.

Suddenly her body began to jerk and heave like a marionette at the mercy of a vicious handler. Before the women could move Tokuko gave one great cry and pushed her son into the world.

Kiyomori, in the Rokuhara Palace, was exultant at the birth of his grandson, the first Imperial heir with Taira blood. Go-Shirakawa, in the Hojoji Palace, had other sons and grandsons who were possible heirs to the throne, and was less interested. Emperor Takakura, in the Imperial Palace, wearily composed a poem to celebrate the birth of his son and then returned to the pet kitten whose antics brightened his tedious existence. The people in the streets sighed and clicked their tongues over this unfortunate scion of the samurai Taira and the Imperial family.

Antoku, first son of Emperor Takakura and Empress Tokuko, grandson of Go-Shirakawa and Kiyomori, had elected to be born on an unlucky day and although the monks doubled their efforts to preserve the child from an evil karma by their prayers, at the hour of the Rat on the

night of the Crown Prince's birth a violent earthquake shook the Capital, killing hundreds and destroying houses, shops and temples. Even the Imperial Enclosure was not spared – a water pavilion shuddered and sank into one of the ornamental lakes.

*

Oni-ichi Hogen lived in a teeming district in the north-eastern quarter where the Yin and Yang masters were centred. Not only the common people but the samurai and the Court depended on their chosen diviners for advice on auspicious days for marriages, journeys and battles and of these diviners Hogen was the most successful. Although a Buddhist monk, his fame was not as a holy man but as a diviner, a tactician, a swordsman and a trainer of fine warriors. A warrior himself, he was rumoured to have six thousand disciples, all allied either to the Taira or the more aggressive monasteries, and all eager to absorb his wisdom and the tricks of his swordplay. He had become rich and respected if not admired or revered; a cold, efficient soldier who at least had the honesty to don a corselet and carry a sword rather than mock the holy saffron of a monk's robe by wearing it.

Shomon suggested that at first Yoshitsuné should visit Hogen's mansion-fortress inconspicuously. So, barefoot, in a loin cloth and with his hair tied up in a twisted cotton band and his face smeared with dirt, Yoshitsuné wandered around the diviners' district looking, he hoped, like a farm lad or an apprentice on a job for his master. Most of the diviners lived in humble one-storey long-houses with the Yin and Yang symbol painted on their wattle gates. But this was not the style of Oni-ichi Hogen, adviser to the Lord Chancellor, Kiyomori. Yoshitsuné grinned when he found the mansion – a vast, quasi-fortress with thick steeply inclined walls punctuated by eight watch towers bristling with guards. There was even a moat, stagnant and slimy, and a drawbridge across which soldiers and Taira officials streamed on business. Several clumsy hand carts laden with aubergines and cucumbers for the kitchens

were manoeuvring in the crowded narrow road to cross the bridge which was jammed with people and horses. Among the shouting farmers were several unkempt boys and Yoshitsuné overheard one ask a sweating, irate farmer if he could help unload the carts for a handful of vegetables. Yoshitsuné quickly joined the confusion and when the bridge was reasonably empty, walked coolly across, one proprietary hand on a swaying load of aubergines. The guards ignored him and once in the main courtyard he found that there was so much activity that he did not need to worry. He drifted over to one of the tall inner gates leading off the courtyard. Peering through, he saw stables with stalls for fifty or more horses. He shook his head. This was a very impressive establishment – that meant that fifty mounted retainers could be mustered at a minute's notice. The farmers, grumbling and swearing, were pushing their carts through a second gate on their way to the domestic quarters so he avoided them and went to the third gate. A huge yard opened up surrounded on three sides by long low buildings, one apparently an armoury and a sword-smith's, the others, barracks. Pairs of sweating men in corselets circled the yard practising stick-fighting or swordplay. A few soldiers sat on the verandas dozing and drinking. One or two looked at Yoshitsuné, decided he was harmless and forgot him. He watched for a while, enjoying the familiar clink of steel on steel and then decided to return to the domestic quarters.

As he lifted a pannier of aubergines a scrawny house servant yelled at him, 'Here, you, take those to the barracks kitchen, through there. There's plenty to do.'

Grimly reminding himself that he was a temporary servant, Yoshitsuné followed the pointing finger along a narrow passage between two walls to a small yard behind the barracks. There was a cooking hut with vegetables and millet piled in front. He dumped his pannier and looked around – a kitchen garden, a well, a pond with fish and ducks and a wicket gate which he peered through into another tiny yard with high blank walls. In the centre were three small stone buildings with heavily barred wooden

doors. The storehouses – relatively fire proof, earthquake proof and thief proof and undoubtedly where Hogen kept his valuables and the Taira scrolls.

'And what do you think you're doing, boy?' The sharp female voice made him jump. He wheeled around and saw an elderly pock-marked maidservant standing by the piled aubergines.

Yoshitsuné gave the woman a friendly smile. 'I was unloading those vegetables and was just curious. That's all. Are those storehouses for grain?'

'Never you mind what they are.' Her eyes narrowed to cracks in her pitted cheeks. 'You don't talk like you look. What's an educated boy of your class doing dressed like that? Why are you unloading vegetables?' Curiosity had replaced the sharpness in her tone.

He walked across and smiled into her eyes. 'If you promise not to give me away I'll tell you.' The response was amazing. The pocked face creased with joy, she grinned a happy, crooked smile and crowed, 'You've come courting! You heard about my mistress and you've come courting! A well-spoken gentleman in disguise – that's what you are!' She chuckled. 'I'll help you, deliver letters or whatever you want. Oh, a nice love letter would please her! She's a lovely girl, she really is, but so lonely. The master is taking his time choosing a husband for her but young girls shouldn't have to wait, I always say.' The grey head shook vigorously.

He remembered that Hogen had two wives and quite a few children, all married but one last daughter. It must be this girl the old woman was talking about. Ugly or beautiful, old or young, she was Yoshitsuné's chance.

'You have found me out,' he said eagerly, 'but I will need your help. I have heard your mistress praised for her beauty and charm, but she is very young, I understand?' he asked tentatively and thought, Please, Lord Buddha, let the old crone say the girl's name. I'll have to have her name to write a letter.

'Oh, my Lady Asuka is young, of course, but not too young,' she added hastily. 'No girl is too young for

40

romance, that's what I always say.'

His relief was obvious but she took it to be over Asuka's age. 'Shall I take her the letter?' she urged.

He gestured to his bare chest and loin cloth. 'As you can see I haven't got it with me. I was just, well, scouting.' He flashed his most winning smile. It was beginning to occur to him that, given his total lack of experience with women, he might not be a very convincing lover. Well, he would worry about that later. 'I'll bring one soon. How do I find you?'

'Naturally, I'm usually in the women's quarters and you can't go in there, except after dark.' She winked. 'But sometimes I go to the kitchens to pick out vegetables or fruit for my mistress. I only came in here to make sure they hadn't given the best stuff to the barracks.' She looked around, puzzled. 'This place isn't usually deserted and the storehouses are always guarded but the master's gone to the Rokuhara this afternoon so the men are a little lax. We had better meet in the other yard, where the carts are, in a few days.' She smiled. 'And when you meet my mistress, come as a gentleman. By the way, my name is Koju. Ask for Koju and someone will find me.' She bowed and hurried off.

Congratulating himself, Yoshitsuné avoided the kitchens and strolled back to the practice yard, settling himself just inside the gate to watch the stick-fighting.

An off-duty samurai with a shining red nose slid off the veranda and walked purposefully towards him.

'You! Get back to the kitchens where you belong! Keep away from here.' His breath, hot in Yoshitsuné's face, stank of saké and old pickles.

Yoshitsuné, forgetting his disguise as a street boy, was astounded to be accosted by a drunken samurai and reacted instinctively, snapping out, 'You go to the kitchens! You stink of them.'

Too late, as he saw the man's eyes harden and his hand drop to his sword, did he remember that he was in a loin cloth and unarmed, without even a dagger. He glared imperiously into the red-rimmed eyes, daring the soldier to

strike. Red-nose returned the stare for a second and then his eyes slid away and he sneered, 'I wouldn't dirty good steel on vermin like you,' and one fist shot out, into Yoshitsuné's belly, a quick, vicious rabbit punch. The boy gasped, but he was young and Red-nose's strength was diminished by saké. Angered by the blow and the insult to his samurai pride, Yoshitsuné grabbed the man around the throat with both hands and tried to force him to the ground. Red-nose flailed his arms wildly.

Suddenly a hand gripped Yoshitsuné's shoulder, pulling him firmly off his prey. A tall samurai, streaked with sweat and dust, stepped between the two men and gazing down at Yoshitsuné said loudly, 'Can't you see the boy's unarmed, Jiro? You mustn't hurt an unarmed boy. He was defenceless against your might.' Harsh guffaws broke out from the verandas and Red-nose's face darkened. Pushing himself around the tall samurai he spat at Yoshitsuné and then he turned on his heel and marched to the barracks accompanied by the chorus of his colleagues' laughter.

The tall samurai nodded at Yoshitsuné. 'Get along. You were lucky he didn't stick you like a pig.'

Yoshitsuné straightened and squared his shoulders, hoping that his proud carriage belied his grubby costume. He looked directly at the samurai and then around at the men in the courtyard and announced in ringing tones, 'That man is a drunken worm. I shall deal with him another time!' Ignoring the murmur of amusement he turned and walked slowly, with dignity, through the gate and out of the fortress. Inside, he was shivering with nerves and pride. He felt no fear.

*

Wisely, Yoshitsuné decided not to tell Shomon about his encounter in the yard but the Holy Man was delighted by his luck with Koju; the girl seemed an ideal way to get to the Taira texts. He ignored the boy's worried questions about love-making, remarking dryly that any son of Yoshitomo should be able to cope with that side of things. But now that Yoshitsuné had time to think he was

becoming nervous about the whole business. At Kurama he had listened to the gossip of those monks who womanised, but he wondered if the information garnered from this source might be suspect. It had been part of his education that in monastic and samurai circles men preferred the company of men, and naturally he had had sexual experience with other temple pages and with a few of the monks. He supposed that with a woman it would be about the same as with a boy and he hoped he could deal with the situation, but never having lived with women, not even his mother, he knew nothing at all about them.

With Shomon's help he composed a letter to Asuka, filling it with praise for her unseen beauty and pain-stakingly writing it all in his best calligraphy on a sheet of Korean paper obtained from Yorimasa. The old poet also provided him with a silk jacket and leggings since the Shijo monastery did not possess such things. He too was pleased with Yoshitsuné's lucky visit to the fortress. Events were beginning to favour the Minamoto, he felt. Droughts in the farm districts west of the Capital had led to a scarcity of food. Prices were rising and while the Taira made money, the people grumbled. There had been a serious riot brutally put down by Taira soldiers from the Rokuhara Palace and, furthermore, it was common talk that most of the rape, murder and robbery in the Capital was the work of the Taira Special Guard whose official task was to keep the peace. Older citizens could remember times when soldiers did not roam the streets and when the only violence came from nature – if the samurai all went back to their provincial estates and left the Court to run the country perhaps calm and peace would return. Kiyomori made less and less effort to placate the population or the courtiers, caring only for his Imperial grandson and his trade profits. Perhaps Yoshitsuné's stolen information might be useful sooner than Yorimasa had dared hope.

Yoshitsuné, dressed in his new clothes, had to make two trips to the fortress before he could give his letter to Koju. Once, he saw Red-nose, but because he was decently dressed he went unrecognised. The second time he saw the

tall samurai who nodded curtly – a change of dress did not fool him.

Koju accepted the letter coyly. 'Of course, I shouldn't. The master has great plans for my Lady Asuka. Her sisters married into the Taira aristocracy and he hopes for even more for her,' she said in an impressive whisper. 'Concubine or even second wife to Lord Munemori, the eldest son of Lord Kiyomori himself. He is old but ... suppose a principal wife died? What then, I say?' She nodded her head gravely at the thought of such social heights for her mistress.

'You don't know anything about me,' said Yoshitsuné and then was appalled at his carelessness. He was letting his apprehension get the better of him.

Koju smiled at the youth. The smooth, delicately-featured face, the full lips, the slim build were to her liking. He was polite and respectful, a gentleman, no doubt about it, and he would be kind to her lonely, waiting Asuka.

'Romance is important too, that's what I always say. There will be time for Lord Munemori later, if needs be. Most young girls have lovers!' Having cleared her conscience she instructed him to come the night of the full moon, enter the fortress before the drawbridge was lifted and hide in the garden of the women's quarters. She would fetch him later. She patted his arm, then bowed formally and with a sentimental glow in her rheumy eyes watched him walk away.

*

During the next few days he went several times to the fortress to watch the soldiers in the practice yard. They noted his presence but he was not challenged. Assessing the men's skill, he decided that he was as good as most of them and it annoyed him that he could not show off his prowess. What was the point of being an excellent swordsman if no one knew? But Shomon had forbidden him to wear the Hachiman sword to the fortress or in the streets, except late at night for necessary protection. He might be provoked into a fight, Shomon had said coldly, might have the bad luck to meet someone better than he

44

and that could cause disaster. But Yoshitsuné chafed at the restriction, longing to test his swordplay against a real rival. One samurai in particular was tempting – the tall captain who had separated him from Jiro Red-nose. He was a superb swordsman with powerful shoulders and arms who defeated every comer. If I could beat him, thought Yoshitsuné, I could take on the great Hogen himself.

The day he was due to meet Asuka, Yoshitsuné calmed his nerves by wandering through the Gion quarter of the city. The famous shrine was preparing for its autumn festival to celebrate the harvest, disappointing though it had been, and the streets around the shrine precinct were jammed with townsmen anticipating the festival by shopping for gay altar decorations and special seasonal food. Yoshitsuné bought himself a sweet beancake and munched it as he watched the jugglers and street musicians who competed for the crowd's attention. The muggy heat hazes had passed and everyone revelled in the crisp air and clear blue skies, relieved that summer was over and that they had survived the mosquitoes and fevers and merciless heat.

Gradually, as he worked his way towards the tall, red gateway of the shrine, Yoshitsuné became aware that the crowd was thicker there. At first, all he could see over the mass of heads and headdresses was a giant monk, a huge bull of a man. Suddenly the monk lifted his thick arm, pulling up with it a startled Taira soldier, dangling from the massive limb like a small child.

'Let go of me, you Taira worm,' the monk bellowed. 'Are you blind as well as stupid? You can see I am a monk. How dare you interfere with clergy!' He shook the man and then dropped him.

Pushing through, Yoshitsuné saw the monk and a smaller man, apparently a pedlar of coloured paper, surrounded by six soldiers dressed in the red armour and tunics of the Rokuhara. The pedlar, clutching his tray of vivid Chinese paper to his bosom, was sheltering behind the bonze.

One of the Taira, a bandy-legged man, brandished his short sword and yelled, 'Monk? You're a bloody agitator! Everyone here heard what you said about the Lord Chancellor. Didn't you?' He glared at the crowd who kept a wary silence, just out of sword's reach. 'Well, speak up or we'll cart some of you off to the Rokuhara for questioning. You all know what that means!'

A man in a farmer's muddy straw boots answered sullenly, 'All the monk said was that he didn't want red paper. He said red was a bad colour. It was a joke. The pedlar here – he didn't say anything.'

The soldier spat with satisfaction. 'Right. An eye-witness. What do you have to say to that?'

Yoshitsuné watched the monk with fascination. His huge muscular frame and ferocious scowl looked peculiarly out of place with his aged saffron robes and badly shaved skull.

'I will say again that red is not my favourite colour. It reminds me of the worms that wriggle around in carrion, taking sustenance from a corpse. Colour of greed, that's red.' He rolled the words off his lips with relish.

'Aha!' cried the Taira. 'So, it's white for you, huh? White for death and the Minamoto. You're a Minamoto agitator. I knew it. You stink like a traitor stinks!'

The bellowed response could have been heard in Northern Oshu. 'I, Saito Masashibo, known as Benkei, of Mount Hiei, do not give a damn for red or white. Red is the colour of maggot-ridden carrion. White is the colour of death. What's the choice? None to Benkei! I am a man of Buddha and you do not bother me with the petty politics of a transitory world.' The bellow rose in volume. 'Your master will not appreciate your ruffling the feathers of Mount Hiei.'

Another Taira soldier poked his short sword at the pedlar who pulled back, shaking his head in terror. 'And what do you say, you little rat? You're not a monk. We can do what we want with you.'

Benkei seized the soldier by his scarlet tunic and shook him until his head waggled. 'He's dumb! How can a dumb

46

man speak treason or defend himself? Go and bully someone your own size!'

The crowd were now definitely on the side of the monk. There were appreciative titters as the Taira's teeth rattled and a few braver members muttered invective against soldiers who terrorised innocent monks and dumb men.

It was a mistake. Kiyomori's men could not back down now. Out came their swords and they began to jab at the crowd. The bandy-legged soldier turned on the quivering pedlar.

'You! You're not dumb.' He pricked the little man with his sword. 'You're making a noise. Say something!' He pricked harder. The pedlar clutched at Benkei's cloak, his tray clattering to the street; the bright sheets of paper caught in the light wind and fluttered away into the golden trees. He held both hands up to the red hole of his mouth where a tongue should have been. The soldier bore down on him poking and jabbing, his eyes evil chinks as he thrust out sharply with his blade. A quick upward yank slit the little man open. Benkei's sword flashed out. The Taira soldier screamed once as the blade half severed his neck from his shoulder, and then he fell across the pedlar's corpse.

Benkei crouched, his dripping sword ready. The huge voice sank to a low snarl. 'Which of you Taira filth wish to die next? None of you are worthy. Where is your captain? Let me take his gizzard.'

Suddenly a group of horsemen appeared at the edge of the crowd, urging their mounts forward. Those who did not move fast enough received a sharp tap from the iron fans carried by the samurai. The soldiers tried to slink away but two of the riders boxed them in.

'What's going on here?' barked the leader, a square-shouldered, red-faced man. He glared contemptuously at the Taira soldiers and then shouted angrily, 'Well, someone speak. You, the monk with the bloody sword, are you responsible for these corpses?'

'In a way, my Lord Tomomori, I am,' Benkei replied with great dignity. Yoshitsuné stared at the samurai soldier

son of the Lord Kiyomori, Taira Tomomori, a man he was committed to destroy. It would not be easy. The way he handled his horse, the set of his shoulders, the quick, shrewd eyes indicated a formidable opponent. He wondered if the rest of Kiyomori's family were as impressive as this member.

'What do you mean "in a way"? Make yourself clear.'

'I am Saito Masashibo, known as Benkei. I was looking at the pedlar's wares for some fine paper on which to copy out a few sutras.' The monk paused briefly to let the piety of this sink in. 'When this scum,' a fierce glance at the soldiers, 'attacked the pedlar and myself shouting nonsense. They killed the pedlar because he was dumb and couldn't answer and because he was little and unarmed. I avenged his death and defended myself.' He ended with a flourish that delighted Yoshitsuné, 'And now, if your lordship is satisfied I shall return to my temple for evening prayers.'

Tomomori regarded the monk and the soldiers sourly and then turned in his saddle to survey the crowd. Yoshitsuné caught his eye. 'You have an honest face. Does he tell the truth?'

'He does, my lord.'

Tomomori looked at their dirty, torn red tunics. 'You are undisciplined. Look at the condition of your corselet.' He struck one with his fan. 'And you, there, your sword has rust on it. You are Taira? Who do you serve?'

'Goro is our captain, in Lord Munemori's household guard,' one said sullenly.

'I should have known. My brother has no sense of discipline. Get back to the Rokuhara where my men will beat some order into you. Benkei, or whatever you are called, no doubt you are lying but the sight of one cowardly soldier irritates me more than just another loud-mouthed monk.' He kicked his horse forward through the melting crowd and disappeared through the shrine gate.

Benkei wiped his sword clean on his cloak and replaced it in his sash. He walked over to one of the Taira soldiers, giving Yoshitsuné a polite nod as he passed, and seizing the

48

man by the shoulders he lifted him up to his own eye level, the man's feet dangling inches off the ground. Suddenly the monk released the soldier and let him crash heavily to his knees, then strode off down the avenue, leaving Yoshitsuné gazing after him in fascinated admiration.

*

Just after dusk Yoshitsuné slipped into the garden of the women's wing of Hogen's house. Lanterns glowed through the reed blinds and the high lilt of female voices drifted out into the night. Yorimasa's jacket stretched tight across his shoulders. He had not worn silk before and the luxurious feel of it gave him some courage as he settled into his hiding place behind the magnolia bushes. Since he had not practised much with a sword in the last few months his hands were smooth as he rubbed them together – smooth and moist. Well, at least callouses would not hurt her tender skin. Oh, Lord Buddha, let it start soon and be over soon, he prayed. Nothing could be worse than this waiting.

Gradually the women's quarters darkened and fell silent. The garden was full of night sounds – frogs, late insects, the gentle movement of leaves under a clear round harvest moon. He tried to ignore his pounding heart and dry mouth; women should not make Minamoto warriors nervous.

Koju appeared silently at his elbow. She held one wide sleeve over the bottom half of her face, presumably for modesty but in fact to hide a giggle. He followed her through the garden to another smaller one – she gestured towards a sliding door that was just ajar. He slipped off his sandals and plunged into the blackness. Slowly he distinguished large screens concealing a sleeping pallet. Intermingling with the natural sounds of the garden came the slither of silk upon silk; the air held a gentle confused scent – the autumn garden, almonds, wood, incense, sweat. He felt a quick shove in the small of his back. 'Go on,' whispered Koju, 'she is waiting. Remember, samurai, she is very young and you are the first.' Then she disappeared.

He stepped round the screens. A single shaft of

moonlight fell through the half-opened window onto a tumbled mass of folds and textures; the mass stirred and a small pale face peered up at him. Momentarily he was unsure what to do, then he knelt and stretched out his hand.

'Don't be afraid.' He might have been talking to himself.

Asuka said shyly, 'Your letter was so beautiful. It made me want to meet you.' Her voice was childishly high. The moonlight caught her face; it was very beautiful, a perfect oval with tiny delicate features. Her hair, like a spill of ink, fell back along the full length of the pallet. He lifted a strand and let it slide through his fingers. The girl shivered.

Yoshitsuné lay down beside her and fumbled with the various layers of robes. Each time his hand found one parting another garment would billow over to enfold and imprison it in silk. Gently she took his hands and guided them through the soft maze to her warm body. They explored and caressed and experimented until, after a short nervous explosion of pain and pleasure, they slept wrapped in each other's arms.

Asuka proved to be altogether different from a boy, not only her soft, willing body but her gentleness were unlike anything he had experienced. He was amazed that something so vulnerable and dependent could exist, even in her cosseted, protected world of silk and music and languid days. Koju, who joyfully aided the lovers as messenger and sentry, was tough and resilient and comprehensible to the boy but Asuka, frail, shy, proved an endless wonder. Orphaned early, raised in a temple by monks, he had never known the warmth and feminine affection that surrounded most young boys during their years of living in the women's quarters. The monks, especially the Abbot, had been kind when they noticed him, but he was only a flicker in the corner of their busy lives, an attractive amusement rather than a vulnerable child needing love and attention. No one had touched, stroked, petted Yoshitsuné as Asuka did and he responded and expanded under her caresses. Asuka, pampered by

doting parents, fussed by Koju, knew nothing but love and she lavished it on a grateful Yoshitsuné.

Shomon grumbled once or twice at the nights spent in the scents and silks of Hogen's women's quarters, warned Yoshitsuné against being weakened by women and their ways and reminded him that Asuka was to be used to serve the Minamoto cause. And in fact the nights were so sweet that he nearly forgot the purpose of the seduction. Finally, with great regret, one dawn as he lay in her almond-scented arms, he spoke of Hogen.

'Do you think your father would accept me? Someone is bound to find out about this and tell him.'

'Oh, my lord. Even I do not know who you are or where you come from and unless you are a great Taira noble he will not tolerate you. I do not ask you who you are because you do not wish to tell me,' she added wistfully.

'I can't tell you, Asuka. But there is one thing I would like you to do, something important to me.' He slid his hand up her slim arm, under the wide sleeve.

'Oh, anything, my lord. I love you so much I would gladly die for you.'

He ignored this childish promise. 'Your father has some books, records of boring military matters that I would love to see. Can you help me?'

She pulled back and looked at him in horror. 'You wish me to open my father's treasure box! Oh, my lord!' Asuka fell back on the pallet. Tears gathered in her eyes and began to spill down her nose.

As he soothed her, Yoshitsuné worried that she seemed to understand how valuable the texts were. Unhappily, he pursued his task. 'But, my sweet love, if you simply borrow the scrolls and bring them here I can look over them myself and then return them. No one will ever know they are missing because they will be away for a very short time. They are just some lists and records that I am interested to see, as a samurai, you understand.' He resorted to wheedling. 'Please, my rose.'

This idea seemed to interest her. 'You will stay here in my room to copy them, not take them away? Ah, that

would not be so disloyal, would it? I should not be such a wicked daughter. My father would certainly kill me if I stole anything, but to borrow is not so wrong.' Rather more cheerful, she sat up and smiled. 'I shall do it for you to prove my love. Koju will help me. She knows that part of the house well. I promise you it will be done.' She settled down on the pallet next to him and, briefly, they forgot the scrolls.

*

Koju asked no awkward questions and agreed to help but she explained that nothing could be done until New Year when all valuable possessions were removed from the guarded storehouses to be checked and aired. Asuka reassured and his own plans advanced, Yoshitsuné relaxed again and brushing aside Shomon's disapproval – samurai didn't need women, the Holy Man said – enjoyed the warm sweetness of the women's quarters. He occasionally made daytime excursions to the fortress and once the drunkard Red-nose recognised his young enemy in a decent kimono; they met on the drawbridge and Red-nose barred the way.

'Why don't you wear a sword? You think you're so fine putting me down in front of my comrades but you're afraid to wear a sword for fear you'd have to fight and hurt that pretty face.'

Yoshitsuné ignored him and tried to pass but Red-nose grabbed his sleeve. 'Wear a sword and then meet me,' he hissed. 'You wouldn't be so pretty after I'd finished with you.' Yoshitsuné reeled back from the sour saké breath. He wrenched his kimono free and spat into the pitted, twisted face. Pushing the drunk aside, he marched out of the fortress leaving Red-nose once again to the laughter of the guards and by-standers. Yoshitsuné, although furious, kept his face frozen. What sort of samurai did he make without a sword? If only he could meet that drunken lout when he was armed, then he would prove his swordsmanship to at least one of Hogen's guard.

*

'Ah, Lord Yorimasa, we are pleased to see you. Take this

place next to us,' Go-Shirakawa whispered. 'We will talk after the music.' Yorimasa, flattered and honoured to be on the Imperial dais, sank into the silk cushion and tried to absorb himself in the performance, but he was aware only of the plump, subtly scented man next to him. As Go-Shirakawa's pale dimpled fingers played with the tassels of his fan an unusual perfume of apricots and sandalwood wafted to Yorimasa.

The music ceased and the musicians bowed stiffly in their archaic court dress. Go-Shirakawa nodded and smiled his cool regal smile. 'The large drum and the flute were particularly fine, did you not think, my lord? Ah, some fresh saké, and try these pine seeds and preserved cumquats. Quite delicious.'

Yorimasa sipped and ate and discussed poetry and all the time wondered what Go-Shirakawa wanted. His invitation to the dais had been very public and when in conversation Yorimasa had turned to address another courtier he had glimpsed Kiyomori and Tomomori sitting among the guests, peering alertly at the Imperial group behind their thin gauze curtains. Kiyomori's cheeks were flushed an unhealthy pink, but whether from curiosity or one of the fevers he periodically suffered from, Yorimasa could not tell.

Suddenly Go-Shirakawa appeared to notice Kiyomori. 'Ah, the Lord Chancellor. We must thank him for the pheasants he sent from his western estates.' He looked directly at Yorimasa. 'We understand there is plague in the west?'

'A sad aftermath of the drought, Your Highness. It came about because there is simply not enough food and now it has spread to the Capital, increasing the suffering of the people here. Corpses are piled in the streets.'

'Indeed? We had been told of riots in the city. Is it true that several temples have been attacked?'

'Mostly granaries, of course, since the people need food, but the temple to Kannon in Shirakawa is in flames now. On my way to the Enclosure I saw the smoke and the mobs ...' Yorimasa paused, not sure if it was wise to mention

what the people were doing.

'The mobs?' Go-Shirakawa demanded.

'The winter has been very cold, Your Highness. They are looting the gold and brass to sell, although to whom the Lord Amida only knows, and they are using the wood from the buildings and the idols for firewood.'

If Go-Shirakawa had not had his eyebrows plucked entirely away, he would have raised them. 'For firewood? How appalling. And what does the Rokuhara do about this sacrilege?'

Yorimasa replied with relish, 'Nothing, my lord.'

Go-Shirakawa permitted himself a few tuts. 'Indeed? The Lord Chancellor is not well but he should order his minions better. They are actually dying in the streets? How unpleasant.'

'Your Highness, they are dying all over the city and the stench will soon be terrible. People are starving. If the rains do not come and the crops do not improve we will all have a difficult time. I pray it will not touch the Imperial Enclosure.' Yorimasa bowed.

'It seldom does. We did not know there was a shortage of food, but then we hear so little, although we did know about the riots.' He glanced across at his Lord Chancellor who glared back. 'The Minamoto estates are centred on the eastern plains — have they suffered from the drought as well?' he asked with unconvincing innocence.

Yorimasa could barely cover his surprise. It was unusual for the Cloistered Emperor to acknowledge the existence of any life beyond the Court, certainly not interest himself in such mundane matters as crops and dying populations; furthermore, it was an unusual assumption that Yorimasa would have any practical information since his reputation was as a courtier and poet, not a warlord. Yorimasa realised that they were coming to the purpose of the conversation — he was being consulted as the elder statesman of the rival clan to the Taira. He glanced at Kiyomori, who was watching a flautist prepare for the next song, but Tomomori's eyes were fixed on the Imperial dais. Yorimasa smiled and replied, 'We have suffered very little, Your

Highness. Some grain has been sent to the Capital but of course the highways are infested with bandits and it has been necessary to travel with bands of samurai to protect the grain carts.'

'Ah.' Go-Shirakawa stroked his smooth, plump chin with satisfaction. 'We have heard that time has eased the disgrace of the Minamoto warlords and that their estates are productive again. How very convenient. Their retainers are in fighting condition?' He smiled his sweetest smile. 'Shall we ask Kiyomori to join us? Call over the Lord Chancellor,' he purred to a servant. 'We wish to thank him for his pheasants. Such lovely birds. But personally we don't care for pheasants.'

*

Tomomori strode around the dim room, impatiently kicking at his cumbersome court trousers. He glared at his father, sitting, head lowered, sipping bitter tea, and at his brother, playing nervously with the rosary he sometimes affected.

'My lord, I have called Hogen here tonight, at this hour, because this matter could be serious,' Tomomori explained crossly for the second time. 'Yorimasa called publicly to the Imperial dais! What does Go-Shirakawa want with him?'

'He is a distinguished poet,' murmured Munemori. 'He's not interested in politics.'

Tomomori ignored him. 'I told you last week that Hogen has had reports of a Minamoto armoury uncovered in Hitachi. There are herds of Minamoto horses on the Musashi Plain and there isn't a drought in the east. Our recruits are pathetic weaklings who die of plague before they lift a halberd, but the eastern samurai are well fed and healthy.' Tomomori's face flushed even redder with anger. 'Yoritomo is in Izu and married to Hojo Tokimasa's daughter. This must be taken seriously, father.'

Kiyomori turned the oil lamp away from him. The light hurt his eyes. His complexion was pale, but two red spots glowed on either cheek and he was sweating. Another fever

attack was on its way and he dreaded it more than a Minamoto revival – the searing headache, his body burning and dry. He couldn't think clearly now and it would be worse later.

Oni-ichi Hogen strode into the room. He always reminded Kiyomori of an evil toad with his squat, square shape. His face was broad and flat, punctuated by a squashed nose, two bulging eyes set far apart and a thin-lipped slash for a mouth. The diviner bowed, glanced with distaste at the braziers around Kiyomori and squatted down as far away from the heat as possible. Just a crude soldier, thought Kiyomori, running his palms over the smooth, cool, comforting violet silk of his court robe.

'Yorimasa and the Cloistered Emperor together? That's bad. Minamoto getting organised. One good thing. No generals. No Minamoto generals with experience, eh?' Hogen squinted at Tomomori who nodded thoughtfully.

'Yoritomo and his brothers are unknown quantities, so is the cousin, Kiso. Yorimasa is too old and Yukiiye is a fool,' said Tomomori.

'Quite,' croaked Hogen.

Munemori suddenly spoke up. 'Of course, if they attracted other families – for example, the Miura are Taira, our people, but they are not very loyal and Lord Miura would make an extremely competent general for the Minamoto. Then there is Fujiwara Hidehira in Oshu – he is old and independent, I know, but he has been a magnificent warrior in his day and he is very rich. Suppose the Oshu Fujiwara come in with the Minamoto?'

Hogen and Tomomori looked at Munemori in surprise. Hogen said, 'Better watch the Miura, eh? Keep an eye on Izu. Double up the guards on the barriers at the passes both to Izu and the North. Minamoto are bound to try Hidehira. Better send a man there yourself?' Tomomori nodded and sighed.

Kiyomori's head buzzed. He staggered to his feet and began to walk towards the blurred outline of the doors, but four steps across the room he wavered, falling heavily against his second son who caught him. Rage surged

through him. How dare the Minamoto challenge him, Kiyomori. He whispered harshly, 'Kill them – Yoritomo, Miura, Go-Shirakawa, Hidehira, the lot!' He slumped in Tomomori's arms.

The three men looked uneasily at one another. 'I think that my father's orders might be reconsidered in the morning,' Munemori said cautiously. 'We would do well to put him to bed ourselves and not mention this to anyone.' Together they lifted the unconscious chieftain and carried him to his pallet.

*

The night was windy and bitterly cold. Occasionally, in open spaces – deserted gardens or the ruins of a burnt-out house – piles of corpses lay unattended, unmourned, victims of plague and famine. At least, thought Yoshitsuné, avoiding one such open mortuary, the cold has frozen the poor devils so that they don't stink, but what an awful, lonely death; no one caring enough even to burn the corpse and mutter a few prayers to help the soul to Paradise. May my karma be better than theirs!

He was striding towards the Gojo Bridge, bearskin boots cracking on the icy road, after an evening spent in the saké shops listening to the idle chatter of the maids and Taira soldiers; wine and lust often loosened men's tongues and he had found he could pick up scraps of gossip by remaining quiet and listening. Eventually he had grown bored and sleepy over his saké and now he was eager to cross the river to the Shijo Temple and his pallet. Tonight – and the last few months, with Shomon away on his travels – Yoshitsuné had defied his orders and decided to wear the Hachiman sword, excusing the disobedience to himself on the grounds that many bandits prowled the streets of the Capital.

The bridge loomed up. Before it the crossroads were in deep shadow and remembering that the threat of bandits was a very real one, it suddenly seemed foolish not to have a lantern as well as a sword.

A voice barked out of the darkness, 'Halt, my good

friend, we may have something to discuss.'

Yoshitsuné could just make out a bulky figure in a cloak that tossed and snapped in the wind.

'I am a collector of swords, sir, and it occurs to me that a fine young samurai like you might have a blade to interest me. Hand it over so that I may examine it.'

The booming voice was familiar; Yoshitsuné reached into his memory to place it as he dropped a hand to the hilt of his sword. 'Come and take it yourself,' he said softly.

The figure leapt forward, cloak billowing out behind him like a flag. 'Don't be argumentative, young man.' A very long sword appeared from under the cloak and whistled in the air. 'Hand it to me or I shall be forced to take your arm with it.'

Momentarily, Yoshitsuné was seized by terror; until this moment his opponents had been pine trees or monks whose purpose was to instruct, not destroy. His blood had been drawn often but each time he had learned something important. Now, this lesson could be his last. His stomach churned and his head whirled with half-remembered instructions, tricks, admonitions. But as he drew the Hachiman sword the familiar balance steadied him and his breathing settled.

He glanced around to assess his opponent and his position. The river embankment was on one side and a plaster-and-lathe wall on the other, limiting his mobility. The big man had all the space that the crossroads allowed and, aware of this advantage, he began manoeuvring Yoshitsuné towards the wall, striking out hard several times. Yoshitsuné warded off the blows, but he was perilously near to the wall. The man's long sword was a fearsome weapon and it was difficult to get near enough to threaten, but Yoshitsuné's concentration was absolute, the terror had charged his energy and his wits. Once he managed to rend the voluminous cape and several times the giant had to jump back. They fought back and forth for what seemed hours, while the moon moved across the sky and flooded the crossroads, gleaming on the giant's bald skull.

Again the great voice bellowed, 'Well, young man,

although you look frail as a daisy you're no weakling. You can handle yourself and that makes your blade all the more of a prize. But it's a cold night so let's end the affair at once.' He swung his sword with terrifying force. Yoshitsuné ducked. The long sword, propelled by tremendous strength, flashed past him deep into the plaster wall where it held fast. With a shout of triumph, Yoshitsuné kicked at the man's massive chest and sent him reeling and staggering back into the moonlit crossroads where he collapsed, the breath rushing out of him into the frozen air.

The boy gathered up the two swords and went to stand over his fallen rival. 'By the Holy Sutras, it's the monk who killed the Taira guard at the Gion Shrine and walked away free.'

The prostrate monk groaned and pleaded with a gesture for time to regain his breath.

'Your big mouth brings you much trouble but you're good with that oversized sword. Here, take my hand and I'll see if I can raise your bulk from the ground.'

Benkei heaved himself up and panted, 'You ... are ... the young fellow ... who spoke for me. Whew! I don't know which is more lethal, your sword arm or your kicking leg. I didn't take you seriously enough, little shrimp that you are.' He flopped over from the waist and took a few deep breaths. When he was breathing easily again he said, 'Now, how about a drink? There's a saké shop under the bridge. The lights are still on so there must be something left in the jugs.' He started down the icy embankment and Yoshitsuné, ebullient with his victory and pricked by curiosity, followed. What a pity he would not be able to boast to Shomon.

The shop was little more than a lean-to with a dirt floor and a small platform where they settled themselves beside an earthenware brazier. The landlord slopped two coarse jugs full of saké down next to them and then went to a corner where he settled down with a jug of his own. In another corner a drunk was curled up, snoring noisily. The only light came from a bowl of oil with a dirty wick, smoking badly.

59

'Not a very salubrious spot, I'm afraid, but the Taira thugs don't leave many places in the Capital where a man can drink in peace. Here's to you!' Benkei lifted the large jug and drained half of it.

Yoshitsuné drank. As at the Gion Shrine he found himself much taken with the monk – not only his size and voice but the immense gusto of the man. Political lambasting, revenge, sword stealing, now drinking; he tackled everything with irresistible energy and noise. Saké was pouring down his throat as though this miserable shed contained the last few barrels on earth.

'Well, young man, what about you? You fight like a samurai but nobody would guess what a fighter you are with that pretty face. Where do you get the power? What is your name? Where do you come from? You're not one of the Rokuhara's mob.'

'My name is . . .' He paused. A sudden impulse made him tell Benkei his real name. 'Yoshitsuné. I . . . er . . . come from Kurama, a foundling raised in the temple.'

'You are quite a swordsman, Yoshitsuné. I had hoped to take my thousandth sword tonight but you foiled me.'

'Thousandth sword?'

'I set myself a goal to relieve a thousand samurai of their weapons, you know, here and there, around the countryside. Nine hundred and ninety-nine men have generously made me presentations and tonight I was to reach my target. Ah, well,' he relaxed and drank, 'there's always tomorrow. No hurry.'

Yoshitsuné laughed. 'What do you do with them? I don't believe you. I've never heard of a mad monk stealing swords. It would be the talk of the Capital.'

Benkei leaned across and grinned at the boy. 'Ha! That's the beauty of it! Now, would a samurai admit he's had his sword taken? Sooner confess castration, most of 'em. Arrogant bastards. Anyway, once I've beaten a man and satisfied myself, I stick his sword in the ground nearby so the poor fool will find it again. But let's see yours. It looks a fine one.'

Yoshitsuné paused for only a second, and then drew the

Hachiman sword and passed it, hilt first. He trusted the monk and in any case what would a renegade know about a famous Minamoto blade? Benkei studied it intently for a few minutes and then shot him a shrewd, appraising look that made Yoshitsuné uneasy.

'This is quite a weapon. It would have added a fine flourish to my collection. Bizen School. This engraving to Lord Hachiman – unusual, isn't it?'

Yoshitsuné took his blade back. 'It's an heirloom. I treasure it above my life.' His tone allowed no more questions to be asked. 'You don't seem very fond of the Taira. Surely they are allies of Mount Hiei, as you pointed out to those soldiers?'

The monk drank, belched and pounded his thick chest. 'My father was the abbot of Kumano Temple. I was sent as a novice to Mount Hiei where I took my vows but my connection with the monastery was severed some time ago. Perhaps I was a little exuberant even for them and it seemed wiser to make my way alone. They call me a renegade but I think that's too strong.' He chuckled. 'Mind you, I know my sutras and can do a good string of prayers as well. But Mount Hiei was too small for me and some of the others.' He whirled round to throw a lump of charcoal at the landlord. 'Here! Wake up and bring us more saké. That's right! Move your bones.'

He continued cheerfully, 'So I am a wandering carefree soul, but the robes and bald pate are useful, just as you saw with those Taira. They didn't dare touch me because of my vocation, but look what they did to that poor bastard, the paper seller, and then you ask me why I dislike the Taira?'

He was now well launched on his theme. Yoshitsuné sat back, sipping from his jug, watching the broad, mobile, pock-marked face with fascination.

'I move around a lot – I've seen the Taira, not only in the Capital but in the countryside as well. They'll take the one son of a widow for a soldier and then rape her daughters and clear her out of grain as well; fire her house and fields. They take what they want from a shopkeeper and carve him up if he complains. You've seen what the Special

Guard do to the taverns and any poor girl they can get their hands on. None of it is necessary, but they like killing. The regular foot soldiers and the samurai are all right – good fighters, good horsemen – same as any warriors.'

'What about the Lord Chancellor?' the boy asked.

'Kiyomori? I'll grant you I prefer a samurai to those flowers who used to run things, but the Court has corrupted him. He's soft. Not really a courtier, not really a samurai; a sort of bellicose merchant with culture.' He stroked his fourth jug of saké with inebriated affection.

Yoshitsuné decided the monk was too drunk to remember the conversation so he said, 'If you are tired of Kiyomori and the Taira, what are the alternatives? The Cloister Court can advise but it must have muscle behind it; that's why the Taira seized power.'

Benkei's drunkenness dropped away. He eyed Yoshitsuné coldly. 'I'm not as stupid as I apparently look, boy.' He pointed to the scabbard. 'That is the Hachiman sword, made for Minamoto Yoshiie, known as Hachiman Taro. It went down the family to Minamoto Yoshitomo. You said you were a foundling at Kurama and your name is Yoshitsuné. How old are you? The right age, I'll wager, to be the youngest son of Yoshitomo. Now that the record is straight, what are you asking me?'

Shomon's voice in his head ordered him to back down but the boy, sure of his judgement, was too attracted to the monk. Squaring his shoulders, he said imperiously, 'Would you serve the Minamoto?'

'I give my loyalty to men, not politics or clans,' Benkei replied curtly.

There was a long pause. Benkei finally broke the silence. 'I had thought to stay free, but I will serve you – not the Minamoto. You. If ever the two clash, my loyalty will be with you. Don't expect any bowing and scraping because it's not my style. But I'll die for you or with you.' He lifted his jug and drank. Yoshitsuné sat back on his heels and grinned. His luck had held.

'There now, boy, or should I say Lord Yoshitsuné, you have your first retainer!' Benkei's laugh was rich and deep

and he slapped his jug on the floor.

*

The Chinese leather box containing Hogen's prized military treaties and records was removed from its fortified treasure house in the week before New Year so that Hogen could check that there had been no deterioration. The day after the removal all three storehouses mysteriously caught fire; the outer stone vaults survived the blaze but with the wooden structure in ashes there was no way of securing the contents so Hogen decided to keep the box and documents in his rooms until the storehouses were rebuilt.

This was exactly what Yoshitsuné had planned. With the help of Koju he acquired one of the kimono worn by Hogen's house servants and one afternoon, while the master was at a Rokuhara archery contest, Yoshitsuné slipped into Hogen's room dressed as a servant and carrying polishing rags. A few minutes later he emerged again and made his way to the garden where he met Koju who took the scrolls he had chosen and hid them in Asuka's quarters. That night and every night for the next few weeks Yoshitsuné spent at Asuka's low writing desk with a shaded lamp at his elbow.

The documents took several weeks of concentrated labour to copy, but as he pored over the cramped Chinese script and faded diagrams, Yoshitsuné's knowledge of the enemy expanded. He found important maps of Taira strongholds, and offensive and defensive tactics for every possible route of attack on those strongholds and the Rokuhara. All these he copied carefully, committing as much as possible to memory. When a text was finished he slipped into Hogen's quarters and exchanged it for a new one. Not once was he challenged. Any copies he made were stored at the Shijo Temple in Shomon's chest.

Asuka, pleased just to have him with her, played the zither for him or simply sat watching as he worked. From time to time he paused to caress her, deeply conscious that by betraying her father she had entrusted her future to him and although she was only a woman, she was now his

responsibility. Stroking her creamy, warm skin and gazing into her pretty, adoring little face, the responsibility seemed grave but not unpleasant.

However rewarding and profitable his nights in Hogen's fortress might be, Yoshitsuné was still dissatisfied. The Hachiman sword lay unused in the Shijo Temple and he knew that he needed practice and testing. One of his reasons for wishing to join his brothers in Izu had been to live the life of a samurai and this he was certainly not doing in the Capital. Benkei did not conceal his surprise or disapproval when he learned that Yoshitsuné seldom practised. 'After all,' roared the monk, 'you didn't really beat me in swordsmanship, you know, boy. You just proved that you can duck and kick – both important, I grant you – but you haven't really proved to yourself what kind of fighter you are. It's no good looking at Hogen's guards and wondering if you can beat them. You have to find out.'

Shomon shrugged and said the time would come and that just now learning Taira secrets was more important than brawling, but Shomon was away the afternoon that Yoshitsuné came across Red-nose and two friends on a deserted street in the burnt-out southern quarter near the river. They stood, swaying slightly, grinning and whispering together, as they watched the boy approach. Yoshitsuné had no sword and although he knew Red-nose loathed him and was prepared for trouble he could do nothing but curse Shomon when all three jumped on him and dragged him into the empty courtyard of a charred shop. He struggled and fought, but they were vicious; Red-nose because Yoshitsuné had defied him, and the others because he was young and helpless. But they were also drunk and inefficient, and when they finally became bored and left him, Yoshitsuné was beaten but not too badly injured. He lay sprawled in his own blood, his throbbing head against the blackened step of a ruined veranda, until dusk, when he staggered down to the river and bathed in the dark water. One eye was closed and he was bruised and stiff but everything seemed to be working. He waited, angry and

depressed, on the river bank until after dark when he crept unnoticed into the Shijo Temple. Before collapsing on to his pallet, he took the Hachiman sword from its hiding place and, holding the beautiful blade in front of him, he swore an oath that its perfect steel would take the blood of Red-nose before another sun had set. He had been a lover, a clerk and a spy too long. Now he must prove he was a swordsman.

He slept heavily for a few hours but woke before dawn to watch the sky gradually lighten, impatient for his day of revenge to begin. That he, Minamoto Yoshitsuné, had been ignominiously beaten by a drunken common samurai just because he had rightly treated him with contempt was a degradation his youthful pride could not tolerate. His nerves screamed at the memory of the vulgar feet and fists on his body. Red-nose must die for this insolence. Shomon's warnings against any confrontation were not even ghostly whispers – the Minamoto plot and fear for his own safety were submerged by his fury and obsession with his humiliator's death.

*

Three men stood on the veranda of the barracks, stamping their feet against the cold, watching a few men stick-fighting. One, squat and thickset, was Hogen; the other two were tall, Tomomori with his ruddy complexion and general's bearing stood next to Hori Yataro, the captain who had first intervened between Yoshitsuné and Red-nose. Hori Yataro possessed the natural arrogance of a superb fighter; his long, narrow eyes were alert and watchful, his expression could change from genial good humour to cold concentration in a moment. But now, as he listened to Hogen and Tomomori, he looked perplexed and unhappy. He knew that he had no real choice – if Hogen and the Rokuhara agreed that he should transfer to Kiyomori's Special Guard he must go. But he was a warrior and the tactics of the Special Guard appalled him, roaming the streets like common policemen in their red garb, doing the dirty work of their Taira lords. Hori Yataro liked a

clean fight – no malice – and it was for this that he had joined Hogen's household. Now he heard Tomomori's voice telling him what an honour it was to be chosen. Hori Yataro took advantage of a pause in Tomomori's lecture.

'My lord, I appreciate the honour, but I am a retainer of Oni-ichi Hogen.'

'Nonsense.' Hogen snapped his wide, toadlike mouth shut on the word. 'You're a good fighter, but I've got good fighters. The Guard needs strong men. Too many bullies. Can't control the rabble when they're hungry. Your obligation to me is finished.'

Hori Yataro shrugged. 'As you wish, Hogen, but . . .' He stopped abruptly. Yoshitsuné stood in the inner gateway. His face was bruised and swollen but he wore a corselet of primrose yellow lacquer and his right hand rested firmly on the hilt of his sword. Hori Yataro unconsciously touched his own sword. He murmured to Hogen, 'There's going to be trouble. Jiro, that drunken bastard, has been boasting that he would teach that boy a lesson and from the look of his face Jiro has used his fists and probably had help to do so.'

Because of the intense cold there were not many men in the courtyard, so Yoshitsuné's entrance attracted immediate attention, as he had hoped. His strongly developed sense of the dramatic told him that his revenge would be less sweet if he had to shout and wave his arms to be noticed. Now his young voice rang out sharply. 'Where is the samurai known as Jiro, the bully with the red nose? I have business with him.'

The soldiers glanced at each other and then back at the youth standing like a battered cockerel in the gateway. Hogen said to Hori Yataro, 'Boy puts up a good show, eh? Know anything about him?'

Hori Yataro raised an eyebrow. Stories about visits from the mysterious youth to Hogen's daughter had been rumoured around the guardroom for weeks. It amazed him that Hogen had not heard them before, but Hori Yataro decided he had better hear them now.

'I don't know much. He comes here from time to time

and has had a few clashes with Jiro. It is said – I don't know if it is true – that he ... ah ... visits your daughter, Asuka.' He steadied himself for the blast to come.

'What?' shouted Hogen, and started for the steps.

'Wait!' Tomomori commanded. 'Here comes Jiro. Let us see what happens. The youth looks worth watching.'

Jiro waddled down into the yard, his red nose bright as a persimmon. At the sight of Yoshitsuné he froze and then quickly pulled out his sword. Soldiers were beginning to collect on the verandas, hugging themselves against the cold and shouting jeers and encouragement.

One hand on the Hachiman sword, Yoshitsuné walked towards Jiro. His mind was completely clear. He saw only his opponent and concentrated on the man's size, strength, age and sword as he approached. Neither spoke. At a few paces Yoshitsuné drew his blade and they crouched; swinging their swords in both hands, they began circling slowly. Yoshitsuné could feel Red-nose's nerves; the man constantly licked his lips and the slim sword quivered in his hands. The boy suddenly feinted, Jiro charged foolishly and took the Hachiman sword straight in the shoulder. He hung for a second or two on the point until Yoshitsuné jerked it away and Red-nose fell forward with a sigh, too wounded to continue the fight.

Yoshitsuné stared down at the writhing figure, disappointment surging through him. It had been too easy and too little – an anti-climax with no satisfaction. He had wanted to see his humiliator die, but now that figure of evil was no more than a wriggling, bloodied worm. He turned away in sick disgust. It had not even been a real fight.

Hogen's voice cracked across the still yard. 'Yataro, kill that insolent intruder!'

The captain could not object. It was a challenge as well as a command. He drew his sword and jumped off the veranda. The boy stood dazed, sword lowered, watching him approach. As he drew nearer Hori Yataro could see how badly beaten he was, one eye swollen shut, his face puffy and bruised. But pride gave his distorted face dignity and Yataro respected him. This would be no easy victory.

'My name is Hori Yataro, *former* captain of Oni-ichi Hogen's guard.' He emphasised the word 'former' slightly, for his own satisfaction. 'Who do I have the honour of fighting?'

Yoshitsuné's lips moved stiffly but his voice was precise. 'My name does not matter. I will fight you.' The man was too good for him, he knew, but this would be better than the continuing emptiness and self-contempt of dirtying his hands on Red-nose.

The two men waited as Jiro was helped away and then they turned to face each other. The courtyard and verandas were now packed with silent, tense men. Yataro was one of Hogen's prize swordsmen and it was amazing that he had been ordered to take on this youth, so amazing that the grim audience was uneasy. Fights were hardly unusual now the atmosphere was electric. Hogen restlessly fingered the hilt of his dagger but Tomomori stared intently at Yoshitsuné.

The opponents bowed. Yataro said softly, 'Are you ready, boy? We will not start if you are tired.'

Yoshitsuné snapped his head up. 'I am ready,' he replied coldly.

Facing each other, eyes locked, the two began to circle, each waiting his chance. Occasionally one would shout or stamp to startle the other. The beautiful, deadly blades sparkled in the winter sun. Once, twice, Yataro attacked with a scream but each time his blow was warded off. The circling continued. The sweat on their faces glistened in the cold air. Yoshitsuné's eyes were fixed in concentration. Nothing existed but the sword in his hands and the figure crouching opposite. Quickly he thrust at Yataro, who leapt aside with a bellow and slashed out. Yoshitsuné yanked his sword upwards and caught Yataro's at the hilt. There was a jarring crash of metal on metal as Yataro's sword flew into the air, over the high fortress wall and struck the thin ice of the moat with a vibrating slap. The captain stood stunned, arms outstretched to strike again with his vanished weapon.

The quiet courtyard exploded as the soldiers poured off

the verandas. For a few moments the two men were left undisturbed in the confusion. Yoshitsuné bowed, his good eye glinting. The fight had been a proper one against a superb opponent and he had acquitted himself well. His confidence was suddenly boundless and only a very tenuous hold on reality prevented him from taking on the entire courtyard. Yataro caught some of the youth's ebullience and grinned. The humiliating loss of his sword suddenly seemed unimportant. It was impossible to dislike or resent a boy who fought so well.

'Hogen,' said Tomomori softly, 'there is something about this youth. Don't set anyone else on him. Damn your daughter and your whole family's honour! I want to talk to him inside.'

Yataro bowed. 'I imagine you have finished with me now, Hogen. I'll leave.'

Hogen's sneer was wide and lipless. 'Wait in the barracks. Don't know if you're worthy of the Rokuhara now, eh? You,' he snapped at Yoshitsuné, 'come.' Yoshitsuné bowed and followed. He had never seen his mistress's father before but even in his exultant state he was amazed that such an ugly man could produce such a lovely child. Walking through the crowd he himself was studied and discussed loudly, several remarking on his smooth face and deceptively frail physique. Yataro's defeat was being taken seriously.

Not trusting himself to speak, Hogen slid open the door to a small room off the main barracks and gestured Yoshitsuné to enter. The boy had not noticed his audience but now he recognised the Taira general. For the first time that day he realised the danger he ran for himself and his clan. Involuntarily he glanced at the naked blade in his hand and then at Tomomori who watched him patiently.

'It's a fine sword.' Tomomori's tone was gruff but not unfriendly. 'May I see it? I fancy myself as an expert.' Yoshitsuné considered quickly. The Hachiman sword with its engravings was famous and Tomomori was sure to recognise the heirloom of the rival clan, but to refuse to show it would arouse even greater suspicion. How foolish

he had been! His only hope if challenged was to say he had found the blade, a just plausible explanation since the Hachiman sword had disappeared after Yoshitomo's death.

He rested the point on his arm guard and passed it hilt first to Tomomori. The Taira took a sheet of paper from his sleeve and used it to protect the steel from the moisture on his hands. Although he studied the blade minutely he concentrated on the balance and the cutting edge, giving the engravings only a quick glance. Scrambling to his feet, the general swung the sword as fully as the low thatch would allow and then returned it to Yoshitsuné, who had watched the whole procedure with ill-concealed tension.

'What a superb specimen. That dedication to Hachiman is unusual but fitting when one comes to think of it. If for any reason you want to sell it ... but no, I am sure you wouldn't.'

'No, my lord. I came by it by chance and ...' Yoshitsuné blurted his story half out and then stopped.

Tomomori finished for him, 'And of course you don't want to part with it. I don't know what master you serve but if you ever wish to join the Taira, come to me, Tomomori.' He nodded dismissively. Yoshitsuné bowed and, ignoring Hogen, left the room, his heart beating so hard he thought the two men must hear. He took three or four breaths of cold air outside to calm himself down.

Across the now empty yard Yataro came towards him.

'I have seen you practise,' said Yoshitsuné, 'and I admired your swordsmanship. It was an honour to fight you.'

'And an even greater one to win, no doubt,' the captain replied drily, looking down at the boy. 'Perhaps we shall meet again – after I've retrieved my sword from the moat.'

Shortly after Yoshitsuné left the fortress Tomomori also departed, leaving behind Hogen, puzzled and angry, pondering his curt instructions to bide his time.

*

Tomomori watched his father with impatience. Kiyomori caught the large cotton ball and rolled it back to the fat, giggling bundle of padded green brocade. Antoku

tottered out to get the ball, over-balanced and teetered perilously close to the brazier heaped with coals. Both men and the nurse leapt to help the Crown Prince but the child grasped his toy and waddled off into the gloom behind the lacquer screens. Although wooden shutters were drawn against the night and braziers were scattered around, the room was cold enough to see one's breath. A spray of early plum, tiny icy white flowers on a bare branch in a grey-green celadon vase, seemed to increase the chill.

A grown man playing with a child was not an edifying sight to Tomomori but he accepted that his father needed some relaxation; Kiyomori was not in good health and the drawn grey face and erratic temper were worrying as was his increasing preoccupation with making his grandson Emperor. An Imperial ruler with a mother from the samurai class shocked Tomomori's conservative soldier's mentality, even though that mother was his own sister.

Antoku came from behind the screens. 'Here, Antoku, roll the ball, roll it. Roll it to me. There, what a clever boy you are. Come and embrace your old grandfather.'

The rotund child toddled to Kiyomori, chortling with excitement. He clambered on to his lap and put his fat short arms around the bent neck. He settled comfortably into a swansdown embrace and began to bat at the amulets dangling against his grandfather's chest.

'What a lovely boy you are. What a marvellous little Emperor you will make. Look at him, Tomomori. Really, he is extremely quick for his age, more like a five-year-old. Here, my little bean cake, have a dried apricot.'

'Father, please give the boy back to his nurse. We must talk.'

Kiyomori shot his too-efficient son an irritated glance. 'I am not getting any younger and quite frankly I am not getting any stronger. It becomes harder each day to face the dawn and to face the world. What harm can it do to take a little pleasure with a future Emperor who is also my grandson?' He tickled the child until he shrieked with laughter. But when Kiyomori beckoned to the nurse the child's face crumpled and turned to shrieks of fury.

71

Firmly, the nurse bore the flailing Crown Prince away. The Lord Chancellor, chewing on an apricot, turned reluctantly to his stern son.

'Now, what is it that brings you to my quarters? Could it not wait until tomorrow?'

'No, father, I don't think it could. I spent this afternoon at Oni-ichi Hogen's fortress and while I was there an unknown boy came to challenge one of the guard, whom he defeated. He then took on Hori Yataro and beat him too.'

'Well, what of it?' asked Kiyomori coldly.

'Father, I know who the boy is,' Tomomori said quietly.

'Well?'

'He is the son of Yoshitomo, probably the youngest. He carries the Hachiman sword; you'll remember it wasn't found with Yoshitomo's body. That wretched servant stole it when he escaped and somehow he managed to pass the sword to the baby you placed at Kurama. It must be him, the youngest one. Yoritomo is certainly still in Izu and our spies say Noriyori is with him. This boy has fine features and an oval face, an unmistakable Minamoto.'

Kiyomori leapt to his feet, scattering the tiny tea table beside him and its contents across the floor. His face convulsed and he shook violently as he bellowed. 'And he was in Hogen's compound! The man who trains our warriors and plans our campaigns has allowed a Minamoto – a son of Yoshitomo – to wander around to his heart's content?' Kiyomori strode over to his son and hissed into his impassive face, 'Kill them! Kill them all tonight!'

Tomomori changed to a soothing tone. 'Hogen is valuable to us. We need him, Father. We need his skill and his knowledge. But the boy . . .'

Kiyomori slumped on his cushion, exhausted. 'All right, forget Hogen but kill the Minamoto. I spared them once because I was tired of death, but it gets easier to kill as you get older. Life becomes simpler, easier to dispose of. I want them all dead.' With a tired wave of his hand he dismissed his son and gestured to his servant to clear up the mess of broken porcelain.

*

Moments after Hogen received his instructions from the Rokuhara Palace he strode into his daughter's room. Asuka was kneeling behind a screen of Korean damask, plucking at the long zither on the floor beside her. To her left was a low, ebony writing desk set up with an ink slab of fine carved stone, a cake of ink ready on its jade rest, a red lacquer container for brushes and another for water; candles stood in elaborate iron holders illuminating the utensils and a roll of pale grey paper. Porcelain braziers stood about the room. Behind another pair of smaller, footed screens, exquisitely painted with tree peonies, was a sleeping pallet and a wooden pillow. A pile of leather clothes boxes and a red lacquer frame supporting a heavy winter Court robe were just visible outside the candlelight.

The scene could not have been more peaceful: a young girl playing to herself before retiring, perhaps after an evening spent practising calligraphy, but to Hogen the room reeked of intrigue. The bed mat spread waiting, sticks of incense smouldering in the bronze holder beside it, Asuka's carefully applied make-up – it all suggested an expected lover. He glared at her.

'Your maids? No attendants? Where are they?'

Asuka stared at her hands lying in her lap, a flush spread slowly up her throat to her cheeks.

'Waiting for that samurai, eh? Know who he is?' She did not look up. 'Minamoto. Chieftain probably, maybe Yoshitomo's son. A Minamoto lover for the daughter of Oni-ichi Hogen! You have ruined me. I felt compelled to take my life but Lord Tomomori begs me not to. Says my value to the Taira is so great that I'm forced to live on in humiliation. Dishonour. Nothing to say?'

Asuka could not speak. Confused, she glanced fearfully at the ebony desk. Hogen followed her eyes. He seized the grey paper. There was nothing written on it.

'Too fine for practising and too long for writing letters or poems. Good paper for making copies of Taira documents like the ones missing from my room. Why are you up at this time of night, eh? You and your traitor lover and – ink stones – and brushes – and water – and long rolls of fine

73

grey paper!' As he named each utensil he kicked it viciously off the low desk. Ignoring Asuka he charged around the room, knocking over the screens. With his dagger he slit open the sleeping pallet and hurled straw around him. Then he pulled the kimono from its frame and ripped it apart, swansdown swirling and floating in the air. Finally he turned to the clothes boxes. He pulled out the heavy robes, scattering them on the floor until the winter box was empty. Then he slashed the spring one, rending it wide with his dagger. He dragged out the fragile clothes of willow green, primrose and apricot and rooted around in the corners of the box. Suddenly, with a yelp, he wheeled on his daughter, who was watching him in horror. In his hand was the scroll containing a description of the Taira strongholds on the Inland Sea.

*

Crunching across the frozen garden to Asuka's room, Yoshitsuné glanced covertly to left and right. He had not dared come to the fortress again in the daytime, even though there had been nothing suspicious in Tomomori's or Hogen's behaviour. However, for this last visit to Asuka he wore his sword, just in case. He must see her and tell Koju to return the Taira document to the strong box. He dreaded the farewell to Asuka almost as much as he dreaded confessing his rash act of revenge to Shomon. He now saw that his impetuous attack on Red-nose, necessary as it had been to him, had been disloyal to Asuka and Shomon. Still, he thought, he had gained something – the satisfaction of his victory over Yataro.

He reached the sanctity of her room without ambush and with a sigh of relief he slid the door open. At first it seemed that Asuka had fallen asleep across the zither with her long glossy hair fanned out over the instrument and onto the floor; then he saw blood seeping into the fine wood, smearing her pale temple, staining the lovely hair. He shook her shoulder. It was limp. He rolled her back from the zither. She had fallen face down in the blood that oozed from the slash in her throat.

74

He barely had time to take in the ravaged room and draw his sword before Hogen burst through the sliding door from the corridor. The diviner was followed by five men, the last of whom was Hori Yataro. The others spread out across the room, kicking writing tools and robes out of their way. Yoshitsuné stood behind Asuka's body. There would be no choice but to fight over it. As he surveyed his opponents he saw that Yataro had not moved from the doorway behind Hogen and the other men. Their eyes met briefly. Yataro gave a curt nod of his head towards the stocky warrior on his right. Suddenly he plunged forward, his sword cutting across the candles flickering in their iron holders. They fell, spluttering, and went out on the wooden floor. Just as the light failed Yoshitsuné saw the stocky warrior topple forward, shock in his eyes and gaping mouth. The boy swung to take on the two men nearest him, trusting to Yataro's advantage of surprise to kill the others. He engaged one and saw in the dim glow from the corridor that it was not Hogen. The diviner had wheeled away and was pulling at the garden door, presumably to let in more light. There was no sound but splintering wood and the curses and grunts of fighting men. The floor was slippery with long polishing and with rivulets of blood. Yoshitsuné often stumbled and staggered to keep his balance and once, to his horror, he tripped on Asuka's body. He disposed of the second of his opponents with a deft slice and turned to Hogen. Moonlight spilled erratically across the room but Yoshitsuné dared not look to see how Yataro was faring. He heard a crash as the incense holder went over, the strong scent briefly obscuring the smell of sweat and death. One man, not Yataro, screamed with pain as he fell across the brazier, banked with softly glowing charcoal. The man screamed again but this time it was cut short.

Hogen was, as Yoshitsuné expected, a fierce fighter, cunning, quick and with the strength of ten men in his stumpy frame, but he had one disadvantage – he stood out in the moonlight against the dim square of the garden while Yoshitsuné was invisible in the shadows. Moving very swiftly he made several surprise attacks on the diviner.

Hogen was famous for his warding tactics and now Yoshitsuné discovered why – the man reacted with the speed of a snake, every blow efficiently blocked. Gradually, Yoshitsuné managed to manoeuvre him into the dark mêlée of bodies and broken furniture. The diviner swore as he trod barefoot on a burning stick of incense. His footwork became restricted. Yoshitsuné heard the twang of a zither string and assumed Hogen had backed into a body wedged against the splintered instrument, perhaps his daughter's. From the corner of his eye he saw Yataro silhouetted against the corridor, panting but apparently unhurt. At that moment Hogen cursed and fell backwards in the dark, sprawling over the dull red coals scattered over the floor. The boy paused only a second and then plunged his sword into the diviner's throat.

Yataro grabbed his arm and as they fled down the corridor towards the garden he muttered to Yoshitsuné, 'I hope you can swim, boy. If we escape from here we still have that moat to cross.'

*

Benkei lived near the Rashomon Gate in the burnt-out ruins of a temple. The main hall was gutted and roofless, the altar, where a goddess had stood smiling graciously at her flock, was a charred stump. The big monk's quarters were in a small separate chapel. It needed strong nerves to stand the place because each wall was painted with lurid visions of hell; horned, staring-eyed demons applied indescribable tortures to their eternally screaming victims while fire, earthquakes and typhoons raged. Every time Yoshitsuné saw the paintings he was profoundly thankful he had never met the artist. Benkei, however, was perfectly at ease. He had a straw pallet, a brazier, a lamp, a chest for his armour and the demons for company.

Yoshitsuné and Yataro escaped from the fortress with little difficulty and swam the icy moat. When the bodies in Asuka's room were found they would become hunted men and Benkei's isolated hide-out seemed the best place to go. Yataro said most of the guardroom knew about Hogen's

orders to kill Yoshitsuné and if Yataro's body was missing it would be known that he had betrayed his master, a crime of great magnitude to a samurai. As they raced through the cold streets in their wet clothes Yoshitsuné tried to question him about his sudden defection. Yataro's answer was to grab him and pull him into the gateway of a mansion. 'Hush,' he whispered, 'the Taira nightwatch! I'll tell you when we are safe.'

Benkei's chapel was empty but they found charcoal, built a fire and carefully cleaned their weapons. Yoshitsuné tried to concentrate on scouring the brown crust from his blade, striving to keep mindlessly busy, but the congealed blood brought ghastly memories back into his numb brain. It was no good. Finally, aching and exhausted, he pushed the sword away, squatted in front of the fire and gazed into the flames, unable to avoid his thoughts any longer. Asuka – limp, soft, empty, horrible. He shuddered, remembering her smooth, warm skin under his caresses – and then – her hand, waxy, cold, like a terrible doll. Blood, so much blood. Red slime from her throat, the throat he had so often kissed. Blood on her face, across her breast, on his hands. He retched and rubbed his palms wildly on his stained jacket. My fault, he thought, frantic. I made her into that awful ... thing. My fault she's dead. My fault Hogen's dead. He had to die. But again the sight of it; the feel of the blade pressing against Hogen's throat; elastic; grinding bone; piercing muscle; spurt of blood; a half-cry of death – the bone, muscle, blood, a gasp. He deserved to die but, great Amida, is it always so ugly? Is killing always so difficult, so terrible? Holy Amida, how will I go on? The bile rose again and he staggered out into the courtyard to heave up the horror, alone under the stars.

Shivering, he returned to the fire and tried vainly to warm his blood, to still his chattering teeth. Yataro looked up. 'Your first?' he asked, handing him a cup of saké. Yoshitsuné nodded. Yataro studied his white, miserable face.

'It's always bad. Don't brood on it,' said the samurai gruffly. 'It was Hogen's karma to die by the sword, but few

men could have fought him as you did. His death is your honour. It's the warrior's way. Dog that he was, he would have accepted that.'

'And Asuka?' Yoshitsuné spoke through a throat aching with tears that must not come.

'She was only a woman, and his daughter, but ... I understand.' His square hand dropped on the boy's shoulder. 'Look, we have decisions to make. Samurai kill, that's a fact of life. Forget it.'

Yataro stretched out beside the brazier and went on, 'Rumour has it you're a Minamoto, one of Yoshitomo's sons.' Yoshitsuné looked back at the fire. 'All right. Be secretive,' Yataro said, 'but without me your head would be skewered on a pike on the Rokuhara gates by now.' He sipped his saké and they sat silently for a few minutes.

Suddenly, Yoshitsuné asked, 'Why did you help me?'

Yataro sat up. 'Two reasons. One, my father was a samurai in the service of a Minamoto warlord in Mino Province. He died in bed but the rebellion frightened my mother and she had me sent to learn my trade from Hogen, assuming that I would be safe in the Taira camp. Although I have Minamoto loyalties, I'm not a political animal and Hogen was a good teacher until yesterday afternoon. That brings me to the second reason. He was sending me to the Rokuhara Palace to serve in the Taira Special Guard and that cancelled my obligation to him. My last task was to kill you, but as you can see ...' He gestured with his broad hands.

'I am Minamoto Yoshitsuné, last son of Yoshitomo,' the boy replied simply. 'If you have no lord now, will you serve me?'

Yataro grinned. 'I thought you would never ask. You killed one of the greatest swordsmen in the Capital tonight. Let's drink to it.'

They drank until Yoshitsuné's eyelids began to droop. Just before he fell into an exhausted sleep he remembered again Asuka's gentle touch, the almond fragrance of her hair, but he was too tired, too drunk, too empty to cry now.

*

Benkei shuffled in soon after dawn, appraised Yataro and heard their tale. He reported that Hogen's men and Taira soldiers were swarming the streets looking for Yoshitsuné and possibly a tall samurai. Any suspicious-looking man was stopped and the wine houses and brothels frequented by warriors had been searched. They decided the fugitives would be safe for a while in the derelict temple – the Capital was too large and too full of hiding places to scour thoroughly.

After a few days Benkei went to the Shijo Temple to find Shomon, who was just back from a visit to Izu. The Holy Man already knew about Yoshitsuné's foolhardy revenge and Hogen's attack; his deep-set eyes blazed with fury that startled even Benkei. 'The boy wants to be a samurai, to emulate Hachiman Taro! Well, Hachiman Taro didn't endanger his clan just to soothe his idiotic pride. What sort of samurai will he be if he doesn't take orders?'

Benkei, who had found obeying orders at Mount Hiei rather tiresome, said nothing. But he took Shomon's point and wondered if the boy really did appreciate the irresponsibility of his actions. He seemed full of remorse, but how much of that was shock after his first kill or regret over the girl, Benkei was not sure. Independent renegade though he was, the monk could still understand Shomon's worry. 'A samurai should never put personal business above his duty!' the Holy Man snapped.

'He is young and has had no one to guide him. He was bound to be headstrong.'

'Well, now he must grow up. He's being sent to Kiso, and then to Oshu. That's what Yorimasa wants.' He remembered his conversation with the old poet, just the night before, as the two of them drank warm saké by a brazier.

'He may have ruined everything,' Shomon had grumbled. 'The sword must have been recognised.'

'Obviously he must leave the Capital,' agreed Yorimasa, pulling his padded kimono closer around his thin shoulders. 'But we can make use of his flight. First he'll go to Kiso to meet his cousin and have a partial family

reunion. Let them sniff each other over – it may save us time later. And then after Kiso he must go north to Oshu. Fujiwara Hidehira is not only the richest warlord in the country after Kiyomori, he's also the epitome of a samurai; he'll know how to train a headstrong youth. And Yoshitsuné does need discipline.'

He had smiled at Shomon. 'We need Hidehira's help against the Taira or, at the very least, his promised neutrality. I know you're angry with the boy. So am I. He is arrogant and impetuous and does not respect his elders, but he has tremendous charm and Hidehira's a very old man with sons who disappoint him. Yoshitsuné wants to be a great warrior and that will attract Hidehira's interest. The boy may accomplish more than we old men ever could. He may bring us the Oshu Fujiwara as allies.'

Shomon did not share Yorimasa's confidence in Yoshitsuné's charm, so he did not repeat the gist of the conversation to Benkei. The monk was informed of Yorimasa's wishes, given a letter of introduction to Kiso for Yoshitsuné and then curtly dismissed. Shomon wanted no more of Yoshitomo's wayward son and his unsavoury companion.

*

Within the month spies brought news that an attempt had been made on the lives of Yoritomo, Noriyori and Hojo Tokimasa in Izu. They had escaped to the hills with Yoritomo's wife, Lady Masako, but there was no longer any doubt that Tomomori had recognised the Hachiman sword and that the Taira were warned. Now Go-Shirakawa had only to ask the Minamoto to take up arms. The sides had been drawn.

4. The Mountains

Spring followed the three companions into the mountains. They left the Capital with the falling plum blossom and crossed the Home Provinces as the apricot and almond trees made their pathetic display in a land hard and cracked after a dry winter and where the rains were already late. The hard-pressed peasants did not welcome extra mouths, and in several hamlets dogs were let loose on them. Frequently, however, they brought down game, and with a badger or deer as an offering to the pot they were allowed to huddle in a smoky corner of a farmhouse, with the farmer's family and animals keeping suspicious watch. Shabby samurai were not unusual in districts around the Capital but they were not loved, armed monks even less.

Occasionally they had to avoid parties of retainers wearing the insignia of local Taira warlords. Twice in one stretch of forest the fugitives met horsemen on the narrow paths and, rather than risk a challenge, they plunged into scratchy thickets until the riders had passed. Both times the parties proved to be bandits, starved-out peasants with no other future but robbery and murder.

As they went higher into the forests of camellia, oak and cedar they saw few people – only a woodcutter and an occasional farmer scratching out an existence in a clearing. One day they came across an incredibly old hermit, chattering cheerfully to himself into his straggling white beard as he sat by a crude shrine, a tiny wooden building crouched under a towering cedar. Yoshitsuné and Yataro shared their millet and some pickles with the old man and prayed briefly in front of the closed altar, sacred to the mountain god. But Benkei snorted at such superstition, patted the featureless grey stone images and went off fishing.

They reached the Shinano Mountains and Kiso in the

81

fourth month. The rains had not failed here and the village, scattered around a small wooded valley, was ablaze with magnolia and quince. As they approached the outlying farms the peasants, hoeing in the rough fields, eyed them suspiciously and dogs sniffed and growled at the travellers' leggings. The village consisted of clumps of small wooden houses standing in fenced vegetable plots. There was a dingy wine shop, and a shrine standing slightly apart, shrouded in a grove of trees. At the end of the path through the village was a large open space and a pond fed by a stream where women with babies lashed to their broad backs pounded laundry or scrubbed cooking pots. When the strangers stamped the dust from their boots and went to wash briefly in the pond, the women pulled away nervously, gathering their children around them.

Beyond the pond was a large wooden palisade with a shallow moat. This was the home of Minamoto Yoshinaka, called Kiso, only living child of Yoshikata, the youngest brother of Yoshitomo and murdered by him.

The gates of the palisade were open and they strode straight into a large barren yard. The only occupants were three mangy dogs snarling over a bone and some chickens picking in the dirt. The house was one-storeyed, with not more than three or four rooms under a heavy lowering roof of thatch.

Benkei walked to the veranda and bellowed into the quiet house, 'Hello! May we beg your attention for a moment?' Silence. 'Is there anybody here?'

The slatted wooden door shot open and a burly, bearded man in his twenties stepped on to the veranda, one hand on his sword. The sword was incongruous with his coarse leather jacket and breeches and plaited straw leggings and sandals, but judging by his broad shoulders and powerful legs he knew how to use it.

'What do you want? We don't welcome strangers in Kiso. State your names and business. You first, monk.' The man had a deep voice thick with mountain dialect.

Yoshitsuné stepped to Benkei's side. He bowed. 'Minamoto Yoshitsuné, last son of Minamoto Yoshitomo,

therefore cousin of Minamoto Yoshinaka, known as Kiso. These men are my retainers, Benkei the monk and Hori Yataro, a fine swordsman. We have come to speak with my honoured cousin.'

He stared at the peasant warrior, expecting some sign of recognition and respect, but the man remained unmoved, looking them up and down with stern eyes. 'Prove it,' he barked.

Benkei had been warned by Shomon that Kiso would be wary and unfriendly: 'Kiso is no place for a display of arrogance,' Shomon had said bitterly, freezing the monk with a disapproving glance. Now Yoshitsuné, barely containing his irritation at this crude welcome, drew Shomon's letter of introduction from the sleeve of his jacket, bowed stiffly, and handed it to the man who unrolled it. He scowled contemptuously at the contents and then yelled into the house, 'Imai, Suzuki, come here!' Two men, also in rough leather with tangled hair tied up in twisted bands like peasants, came out carrying swords. 'Imai, get my uncle. Suzuki, watch these three.' They did as they were told. Everyone waited silently.

After a few minutes Imai returned followed by a man in his fifties, who shuffled out on the veranda, his feet concealed by trailing court trousers over which he wore a faded, embroidered kimono of scarlet brocade. His top-knot was covered by a stiff peaked Court headdress, green with age but a Court headdress none the less. He was powdered and heavily made up.

Yoshitsuné stared in disbelief at this apparition, now gracefully seating himself on a low stool. Before him was an aged version of himself – no, not quite himself. Although the face was oval and delicately featured like his own, the eyes were prominent, the cleanly plucked, powdered cheeks pinched and pale, and the curved mouth was petulant and slightly slack, showing too many small, even teeth, carefully blackened. It was a face that was shrewd and foolish, cultured and mean at one and the same time.

With barely a glance at the newcomers he held out a white hand and said in a high, educated whine, 'I suppose

you wish me to read that, nephew.' He shrugged. 'What would you do without me?' He took the scroll, perused it quickly, then turned to Yoshitsuné, smiling with all his tiny teeth.

'You must be Yoshitomo's son. I am your father's younger brother, Yukiiye, humbly at your service. This is your cousin, called Kiso, who has extended his hospitality to me and will no doubt do so to you.'

The bearded man studied Yoshitsuné closely. He gestured to his lieutenants to put up their swords and then exchanged bows with his cousin. 'Excuse my precautions, cousin. Now of course I can see how closely you resemble our honoured uncle, but we have few strangers here in Kiso. It is best to treat them with suspicion at first.' The mountain twang had modified and his language became formal and comprehensible.

The visitors removed their sandals and entered the main hall, a large dim room with latticed windows and a crudely finished wood floor. The only decorations were armour chests pushed against the timber and plaster walls, a huge rack hung with halberds and long bows and an earthenware vase with a branch of golden quince in it lighting up a dark corner. Two men, dressed in hemp, sat throwing dice. These Kiso introduced as the Kato brothers.

Yukiiye giggled as he settled cross-legged on the only cushion. 'I call these four the Heavenly Kings after the four guardians of Buddha. They are never far from Kiso's side and protect him as assiduously as though he were Buddha.' The four warriors certainly looked formidable – broad, taciturn and alert.

Kiso frowned at his uncle and then explained swiftly, 'Imai is my foster brother. His father took me in and raised me after . . . my father died. We are brothers in everything but blood. He, the Katos and Suzuki would die for me and I for them. I trust it is the same in any bond among samurai.'

Yukiiye's eyes flickered over his new nephew, looking for some reaction to Kiso's reference to his father's death, but Yoshitsuné, unaware of the family history of fratricide,

showed no sign of comprehension and continued to study his cousin with interest; dour, Yorimasa had said, but a leader of men. Yes, Yoshitsuné could feel the power of the man.

Suddenly a door in the back of the room slid open. A woman dressed in a faded kimono with a gauze scarf covering her hair and face knelt on the threshold. She touched her forehead to the floor three times and then, eyes lowered, walked gracefully into the room, carrying a wooden tray with coarse jugs and wine cups.

'This is my wife. We live a primitive and informal life in the mountains, my cousin. Our women work and fight by our side. She is also an accomplished dancer, however, and perhaps she will perform later.' The woman knelt and placed the tray before her husband. The three visitors stared, stunned at the incredible sight of a woman moving freely among men. Her face was too heavily veiled to judge her beauty, but Yataro noted that she was tall and slim and moved with as much grace as any pampered noblewoman. It was her hair that really gained his approval, glossy and sleek and so long that it trailed a foot or two on the floor as she backed out of the room.

The men split into two groups. Benkei, Yataro and three of the Heavenly Kings retired to one side with saké and dice and stories. Kiso, Yukiiye and Imai, who was firmly included by Kiso, plied Yoshitsuné with questions about Yorimasa and Shomon and the plans of the Taira. Yukiiye asked about the current fashions in the Capital. The older man had been a wandering exile for eighteen years. He had not directly participated in Yoshitomo's rebellion but unlike Yorimasa he had not been considered safe or useful enough to be accepted at Court, so he had drifted from one Minamoto family to another with occasional incognito visits to his beloved Capital. Although he could use a sword he was not really a samurai but a member of the samurai class raised and educated as a courtier. This had been his life until his older brother's rebellion had cast him into disgrace and out of the Court. Kiso village had been his main base for the last few years. Attempts to instil into his

nephew some basic education and gracious airs had been unsuccessful. To Yukiiye's chagrin Kiso remained firmly a mountain-bred samurai, happiest in the company of his warriors and his horses.

Yoshitsuné told them as much as he knew of Yorimasa's plans. Kiso questioned him about Yoritomo and was disappointed that the boy had not met him. Although he did not mention the matter of the clan chieftainship it was obviously an important issue. He also asked to see, and minutely examined, the Hachiman sword, returning it to Yoshitsuné without comment.

The conversation turned to local conditions. Kiso explained that he was in contact with various warlords all over the mountain province and could raise an army of two thousand men in a matter of days. Some of the men were Minamoto themselves but others were minor warlords – little more than bandit chiefs – who realised that their purposes were best served by an alliance with one of the larger clans. Since Taira presence in the hill regions was traditionally negligible – they liked the coast and rice lands – Kiso had easily established the Minamoto cause as the mountain cause with himself as its leader.

Kiso's wife returned with small tables laden with salted vegetables, red beans, venison and smoked bear meat. Yoshitsuné, used to the delicate taste and texture of fresh fish and vegetables, found the game revolting, but the others ate freely, washing the food down with large draughts of rough rice wine. The hall grew gloomier, barely lit by a few lamps of bear fat. The drinking increased and the conversation became wilder. Eventually Yukiiye retired fastidiously to another room, leaving the now drunken warriors to highly-coloured tales of battle and bravery that went far into the night until, one by one, the drinkers collapsed.

The next few days were spent inspecting Kiso's samurai in the valley and meeting local warlords. The mountain men, crude and unlettered, were lacking the basic graces considered necessary for even the lowest samurai in service in the Capital. None, including the warlords, could read or

86

write; they spoke, if at all, in a terse low dialect that was barely comprehensible, and orders were obeyed with a surly shrug. Clothes were of coarse hemp or battered leather and their long, untidy hair was bound up in greasy rags. There were no lacquered steel corselets, padded silk, neat topknots or stiff headdresses. But discipline was strict, each man knew his place and his duty. Furthermore, the dangers of life in such a rough country made absolute loyalty essential. A man bound himself to a master to train, fight and die without question. In return he received a horse and a plot of land. It was an effective system without subtleties or confusion.

At night, wrapped in fur rugs in a corner of the hall, Yoshitsuné discussed what he saw each day with Benkei and Yataro. Kiso he found mystifying: gruff, charmless, strangely bitter, not at all appealing to the youth despite his obvious ability as a warrior. Acutely aware of his own lack of military experience, Yoshitsuné needed to test his opinions against those of the others. Benkei and Yataro had some reservations about Kiso's ultimate worth to the Minamoto.

'Suppose,' Benkei said, 'there's a conflict over the leadership and Yorimasa and Yoritomo find they are fighting against Kiso. Whew! A couple of thousand of these mountaineers could destroy a fair-sized army.'

'You don't think Kiso would obey orders from above? Yorimasa and the Cloistered Emperor?' Yoshitsuné asked.

Yataro sucked his teeth. 'I think he is very ambitious. His claim to be chieftain is not as good as your older brother's but nevertheless he is a powerful warlord.'

'Of course, it would be easier to assess Kiso if we knew something about Yoritomo and the men he has,' Benkei said between yawns, 'but one thing is certain – these mountain men are magnificent fighters.'

Yataro lay on his back, looking up into the gloom. 'They understand – really understand – duty. I haven't seen any of the quarrels or rivalries like the ones we used to have in Hogen's quarters. They must exist – men are only men – but you feel that not one would let his own emotions

interfere with his duty. That makes them dangerous.'

'But is that good?' asked Yoshitsuné. 'I mean, if a man never thinks for himself . . .'

Yataro replied irritably, 'You have a lot to learn about being a samurai. The trouble with you, Yoshitsuné, is that you've always been on your own, but you'll understand how it works after a few months in Oshu, living like a samurai.'

There was a long pause while each man thought his separate thoughts. Finally Yataro broke the silence. 'Hogen expected loyalty too, but somehow, because he was a monk and not one of us, I never accepted him.' Another pause and then he continued, his voice low and hoarse, 'What I did was still wrong. He was my master.'

'He repudiated you,' Yoshitsuné replied. 'You owed him nothing.'

'Hrumph,' Yataro grunted. 'I wonder. Somehow life seems simpler here in Kiso. A samurai is a samurai, a monk is a monk, a lord is a lord.'

'It's the mountain air,' Benkei muttered, but he was watching Yoshitsuné in the dim light. Did the boy ever think about his own disloyalty? When he disobeyed Shomon's instructions about the Hachiman sword he had nearly ruined Yorimasa's careful plans. Did Yoshitsuné understand that, Benkei wondered.

But Yoshitsuné was remembering Hogen and Asuka and speculating sleepily that perhaps Yataro was too disturbed about the whole business. After all, it had turned out right in the end – except, of course, for Asuka. He drifted into sleep.

*

Kiso assessed his visitors no less keenly; Yoshitsuné's swordsmanship impressed him, but in their discussions he found the boy gratifyingly naïve. One rainy afternoon during a game of chess Kiso questioned Yoshitsuné about his plans.

'Well, we'll go on to Hiraizumi. Someone must talk to Hidehira and the Oshu Fujiwara and try to persuade them

88

to our side.'

'The Oshu Fujiwara have always been neutral. Hidehira is entirely concerned with that province of his and who can blame him? After all, he fought the native tribes for it. They say he has native blood himself and that's what makes him so tough. But how will a boy like you convince the old man to fight in the south? What will he get from it?'

Yoshitsuné rolled one of the smooth chess pieces in his hands. 'I don't know. But if there's to be civil war in the land – and it seems there will be – he has to take sides.'

'Suppose he does help us and then demands the biggest prize of all as a reward? He may be centred in the north, but his clan is the oldest. The Fujiwara have existed nearly as long as the Imperial family. No, he'll want the big prize.'

'What prize? What do you mean?' Yoshitsuné was puzzled.

'Real power lies with the samurai now. Kiyomori is Lord Chancellor – fair enough – but his strength comes from the military. Why not take an appropriate title, a military one, like Shogun? The way I see it, we may do the fighting and then Hidehira will demand to be Shogun.'

Yoshitsuné laughed, surprised. 'There hasn't been a Shogun for – oh, twenty Emperors. I don't know how long.'

'There is no reason why there shouldn't be one now that the samurai rule the land,' replied Kiso placidly. 'General-issimo of the Emperor! Greater than any Lord Chancellor.'

Speculation glinted in Yoshitsuné's eye; how great and how ruthless was Kiso's ambition – and how much was this ambition for the clan or for himself? Isolated in his mountain village, what dreams of power and wealth haunted Kiso's sleep? 'Is that what you want, Kiso? To be Shogun?'

Kiso shrugged. His little cousin was growing rather too sharp. 'You are a good swordsman and you probably deserve the Hachiman sword, if only because it was Yoshitomo's.' He sneered over the name of his father's murderer. 'But you do not understand the important things.'

Yoshitsuné said quietly, 'I understand that you want to

be Shogun, but then Yoritomo will also want to be Shogun and that weakens our clan. You are selfish in your ambitions, Kiso. I hope Yoritomo will not be the same.'

'And you, what do you want?' asked Kiso coldly.

'I want to be the greatest warrior that ever lived. I don't need to be Shogun for that.' Yoshitsuné turned back to the chessboard with dignity; another few moves and he might win the game from Kiso.

When, after a stay of a few weeks, Yoshitsuné and his comrades left Kiso the cousins had a wary mutual respect but understood each other not at all.

As a parting present Kiso gave the three men fine mountain-bred ponies, small, broad-chested, sure-footed beasts that tackled the stony paths with confidence. Pushing their sturdy mounts all day, stopping only to sleep or visit Minamoto sympathisers, the three men arrived in Oshu at midsummer. They rode into the capital, Hiraizumi, on the eve of the Festival of the Dead.

5. The Imperial Blessing

Commotion was unusual in the discreet rooms of the Hojoji Palace. The Cloistered Emperor was aware that something peculiar was occurring in the ante-chamber even before his attendant Tametoki appeared, confused and flustered. Before either could speak Kiyomori strode round the Korean screens, jostled Tametoki aside and made curt obeisance to Go-Shirakawa. He brought with him a sharp smell of outdoors that cut across the perfumed stuffiness of the Palace.

'How surprising, Lord Chancellor. This sudden visit is a pleasure. We had thought you were spending the winter on the Inland Sea with our grandson, the new little Emperor Antoku. Perhaps the seaside has lost its charm for you?' purred Go-Shirakawa. Only his narrow eyes betrayed any nervousness.

Kiyomori's appearance had changed drastically in the last two years. His face and physique had the wasted droop that comes from frequent exhausting fevers and the thin hands tucked in his sleeves shook constantly. Summer no longer brought relief from his ailment and now in the bitter winter cold he suffered more than ever.

'My villa still charms, Your Highness, but Antoku is frail and took cold in the sea air.'

'And since his father Takakura is dead and Antoku is now the Emperor you decided to bring him back to the dour delights of the Capital? It is not a very pleasant place at the moment, or so we understand. Still very little food and a great deal of plague, although of course here in the Imperial Enclosure . . .' He spread out one plump hand to suggest a cornucopia of food and health.

Kiyomori snapped, 'He is your grandson too. And your Emperor. I would have thought you would have wanted him kept safe.'

Go-Shirakawa returned Kiyomori's rudeness with a

well-aimed barb. 'We understand that young Antoku is not always safe in the Capital even under the massive Taira guard that accompanies him everywhere. We were told a madman managed to gain access to the shrine during Antoku's accession ceremony and harangued the child on the ill omens that have dogged his short life. A madman in the Imperial shrine is quite an ill omen in itself, we would have thought.'

'We dealt with the madman. The child was not frightened,' Kiyomori replied sharply.

'Ah.'

Go-Shirakawa took a saké cup from Tametoki. Kiyomori, as usual not offered anything, watched his host sip and then remarked in an unexpectedly pleasant voice, 'Your Highness has been very busy while the Court was resting on the Inland Sea. I find it admirable that, as well as religious duties, Your Highness can maintain such a varied group of acquaintances and keep up such a vigorous correspondence. Imagine exchanging letters with such entirely different men as Minamoto Yukiiye and Hojo Tokimasa, an exiled courtier and a provincial warlord. What an unusual combination! And how clever of Your Highness to discover the whereabouts of Tokimasa when the Rokuhara soldiers have been looking nearly two years for him.' The tone was smooth but the malice was unmistakable.

Go-Shirakawa replied evenly, 'It is kind of the Lord Chancellor, so occupied with his own affairs, to take an interest in ours. But you will appreciate that most of our time is spent in the observance of the holy sutras.'

'It is about Your Highness's religious duties that I came today.' Go-Shirakawa almost blinked. 'The hurly-burly of the Imperial Enclosure must be a terrible distraction for a man of Your Highness's piety. Such a worldly, not to say sinful atmosphere.' Kiyomori caressed his moustaches. 'Therefore I wish to present Your Highness with a token of my respect – a palace, small but attractive, in Higashiyama, just outside the Capital. A perfect place for meditation and repose.'

'Lord Kiyomori, you are always a thoughtful man but we shall not presume on your generosity.' A slight film of sweat spread across Go-Shirakawa's forehead.

Kiyomori pounced. 'It is my pleasure. And to ensure the move to this quiet abode is an easy one I have provided a detachment of soldiers to escort Your Highness.' His voice cut across the discreetly luxurious room like the edge of a polished sword. 'They are in the courtyard, awaiting instructions. Your Highness can – and *will* – leave for Higashiyama immediately.'

He touched his forehead to the floor three times rapidly and prepared to rise. But, as though it were an after-thought, he looked straight into the Cloistered Emperor's eyes and said, 'There are other members of the Court, also close friends of Minamoto Yukiiye and Hojo Tokimasa, whom I should like to honour as well. Each of these men will discover a small band of Taira soldiers outside their mansions for protection in these difficult times.' He bowed again, with a distinct flourish of triumph and left the Sacred Presence fuming impotently on his silk cushion.

*

The sudden summons mid-afternoon had been a great surprise and Shomon worried as he hurried along towards Yorimasa's mansion. In the past it had been considered wiser for monk and poet to meet only at night.

Yorimasa was not alone. Beside him sat a podgy young man munching candied persimmons whom Shomon recognised as Prince Mochihito, a younger son of Go-Shirakawa, a foppish, bland fellow but still the most promising rival to Emperor Antoku that the Cloister Court could produce. The Holy Man bowed low. Mochihito nodded and chewed.

Yorimasa smiled grimly at his clansman. 'No doubt you are puzzled to be called here, Shomon. Well, there is no time to waste. Prince Mochihito and I have drawn up the call to arms against the tyrant Kiyomori and his usurping grandson. Minamoto Yorimasa, loyal servant of the Clois-tered Emperor, is to take up arms against the Taira and

right the wrongs perpetrated against the Imperial family. The Minamoto will remove Antoku, the samurai Emperor, and place this true child of the Sun Goddess,' he gestured to Mochihito, 'on the throne. A messenger is carrying a copy of our declaration to Yoritomo's camp, another has gone to Kiso. It is a pity you could not see the document but there was no time to lose.'

Shomon was dumbfounded. He had waited and planned so long and now it was beginning.

'There are so many questions, my lord. Why so suddenly? What has happened? Are we ready?'

'You don't know? The Rokuhara Palace is seething with suspicion. Kiyomori has returned to the Capital.' Shomon sighed; he had hoped the Lord Chancellor could be deposed in his absence. 'Go-Shirakawa and most of the courtiers sympathetic to our cause have been placed under virtual house arrest. The Cloistered Emperor is now well and truly cloistered in a Taira villa in Higashiyama surrounded by a hundred samurai. The others are imprisoned in their own homes with armed guards at the gates. Apparently Kiyomori does not suspect Prince Mochihito or myself since we have not been questioned, but naturally we cannot take any risks. Alas, we shall not be able to wait for Kiso or the eastern contingents, perhaps not even for Yoritomo.'

'Which leaves us with the personal retainers of your lordship and the Prince and possibly the monks of the old Capital of Nara, who should support us unless Mount Hiei help Kiyomori. Then what will Nara do? This is a considerable question.'

Yorimasa nodded. 'It is. They could give us two thousand men, but the abbots will be unpredictable at such short notice. That is why the Crown Prince will ride there tonight. His Imperial presence leading the abbots and their men into battle will be encouragement.'

At the words 'ride' and 'lead' a spasm crossed Mochihito's plump face. He put down a persimmon and sucked his sticky fingers.

'Riding? On a horth? You thaid nothing about a horth,

Yorimatha. I hate hortheth!' His many chins quivered with indignation. 'I thall lead my troops into battle in a palanquin at the motht. Perferably an oxth-cart. No hortheth. A wave of my Imperial hand from time to time ith enough encouragement.' He affectionately examined his dimpled but unencouraging paw.

The old man sighed, opened his fan, shut it again. 'Your Highness, speed is essential. A palanquin or an ox-cart will take almost a day to reach Nara. It must be a horse.' His voice was honeyed steel.

Mochihito sat enwrapped in plump, stubborn stupidity. Yorimasa said in a low voice, 'Your father would expect it to be a horse. He will certainly hear about this.'

There was a long silence. Finally Mochihito said in a resigned whisper, 'Then it thall be a horth.' Morosely he picked up his fan and pulled his rotund body upright. 'I thall go to prepare for the ordeal. It ith nethethary that the horth be gentle.' He looked hopefully at Yorimasa.

Yorimasa bowed low three times. 'Naturally, Crown Prince. I know that the brave sight of Your Highness will put steel into the spines of the bonzes of Nara. When next we meet you will be Emperor. A thrilling concept!' He bowed again and Shomon touched his forehead to the floor as Mochihito waddled sadly from the room.

'Oh, what a simpleton the man is! Why didn't Go-Shirakawa have him drowned at birth? Still, he is easy to control and that is in his favour.' Yorimasa's voice was tired, his aristocratic face stretched with fatigue and worry. 'I wish that the boy Yoshitsuné were here. The last two years in Oshu must have changed him, but only to make a man of him. He would be an inspiration to the men. Oh, I know you think he is arrogant and would do something melodramatic and silly, but perhaps he has outgrown that. Anyway, I wish he were here.'

'My lord, you must rest. This business will test your strength to the limit. We had, after all, assumed the brunt of the fighting would be carried by the younger commanders.' Shomon spoke gently. Compassion, a new sentiment, touched him, sweeping away his distrust of the

95

poet-politician. Events had happened too quickly for the old man and Shomon shared his depression; all their years of preparation and planning could well come to dust in the next few days.

'You are right, Shomon, my friend. I must give instructions to my captains. They are waiting in the antechamber. Then I shall rest, if Kiyomori leaves me in peace that long. The Nara monks will send their reply by morning and if they will fight, you and I shall ride to meet them. Perhaps you should sleep here as a precaution.' He rose and looked at the Holy Man's gaunt face. 'I had hoped to go to the next world knowing that my task in this one was completed. That is not to be, I fear. Let us hope the younger generation will be able to finish our work.'

*

A few hours later Taira troops entered the Imperial Enclosure to seize Mochihito and accuse him of treason against Emperor Antoku. But the Prince had already fled, helped by his personal attendants. Strapped into his armour, he had been hurried into a palanquin, to his great relief, and borne to Yorimasa's mansion through streets packed with soldiers pouring in from Taira estates.

Mochihito's near arrest warned Yorimasa to move immediately. He forced the wailing Crown Prince on to a horse and with Shomon and two hundred of his personal retainers they left the Capital on the Nara road, pursued by a large Taira contingent. By the time the fugitives reached the bridge at Uji it was obvious that unless the monks came out to meet them the Minamoto were lost. Scouts reported Taira patrols dotted all over the long river valley that linked the Capital with Nara, but there was no sign of a monastic army. Since the Rokuhara forces would also have to cross the river to reach Nara, Yorimasa chose to make his stand at Uji, the only possible fording. Mochihito would be a useless burden in battle so Yorimasa decided that he should continue on to the old Capital to beg for help. The Crown Prince had dressed himself in a white brocade gown over violet lacquered armour, a ridiculous if impressive

sight. However, horses had indeed proved his nemesis and six times between the Capital and Uji he had tumbled off – now he was muddy and pathetic and whining. Yorimasa ruthlessly bundled him back on his horse and pointed him towards Nara, sparing only a few precious samurai for an escort. If the monks would not fight they should at least give him sanctuary.

Yorimasa ordered the bridge destroyed and the white pennants of the Minamoto unfurled on the eastern bank. A temple, long deserted, stood by the famous crossing. Attracted by its peace Yorimasa retired to the wild garden to wait until the Taira arrived. It was all over, he knew. Now he had to compose himself to face the end.

*

Within two hours the Taira had forded the river, surging over the resistance of the outnumbered Minamoto and dragging the white banners into the mud. Shomon died in the first wave of arrows before he had drawn Taira blood. Death came quickly, but before blackness closed over him he whispered not the name of Amida Buddha but of his master, Yoshitomo, whose death he had failed to avenge.

Yorimasa had removed his winged helmet so that he could see what was happening. His white hair and frail figure on a wheeling, excited horse marked him as an easy target for the Taira bowmen. A group of archers remained on the raised river bank to pour their arrows down on the enemy and it was one such arrow that caught the old man in the neck. He slumped in his saddle, dizzy with pain, but managed to force his mount through the chaos until he reached the deserted temple. His thoughts were fogged with weakness but only one thing mattered – he must not die at Taira hands. The failure of the plot was forgotten, only his own death was important now. The cacophony of the battle receded, leaving only the sound of blood thundering in his temples. With difficulty he found a clearing and slid off his shivering horse into the long grass. He could not hold his head up any longer. A hand touched him and he dimly perceived his manservant beside him.

'Help me.'

The man unbuckled his master's corselet and, drawing out the long dirk from its sheath, pressed it into the old man's palm, his tears falling on to the quivering hand. 'I have your sword, Lord Yorimasa, and will use it. Kiyomori will have nothing to gloat over.' The servant wept openly but Yorimasa was past emotion. The poet and courtier had disappeared, only the conditioned samurai remained. Faintly, with his ebbing strength, he dragged the blade across his naked abdomen. The sword flashed instantly, neatly striking off his head. The servant tossed his grizzled prize into an old well and then returned to the battlefield and his own death at the hands of the Taira swordsmen.

Mochihito nearly reached Nara. Taira soldiers overtook him just outside the half-opened gates of the ancient city. They slaughtered the escort and the plump man in white without a word being spoken. The corpse was put on a shutter wrenched from a nearby farmhouse and dragged back to the Capital, muddy white robes fluttering dimly in the dusk, a depressing testimony to the Cloister Court's new allegiance to the Minamoto.

Kiyomori's first act on hearing the news of the victory was to order the destruction of the Shijo and the major Nara temples. His sons and councillors protested that this pointless violence would turn the Buddhist establishment against the Taira, but he persisted. Shigehira, Kiyomori's youngest son, reluctantly attacked and burned the wayward temples. All that remained of the Shijo was a scorched pagoda, and in Nara the huge bronze Buddha smiled serenely over the smoking ruins of the great hall. The surviving monks scattered to Izu where they joined Yoritomo, or to other monasteries where they fed the growing hatred for Kiyomori and his clan.

Go-Shirakawa sulked in his villa, waiting for deliverance from his Taira protectors.

6. The Brothers

Yataro carried a steaming bowl of gruel round the fire to Yoshitsuné, who lay against his saddle watching the shadows of the flames writhe on the dark pines. The youth looked up at Yataro's approach and smiled.

'How much further, do you think?' He took the bowl and then set it down quickly, blowing on his singed fingers. 'That's hot! Your hands are like leather.'

Yataro laughed and squatted down. 'It's cold at night now, real autumn weather. Snow up in Oshu soon.' He squinted at Yoshitsuné, who stared impassively into the fire, the reflected lights dancing across his eyes. 'You miss old Hidehira, don't you?' he asked abruptly.

Yoshitsuné watched the fire. 'Yes, he was a father to me.' His voice caught and then he continued briskly, 'But after two years it was time to go. Yoritomo's message came at the right time. I was beginning to forget my duties as a Minamoto. It was such a pleasant life,' he added wistfully.

Yataro glanced at him again, at the broad shoulders and small head, held so high and with such fierce pride. Well, he thought, the boy's only twenty; he's matured so much in Hiraizumi, become such a leader, that I forget he's still young. He changed the subject and tried to cheer Yoshitsuné. 'Anyway, Fuji's just to the west and we're well into the Hakone foothills so we should reach Yoritomo's camp tomorrow. I wonder how many men they have?'

Yoshitsuné, submerging his homesickness, replied eagerly, 'Yoritomo's messenger said quite a few had joined them, including some Taira. Hojo Tokimasa, his father-in-law, of course, but others as well as the monks and the Minamoto in the area, and anybody else they can convince that the day of the Taira is over.'

Yataro shrugged. 'The Taira is a big clan with a lot of fighting men and many resources – as Yorimasa found out.

99

Even though your brother has outmanoeuvred their army to set up this camp, he hasn't an easy task before him. A pity Hidehira won't help.'

Yoshitsuné took up his bowl and his eating sticks and began to shovel the hot millet into his mouth. Between mouthfuls he said, 'Fujiwara Hidehira had no quarrel with the Taira.' His tone was sharp and Yataro knew well enough to leave it at that.

*

They broke camp at dawn, carefully extinguishing the fire and any traces of their stay, to begin the last lap of their hurried journey from Hiraizumi to Fuji. Yoshitsuné and Benkei rode in the lead followed by the fifty samurai who had joined Yoshitsuné's service in Oshu. Yataro brought up the rear. They travelled as lightly as possible, carrying only the armour on their bodies, weapons, and a few cooking pots. Grooms followed a few days behind with the extra horses and armour chests.

It was a magnificent autumn day, with blue sky, warm sun, crisp air and as they rode from the cover of the forest, Fuji – the sacred mountain – rose up to the west, its lower slopes red with maple spreading up to golden larch, black lava and finally a glistening sheet of early snow. Yesterday Yoshitsuné had had his first glimpse of Fuji and the simplicity and perfection of the great cone burning red and white and gold and black in the last rays of the sun stunned him. Yoritomo had chosen to build his winter campsite in the shadow of the ancient mountain; the gods, pleased, would surely bless the Minamoto cause.

Benkei squinted into the sun. 'Fuji makes an excellent guide. If we bear west we should reach the camp tonight if it's where I think it is.'

Yoshitsuné did not answer; Benkei's knowledge of the countryside, any countryside, was always surprising. No one, probably not even Benkei, knew how old he was, but he had compressed a great deal of existence into however many years it was. Sometimes his knowledge irritated Yoshitsuné, impatient at always being the student, never

the teacher, but this morning, riding in front of men who had sworn to die for him, he could not be angry. He was going to meet his brother, the saviour of the Cloister Court chosen to defeat the tyrant Kiyomori. And he was going as a samurai, bringing his own retainers whose loyalty to him was absolute.

The fifty men from Oshu, trotting briskly along, were samurai, men born into a life of warfare and honourable death, proud, independent, accustomed to a world ruled by soldiers. Hidehira's father had carved out a rich domain in the mountains and valleys of the north, attracting landless warriors and adventurers to fight against the aboriginal tribes in return for a fertile plot of land in this free frontier country hundreds of miles from the petty politics of the Court. Rich veins of gold provided added wealth, not just to adorn the new temples and palaces of Hiraizumi but to trade with China, Korea and hot, mysterious southern lands that had no names. Fine woods, silks, paintings, spices, porcelain enriched the northern city, dazzling even visitors from the Capital.

Hidehira had proved an even greater warlord than his father, ruling his vast isolated territory like a king. It was rumoured he had native blood from an aboriginal maternal grandmother, and perhaps it was for this reason that instead of annihilating the tribes, he exiled them across the straits to the cold northern island of Hokkaido. But with the enemy gone, peace did not suit many of his retainers for whom farming was no substitute for fighting. Furthermore, the future, after Hidehira's death – and he was in his eighties – was not promising. Yasuhira, Hidehira's eldest son, was no warrior. The famous Fujiwara bellicosity had trickled out in him. He cared only for his grain reports and treasury records. Fat, slow, pear-shaped from years at a desk, Yasuhira pored over the accounts of his father's estates and it was said he knew to an egg how many chickens Hidehira owned or to the last grain how much millet was in the granaries or in the ground. Barely able to ride or use a sword, Yasuhira was a great disappointment to his father and to the northern samurai who ached for a little

action to liven their routine of hunting, guard duties and drinking.

Yoshitsuné's arrival in Hiraizumi had provided possible escape and many begged to join the young man's service, tempted by the prospect of a long civil war. Hidehira had understood their frustration and boredom, so he had released the warriors from obligation and encouraged them to join Yoshitsuné. Yasuhira grumbled but was secretly pleased to be rid of fifty men who ate too much and did too little. He preferred a productive farmer or a book-keeper any day; now that the native tribes had been driven over the sea the samurai code was just so much expensive nonsense. And, privately, he regarded his aged father's infatuation with the Minamoto stripling as yet more expensive nonsense. Fearing for his own inheritance, Yasuhira would have gladly lost one hundred men to see Yoshitsuné ride out of Hiraizumi once and for all. He was only thankful Hidehira had enough sense to ignore the boy's pleas for Fujiwara men to fight the Taira.

Tadahira, Hidehira's other legitimate son, was a fine huntsman and a collector of lacquerware but a soldier by necessity only. He reluctantly led expeditions against the aborigines and then hurried back to the luxuries of Hiraizumi; to polished rice and the comfort of his flute, his lacquerware and his women. Hidehira was disappointed in Tadahira too; he was not quite man enough for the tart old warlord, but at least Tadahira was preferable to his elder brother.

Yoshitsuné had come into Hidehira's old age as an unexpected but wonderful gift from the gods. For two years the old man had someone who cared, who longed to be as great a warrior as Hidehira himself had been. Hours were spent supervising the boy's sword lessons and archery contests, while endless tales were told from his own fiery youth as the vanquisher of the tribes. He joyfully hauled his aged bones into the saddle to hunt with Yoshitsuné and improve the youth's rather inadequate horsemanship. A young filly, coal black, was trained especially and presented as the warhorse of warhorses. Yoshitsuné loved her

passionately and did indeed develop into an excellent horseman, delighted to please his doting foster-father.

Although slightly intimidated by Hidehira's great age, Yoshitsuné quickly learned to love and respect the old warlord, accepting his criticism with an equanimity that amazed Benkei. Hidehira discussed with the boy what it meant to be a samurai and after listening and questioning, Yoshitsuné, with the hard assurance of youth, saw his loyalty and obedience to the Minamoto as invincible. Cosseted by Hidehira's affection, secure in the safe, uncomplicated samurai world of Hiraizumi, Yoshitsuné blossomed, not just in his martial skills but as a confident leader, patterned after the warlord of Oshu. Only Benkei, although pleased with the boy's development, wished that life in Oshu was a little more challenging for his master; a little opposition, a few more obstacles would do him no harm. And Benkei's worries increased when he sensed Yoshitsuné's reaction to the dagger.

Tadahira accepted his father's affection for the boy with good nature but even he was upset over the dagger. A Fujiwara family heirloom, forged by the swordsmith Sanjo, the magnificent blade had passed to Hidehira when he was nineteen, but he had never seen fit to hand it over to one of his own sons. 'It is a blade a man would be proud to take his own life with – I cannot see Yasuhira or Tadahira doing that. No courage, either of them.' So Hidehira kept it to himself, tucked into his sash, until Yoshitsuné's nineteenth birthday when he presented the dagger to the youth. Yoshitsuné held it warily, its tempered edge glittering with icy fire. He felt almost faint – it would slice through flesh and muscle and gut as easily as through water. Hidehira had said, 'It is my finest possession. You understand how I feel about it because you have the Hachiman sword. Only a samurai can live with such steel.' But Yoshitsuné knew he would never feel about the Sanjo blade as he felt about the sword, and he shivered each time he touched it, praying that his weakness did not show. Yasuhira, round-hipped and sag-bellied, bitterly regretted the value of the dagger. Tadahira was deeply hurt to see

it leave the clan, but realistically accepted that neither he nor his brother deserved it. Still, he was hurt. Yoshitsuné saw that and was sorry. Now, riding along the forest path, he touched the blade, touched it resting against his belly, quickly, and his fingers did not linger. It continued to rouse in him a sensation of horror that he did not want to understand.

Benkei's horse stumbled and the monk's booming complaint broke into Yoshitsuné's reverie. They looked at each other without speaking; idle chatter was not a part of the bond made during the last two years. Benkei, after a life of physical and emotional independence, now found himself tightly bound to this youth. Attracted to the boy by his skill and his aura of authority, Benkei had come to sense a gap, a need in Yoshitsuné's life that the monk believed he filled – a need for a companion, not a quasi-father such as Hidehira had become, and not an instructor like Shomon, but a companion, whose strength lay in absolute confidence, absolute conviction and absolute loyalty.

Yoshitsuné's early life had been so lonely, so isolated among the monks with few peers as rivals that he had grown up sufficient in the knowledge that his own way was right – and so often events had seemed to prove this true. This self-assurance strengthened during his happy, un-challenged years in Oshu. After the affair of Tomomori and the Hachiman sword, Yoshitsuné realised that he had acted rashly, but he had never really accepted that his rash act was wrong; in fact, things had turned out well, perhaps too well. He had proved himself a superb swordsman and had escaped safely to a proper samurai's life in Oshu. Asuka's death was heart-breaking, but it was her karma to die young. But Yoshitsuné *was* rash, or impetuous, or arrogant, or ambitious or had excessive high spirits. It depended on who was describing him – and these qualities could appear dangerous to some. Shomon did not admire them, nor did Kiso. Hidehira ignored them. Now Benkei wondered about Yoritomo, the unknown brother and chieftain they were soon to meet. Indeed, Benkei himself did not totally admire imprudence, but he recognised it in

himself and believed that only he, as an equal and friend, could curb Yoshitsuné's audacity should it become necessary.

Riding through the autumn morning Benkei wondered too if Yoshitsuné, suddenly drawn into his real family for the first time, working and living with his own brothers, would need him as much as before. The nagging thought that he might not took some of the warmth from the sunshine.

*

The camp spread along the west bank of the river into the red and gold forest sprawling up the foothills. Each warlord had staked a plot and built crude earthworks to contain the shelters for horses and men. Over the wooden entrances to each of these compounds flew the identifying pennant of the lord of the clan.

The Oshu contingent approached from the foothills so that the full size and pattern of the camp was set out before them. They drew up their horses and stared down in amazement.

Benkei whistled. 'Look at it. He must have ten thousand men!'

Yataro pulled up next to him. 'The messenger was right. Not just white banners but red ones, too. There's Lord Miura: well, that makes sense. Hogen always told Tomomori not to count on him. And there, Rokuro, isn't that Lord Doi's standard? He's from your part of the world.'

Rokuro, a scarred, simian archer from the east coast, nodded. 'That's Doi, but it's the young one. He likes a good fight and a chance to make a profit. The old man is dead and he wouldn't have joined the Minamoto. Yoritomo is really pulling the lords to him. There are the standards of Takeda of Kai and Lord Kozuke. They are usually neutral so their presence is a great asset to the Minamoto cause.'

Benkei peered out over the plain. 'Most of the Minamoto are too far away to identify. I can see Lord Wada's banner but there's no sign of Kiso. He'd be near Yoritomo, and

that's obviously Yoritomo's compound near the centre, next to Hojo Tokimasa and the single hut that should be Noriyori.'

'Benkei.' Yataro pointed. 'There, next to the main compound!' The low sun lay on one standard particularly, a flying crane encircled by plum branches. 'Kajiwara Kagetoki. I'd know that crest anywhere.' Yataro sat back in his saddle, his broad face screwed into a tight knot of disapproval.

'A good warrior,' said Rokuro tentatively.

'Have you ever fought on his side? He's arrogant, ruthless, a liar who makes trouble to suit himself. He would skewer his own grandmother if there was something in it for Kajiwara. Yoritomo had better keep him in his place. Miura, for one, hates him. So do most of the Taira.'

'Hm,' mused Benkei.

Looking out over the sprawl, Yoshituné felt the elation of the journey slip away. He had pushed his men and their mounts to the limit, racing toward this meeting with his brothers. Shomon's predictions and the possession of the Hachiman sword had convinced him that he would be an indispensable right arm for his clever, efficient eldest brother, his commander in battle and his protector in peace. The image had blossomed in his mind, crowding out not only Noriyori but any other rivals. Now he stared down at the crests of men he knew to be experienced, war-wise samurai, used to commanding thousands of men, and for a few seconds he wanted to turn back. With hot embarrassment he remembered a frequent fantasy he had had as a child, after Shomon had told him about his elder brothers. All three of them were in battle; Yoritomo was the splendid leader with Noriyori and Yoshitsuné serving as his lieutenants. Suddenly in the chaos of men and horses, Yoshitsuné saw an enemy archer drawing aim on Yoritomo and with one swift fearless leap, the boy interposed himself between his brother and the archer, taking the arrow himself. He died, of course, but not without feeling Yoritomo's hot tears of gratitude and grief on his chill brow. Now he realised the futility of the

memory and his presumption. His imaginings were insane. They could never be realised. Then he straightened his shoulders and kicked his filly forward. His karma was good; he knew it.

'Come. It is time for Yoshitomo's sons to know one another. We must be expected.' He started down the winding path towards the camp.

The captain of the guard received them without interest. Too many important names had passed under his scrutiny in the past few weeks for one more Minamoto to be noticed. They were assigned an area and told that Yoritomo would naturally wish to interview their leader.

In a few hours they had shelter and a huge cooking pot boiling on the fire. Just at sunset a horseman rode up to the hut, a large man in his late thirties with a strong, haughty face dominated by a vast beaked nose. Embroidered on his cloak was a crane enclosed in entwined plum branches. He demanded in a loud voice the whereabouts of Minamoto Yoshitsuné, but when Yoshitsuné stepped forward to introduce himself, he carried on with his own introduction, which was hurled down like a challenge.

'I am Kajiwara Kagetoki, general of Minamoto Yoritomo. If you are Yoshitsuné mount up and come with me. Yoritomo will see you now. Be quick.'

Benkei, standing behind Yoshitsuné, saw one hand twitch toward the Hachiman sword. The monk held his breath. The hand dropped away from the sword and with a quick shake of his shoulders the younger man called for his horse. Benkei took the reins while Yoshitsuné mounted. Looking impassively into his master's tense white face, the monk winked. Yoshitsuné stared back for a moment and then grinned. He wheeled his horse towards Kajiwara and said, 'I am ready to accompany you, my lord,' but the samurai had already started along the twisting path between the various encampments and Yoshitsuné's courtesy was wasted on the disappearing broad back.

When they reached the large central palisade Kajiwara pointed with his fan at a rough hut. 'That's where Yoritomo lives. Go in. He's expecting you.' As he rode

away Yoshitsuné slid off his horse, took a deep breath and pushed aside the leather curtain over the door.

Yoritomo was alone. Piles of rolled documents lay before him and he was reading a report by the light of a wick floating in bear fat. He looked up and gestured, unsmiling, to a fur rug beside him. Yoshitsuné bowed and settled himself cross-legged on the offered seat. The brothers, side by side, studied each other. Yoritomo saw a slight but broad-shouldered young man, with an oval face, full mouth and black eyes who was dressed in hunting clothes and carried a long sword. Yoshitsuné saw a chunky beardless man in his early thirties with an oval head and features similar to his own and Yukiiye's, but Yoritomo's face was fuller, his wide lips aggressively sensual. The delicate features that lent charm to Yoshitsuné's face had sharpened and hardened in the elder brother and his round eyes were cold with intelligence and speculation.

Yoritomo dabbed at his dry eyes with a sleeve. 'Well, my young brother, I am greatly moved to meet you at last. Shomon told me so much of you that I feel we know each other already.' His voice had an unpleasant harsh quality. It was a voice that would always carry above others, distinctive and commanding.

The sentimental preliminaries now obviously over, Yoritomo asked abruptly, 'How many men did you bring? When will Hidehira's troops arrive? Did you meet Kiso on your way?' As he fired the questions his eyes dropped to the written lists in his lap.

It was a few seconds before Yoshitsuné could answer. There was so much he wished to say to this lost brother: questions about their father, Yoritomo's boyhood, the rebellion, exile, the long, long years of waiting for this meeting. Important as these questions might be to himself, he could see that they would not interest the man sitting beside him. Stifling his disappointment he replied, 'I have fifty men, all fine warriors. Hidehira has not yet decided what he will do. We did not see Kiso.'

Yoritomo fastened on Hidehira. 'Hasn't decided what he'll do? Crafty old fox! Probably waiting for Kiso and me

108

to settle our claims first. You've met Kiso, haven't you? We'll discuss him later but now I'll give you a brief summary of the situation.

'We're camped here until spring when we'll move our headquarters to Kamakura. A contingent has already gone ahead to build barracks and organise food supplies, planting and so on. Besides being our ancestral home it is easy to defend – on the coast protected by mountains. Have you been there? No, eh?' He went on without waiting for an answer.

'You'll have seen the various crests of our supporters. A lot of them are Taira and this is good in one way, but . . .' He gave his brother a sharp penetrating look. 'A man who deserts his clan is not to be completely trusted. Agreed? Even the Miura might join up with Kiyomori if things go badly for us, although Tokimasa and Kajiwara are good men. You and Noriyori are my own blood so we are bound to the same things. We place the clan first, above material gain. But the others . . .' He shook his head. 'They are using us just as much as I am using them. Still, without them we would have little hope.' He studied his younger brother again and Yoshitsuné found himself embarrassed under the appraising stare.

'You will have to prove yourself. Noriyori is competent and I've made him a commander, but you are young and my more experienced allies might well resent you. You should be tested in battle, but there are not many fighting Taira around here.' He chuckled. 'They are either licking their wounds or chasing after Kiso or Yukiiye.' Yoshitsuné looked up with interest. He had forgotten his uncle. Yoritomo answered the question before he could ask it. 'He is raising troops south of the Capital. There are many people who would be pleased to see Kiyomori toppled and Yukiiye has volunteered to approach the big families, most of whom he knows from his old days at Court. Of course, there is always the question of who he is raising troops for – Yoritomo or Kiso ? We shall have to see.

'Well, that is all, I think.' He picked up the list and perused it. 'Now go and see Noriyori. I am not your only

brother. From now on you will be included in all the meetings of my councillors and commanders – tomorrow after the morning rice. Be here. You will find Noriyori in the next hut.' He put down the list and picked up another.

Yoshitsuné was dismissed. He had spoken three sentences.

Noriyori was in the next hut apparently preparing to go visiting. In a jacket of padded green silk and scarlet breeches he was seated before a polished bronze mirror carefully plucking the whiskers from his chin. He recognised Yoshitsuné instantly, greeted him with a warm embrace and, dismissing the servants who were helping him dress, offered saké. They settled down comfortably on the straw matting.

'Well, well, my little brother. When last we met you were a babe in arms. I owe my life to your mother, you know; so does Yoritomo although it is not something I would mention to him. Lady Tokiwa is dead now, I understand? What she did took courage.' To Yoshitsuné's pleasure he spoke with admiration. No one but Yorimasa had ever mentioned his unknown mother to him and although he rarely thought of her, it was warming to hear her praised.

Noriyori's charm and friendliness were relaxing and he talked happily about his life in Kurama, the Capital and Oshu. Yoshitsuné found his brother witty and intelligent, though far more interested in gossiping about the past than planning for future battles and revenge. Tall and well-built, a handsome man bubbling with vitality and good humour, he was in startling contrast to the efficient Yoritomo to whom inevitably the conversation turned. Yoshitsuné hesitantly ventured that his brother had been businesslike rather than welcoming. Noriyori nodded and said guardedly, 'His manner is abrupt but his life has been very difficult.'

'You have been with him for over three years. Have you become close friends in that time?'

'No, not close by any means. He is only really close to Lady Masako and her father, Tokimasa. Other than that he trusts practically no one.'

'Not even you, his own brother?' Yoshitsuné asked in surprise. 'We are all Yoshitomo's sons.'

Noriyori poured out more saké and replied grimly, 'You'd better be prepared. He resents you and me as though we were the very devils of hell.'

'But why? How? I haven't met him until today.'

'Because we were children at the time of the rebellion and never understood what was happening, and then we were packed off to comfortable temples, never knowing any real anxiety or hardship. But he fought with Yoshitomo and saw our brother, Tomonaga, dying in the snow. They are only names to me, nothing to you, I expect, but they were a real brother and a real father to Yoritomo. Then he was hunted down and dragged to the Rokuhara Palace to be executed, saved by a whim of Kiyomori's and sent off to a very hard exile in Izu, a godforsaken spot. The monks waived a lot of Taira restrictions for me, and you too, about practice swords and training – I was even given a horse – but Yoritomo was really a prisoner of war. Perhaps the greatest humiliation of all for him was that Hojo Tokimasa wasn't even a Taira noble of high rank but just a provincial warlord in an out-of-the-way district. He was shrewd, though. He saw Yoritomo's intelligence and nurtured it. Do you know something? I think the biggest single reason I believe we'll crush the Taira and take control is because Tokimasa believes it too, so much so that he threw in his lot with Yoritomo. Tokimasa is perhaps an opportunist, but he is a clever one, and he and Yoritomo have plans: a samurai government based in Kamakura with a network of provincial officials answering to Kamakura only. The Rokuhara would just be another branch.' He shrugged. 'I don't really understand all these politics. Politics just lead to more politics as far as I can see, but it is certainly a novel idea. Yoritomo's real advisers are Tokimasa and Kajiwara, who is a dangerous man. You and I are just convenient for our brother – we can be used against Minamoto and Taira alike.'

'But surely he must trust us?'

'I doubt it. Don't say anything controversial in public,

especially when Kajiwara is present. We know he reports what he hears but we don't know who else does as well. Yoritomo learns everything. He has spies everywhere. And he trusts no one but those two and his wife.' Noriyori's sudden grimness was a sharp contrast to the earlier easy charm.

'But if he trusts Kajiwara and Tokimasa, why not us? It doesn't make sense.' Confused, Yoshitsuné stared at Noriyori. How could brothers betray one another? Not just the blood bond but the samurai bond forbade it.

'No, perhaps you're too young to see. We didn't suffer the fear, the degradation and the deprivation he did, and he will never forgive us for that. When he killed his first man he was twelve. I was twenty-one when I killed mine. How old were you?'

Yoshitsuné remembered the dark room, slippery with Asuka's blood. He saw the glow of live coals and smelt the incense. 'Eighteen,' he said.

'Well, maybe he'll take to you. Who knows?' Noriyori rose. 'My long-lost brother, I have an assignation with a lady. Actually, that might be too fine a word for her. She is a good, willing farm wench and I am late already, as Yoritomo, who knows everything, could tell you.' As Yoshitsuné stood up beside him, he dropped an affectionate arm around his shoulders. 'This is a marvellous day for the Minamoto. The three of us. We will be invincible.' Yoshitsuné grinned at him – this was what he imagined having a brother would be like. Happily, he left the tent with Noriyori, Yoritomo's brusqueness temporarily forgotten.

*

The next morning, after a breakfast of bean soup and salted vegetables, Yoshitsuné strolled to Yoritomo's palisade for the meeting. In each of the encampments he passed samurai drilled, groomed their horses or shouted at the foot-soldiers building more lean-tos, more earthworks to shelter the growing army. The stench of half-cooked meat, sweat, excrement and thousands of men and horses

hung in the air like the smoke from the cooking fires.

Noriyori stood by the entrance to the main palisade, his head turned towards several small, nut-brown men arguing over a roll of dice. He gestured to Yoshitsuné to listen to their babble and said, 'Can you guess where they've come from? No? Kyushu! What an outlandish language!'

'I didn't know there were any Kyushu lords here.'

Noriyori put an arm around his brother's shoulder and led him towards Yoritomo's hut. 'There aren't. These are ronin, masterless samurai, mercenaries who come north to fight because the looting is better than on that awful island. They look like monkeys, don't they? I wonder if the women are as ugly. Come inside. They're all here.'

A dozen men were crowded into the room, dim after the bright autumn sun. Some, like Yoritomo, sat cross-legged on the uneven wood floor, others leant against the walls, but each turned to examine the new arrival. Yoritomo said in his harsh voice, 'This is Yoshitomo's youngest son, Yoshitsuné by name. He has just arrived from Oshu – without any men from Fujiwara Hidehira.' He gave a sharp, humourless laugh. 'I won't present you all. It's too confusing, but this,' he clapped the middle-aged man next to him on the shoulder, 'is my father-in-law, Hojo Tokimasa.'

Yoshitsuné bowed to the room in general and Tokimasa in particular; thin, with a lantern jaw and iron grey hair under his headdress, he coolly returned the bow and studied Yoshitsuné indifferently before speaking. 'The family resemblance is certainly strong. It is a pity about Hidehira, we could have used his help. Tell us about Oshu, Yoshitsuné. Has the drought affected them? What about the frontier? How many samurai does Hidehira command?'

A short, bearded man said, 'He must be older than the gods by now. That native blood he's supposed to have must be a preservative. When is he going to die?' Several others smiled uneasily. The concept of Hidehira, too powerful and too independent, was an uncomfortable one to these warlords, still tied to the Capital and their clans.

Yoshitsuné replied coolly, 'His health is excellent. He hunts and paints and is as alert as a thirty-year-old.'

'Quite,' Tokimasa broke in firmly. 'But the drought?'

Yoshitsuné concentrated on Tokimasa, his back to the bearded man. 'There is no drought in the north; the summers have been a little dry but there is plenty of grain. He has about two thousand samurai but many of them are on constant patrol against the tribes, although most of the natives are moving across the straits to the northern island. I have seen that myself. Their boats make the crossing each summer, taking the women and children to settle.'

'In that case, if his men aren't tied up with the barbarians any more, why doesn't he help us? Is he afraid?' sneered the bearded man.

'He has no quarrel with Kiyomori,' Yoshitsuné snapped.

'Of course he hasn't. Lord Doi, would you go marching into a rebellion against a man who has not harmed you?' Noriyori put in smoothly.

'Yes, if there was a good fight and some loot in it. A samurai's life is battle. What do you say, Chiba?'

Lord Chiba, a squat man in bearskin, shrugged. 'Leave it, Doi.' Doi grunted and began to pick his nails.

Yoritomo said, 'Shomon told me you spent your time in the Capital reading Taira records; fortresses, defences, battle strategy, and similar material. What can you tell us? Did you make copies?'

'Most I tried to memorise but some were copied and left with Shomon. They are lost, I suppose, except for a few I took with me to Oshu. I have them here.' He reached into the wide sleeves of his jacket and took out three scrolls of grey Korean paper.

'Let me see those.' Kajiwara Kagetoki shouldered his way to the centre of the room and held out his hand. Subtly, Yoshitsuné felt the atmosphere change. Doi turned his back on Kajiwara and continued to click his nails loudly. Several men glared at the big man but most sat in silence, watching. Glancing at Yoritomo, Yoshitsuné saw that he too was watching, with an amused smile

twisting his full lips. He caught his younger brother's eye and said smoothly, 'Give them to Kajiwara. Unlike Lord Miura and Lord Chiba, our other Taira allies, he has been in Kiyomori's confidence and will tell us if they are valuable.'

Reluctantly Yoshitsuné placed the scrolls on the broad palm, scrolls that had cost Asuka her life and that to him were valuable. Kajiwara snapped the first open, looked it over and dropped it on the floor. 'This is rubbish. I could have told you this. What was Yorimasa playing at? He was a poet. What did he know about military affairs? He should have sent the boy straight to the mountains to make a man out of him. Why waste time on this when I can tell you everything in it?'

Yoshitsuné stepped forward and said evenly, 'When my great-uncle set me this task he did not know that one of the most famous Taira warriors would desert his chieftain for the enemy, bringing all the Taira secrets with him. He taught me that the samurai virtues were obedience, honour and loyalty and he died bravely defending those virtues.'

'Well said,' murmured Noriyori happily.

A ripple of interest circled the room. Kajiwara turned to the gently smiling Yoritomo. 'Your brother obviously needs a lesson in manners as well as warfare and swordsmanship, but it will have to come from his own clan. I am too busy to train a youth.'

Yoritomo stood up. 'We have more important things to discuss. Yoshitsuné, since you apparently have nothing to contribute you must listen and learn.'

Yoshitsuné stepped back to the wall and squatted down against it, next to a man with a long sword scar across his cheek. 'I am Miura,' he said softly, 'I too deserted my clan but I hope I am honest about it and I admire your courage.' He smiled pleasantly. Yoshitsuné returned the smile stiffly, ignoring Noriyori's hand on his shoulder. He missed the sense of the rest of the meeting, because he was smouldering with rage. What sort of brother was this he had waited so long to serve?

*

The winter at Fuji proved physically uneventful. The Taira did not attack the camp. Kiyomori's illness made him increasingly erratic in his judgement and Tomomori gradually took over control of the Taira army. Tactfully ignoring his father's demands for Yoritomo's and Go-Shirakawa's heads on pikes, he concentrated his forces on catching Kiso who was raiding in the west, feeding his mountaineers off captured Taira grain coming by cart from the still fertile north and east. Tomomori knew that his hungry army could not possibly defeat the Minamoto safely ensconced on Fuji but he sent envoys scurrying from the Rokuhara to the Taira lords who had not defected to Yoritomo, forcing them to reaffirm their loyalty. Those who hesitated were threatened and bullied into co-operation; most quickly promised men and horses.

Life for Yoshitsuné was little different from what it had been in Oshu: hunting, archery contests on horseback and endless practice with his sword. As Shomon had predicted, he proved to be a superior swordsman, greatly respected by his peers in the camp. But it worried him that he had not taken part in even the few skirmishes against Taira raiding parties that occurred and he thought constantly about how he would react in battle or how he would command his men. It did not help that Yoritomo and Kajiwara carped continually about his lack of experience.

The main interest of the camp was politics, and Yoshitsuné could only observe and wonder. Yoritomo and Tokimasa controlled the council absolutely – the warlords were permitted a few occasions to bicker among themselves about proposed military strategy for the spring but most of the meetings concerned Yoritomo's plans for the future, after the defeat of the Taira. He wanted a separate samurai government in Kamakura to replace the power of the Rokuhara in the Capital and he hammered out endless details of administration with the senior warlords who would work with him in his proposed samurai-dokoro, council of samurai. A few, like Doi, were bored by the prospect. They had joined the Minamoto to expand their estates and they made no secret of it. But others, Lord

Miura, Lord Wada, and Takeda of Kai, had joined Yoritomo because they were disappointed in Kiyomori.

One day, as they were hunting boar on the slopes of Fuji, Miura explained to Yoshitsuné how excited he had been when Kiyomori was made Lord Chancellor. It had seemed a great opportunity to clear away the fusty, inert Court bureaucracy. But when Kiyomori simply used the Court for his own ends Miura had become disgusted. 'We need roads between the provinces, an office to deal with harvest and grain taxes. This famine is a perfect example. One part of the country has an abundance while the rest starves. Excess grain could be stored and distributed, but now it just fills the Rokuhara coffers and rots.' He unstrung his bow and laid it across his saddle. 'Kiyomori made his branch of the clan rich while the rest of us cooled our heels. He dominates the trade with China and Korea and that's why Lord Tajima is here and not in the Rokuhara. Kiyomori wouldn't let him send ships to Korea – Tajima's a Taira and his people are sailors. Why shouldn't they have a part of the trade? But no, Kiyomori would not agree.' Muira lowered his voice and glanced around the empty forest. 'I'll be honest, Yoshitsuné, I'm not sure I like your brother, or even trust him, but I admire his ideas.'

Although he had initially been somewhat ill at ease with all the defecting Taira warlords, who were after all traitors, Yoshitsuné had come particularly to like Lord Miura, an intelligent, cultured samurai renowned for his efficiently run estates in the eastern province of Sagami. But although he understood the motives of such ambitious Taira as Doi, Tokimasa and even Kajiwara, Yoshitsuné found it difficult to understand how a man so obviously imbued in samurai qualities as Miura could turn against his clan; he was torn between admiration of his independence and suspicion of his treason. Finally, as they walked through the camp one evening after a drinking session with Noriyori, Yoshitsuné, his tongue loosened by saké, asked the middle-aged samurai if his disloyalty to the Taira rested on his conscience. Miura, relaxed by good wine and good company, smiled down from his considerable height at the

younger man.

'When I was a boy, my father, a hard warrior of the old school – he fought against the barbarian tribes – taught me to be loyal and obedient to the Taira chieftain, to serve him and the Emperor and to look after my retainers and my peasants.' He shrugged, 'Well, the world was a simpler place then – samurai were soldiers and landowners, they had nothing to do with the Court.' He strode on in silence for a few minutes, the lantern he carried casting his giant deformed shadow against the split bamboo palisades.

Yoshitsuné was beginning to think the conversation ended when Miura spoke again. 'In that simpler world a samurai knew what his path was, but now . . . That hasn't answered your question, has it?'

'No, it hasn't. Yorimasa gave me the same sort of answer about his support of Kiyomori against my father.'

Miura laughed and stroked his salt-and-pepper beard. 'I don't feel anything about Kiyomori, although if he were blood kin it might be different. I owe my peasants a better life than they will have with the Taira in control and Yoritomo may make the country safer so that they will have that better life. But ultimately, without loyalty and obedience, we can have no civilisation.'

They walked in silence to Miura's compound. The taller man saluted his sentry and then turned to Yoshitsuné and clapped him on the shoulder. 'Karma is karma and cannot be changed, but I think that the future is with Yoritomo – he demands absolute loyalty and we would do well to give it to him. Goodnight, Yoshitsuné.' And he disappeared through the narrow gate, taking the lantern with him.

Walking the short way to his own quarters, Yoshitsuné reflected that Miura's answer had been honest enough, and his respect for him grew. But, waking in the morning, thinking over the conversation, sober in the daylight, it occurred to him that Miura's justifications might have a rather shallow ring if they issued from Doi's greedy lips or were offered by the palpably ambitious Tokimasa. Well, he thought, Miura's wrong about one thing; here, in this camp, life is simple. One obeys Yoritomo.

On another occasion, Lord Wada seconded Miura's views, also adding in parenthesis that, although a loyal member of the Minamoto clan, he did not like or trust Yoritomo. 'I would be happier if Kajiwara didn't have so strong an influence on him. All the Taira who know Kajiwara are wary, but Yoritomo will not listen to our words of caution. Even Tokimasa is not allowed to criticise him.'

Yoshitsuné loathed Kajiwara, but he quickly learned to keep silent in Yoritomo's presence. Kajiwara's spying and words of treachery were a vicious joke among the warlords and Lord Wada's son was everyone's hero when, leaving the camp to lead a scouting party, he shouted to Kajiwara, 'I'll be gone a few weeks at least, so that will give you plenty of time to ruin my reputation as a soldier. Enjoy yourself!' And indeed, on the senior Lord Wada's return from his estates, Yoritomo told him that his son was becoming insolent and perhaps the camp would be better without him. Wada replied that if his son left, he and his one thousand men would accompany him. The matter was dropped, but from then on Lord Wada's opinion was openly ignored in the council.

Yoshitsuné saw little of Yoritomo, who spent his free time with Kajiwara or his father-in-law. Noriyori shrugged at this behaviour. 'Yoritomo is a boring bastard anyway. Who needs endless discussion on how best to tax the monasteries? Pass the saké.' But Yoshitsuné was depressed by his eldest brother's lack of interest in them both. Finally he accepted that to Yoritomo he was just another samurai and that his advantage of blood connexion was only important in that it meant absolute loyalty.

He vented his rage to Benkei. 'He said we three brothers must stand together. Noriyori and I are his commanders – his *special* commanders – but he spies on me as he does the others and he allows Kajiwara to goad me in the council. He treats me like a dog.'

Benkei's reply was firm. 'He's a strange man, but Noriyori is right. Do what Yoritomo says and don't give him anything to use against you. It will all work out when

the fighting starts. Just watch Kajiwara. He's the dangerous one.'

But the resentment simmered and Yoshitsuné complained frequently to Benkei, Noriyori or Wada and
Miura. After the incident of Wada's son, the warlord
slapped Yoshitsuné on the shoulder and said, 'My son is a
good warrior. He has proved himself in battle so he does
not worry about Kajiwara. The same goes for you, boy.
Kajiwara is sly but he's a good soldier and I think you will
be his equal. Then you can ignore him and Yoritomo will
appreciate your worth, as much as he does anyone's.'

Lord Miura, experienced in the ways of war councils and
clan politics, explained it succinctly. 'You do not have to
like your chieftain to respect him. You only have to serve.
Stop looking for a friend and accept him for what he is. His
intelligence deserves your respect.'

'I shall prove myself soon, Miura, and then he will
respect me.'

Miura replied gravely, 'Prove yourself by all means. But
let us hope that when he respects you he doesn't start
fearing you. He will not tolerate competition from any
man. We have all learned that.'

*

Kiyomori's condition deteriorated rapidly as the winter
progressed; by the second month he was bed-ridden,
wracked by high fevers, headaches and violent bouts of
temper. In his delirium he railed against Yoritomo and his
rebellion. Munemori, well-meaning but weak, took over
the political business. Tomomori ran the military affairs
from the Capital, leaving their youngest brother, Shigehira, to command the starving troops in the field.

At the end of the third month Kiyomori's mind cleared
and he demanded that Go-Shirakawa, now back in the
Hojoji Palace but under heavy guard, be brought to the
Rokuhara. The Cloistered Emperor found his minister
fully conscious but in a sorry state, lying back on an arm-
rest. A scarlet-and-white-robed priestess, deep in a trance,
crooned prayers over his restless body, and an aromatic

cone of mugwort smouldered on the grey skin of his forearm. But Go-Shirakawa had seen dying men too often and knew that sorcery could not save Kiyomori now. He shammed no sorrow over his 'protector's' condition. His brief homily on the joys of death, the exchange of false earthly pleasures for the pure freedom of the soul, had a distinctly gloating ring. For his part, Kiyomori showed little of the respect due to a descendant of the Sun Goddess; Go-Shirakawa was given precise orders: Munemori would run the government, Tomomori the samurai, and the young child Emperor Antoku would reign until he could take a Taira consort and they had produced a son to succeed him. When Go-Shirakawa flounced his lavender brocade robes and protested plumply, Kiyomori went into a wild fury, his face scarlet, screaming at the Cloistered Emperor until, shattering his fragile arm-rest, he collapsed back on the pallet under a fine film of mugwort ash. Go-Shirakawa slithered from the room, leaving his Lord Chancellor as he had fallen.

A few days later Kiyomori recovered again and called for his sons and grandsons. They knelt respectfully by the pallet, Munemori weeping uncontrollably. In a hoarse whisper Kiyomori went over the various responsibilities to the clan and to Antoku. Suddenly his voice took on a new intensity. 'There is one thing each of you must swear to do. My soul will not rest until it is completed. I want Yoritomo's head severed from his body and placed on a stake at the execution grounds and I want the Minamoto rebels driven into the Eastern Sea. I want the foul sons of Yoshitomo dead. Only that can give me peace to go on to the next world. Do you understand? All of you. Swear to it!' He dragged himself on to one elbow, eyes staring from his crimson face, 'Swear!'

Munemori wiped away his tears with the sleeve of his robe and put his arm around his father, settling him gently on the pallet. 'We swear, my father.' He nodded to the others who spoke quickly in succession. Before the last had sworn Kiyomori sank into a coma.

The screens of state were pushed aside to admit priests

from all the temples of the Capital. They shook rosaries and recited prayers to help the Lord Chancellor to the Western Paradise.

Kiyomori spoke once more. He gazed dimly at Tomomori and whispered, 'Take Yoritomo's head. It is owed to me.'

A few hours later he died.

Go-Shirakawa, freed at last, amused himself by bullying the quivering Munemori, but the sport was too easy. Tomomori, a more formidable opponent, refused to play at politics and spent all his time with his commanders, interviewing scouts and raging against Yoritomo, Kiso and the weather.

Despite constant surveillance, the Cloistered Emperor frequently received news of the Minamoto armies and he knew things were progressing the way he wished them to. Eventually, after months of watching and waiting, he called for his ink stone and brushes and composed two letters, one to Kiso in the west and one to Yoritomo in Kamakura. Go-Shirakawa was bored with Munemori. It was time to make a move.

*

Yoritomo moved his army and his family to Kamakura in the spring. Yoshitsuné found it a grim, disappointing place although the location was superb. The town was scattered through pine forests to the wide smooth beaches of the Eastern Sea, with the land side completely protected by high, wooded hills, passable through only a few easily guarded valleys. The ancient Minamoto had chosen their stronghold wisely but the town was crude and undeveloped; one wide muddy street lined with low barracks and long houses for the warlords ran from the fortress where the samurai attended the samurai-dokoro into the thickly wooded slopes. Yoritomo promised much for the future – houses, gardens, shrines, temples, armouries and workshops for the artisans who would live in the city under his patronage. Indeed, he started a mansion for himself immediately. But for the present Kamakura was a fortified

fishing village, cold, bleak and uncompromising.

The east proved to be surprisingly inhospitable. Rather than endanger the truce with the Rokuhara several eastern warlords took up arms against their rebel kinsmen. Summer and autumn were wasted in sporadic fighting and although Yoshitsuné was sent out many times in command of small forces he never managed to engage the enemy. To his disgust he remained untried in battle.

One day he urged his black filly through the pines towards the bay. As the woods thinned pine needles gave way to sand and before him stretched the beach and the cold Eastern Sea. Behind him was Kamakura.

He let his horse paw at the sand while he looked around him. To his left on the straggling tree line stood a large sacred gateway, two tall thick wooden pillars topped by two curved crossbeams, marking the entrance to a shrine, the habitation of a god. He dismounted and walked along the beach, through the gate to the shrine huddled in the trees. It was a small, thatched unpainted building sharing a sandy compound with a gnarled cypress and a featureless stone statue draped in red. The tree had a few pieces of paper – prayers, incantations or thanks – twisted on to its branches by hopeful applicants. A faded wind-battered placard announced that this shrine belonged to Hachiman, God of War.

Yoshitsuné washed his hands and rinsed his mouth with water from a crude stone bowl by the porch and, purified, stood before the closed shutters of the sanctuary. The presence of Hachiman seeped through his body, whispering in the pines, filling his ears and telling him to draw his sword. The blade seemed to vibrate, struggling to return to the god in whose name it had been forged. He clutched the hilt firmly in two hands and silently prayed; the god in him welled up in answer to the god of the pines, of the sanctuary and of the sword. Minamoto Yoshitsuné melted into all this, fused with the sword, taking the strength of the steel into his soul. Slowly the presence of the god ebbed, the shrine hut and scent of pines returned. Empty and exhausted he lowered the sword, now a sword again,

bowed to the sanctuary and backed out on to the tiny porch, at peace. He felt, obscurely, as though he had just fought his first battle, the urge to be tested was no longer consuming him and he was sure of his own courage.

He was loath to leave the place, to walk away from the living rocks and sand. A gull screamed as it flew over him out to sea and he turned to watch its flight. Standing between the pillars of the sacred gateway stood Yoritomo. Yoshitsuné glanced back at the shrine, but the spirit was gone. Reluctantly he put up the Hachiman sword and went to greet his brother.

Yoritomo watched his approach with cold, narrowed eyes. 'I did not know you visited this shrine. What were you praying for?'

'What does any man pray to his family's guardian for, my lord? Especially if the guardian is the God of War and the man aspires to be a warrior?'

'Quite so. Have you been here before?'

'No. It is a powerful place. Our ancestor who built the shrine must have felt the presence of the god very strongly.'

'The whole area is sacred to Hachiman so when we build a new magnificent shrine the god's presence will be strong there, too.'

Yoshitsuné was surprised. 'A new shrine? Is there to be another Hachiman shrine in Kamakura?'

'My dear young brother,' Yoritomo gave a short laugh, 'the Minamoto must construct a suitable monument to their deity. The God of War needs an impressive shrine, worthy of him and of the new eastern capital.'

'Kiyomori's contributions to the Inland Sea shrines weren't popular, my lord. The monasteries do not like to see the old religion encouraged.' He found his brother's presence, as always, unsettling and this made him argumentative.

'It does not apply to Hachiman. He is a Buddhist Bodhisattva as well as a native god.' As they walked along the grey sand towards the horses Yoritomo continued, 'Shomon said you were the warrior of the family and that is

why he gave you the sword. By right of inheritance it should be mine.' There was no possible reply to that so they strode on in tense silence. 'You have yet to prove that Shomon was right. These northern retainers of yours may regard you as the finest swordsman alive but the rest of us have still to be convinced. Kajiwara Kagetoki has made this point to me many times.' Yoritomo's harsh voice grated through the sound of the waves and the cries of the gulls.

Yoshitsuné stopped. The two men faced each other on the vast beach under the low, leaden sky. 'Shall we test the sword now? Do you wish to fight, my lord Yoritomo?'

The older man dropped his hand to the hilt of his sword. For a few seconds it rested there, then he shrugged. 'No. My life is far too important to risk in some childish duel.' He laughed his hard, humourless laugh. 'Now, when Kiso finally appears, you may test the sword on him. Then on Noriyori. If you defeat them no one will question your right to it.'

'Not even Kajiwara Kagetoki?'

'He is a Taira and has nothing to do with Minamoto affairs,' snapped Yoritomo. 'But let me tell you of Kajiwara Kagetoki. He is a great warrior, a superb commander of men, and as fine a samurai as we shall see in our own time, worthy of Hachiman himself. You would do well to show him respect.'

Youth prompted Yoshitsuné to retort that he thought Kajiwara had few of the qualities of a Bodhisattva, but he was very wary of Yoritomo and he was just beginning to realise the presumption of his challenge to a duel. They mounted their horses in silence.

'Two more things I wanted to say. I only see you rarely now since you spend most of your time roistering with that revolting monk and your cronies.' Yoritomo turned his horse and started back towards the pines; Yoshitsuné had no choice but to follow.

'You are to report to the fortress of Kawagoe Shigeyori in Hitachi. I want you to marry Kawagoe's daughter – it is all arranged. He is not too endowed with brains, but he is

one of the richest men in the east and as an ally he will bring us some three hundred samurai. You wed the girl and then I don't have to ask him to command his men. You can. They tell me that whatever kind of general you are going to make, you will be better than that fool. Leave tomorrow.'

Since Yoritomo's tone did not invite comment, Yoshitsuné rode sullenly beside him, determined to show no sign of surprise. A marriage wasn't that important but he should have been consulted – she might be the mother of his children and if she was a fool too ... But Yoritomo continued briskly, 'Return to Kamakura immediately after you consummate the business. I have a very important mission for you and your brother.' He gave Yoshitsuné a cool, appraising look. 'Perhaps too important for you to handle, but as you are the only one who has met Kiso I want you to ride with Noriyori to his camp in Kaga. There has been a letter from the Cloister Court; Go-Shirakawa requests our help against Munemori and the usurper child Emperor Antoku and furthermore, there has been some rain in the west. We must strike while the Taira are still weak from the famine so that if the next harvest is successful it is in Minamoto hands. We don't know if Kiso has heard from the Cloistered Emperor, but the business of the chieftain of the clan must be settled before we move against the Taira. Talk to Kiso and make it clear to him that there can be only one leader of the clan and that is me.'

The horses picked their way through the woods. When they reached the muddy track that marked the settlement, Yoritomo tapped Yoshitsuné's arm with the tip of his iron fan.

'I am chieftain of the Minamoto and no one else has a valid claim. I fought at the side of Yoshitomo, our father, and I suffered humiliation and persecution by the Taira while you rested in comfort, your infant mind at peace. Not one of you, Yukiiye, Kiso, Noriyori or you, have suffered as I have for our clan. Absolute control is mine alone and you will obey my orders or I shall rule without you. Is that understood?'

Yoshitsuné replied slowly, 'I am your brother and your

vassal. You are the head of my clan. I shall serve you always.'

'See to it that you do.' Yoritomo reined in by the unpainted wooden palisade of the samurai-dokoro. Yoshitsuné bowed in the saddle and kicked the filly forward along the rutted road, but before he had gone a few yards Yoritomo's harsh voice brought him to a sharp stop. 'Wait. You are not dismissed. Come back here,' and he rode through the gate into the crowded courtyard followed by his younger brother.

Yoritomo slid out of the saddle and looked up at Yoshitsuné, his face as chill and closed as a death mask. 'Hold my horse,' he said in a loud carrying voice, 'I have business inside.' Yoshitsuné stared down at him incredulously. It took a few seconds for the full shock of the order to hit him and by that time the samurai and servants milling in the courtyard had also taken in Yoritomo's words and turned to watch the two brothers. Neither moved. Yoshitsuné said in a low, tight voice, 'That is a groom's task. We had the same father.'

'But different mothers. Mine was a lady of the Court, yours was a courtesan, an expensive one but still a courtesan. I am chieftain and you are my vassal. Hold the reins.' He thrust the reins at Yoshitsuné. A puzzled murmur ran through the crowd.

Yoshitsuné could not move; his face was very white as were his hands, gripping his own reins with terrible strength. All his lessons in obedience, his protestations of service were lost in the red whirl of fury behind his eyes. He neither saw nor heard the crowd – only Yoritomo's oval face dominated by cold eyes.

'That's an order. Hold the reins,' Yoritomo repeated in a low voice.

Blindly he slid off his horse, wrenched the reins from his chieftain's hands and stood, the blood flooding into his cheeks, eyes glazed and unseeing, his self-control total and agonising, as Yoritomo wheeled and strode into the samurai-dokoro. The crowd relaxed and went about its business, avoiding the rigid figure of the youth holding the

horses by the veranda steps. Among themselves some muttered that Yoritomo's action was justified – he was the chieftain – but others agreed that the public and deliberate humiliation of his own flesh and blood was not necessary.

Lord Miura had entered the courtyard just as the incident began. His heart ached for Yoshitsuné, remembering his own youthful pride, but he reflected that perhaps the boy now understood how very difficult his questions about loyalty and obedience and honour were when transferred from mere words to people.

Yoshitsuné, his heart pounding, his face a disciplined mask, understood nothing at all but that he had been humiliated and treated as a servant by his own brother for no reason. He held the reins for ten minutes, his mind a blank, cold and emotionless as he knew a samurai should be. But when a groom, sent by Yoritomo, came to take the horse to the stable and he could return to his quarters, confused anger surged through him. He was proud of his own self-control, but he could not comprehend why Yoritomo had acted as he had. The question haunted him, day and night, until, eventually, his mind, puzzled and exhausted, pushed it away. He understood nothing.

He never spoke to Benkei about the incident, although the monk had heard of it from others. Like Miura he felt sorry for Yoshitsuné but he saw that, after a period of depression and self-questioning, during which not even his friends could reach him, the young man had hardened. His questions became fewer and less naive; he was more definite with his men. The authority that had always been there strengthened. Yoshitsuné had come of age.

*

Yoshitsuné and his retinue were greeted enthusiastically by Lord Kawagoe, a slow-witted ox of a man. His daughter proved as stimulating as a well-fed carp, a creature to which she bore a close physical resemblance. Yoshitsuné wrote her some poems, played his flute, spent three nights with her, exchanged wedding cakes and then gathered up his celebrating companions and galloped back to Kam-

akura. The austerities of that grim port were a welcome relief.

Within three months three hundred samurai arrived from Hitachi to be led into battle by their lord's new son-in-law. His wife wrote to Yoshitsuné several times and although he answered kindly with a poem or two he hoped fervently that he would not have to visit her again, alliance or no alliance. And again he mourned for his lost Asuka, so warm, so sweet, so loving.

Noriyori and Yoshitsuné led the expedition to meet Kiso. Winter was still in the mountains and the journey was difficult and slow. Reaching Kaga they learned that Kiso had broken camp and was moving south. They caught up with the large army spread out around the Heizenji Temple that was playing host to Kiso and Yukiiye during the ceremonies marking the anniversary of the birth of Buddha. The bellicose abbot had offered a hundred of his best fighting monks to the Minamoto as well as a guarded half-promise that the monasteries of Mount Hiei might decide to support the rebels against the Taira. Many of Kiso's lieutenants were from Taira or other important samurai families and although he had not attracted warlords as famous as Lord Miura, his army, built around the core of loyal mountaineers, was organised, moderately well-fed and itching to fight. Yoshitsuné found Yukiiye much the same, vain and wittering, but Kiso had become a commander of men. Even more stern and laconic than before, he lived in full armour, spending days and nights in the saddle, riding from one group to another, discussing, planning, organising. Except for the four Heavenly Kings he appeared to trust his assistants even less than Yoritomo did.

The eastern Minamoto received a curt welcome. They were greeted by Imai, Kiso's foster brother, and informed that the next morning the army would break camp, split in two and proceed, one part under Kiso and another, smaller part, under Yukiiye, towards the Home Provinces. However, the present afternoon was devoted to the festival of the observation of Buddha's birth and the men were being

given a chance to enjoy themselves before the campaign.

The festival was in full swing; the main temple buildings were decorated with paper flowers while archery contests and horse races on the river bank drew hundreds of participants and observers from the ranks. Roped off areas were set aside for Sumo wrestling; musicians, masseurs and acrobats had poured into Heizenji to entertain and fleece the relaxing army. Prostitutes in their best kimono minced giggling through the throngs, their long black hair oiled and glossy. Pedlars, strange travelling fairmen with hard secret eyes, touted their wares. There was a jumble of noises – drums, flutes, laughter, shouts, hawkers' cries, angry arguments. As the afternoon progressed fights became frequent. Mounted samurai urged their horses through the crowds cracking heads and pulling apart battling drunkards.

Kiso, Imai, Yukiiye, Yoshitsuné and Noriyori met in a small pavilion in the temple compound. The cacophony of the fair made conversation difficult and they were forced to sit close together in a circle to be heard. Food was sparse and unexciting but there was saké, to which Yukiiye and Noriyori addressed themselves enthusiastically.

Kiso proved cool and unforthcoming: yes, he had been in communication with the Cloister Court; yes, the drought had broken; yes, now was the best time to move because later there would be food to feed the Taira army. What did Yoritomo propose?

Noriyori countered: what did Kiso propose? Would he wait in the Home Provinces until Yoritomo was ready? Some of the big families in the east were still troublesome and could mount a dangerous counter-attack on the Minamoto rear, but when they had been dealt with the two branches of the clan could converge on the Capital together – by summer at the latest.

A long pause. Kiso said, 'Who would lead this joint army?'

'You mean who will be chieftain of the Minamoto?' replied Noriyori. 'Yoritomo, of course. Yoshitomo was the eldest son and Yoritomo is his eldest surviving son. He

already has experience as a commander.'

'So has Kiso, now,' put in Yukiiye maliciously.

Noriyori ignored him. His handsome face was flushed with wine. This politicking was not something he felt happy with. Why should Kiso care if Yoritomo was chieftain? For that matter, why should Yoritomo care? They were all the same clan, sharing the one aim. Yoritomo had given Noriyori another offer to make to Kiso. Was now the right time? Why didn't Yoshitsuné say anything? He had met this cousin before and he knew what Noriyori had to offer. What did he think? He glared at his younger brother who was studying the impassive Kiso with absorption. Noriyori had a headache. Fifteen minutes with one of those solid country prostitutes would cure it. Oh, well, he would see if he could bribe Kiso, as Yoritomo had instructed.

'My brother does not want to live in the Capital. Naturally he will be leader of the clan, but he intends to remain in the east and therefore he proposes that Kiso Yoshinaka take over the Rokuhara for the Minamoto. The authority will be almost equal but the final word will lie with Kamakura.' Noriyori spoke rapidly.

'He really is going to *live* in Kamakura?' asked Yukiiye incredulously. Noriyori nodded. 'The place stinks of fish.' The old man snapped his tiny teeth in disgust.

'He does not want to operate through the Court as Kiyomori did but to set up a separate government away from the Capital, run by samurai and using samurai to administer the provinces, reporting to the samurai-dokoro.' Noriyori recited his information by rote – he had heard it all so many times.

Yukiiye shrugged. 'I don't see anything wrong with the way things are. The Capital is the heart of the country. It is the only civilised part. Don't you agree, Kiso?'

But Kiso was not listening to his uncle's prattle. He had been watching Yoshitsuné with as much keenness as Yoshitsuné had been watching him. Now he addressed him sharply. 'If Yoritomo is in Kamakura – as chieftain – and I am in the Rokuhara – as deputy – where will you be?'

Startled by the question, Yoshitsuné paused. 'What have I to do with it? I am not a candidate for chieftain of the clan.' He added tartly, remembering the incident of his brother's horse, 'I am just my brother's vassal.'

'Will you command the Minamoto samurai – or will Yoritomo?'

Yoshitsuné gestured to Noriyori. 'Perhaps Noriyori and I . . .'

'Never mind Noriyori!' snapped Kiso, abruptly and rudely. Noriyori raised an elegant eyebrow and returned to his saké, observing silently that it was lucky he had less than the customary share of family arrogance. Yoshitsuné, appalled by Kiso's discourtesy, glanced sideways at his unperturbed brother and for the first time realised that Noriyori did not really matter. The conflict was between Yoritomo and Kiso – and himself.

He turned back to Kiso, who had just revealed himself as a rival. 'My ambition is to serve my brother as a warrior as valiantly as possible. Politics do not interest me.'

'So Yoritomo will be in Kamakura and I will be in the Rokuhara – and you will be a hero. Eh?'

'If that is settled, let us continue,' muttered Noriyori to himself.

Kiso's sneer was unmistakable. 'So Yoritomo will be Lord Chancellor or Shogun. I will be chief clerk in the Rokuhara. What will our hero do? Lead parades? Polish his sword?'

Yoshitsuné stared at him. 'I shall serve my brother,' he repeated firmly, 'in the provinces or . . . whatever he commands.'

'A retired hero,' chortled Yukiiye who was enjoying this immensely.

'Did you know,' Kiso asked in a suddenly conversational tone, 'that your father murdered mine?' Imai laid a steadying hand on Kiso's arm while Noriyori sighed and Yukiiye giggled. 'Did you know that?' repeated Kiso.

Yoshitsuné looked at Noriyori who shrugged and nodded.

Kiso continued fiercely, 'He didn't like competition so

he killed him. I wonder if it is a family trait? I'd bear it in mind if I were you.'

Yoshitsuné, struggling to cover his shock, said, 'I didn't know my father but there must have been reasons.' He thought of Shomon's passionate loyalty and of Yorimasa's reservations: brutal and muddled, he had said of Yoshitomo. Perhaps he was not surprised after all.

Kiso drained his saké cup and snapped shut his iron fan. 'This has been an interesting if futile meeting. We speak bluntly in the mountains. I don't trust Yoritomo and I find his plan to turn samurai into tax collectors and provincial officials ridiculous. Kiyomori at least knew the difference between a samurai and a bureaucrat.' He snorted. 'Government is a job for clerks, not soldiers. Soft men who can read and write. Kiyomori enjoyed his success and he lived in luxury. Perhaps he never was much of a warrior and that is why he became soft and idle, but I am a warrior. When I have destroyed the Taira I will still be a warrior, not a clerk. Weak men are corrupted by Court life. I am not weak.' He rose abruptly. 'This talk is pointless. My men are ready and we will march on the Home Provinces now. Go back to your bureaucrat of a brother and tell him if he is ready we will attack the Capital together. Let the best general – Kiso or Yoritomo or Yoshitsuné – be the leader of the Minamoto. The rest can be decided later. Come, Imai, we have work to do.' He strode from the pavilion.

Yukiiye rose to follow him, one elaborate sleeve held daintily over his lips. 'Oh dear, oh dear,' he giggled.

Noriyori sighed and stood up. 'What an unpleasant man. I'm going to enjoy the fair. If I were you, Yoshitsuné, I'd do the same. There is not going to be much fun to be had in Kamakura after we report this.'

Yoshitsuné gazed at Noriyori, amazed at his calm. How could he accept Kiso's insult to his honour and their father's memory? Where was his pride? Yoshitsuné knew the laziness in Noriyori's good nature. His indolence, so appealing when compared with Yoritomo's harshness, suddenly became a weakness and Yoshitsuné realised, in a cold flash of insight, that he himself was more like

Yoritomo than like this charming, feckless brother. He said firmly, 'We should leave for the east immediately, I think. Yoritomo must know what is happening.'

He began to gather up the maps but Noriyori laid a hand on his arm and shook his head. 'Tomorrow, little brother, tomorrow. We gain nothing by riding out tonight.'

*

Later in the evening Yoshitsuné and Benkei retired to their quarters in the temple. The others were carousing among the ruins of the day's pleasures but Yoshitsuné was tired and confused after his interview with Kiso. The news of his father's fratricide horrified him all the more because he found he could easily believe it, especially now as he discussed it with Benkei. The monk, moderately sober, lay flat on the floor, his head resting on his saddle. 'Your father must have had very good reasons for what he did. He wouldn't go against the God Hachiman's strictures on family murder without good reason. Kiso's father was probably weak or disloyal, but you'll never know, Yoshitsuné. It's all lost in time now and anyway it was karma. You don't want to confuse politics with soldiering, my friend, as Yoritomo does.'

'Yoritomo has never struck me as being a real samurai, not in the true sense,' mused Yoshitsuné.

There was a quick furtive tap on the shutter, it slid back and to their surprise Yukiiye slipped into the room. He made a fastidious face at the sprawled Benkei and turned to Yoshitsuné.

'Nephew, I have something to tell you. It is most important. However, I'll want a favour in exchange. You must commend me to Yoritomo. It is my deepest desire to serve him – but at the Court.'

Yoshitsuné regarded his uncle with some distaste. 'I will speak to Yoritomo. What is it you wish to say?'

'Kiso has had several letters from the Cloister Court. Not just the one.'

Yoshitsuné reacted with rewarding surprise. 'What were the letters about? Do you know?'

134

Yukiiye smiled. 'Yes.' He paused dramatically. 'Go-Shirakawa will make Kiso Shogun if Kiso drives the Taira out of the Capital and deposes the child Emperor Antoku.'

'Shogun!' Benkei sat up, startled. 'There hasn't been a Shogun for generations. That means that Kiso becomes the supreme military commander. The first servant of the Emperor. It would be a more powerful position than Lord Chancellor.'

'Kiyomori would have dearly loved to be Shogun but Go-Shirakawa wouldn't co-operate. Kiso will live off polished rice and sweet fish while Yoritomo swallows millet as a country samurai in that stinking fishing village,' sneered Yukiiye. 'If Kiso is not stopped Yoritomo will wish Kiyomori had slain him as a boy. Kiso will have the entire force of the Empire to turn on his rivals. He will have more power than Kiyomori ever did.'

'Are you sure this is true?' asked Yoshitsuné sharply.

Yukiiye bridled. 'I read the letter to him. Our future Shogun cannot make out Chinese characters. There is a bargain between them. Kiso will join with Go-Shirakawa on Mount Hiei – the monks are in the conspiracy – and march on the Capital. Once in the Rokuhara Palace he will be appointed Shogun.'

Yoshitsuné turned to Benkei. 'Find the others. We start tonight.'

*

Yoritomo received the news with a delighted chuckle. 'Sly fox, Go-Shirakawa. I thought he might try this. We shall just sit back and let Kiso begin his battle. He should do a fair amount of damage with his army and make it easier for us ultimately to defeat Tomomori. At the very least, he should drive the Taira out of the Capital and I do not think the Cloistered Emperor will find Kiso or his army easy to control afterwards.'

Yoshitsuné, exhausted and coated in mud and sweat from a fortnight's hard riding, stared at his brother in amazement. 'You mean we just let Kiso take the Capital alone? In the name of the Minamoto?'

'We let Kiso take the Capital alone. Not in the name of the Minamoto. I am the chieftain of the clan. If he usurps my position, shows disloyalty to his lord – me – then we take steps to reprimand him.' Yoritomo smiled. 'The moment he ceases to obey my orders or takes rewards or titles on his own initiative he is an outcast from his clan. Death is the only answer to such dastardly behaviour. My father destroyed his father. I shall destroy him. But in the meantime he will have cut down the Taira.'

'Suppose he fails?' asked Noriyori wearily.

Kajiwara, standing by, regarded the two younger brothers patronisingly. 'He won't fail, his army is fresh and well-fed. Tomomori and Shigehira are good generals but their men are starving.'

'Suppose we fail?' asked Yoshitsuné.

Yoritomo put an arm round him and smiled coldly into his eyes. 'It is your job, and that of your famous sword of Hachiman, to see that we don't.'

7. The Victory

In the next four months Kiso and his army swept across the Home Provinces, scattering Taira before them. Yukiiye was less effective and tended to avoid any serious engagements but, in a small way, he helped. Mount Hiei, irritated past endurance by Munemori's arbitrary and very stupid confiscation of some of their best estates, welcomed Kiso to their temples where Go-Shirakawa, by careful coincidence, was making a pilgrimage. The Cloistered Emperor was packed into a palanquin and escorted by Kiso's army back to the Capital and his beloved Hojoji Palace.

The Capital could not be defended by the shattered Taira and Munemori had no choice but to fire the Rokuhara and flee with the child Emperor Antoku, former Empress Tokuko and Kiyomori's widow, the little Emperor's grandmother. Nestled with the Imperial family in the ox carts was a large gilt and ebony box containing a sword, a bronze mirror and a seal: the Imperial Regalia, a gift from the Sun Goddess to her descendants on earth. As long as they were in Antoku's possession, he was the true Emperor in the eyes of the people and the gods.

Kiso's triumph proved brief. The Cloistered Emperor did resuscitate the title of Shogun for him, although he resented bitterly the loss of the Regalia since no new Emperor could be created without the sacred symbols. The Rokuhara was hastily rebuilt, white banners flew from the flag poles and Kiso ate polished rice and wore silk for the first time in his life. His men, stunned by the luxury of the Capital, even in its battered, half-starved state, grabbed, looted and raped, terrifying the Court and the defenceless population. Only the news that Shigehira had regrouped his army stopped the carnage. Kiso, who had planned to devote his autumn campaign to wiping out Yoritomo and had already appealed to Wada and Miura to

join him, was urged by the Cloister Court to defeat the Taira first and regain the priceless Regalia. Shigehira, now in command of a large body of desperate troops, met Kiso in Bizen and routed his dissipated army. The defeated Shogun hurried back to the Rokuhara and more bad news – scouts reported a large force on the highway from Kamakura, at least five thousand men, led by Yoritomo's brothers coming to the assistance of Go-Shirakawa. The Cloistered Emperor was appalled by the unexpected violence of Kiso's barbarous mountaineers, but he was not one to linger over his mistakes when there were alternatives. He knew that he had chosen the wrong branch of the clan, he regretted it, and he switched his patronage to Yoritomo, calling for his help. The eastern warriors could hardly be cruder or more destructive than the mountaineers and he did not fancy a whole winter of Kiso and his men.

Yukiiye was not one to linger over his mistakes either. He rapidly withdrew south of the Capital with his part of the army. There he waited to make peace with Yoritomo.

The Shogun, pausing only to set fire to the Hojoji Palace in revenge, escaped from the city with the four Heavenly Kings and a hundred and fifty samurai. The Kamakura army had to cross either the Seta or Uji rivers to enter the valley where the Capital lay or they would have to march several hundred miles out of their way, circling Lake Biwa, to attack from the south-west. The Shogun's only hope was to reach the Seta and Uji bridges, burn them and hold the bank until his scattered army could be re-grouped.

*

Yoritomo's announcement that the punitive army would be led by his two brothers received a mixed reaction in Kamakura. Yoritomo's explanation – internal Minamoto disputes should be solved by Minamoto commanders – seemed valid enough, but while Noriyori had a little experience, Yoshitsuné had none. The dissenters were somewhat mollified, however, when Lord Miura and Lord Kajiwara were ordered to accompany the army in an

advisory capacity. Miura was agreeable but Kajiwara remained disgruntled until Yoritomo, in a private interview, explained his motives. 'The feeling is that Yoshitsuné will make an excellent commander. Well, we will have to find out. Miura, Wada and Noriyori are adequate, competent, but we have a commander of genius only in you.' He clapped Kajiwara on the shoulder. 'Let us see what the boy can do. He may prove too rash to be of value – in a way I hope he does, he is arrogant – but the men like him, he seems to have control over them, so we will take the chance.' What Yoritomo did not add was that Yoshitsuné was also a Minamoto and although he distrusted his charismatic younger brother, he would feel a great deal easier with one member of his own family, respected and obeyed, as Commander-in-Chief. The bland, charming Noriyori, although easier to control, would not do.

Yoshitsuné accepted the challenge with an outward confidence that surprised no one. He had proved himself excellent in every aspect of the martial arts: on a horse, with a bow and particularly with his sword; he was liked and respected by his peers. Only Kajiwara and Doi actively resisted his charm.

As for himself, since the afternoon in the Hachiman shrine, Yoshitsuné had believed, in the very depths of his soul, that he was indeed one of the chosen of the God of War and that that set him apart from other samurai. But would he fear death? Only if it came before he had proved himself. He had learned on that same agonising afternoon that he feared humiliation far more than he feared death. And that, thought Yoshitsuné, makes me invincible!

*

'But if we cross the river at Uji we have surprise on our side. We can be in the Capital by tomorrow night,' Yoshitsuné said briskly.

'Nonsense,' retorted Kajiwara. 'The Seta bridge is long and narrow and thirty men could hold it for days. Scouts say that the bridge at Uji is down and the river is so swollen with this heavy rain that we'd never get men and horses

across. There is no choice but to move around Lake Biwa and attack from the west. Noriyori, you at least can see that.' Kajiwara paced furiously round the smoking fire. The Kamakura army was camped a few miles from the Seta bridge and the brothers with their advisers were huddled in a makeshift pavilion against the pouring rain, arguing about the next step. Yoshitsuné wanted to cross the Uji river and surprise Kiso; Kajiwara regarded that as the rash plan of an inexperienced general; Noriyori and Miura wavered. The argument had raged for over an hour.

'There is the problem of Yukiiye,' put in Noriyori.

'Exactly,' Kajiwara pounced, but Yoshitsuné and Miura were unimpressed.

'He waits south of the Capital. He won't move until he sees what happens to Kiso,' said Yoshitsuné.

Miura thoughtfully scratched the long scar in his beard. 'Lord Yukiiye has a large army and if he were still sympathetic to Kiso surely he would have already moved into the Capital or helped to defend the bridges. Our scouts confirm that there are no more than fifty men defending Seta and only about a hundred at Uji.'

'This is what worries me. Where is Kiso's army?' said Noriyori.

'Gone!' snapped his brother. 'That's obvious too. We know Shigehira beat the bulk of it and Yukiiye has the rest. Kiso has only his mountain samurai and not too many of them. But Kajiwara is right. Thirty could hold Seta bridge for a long time so we must take Kiso by surprise before he gets away. If he gets across the river he can start all over again. He has already proved his skill at raising troops. The only way to stop him is to take his head.' His voice was harsh with irritation at their obtuseness.

'Pure speculation. No experience to back it up. And you have not convinced me about Yukiiye,' Kajiwara retorted.

'My dear Kajiwara, surely, if necessary, you could defeat Yukiiye? Everyone else has. Look, I have a simple proposition.' Yoshitsuné tried to force patience into his voice. 'We have nearly five thousand men and Kiso may think we have more. You three stay here and attack the Seta

bridge and, once you're across the river, go to the Capital and look for Yukiiye. I'll take my men and we'll ford the river at Uji, down from Kiso's camp, and attack at dawn. The rain will give excellent cover. With the element of surprise we should be successful or at least hold them until the main bulk of our army has crossed the Seta. Don't let them fire the bridge. The river there will certainly be too swollen to ford.'

'I think this is a chance worth taking,' Noriyori said pensively. 'If Yoshitsuné fails we can split our troops and Kajiwara can take a contingent around Lake Biwa to attack from the west. We have enough men to risk it. Yoshitsuné will at least block Kiso's escape at the Uji crossing and perhaps force him to run south where he is unknown. Lord Miura, what do you think?'

'I agree. Yoshitsuné may be inexperienced but the plan is a valid one, dangerous for him but definitely valid.' He smiled at the young man.

Kajiwara glowered. 'All right, Yoshitsuné. I'll give you until midday. If we don't hear of a victory by then we do it my way, the proper way, circling Biwa and meeting Kiso face on. Sneaking across rivers and taking an army by surprise is not the proper way to fight a battle. In any case your brother will have a full report of this meeting.'

'I'm sure of that.' Yoshitsuné bowed curtly. 'I'll leave within the hour.'

*

'Look at that river!' said Benkei in disgust. 'But there, I can't get any wetter than I am now. What a cold foul night. I had forgotten how it can rain in the west.'

'Oh, your fat will protect you,' Yataro muttered, untying his leg greaves. 'Hold my horse while I lash these greaves to the saddle.'

At the sound of Yoshitsuné's laugh both men looked up from their task to watch him weave his way through the sodden men and horses. 'This rain is good cover but your horses look as though they have already been in the river. So do you!' The men laughed, good-natured despite the

141

rain. 'Here, Rokuro, get those arm bands off. Do you want to arrive on the battlefield rusted into a piece of statuary?'

He saw Benkei and Yataro and started towards them, inching cautiously round the rump of Rokuro's uneasy warhorse. But Rokuro, one of the Oshu men, grabbed his arm, 'Careful, commander! You're going to ride into your first battle wet as a new born babe and in my part of the world, they say that's lucky.'

Yoshitsuné laughed again, a young, excited laugh. 'I know the superstition so I fell on my knees and begged the other commanders to let me lead you through the Uji river in the rain into battle.'

The men chuckled, trying to forget the water pouring down their necks and the cold treacherous river a few feet away. Rokuro muttered, 'Kiso should have good quality saké for once, stolen from the Capital, and if those mountaineers of his haven't drunk it all there should be some worthwhile drinking tonight!'

Yoshitsuné, wiping the rivulets running down his face, said, 'Every minute wasted on this bank of the river is giving those disloyal dogs an advantage.' He raised his voice. 'Form into your groups and get ready to go.' He pulled himself up on his mare where he could be seen by his captains grouped around. His corselet was of brilliant primrose-yellow lacquered plates, visible even in the moonless murk. Like his men, he wore a short leather skirt to protect his groin and upper thighs and also like them his helmet, shoulder, arm and leg protectors had been removed to facilitate the river crossing and his sword was wrapped in his cloak to guard the precious steel. A long bow and a quiver of arrows were strapped high on his back. He looked down on the men milling about him and felt his stomach contract and his bowels loosen. They stared up at him, waiting for his words. For a second he was speechless, caught in the moment, in the reality of his first command. Then with a great burst of energy he rose in his stirrups and shouted over the pounding rain and grunting horses, 'Right, you know what to do. Lead your men, not more than fifteen to a captain, across where the ford looks safest

and we'll collect again on the other side. Yataro and Rokuro will go first and if they lose too many men we'll move down river. This whole manoeuvre has been planned to surprise Kiso so keep the noise down, especially once across. Rokuro, send out scouts on the other bank.' His young voice carried easily and the men, all experienced warriors, listened and nodded, faces screwed into grimaces against the rain. 'If Rokuro is right the spoils of war should warm your bellies by midday. Good luck.' A gruff murmur of excitement spread through the samurai as they grasped their horses' bridles and moved towards the river.

Yoshitsuné pushed through to where Yataro stood and leaning over in the saddle, he said in a low voice, 'The rain is not so heavy now so we must move quickly and get to Kiso's camp before dawn. If his scouts catch us half in and half out of the river we shall perish. No one could fight in those currents.'

'We're ready.' Yataro tugged his horse into action. He grinned back over its sturdy neck at Yoshitsuné. 'Good luck!'

'I've been waiting for this for too long. My karma is good, Yataro. I feel it. The time is right for Yoshitomo's sons. All right, in you go and don't drown!'

Yataro signalled to his men and with a quick glance at Rokuro, started down the bank into the river. Yoshitsuné, one eye on their progress, moved over to Benkei with whom he planned to cross the river.

Making room for him, the monk ran an appraising eye over his master. 'Nervous?' he asked.

'I don't know. I should be – I'm the least experienced man here.'

'These lads know what they are to do. No worry there.'

Yoshitsuné held his hands out flat in front of him; they shook slightly under the diminishing rain drops. Benkei looked at them. 'No worry there, either. Any warrior with steady hands before a battle is either dead or a fool.'

Yoshitsuné laughed. 'I feel as though every nerve in my body is doing a wild dance, but oh, Benkei, I can't wait to go!'

143

'Some of Rokuro's men are down but from here it looks as though Yataro's doing better. He's lost one but that seems to be all.'

Yoshitsuné moved down the line of waiting men, instructing them to follow Yataro downstream. As he went from group to group the men fell silent. Amazing, Benkei thought, for a novice to command such confidence from so many hardened warriors. For the thousandth time, the authority of the young man impressed him.

The men went into the river slowly and carefully, for one false step could mean an icy death. Yoshitsuné and Benkei watched from the bank as they struggled into the water, but Yoshitsuné could only bear the inactivity for a few minutes. His first battle lay beyond the river and his blood bubbled in his veins. He longed to feel the cold river current against his legs.

'Benkei, come. There on the left. They've all got through. Let's go.'

'My blood is already half frozen. The river will finish the job,' the monk grumbled.

They led their reluctant horses to the bank. The men waiting moved aside to let their general pass. Although they might not like fording the river, they trusted their commander and their karma was tied to his.

Yoshitsuné pulled his mare after him down the slippery slope to cold water that struck his legs like needles. The horse jerked back in terror but she was well trained and responded to firm commands and the pressure on her bridle. The water rose to Yoshitsuné's waist. The current was swift and the river bed uneven and cluttered with stones and debris. On his left the corpse of a soldier, lodged with flotsam between two boulders, fought a silent battle against the barrier that delayed his last journey to the sea. An abandoned horse struggled mid-stream, wheeling in circles, too terrified to go forward or back. Benkei grabbed the animal's reins and tugged it after him. The water, now at chest level, had driven all feeling from their lower limbs and it was sheer will that drove them to put one foot down before the other to fight against the current. Gradually the

level fell and they were stumbling up the bank. The winter air enfolded their soaking bodies in a freezing blanket.

Benkei spluttered and stamped. 'Hate water. Revolting stuff. Get your blood moving, boy, or you'll freeze in the saddle.'

Cold, bedraggled warriors were assembled by the captains who reported their losses to their commanders. Scouts had been sent out from Rokuro's group to locate Kiso's camp but it took well over an hour to get all the soldiers across the river and at any moment patrols might discover them and give a warning. The gift of surprise would be lost. The rain had ceased and a rising winter sun flooded the sky pale blue and yellow as they fanned out and rode silently across the bleak terrain to the Shogun's camp, a miserable clutch of tents huddled in a field.

Yoshitsuné rode the black mare along the bank of an irrigation ditch, in full sight of the enemy. Standing in his stirrups he shouted out his challenge to Kiso.

'Here before you is Sama Kuro Yoshitsuné, son of Minamoto Yoshitomo, brother of the Lord of Kamakura, the chieftain of the Minamoto. I want the head of the traitor, the false Shogun. Come out and fight me if you dare, Minamoto Yoshinaka, called Kiso!'

The yellow armour glowed rose and then gold in the early sun, the crest of the helmet blazed like a holy fire and the mare's black coat gleamed rich purple. The magnificence of the prancing horse and rider, aflame against the full glory of the eastern sky, astonished the warriors on both sides. All stared at the magical sight for a few seconds, then with a fierce roar the Kamakura men galloped over the bank and rushed past Yoshitsuné into the camp. The enemy had rested in full armour but they had to scramble on to their panicked horses.

The easterners plunged into the screaming knot of men and animals, shouting their names and their challenges to the mountaineers who prepared to defend the Shogun. Yoshitsuné saw his men, experienced in the rituals and formalities of warfare, get on with the business of fighting and killing while he sat, momentarily too confused to know

145

what to do. His archers had been forgotten in the rush and now they milled unhappily on the bank, not daring to fire for fear of hitting their own men. Yoshitsuné realised he should have used them before the charge and he wheeled the mare in a frantic circle while he ordered his thoughts. Snarling pairs of men slashed and hacked at each other. Benkei, a giant on a huge horse, wielded his great Rock Cleaver sword at a shaggy mountain man nearly his size. Yataro had taken on two, his wide face frozen into a killer's mask. The black mare, impatient to join the action, trumpeted and reared. Her neat hooves drumming on the hard ground brought Yoshitsuné to his senses. Kiso! He must get to Kiso – his men knew their task, his was the Shogun. There, across the field he saw his cousin and two of the Heavenly Kings engaged with three Oshu men, one of whom was just going down before Imai.

With a shout Yoshitsuné charged off the bank and directed the mare around the edge of the field through fighting groups. A mountaineer whirled his horse away from a fallen opponent and shouted his name at Yoshitsuné, sword sweeping over his head. Yoshitsuné pulled up the mare, feinted and struck at the man, throwing him off balance. He kicked the mare past before the mountaineer could recover, eager to get to more important challenges.

Suddenly a burly figure loomed up. 'I am Suzuki, retainer of the Shogun. Prepare to die, Yoshitsuné.' One of the Heavenly Kings made an opponent worth fighting and Yoshitsuné stopped to meet him. Instinct and long training blanked out everything but Suzuki and fighting: the shrieks, the fear, the jostling horses, the pain, the weariness, the deadliness of the game became part of him. He fought Suzuki long and hard and when he finally killed the Heavenly King he did not pause but urged the mare over the jerking body towards his goal. Another samurai and another blocked his way with challenges and were killed and discarded until before him he saw Kiso, protected by Imai and one of the Kato brothers who, with a mighty roar, wheeled to face Yoshitsuné. He had no choice but to fight, leaving Kiso unchallenged.

Somewhere, he heard Benkei bellow, 'My lord, Kiso and Imai are escaping towards Seta.' Kato, encouraged by the news of his master's safety, fought harder to protect it. But he was fatigued and desperate and finally reckless. Yoshitsuné broke through his guard and skewered him under the shoulder. Stunned and spouting blood, Kato toppled off his horse, also staggering from too many sword thrusts, and fell into the mud.

Kiso was indeed gone. Benkei, ragged and bloody, rode up. 'What a fight! There are only a few of them left.' Yoshitsuné looked round him for the first time; the field was covered with horses and men, some writhing and screaming, some still. Crows flapped around the quiet ones. Those animals and men still on their feet stood in inches of red slime – the hoar frost had melted under a flood of hot blood. Here and there a few pairs of men fought but most, dazed and exhausted, swayed stupidly as they looked at the carnage. Yoshitsuné was brought to his senses as Kato's wounded horse, kicking and thrashing in its death throes, started the mare into a nervous dance. He slid off her back and walked to Kato, who had hauled himself onto his left side. His right arm dangled uselessly, but his left hand held a dagger. His eyes were open, glazed with pain, and he did not sense Yoshitsuné by him as he struggled to rest the pommel of the dagger on the ground, the point under his chin, against his throat. With a deep shuddering sigh, Kato collapsed his full weight on to the point of the blade. Yoshitsuné gasped and his hand went, involuntarily, to the Sanjo dagger thrust in his belt. As his fingers brushed the hilt a quick violent spasm shot through his nerves, leaving him suddenly weak and sick. His hand jerked away from the dagger; he turned, and leant against the mare's hot sweaty flank, his eyes closed, the morning sun seeping into him.

'By the Lord Buddha, you're a fine mess. Are you hurt?'

Yoshitsuné opened his eyes and stared at Benkei. 'What?'

'Hurt? Are you hurt? No? Well, pull yourself together. You, Rokuro, finish off Kato's horse. Yoshitsuné, we have

to strip and burn the dead and deal with the wounded.'

'Kiso?' asked Yoshitsuné.

'Gone to Seta, I imagine. Look, boy, I sent a messenger to Noriyori half an hour ago when the battle was won. You were having the fight of your life with Kato so I thought I'd better let them know we'd done it. We don't want Kajiwara marching around Biwa for nothing, do we?' He chuckled and patted Yoshitsuné on the back. 'They'll get Kiso. He'll probably make for Awazu so he can cross the lake.'

Yoshitsuné nodded stupidly. Benkei stepped closer and gripped his aching arm. 'Pull yourself together. We've had the battle, now comes the hard part, cleaning up and remaining on our feet. Take Kato's and Suzuki's heads. They're yours. You have proved you can fight, now prove you're a real commander. Go and tell your men how well they fought.'

He pushed Yoshitsuné up on to the mare and slapped her rump. As she trotted into the stinking horror of the battlefield Yoshitsuné forced a smile onto his stiff lips and cried, 'Hey, Yataro, what a fight that was, eh? Rokuro, how many heads did you take?'

*

An early moon spilt its chill light over the fields. The ground had frozen again and the horses had to pick their way carefully over thin, brittle sheets of ice covering ruts and holes. The animals frequently stumbled and cut their legs. Dotted about were small farmhouses, sealed off for the night behind wooden fences. Dogs occasionally barked but no wise human showed himself when rival armies were on the move.

Imai reined in his horse. 'Listen! Do you hear it?' They strained for any noise; a dog howled; silence; then came the rumble of trotting hooves and men's voices.

'How far away do you think they are?' asked Kiso calmly.

'Two fields? Three? They must have guessed we are going to Awazu.'

'We must split up. At least they will have to work a little harder.'

'If I make myself obvious it will distract them,' said Imai briskly. 'I'll ride along the embankment. You go left across the fields.'

The foster brothers did not look at each other. Death was the enemy they would fight separately. Imai muttered hoarsely, 'We'll meet in the next world.' He spurred his horse on to the irrigation bank where, illuminated by moonlight, he would be visible for some distance. With a wave of his hand he turned towards Awazu.

Kiso set off across the paddy fields. If he could find a sheltered place it would be as well to end his life now. A frozen patch in a peasant's field seemed a sorry resting place for the Shogun of the Emperor, but it was his karma.

Suddenly his mare lurched, breaking through the thin, deceptive ice. She struggled helplessly in the cold muddy water, sinking deeper with each effort, jagged ice slashing her fetlocks.

Three men wearing Miura's crest rode along the embankment towards Kiso, attracted by the moonlight flashing on his silver spiked helmet. Kiso tried to reach his sword but the action sent the floundering mare pitching to her knees. An arrow droned through the silence and the animal jerked and screamed. Kiso staggered to his feet, sword in hand, but the three were moving down the slope, approaching in a semi-circle, closing in and backing him against the twitching horse. Kiso shouted and raising his sword he charged at the nearest man. The samurai wheeled his horse to the left and plunged. Kiso took the blow full in the diaphragm, impaled on the Kamakura blade. The second horseman struck off the Shogun's head with one clean sideways swipe. The trunk, spouting blood, collapsed into the mud.

At dawn, a farmer crunching across his fields found two headless corpses half a mile apart. The mud around both had been churned by horses' hooves. He quickly stripped off the armour, valuable even though battered and pierced, and burnt the corpses. But since he never dared sell the

armour, nor confess to the local officials what he had done, the bodies of Minamoto Yoshinaka known as Kiso and his foster brother, Imai, were never traced.

*

Three years after he had fled the Capital, a fugitive from the Taira, Yoshitsuné returned there. It was hardly an impressive entry. His men, tired from their long march south and from the fighting, straggled through the southern outskirts to camp by the dilapidated Rashomon Gate, contesting the wild dogs and beggars for space.

The young general, warily jubilant, rode to the Rokuhara Palace where he met Noriyori, Kajiwara and Miura. Kiso's fifty men had sold their lives dearly on the long narrow Seta bridge and it had been mid-afternoon before the easterners, aided by a rear attack from some Oshu samurai straight from the Uji battlefield, could fight their way across and send samurai after Kiso and Imai. The traitors' severed heads were carried by courtiers to Kamakura along with a full report of the battle. Noriyori had arranged for scouts to search the countryside for the skulking Yukiiye.

The commanders had just begun to relax in the former Shogun's quarters when an Imperial messenger arrived from the Cloistered Emperor who wished to thank his Minamoto saviours personally. And immediately. As an advance token of his gratitude he sent superb Court dress. Yoshitsuné and Noriyori washed and wearily clad themselves in the complicated layers of silk and brocade, but they were too tired and too numb to appreciate the beautiful colours and exquisite embroidery.

Go-Shirakawa kept them waiting in an ante-room for twenty minutes. Once again it gave him great pleasure to make samurai leaders cool their heels. There had been much gossip about the sons of Yoshitomo, and Go-Shirakawa inspected these with interest when they finally knelt before him. Noriyori was what he had expected, an uncomplicated warrior, but he was intrigued by

Yoshitsuné's appearance. Exhaustion lent the young man's face a pallor which was accentuated by dark hollows under the eyes, and his movements displayed a grace and style that the Cloistered Emperor found amazing in a samurai.

However he had more important things to do than dwell for long on charm. As if to remind them of their humble status he offered no wine or fruit, although he himself accepted a cup of tea from Tametoki, his servant.

'Our gratitude to the Lord of Kamakura is boundless. His kinsman, Kiso, behaved abominably, forcing the Cloister Court to obey his demands. Violence was used. Disgusting!' He shivered. 'Kiso even went so far as to burn our favourite palace. But you have dealt efficiently with him and we are pleased.'

The brothers bowed and murmured that it was their duty and pleasure to serve his Sacred Highness.

Go-Shirakawa continued, 'We have communicated frequently with the Lord of Kamakura and he appreciates that there are still many problems to solve. Kiso did drive the Taira from the Capital but, alas, they took the young Emperor and the Imperial Regalia with them. Antoku was imposed upon the Court by his grandfather, Kiyomori, and will be replaced, but the Regalia – the Mirror, the Sword and the Sacred Seal – must be returned. We have offered Munemori a truce if he brings the Regalia to the Capital immediately.' He paused to watch the effect of this on his listeners. A truce with the Taira would not be well received by the youngest Minamoto and his face reflected his disapproval. 'But,' he continued, 'it seems likely that he will refuse. Therefore we have prevailed upon Lord Yoritomo to send you after the Taira. As our envoy.' He smiled sweetly and sipped his tea.

They were dismissed a few minutes later and returned in separate palanquins, so conversation was impossible until they were in the Rokuhara, joined by Kajiwara and Miura. To Yoshitsuné's surprise Noriyori was depressed by the command to pursue the Taira.

'How do we know this is what Yoritomo wants? He seems more interested in the samurai-dokoro than in

fighting, and if the Taira are in flight will he want us to pursue them now? We have only Go-Shirakawa's word and he is an old fox.'

Kajiwara, irritated by Yoshitsuné's success at Uji and by exclusion from the Imperial audience, said shortly, 'It is a pity Miura and I did not accompany you. We are experienced in political affairs and our judgement would have been useful.'

Noriyori answered morosely, 'Useful, of course. But we would still have to obey the Imperial orders.'

Through a haze of fatigue Yoshitsuné said quickly, 'But Yoritomo certainly wants the Taira crushed once and for all. We know Shigehira and Tomomori are dangerous and have large armies – look how they defeated Kiso. Whatever Go-Shirakawa is plotting, the defeat of the Taira is still essential to *us*.'

'The boy is right,' said Miura, 'but I see Noriyori's problem. The Inland Sea is the Taira stronghold and they'll be nearly impregnable there. If we start immediately we shall be inferior in numbers in enemy-held territory and yet if we wait they will be even stronger.'

Noriyori nodded. 'That's part of it. And we have virtually no ships. That's a problem too. And, frankly, none of us know much about naval warfare. The Taira do and the Inland Sea pirates are their allies. We have no choice – since we must follow the Cloistered Emperor's command – but I don't like it.'

Yoshitsuné said eagerly, 'Yoritomo would want us to pursue our advantage.'

Kajiwara glared at Yoshitsuné. 'Yoritomo's mind is not so easily read.'

The three men stared at Kajiwara, restlessly tapping his iron fan on his knee. Miura said softly, 'What worries me is that Yoritomo will be the fourth faction Go-Shirakawa has supported in five years. Kiyomori, Yorimasa, Kiso, Yoritomo. Who will be next, I wonder?'

After the others had dispersed to get some sleep, Kajiwara took his writing box and prepared ink. As the rising winter sun sparkled over the frosty Rokuhara

gardens, he settled down to compose a separate secret report to his master in Kamakura.

*

Yoshitsuné's second battle and his first venture against the Taira came almost immediately. The child Emperor Antoku, Munemori and the remnants of the Imperial Court still loyal to the Taira took refuge at Yashima on the island of Shikoku, although Shigehira and Tomomori remained on the mainland in possession of a Taira fortress at Ichinotani. Scouts reported that the fortress was on a strip of land between the mountains and the sea, easily fortified and held: the steep cliffs and the sea made natural defences and the east and west flanks had deep ditches and palisades. A large Taira fleet was anchored in the harbour to ward off a sea attack.

The plans for Ichinotani had been the last of Hogen's documents that Yoshitsuné had seen – it was the document found by the diviner in Asuka's clothes chest and Yoshitsuné was sure he remembered that somewhere in the mountains behind Ichinotani there was a ravine, treacherous but just passable, leading down to the fortress. It would be difficult to find and dangerous to use but a small group of men might be able to surprise the fort. The Minamoto commanders, excepting Kajiwara, decided that this news made an immediate attempt on the Taira desirable and Go-Shirakawa agreed with alacrity. Tomomori was attracting a lot of local support so prompt action was advisable, and Yoshitsuné declared that there was no time to communicate with Yoritomo or wait for Yukiiye. Kajiwara grumbled and pointed out obstacles but Noriyori and Miura agreed with Yoshitsuné, impressed by his plan. The weary army marched out of the Capital only a week after it had arrived.

Yoshitsuné and Noriyori formulated a strategy. The army would appear to split in half, Noriyori and Kajiwara attacking on the eastern flank and Miura and Yoshitsuné apparently leading an attack on the west, but Yoshitsuné would quietly leave Miura's army and, with his retainers,

find the ravine and start a diversionary rear action after Miura and Noriyori had launched their offensives, giving them a better chance to breach the palisades.

The plan went perfectly. After several hours' searching, the party found the ravine, steep and thick with icy brambles and boulders, but the fifty determined samurai and their horses stumbled and slid down, spewing rocks and soil, with Yoshitsuné in the lead. He burst into the Taira camp wearing no helmet so all could see his face, the Hachiman sword gleaming in the sun as he swung it over his head, roaring challenges to the Taira commanders. Benkei seized a torch as he rode by and fired a line of wooden huts. The strong wind whipped the flames into an inferno, blinding and confusing the soldiers, but Yoshitsuné's cries kept his men together and they slashed ruthlessly through the enemy. In the confusion the Taira abandoned their defences, allowing Noriyori and Miura to break through easily. Wedged between the three fronts the Taira had no choice but the sea. Over a thousand were killed and among the prisoners was Shigehira, Kiso's victor; but many escaped to the junks anchored in shallow water, among them Tomomori and several thousand men, who left their camp a smoking ruin. Unable to follow the sea-going junks the Minamoto milled along the coastal strip, trampling and killing and burning in frustration. Yoshitsuné, outraged to see his victory snatched away, urged his mare out into the breakers. He lifted the Hachiman sword, crimson with Taira gore, and bellowed into the wind, 'We shall meet again, Tomomori, and you will not escape.'

*

Although Ichinotani was hardly a total success it diverted the danger of a Taira attack on the Capital. The weary population of the city had anticipated an invasion, but now that the dreaded enemy had been driven to some isolated spot where they could only terrorise uncivilised provincials, the Kamakura army were regarded as saviours and, when they returned, were bombarded with paper

154

flowers and sprays of plum blossom. Stories of Yoshitsuné's exploits at Uji and Ichinotani had already spread through the people, hungry for a hero after years of grim military rule. His bravery was embellished – there were rumours he could fly like an eagle and kill six men with one arrow. Mud-spattered but radiantly happy, he sat on his black charger, glowing in his battered yellow armour, accepting the cheers. Hachiman had spoken in the shrine and now the God's whisper mingled in his ears with the cries of the jubilant crowd. The hero of Ichinotani raised the Hachiman sword and saluted the people. Noriyori, Kajiwara and Miura rode behind him, virtually ignored by the excited throngs. If they resented Yoshitsuné's popularity and their own relegation to mere mortal status, they wisely said nothing – for the time being.

*

A few weeks after Ichinotani Kajiwara Kagetoki arrived in Kamakura. He rode along the avenue that stretched from the raw precincts of the new Hachiman shrine to the samurai-dokoro, headquarters of Yoritomo's samurai administration. As the first important commander to be interviewed he had an advantage that he was all too well aware of. His account of the battles was straightforward, unexaggerated; he mentioned Yoshitsuné's exploits without emotion but emphasised that Kiso had escaped from the battlefield at Uji and Tomomori from Ichinotani. His venom was reserved for the details of the reception in the Capital, the legends and miraculous tales already accruing around the young hero. He dwelt at length on the interest shown by the Cloistered Emperor; on the many banquets and entertainments lavished on Yoshitsuné by frivolous courtiers ever eager to take up a new favourite. He also mentioned the growing belief among the common samurai that Yoshitsuné was the reincarnation of his great warrior ancestor, Hachiman Taro.

Yoritomo listened, his eyes hard and cold. Noriyori's competence, Miura's experienced advice did not interest

him. He returned again and again to his youngest brother's glory.

When Kajiwara left the samurai-dokoro, rain was falling heavily. As his tired horse plodded along the churned muddy avenue, Kajiwara, hunched in his saddle, a cloak swathed around his face, smiled with rich satisfaction.

*

Yoshitsuné was preparing for a blossom viewing. He knelt before the mirror stand as his attendant arranged the stiff black tubular headdress over his topknot. His heavy brocaded outer kimono was a rich grass green blending with the lighter shades of green and primrose in the under kimono, and his Chinese silk trousers were embroidered with a pattern of peony blossoms. All the clothes were gifts from the Cloistered Emperor.

Benkei hurried into the room. 'What are you doing? This is no time to be enjoying yourself. Haven't you heard the news from Kamakura?'

'It is a beautiful afternoon and the cherries are at their peak, in another day they will be falling. The Lord Privy Seal is giving a splendid party with dancers from the Inari Shrine and I do not want to hear about grim doings in the frozen east. The light greens and yellows are good together, don't you think? Go-Shirakawa is a generous old soul. This embroidery is magnificent.'

Benkei stood spread-legged in the centre of the room, arrogant despite his stained saffron robe and battered monk's bonnet. He glared at his master, 'You *have* dressed up like a little Court flower. You've bathed again. It'll weaken you, you know. Already I barely recognise you and I am sure the lads who followed you into Ichinotani would think you were some Fujiwara bath attendant. And as for taking presents from the Cloister Court...'

'Oh, don't be so bad-tempered. You enjoy the living here, but your religious training has made an uncultured prig of you. As well as a dirty one. Maybe if you bathed Go-Shirakawa would give you a new robe. He is a monk, too,

after all.' Yoshitsuné chuckled as he tapped his headdress into a firmer position.

'The news is not good. Do you want to hear it?'

'Hm?'

'Yoritomo has requested that Noriyori be made a courtier of the Fifth Rank and Governor of Omi Province as well. Even more sinister, he has been appointed Commander-in-Chief of the Minamoto forces. My information is that Yorimoto specifically instructed the Cloister Court that you were to receive no Court rank, no titles and no estates. There is no mention of you in the list of commanders for the new campaign. It seems that the Lord of Kamakura is upset.'

Yoshitsuné stared at his reflection shimmering in the flat bronze oval mirror.

Benkei added, 'Kajiwara returned to Kamakura last month. He has always loathed you, but after Ichinotani I think he would do anything to bring you down.'

'But Yoritomo can't just accept Kajiwara's word. What about Miura? Noriyori? What do they say? After all, I am his brother, his own blood, and I proved myself to be a good commander. That is what he sent me out to be. And since then I've worked hard on the new campaign, just as hard as Noriyori. Harder. What's wrong with him?'

Benkei ran an eloquent eye over Yoshitsuné's clothes.

'All this? But this isn't my doing – I can't refuse. You know that. Besides I don't entirely share my brother's insane views on the Court. I have been to a few entertainments, made love to a few Court ladies, but I haven't been disloyal to the samurai-dokoro. I'm still a samurai. Am I corrupt if I don't spend all my time with soldiers' whores stinking of garlic? Am I supposed to be like Noriyori?'

'Granted that his tastes are low, at least the women Noriyori associates with are not likely to be playing political games. The scent of garlic would seem like the finest Chinese perfumes on those females, but they are no threat to Yoritomo.'

'Neither am I.'

'Yoshitsuné, your brother is not like other men. He

distrusts everyone – you, Noriyori, perhaps even Tokimasa and Kajiwara.'

'Very possibly, but I won two important victories for
him. Oh, I know Kiso got away at Uji but I was not to
blame. Neither was I to blame for the escape of Tomomori.
Yoritomo told me I would have to prove I deserved the
Hachiman sword; well, I have. Now he tries to humiliate
me! My brother is to be received at Court while I, the hero,
am no more than a common samurai.'

'It will be embarrassing,' agreed Benkei.

The flush of temper in Yoshitsuné's cheeks was not
becoming against the green brocade. He began to stalk
around the room, swishing and swirling his robes like an
angry cat twitching its tail. 'I am going to the viewing this
afternoon. If anyone asks me why I have been passed over I
shall tell them! Let them know what an ingrate Yoritomo
is. I don't have anything to be ashamed of.'

Benkei nodded.

'And tomorrow,' added Yoshitsuné, 'I will compose a
letter to the Lord of Kamakura pledging my loyalty to him
and to the clan – as a precaution . . .'

Benkei nodded again.

Yoshitsuné turned to the sword stand where the Hachiman sword rested; below it, on a similar stand, lay the
Sanjo dagger, Hidehira's present. He took up the sword
and thrust it in his sash but the dagger he left on its stand.
The sight of it, even more than usual, repelled him.

*

The cherry viewing was not held in the Imperial
Enclosure but along a particularly lovely stretch of bank on
the Kamo River, a distinction, Yoshitsuné thought sourly
as he slid his complicated costume out of his palanquin,
that would be lost on Yoritomo. This was simply a party
given by a man who happened to be a Court official, and
most of the parties he attended were the same. Politics were
never discussed, everything was civilised and pleasant. He
looked around at the groups of men fluttering their silks

158

and embroideries like so many clumsy butterflies under the dipping willows and frail clouds of blossom. What was the harm in it?

The women remained in the ox-carts, the bridles of the huge impassive animals held by sumptuously dressed, equally impassive servants. Although nominally hidden from masculine scrutiny by rattan blinds, the women were in fact flirting and giggling and flouncing their carefully planned, complicated kimono to attract possible suitors. He smiled and bowed to one all but invisible lady whom he had recognised by her famous and much praised shades of pink and rose. The sleeves shivered enticingly and Yoshitsuné, who had made love to her several times before, noted that she might be worth a visit later that night. Yoritomo would apparently expect them to talk politics on her pallet until dawn. Even his few courtesy visits to Go-Shirakawa had been devoted to discussions of poetry, music or the seasons. Really, thought Yoshitsuné, Yoritomo knows nothing of the Court. Because he eats, sleeps, and lives intrigue and administration he thinks the rest of the world does the same.

Among the guests he found that most were aware of Yoritomo's deliberate snub; one or two were openly sympathetic but several cut him. To his surprise he saw his brother in a group of livelier Court gentlemen. Noriyori avoided most invitations to Court circles, by choice as much as Kamakura policy, and had found his way into somewhat sleasier echelons of Capital society where he drank, gambled and whored happily. But with promotion to courtier of the Fifth Rank he apparently felt it behoved him to appear at an important official's entertainment. He accepted Yoshitsuné's congratulations with an embarrassed shrug.

'Thank you. I won't say I am not pleased, but I would be much more so if you had not been slighted. What does Yoritomo mean by passing you over completely? Has he sent you a letter at all?'

'No, nothing but instructions about our duties here. What about you?'

'No, nothing, but ...' Noriyori paused, nervously opening and closing his fan.

'Well?'

'Kajiwara went to Kamakura and, frankly, it is not difficult to guess what he told Yoritomo without me or Miura to defend you. I am sure you were right to make the surprise attacks at both Uji and Ichinotani in the way you did, but Kajiwara is old-fashioned about strategy and unfortunately so are most of the warlords in the samurai-dokoro. You did things in a different way and it has made them suspicious and uneasy. I am delighted to be Commander-in-Chief but you are the better general even if a little unconventional.' He sighed. 'It is certainly Kajiwara who has prejudiced Yoritomo against you and made him ... distrust you.'

'You think Kajiwara made me look too ambitious? Too anxious for glory?' Yoshitsuné found a certain relief in being able to lay the blame squarely on Kajiwara. It enabled him to push other, murkier, less pleasant ideas to the back of his mind.

'I do,' Noriyori said unhappily. 'Yoritomo sneered at you because you had no experience. Well, now you have it and have made yourself popular and, perhaps unwisely, shown a little independence he is worried.' He looked around at the other guests, most of whom by now were seated in pavilions under the trees devoting themselves to saké. 'I hate this sort of thing,' he said, but whether he meant parties or intrigue Yoshitsuné could not tell.

A small brilliantly attired figure was approaching across the grass; it was Yukiiye, entirely in his element, superbly and expensively dressed, exquisitely made up. After Kiso's death he had applied humbly to Yoritomo for mercy and forgiveness, but no one would believe it to see him now, an elegant habitué of Court circles.

'My dear boy.' He flickered his fan towards Noriyori. 'The hero of the day and the victor of the future. Now that you have become such a distinguished gentleman I see that you no longer worry about your brother's idiotic strictures on the Court. It is good to see you in civilised company.'

His lips drew back in a tight smile revealing his fashionably blacked teeth.

'Thank you, uncle. None of this would have been possible without your help.' The slight tinge of sarcasm was lost on Yukiiye.

'Good evening, uncle.' Yoshitsuné smiled and bowed.

'Oh, yes, Yoshitsuné. Now, Noriyori, come with me. There are several important people I want you to meet and of course you must see Shizuka Gozen dance – such a marvellous performer and so incredibly beautiful. Come.' Without a backward glance at Yoshitsuné he led a reluctant Noriyori away.

Yoshitsuné stood still for a few seconds until his irritation was under control – snubbed by his own uncle, that old fool Yukiiye! Suddenly the unpleasantness of his situation came home to him; from being everybody's favourite he was now almost a social nuisance, an outcast. He began to walk back to his palanquin, bent on taking temporary refuge at the Rokuhara, but as he moved up the slope towards the ox carts, the guests were summoned to the dances. He could not leave now, and even as he turned back one of the stewards approached him and, bowing politely, informed him that Shizuka Gozen had heard of his skill as a flautist and would be honoured if he would accompany her. Slightly mollified, he removed himself to the wooden platform for the dancers and musicians, most of whom were also guests known for their musical accomplishments. He knelt between two courtiers, one with a lute, the other with a large drum, both of whom bowed rather coolly. Shizuka perhaps did not know of his disgrace or, if she did, was deliberately ignoring it. He was unaccountably pleased.

As she appeared there was a murmur of appreciation. Dressed in trailing trousers and kimono of pure white silk, her long gleaming hair bound to give her freedom of movement, she was heavily made up, but the thick powder and tiny rouged mouth accentuated rather than concealed her beauty, perhaps because her perfect almond eyes glowed mysteriously in the white mask. She tapped the

small drum she carried and began to dance. Compelled by her beauty and charm, the accompanists played with inspiration as she moved through the complicated patterns and movements. Yoshitsuné watched, fascinated by her grace. Several times their eyes met briefly and he felt his heart jump with excitement. Before she had completed her performance he had forgotten Yoritomo.

The host presented gifts of gratitude to Shizuka and the musicians. Lanterns were lit and the party continued with informal music, but Shizuka had vanished. It was a beautiful evening, clouds scudding across a sickle moon in a pearly grey sky, the air scented with blossom and the guests' subtle perfumes, an evening far too beautiful to waste with people who despised him. On impulse, he sent his servant for the palanquin and set off for the Nijo ward where he had heard Shizuka lived.

Her house was set in a garden behind a thick hedge of lavender and bush clover. It had occurred to Yoshitsuné that the dancer might not have returned home – there was no reason why she should not linger by the river to enjoy the evening. Resigning himself to failure, he sent his servant to enquire while he, unable to bear the confines of the palanquin any longer, stepped down and paced the narrow road.

A late-blossoming almond tree stood beside the wicket gate and its lovely odour brought back the music and Shizuka's dancing. And another memory. Asuka had loved the sweetness of almond oil and, night after night, lying in her arms, he had absorbed the fragrance. He paused, saddened by the evocation of her, by the futility of her death, by how much he still occasionally missed her. Momentarily the anticipation of Shizuka's beauty faded. She would be just another conquest, just another hour or two of flirtatious manoeuvring, then a few moments of pleasure followed by – nothing. He had come to know it all so well. There would be no warmth, no tenderness, no purpose. An aching misery swept through him. He stopped and gazed up at the cool, unhelpful moon and then stepped back towards the palanquin. His servant's stealthy

reappearance arrested his departure.

'The house is shuttered but one room is open. The interior is dark but I could see a woman's figure. Shall I go and announce you, my lord?'

Yoshitsuné hesitated. Asuka's memory had deadened his desire, but where would he go, what would he do? With a sigh he turned to the little wicket gate. 'No, stay here. I shall go myself.'

The house was small but well kept. He followed a raked gravel path round it until he found the open room where a shadowy figure was just visible seated beside a lattice screen. Yoshitsuné wondered whether it was Shizuka, watching the moon or waiting for someone, though he suspected it might be a female relative or maidservant. Keeping to the obscurity of the veranda, he moved nearer to the window. Another fragrance floated into the spring night – there could be no doubt, this was Shizuka. The subtle scent of her robes released by the evening warmth excited him again and he whispered her name. The figure moved slightly and inclined forward. She murmured, 'Who is it? Speak or I shall call the servants.'

'It is Sama Kuro Yoshitsuné. I had the honour of playing the flute this evening. Your dancing moved me so greatly that I could not resist ... I know it is late but ...'

'The evening is beautiful, I understand.' There was a rustle of silk and a pale gleam as she withdrew her small hand from her sleeve and extended it toward him. 'Please come closer or you will wake the household.' She peered at him through the dusk. 'Ah, so it is indeed the famous victor of Uji and Ichinotani. You are not what I expected.'

'What had you expected?' He sat on the edge of the veranda, asking the usual questions, following the expected pattern, anticipating the usual result and its ensuing emptiness.

'We had heard in the Capital that the samurai of Minamoto Yoritomo were rough coarse fellows like the followers of Minamoto Kiso, so naturally I dreaded the arrival of the Kamakura army. But you do not seem uncultured or brutal.' She paused and then added quietly,

'It was rumoured that Yoshitsuné was different. That is why I requested that you accompany me and I saw at once that the rumours were true.' He wondered if she had also heard about Yoritomo's orders and decided that it did not matter anyway. She seemed unusually serious for a woman; it was difficult to imagine her coyly fluttering her sleeves from behind a rattan blind. Asuka had never been coy, but Yoshitsuné realised after later experiences that this was because she was too young to know how to play the games of love.

Shizuka, however, was watching him, her gaze calm and direct. Interested, he asked, 'Did you know the famous victor of Uji and Ichinotani has been ignored by the samurai-dokoro and relieved of his command?'

'I did know that, and it must be painful for you. It is karma but it is painful all the same.' They were silent for a few moments, listening to the night sounds of the garden. Suddenly she said, 'Perhaps if you were less cultured and more brutal you would be more acceptable to the samurai-dokoro?'

'But samurai don't have to be barbarians; that is as foolish as the theory that the Capital is feeble and effete.'

'Of course. I'm sorry.' Another pause and then she added, 'Would you like some saké? There is some here, only a little, but the servants are asleep and I would prefer not to wake them.'

Custom demanded that he accept the saké, but he did not want any and he felt that this woman would understand. 'No, thank you.' Through the gloom he could see her smile and nod. He said in a low voice, 'I am no longer a favourite in the Capital, you know.'

There was no reply. She had retreated only a little way behind the lattice screen, just the distance modesty required. He could barely see her face but by reaching out he could touch the hem of her robes – he placed a hand on the silky material. When she did not pull away, he slipped off his sandals and stepped across the narrow veranda, into the warm darkness where she waited.

*

He awoke before sunrise and lay on the pallet, confused by the unfamiliar surroundings but at peace. Shizuka moved in her sleep and he remembered – her body smooth and yet firm with muscle, yielding and yet demanding, her tenderness and her friendliness. There had been no sparring, no holding back. Yoshitsuné stretched with deep contentment. He had forgotten what it was like to make love to a woman and feel joy, not just satisfaction or accomplishment but warm joy seeping through his body, filling his lungs, expanding his soul. He looked again at Shizuka and her eyes, open now, glowed softly. 'I am no longer a favourite,' he repeated.

She smiled. 'My karma is tied to yours now.'

When he left the little house, walking into the golden spring road, he paused by the almond tree and inhaled. A whiff of sadness lingered perhaps for a futile death, but what was a little sadness in the midst of so much happiness?

*

Go-Shirakawa, seated on a cushion with his robes plumped round him, received Yoshitsuné affably, impressed again with the boy's charm – really a most attractive individual for a samurai. His approach and obeisance were modest enough but the Cloistered Emperor's sharp nose for human frailty caught a whiff of arrogance behind the pose. Yukiiye's stupidity and Noriyori's laziness were dismissable but this youngster's pride might be very useful in the inevitable struggle with Yoritomo, who could not but be aware that he had a potential rival here. Go-Shirakawa smiled to himself; he would enjoy a little intrigue again. Life had become so quiet.

'Are you and Noriyori comfortable in the Rokuhara? We cannot imagine that the fortress can be very luxurious?'

Yoshitsuné bowed again. 'Not luxurious, Your Highness, but bearable.' He smiled politely. Through all his adult life he had heard the Cloistered Emperor discussed merely as a tool to be manipulated by the Minamoto against the Taira. All the obsequious phrases and titles had

been used, but Go-Shirakawa had been essentially represented as no more than another politician. Now, alone in the presence of the sacred monk, descendant of the Sun Goddess, Yoshitsuné was somewhat awed in spite of himself. The Cloistered Emperor dwelt behind a patina of history, a special unknowable, impenetrable mystery that separated him from other men; although he might extend gracious patronage, he could never extend friendship. One would never know what he was really thinking. He was, Yoshitsuné reflected, very like a finely bred cat.

Go-Shirakawa offered some saké to Yoshitsuné and then began his game. 'We were very surprised to find that although Yoritomo requested Court rank for Noriyori, he did not wish the request to include you – an oversight, we think.'

'Perhaps, Your Highness,' Yoshitsuné replied warily.

'We are sure that it was. Therefore we have promoted you to Courtier of the Fifth Rank as well – to remedy the oversight.' He beamed benignly at Yoshitsuné who touched his forehead to the floor, partly in courtesy but mainly to hide his confusion. He knew that Yoritomo's command was definite – no rank or honour to be received from the Court except at the express order of Kamakura. What was he to do? If he accepted ... but he could not refuse the Cloistered Emperor. Kiso had accepted Court favour and Yoritomo had destroyed him. Kiso had been of course disloyal, and Yoshitsuné knew he himself was not. But did Yoritomo?

'Yoshitsuné, are you so overcome you cannot speak?' asked the sweet dangerous voice.

He raised his head, his face pale. 'Yes, Your Highness, I am deeply honoured.' Inwardly he shuddered.

'You and Noriyori will now have equal rank in the Court and on the battlefield – a good idea.'

'Oh, no, Your Highness. I shall not be participating in the spring campaign. Noriyori is the Commander-in-Chief.'

'How surprising,' murmured Go-Shirakawa but he did not seem at all surprised. 'Then we must find something

for you to do. The Imperial Guard can always use new blood, and what could be more fitting than samurai blood?' He chuckled. 'And now that you hold Court rank no one should really mind. In any case, we believe there are already a few samurai in the guards. Lieutenant. That will make quite a promotion from commander of a raggle-taggle army.'

Shocked and appalled, Yoshitsuné stared at the Cloistered Emperor – a commission in the Imperial Guard in itself meant nothing, for the guards had not fought in years, not even against Kiso, but the title was a great honour. Precisely the sort of honour that Yoritomo did not want his vassals to accept from the Court. It was as if Buddha had taken away his will, his ability to choose, to say yes or no. It was karma.

'And , of course,' Go-Shirakawa continued, 'you must have a proper house. The Horikawa mansion would be perfect. Indeed, it has just been refurbished for an occasion such as this.'

'Most Sacred Highness . . .' Yoshitsuné began.

'We understand that you are overwhelmed, Yoshitsuné, but you have proved yourself a fine general, really quite extraordinary, we are told, and such gifts cannot go unrewarded. These honours are your due,' the Cloistered Emperor purred. Ah, the boy was caught. He could not really refuse and, more important, he genuinely believed that he deserved this recognition. Yoritomo was a fool to leave open such an opportunity.

Yoshitsuné sighed, a deep, resigned, exhausted sigh. 'Your Highness, how can this humble samurai ever express his thanks?'

Go-Shirakawa smirked sweetly. 'We may find a way.'

*

Out in the fresh spring air, Yoshitsuné stared around him in dismay. The sky was still blue, the trees were still in blossom, the warblers still sang, the Imperial Enclosure had not disappeared. Courtiers and servants moved sedately about their business, bright in their spring silks.

He caught a sudden glimpse in a further courtyard of a detachment of the Imperial Guard and a shiver ran up his spine.

Where should he go? His first impulse was back to Shizuka's but no, that was not possible in the middle of the day. He thought of Benkei, but perhaps a visit to Noriyori first might be wise.

Noriyori's quarters in the Rokuhara were simple without being severe: a grey Korean vase filled with branches of starry white magnolia, a lacquer weapon rack, a scroll with a poem written in his own surprisingly fine calligraphy. As usual a small paulownia wood table was littered with saké cups and porcelain decanters. Noriyori sat cross-legged on a straw mat within easy reach of the cups.

'Hello, young brother. We missed you the other evening when you vanished so swiftly. Not that I blame you after Yukiiye's discourtesy. Saké?'

Yoshitsuné took the cup gratefully.

'Anything wrong?' Noriyori asked, filling his brother's rapidly emptied cup.

'You are looking at a new lieutenant in the Imperial Guard and the new owner of the Horikawa mansion. And a courtier of the Fifth Rank,' Yoshitsuné replied numbly.

'What?' Noriyori sprang to his feet. 'So Yoritomo has changed his mind. I am happy! More than happy. Are you commanding the army too? Let us drink to it!'

Yoshitsuné looked wanly at his smiling brother and said in a tired voice, 'No, Yoritomo has not changed his mind. The Cloistered Emperor has honoured me. But we can still drink to it.' He raised his cup.

Noriyori sank down on his mat. Blood drained from his cheeks leaving him as pale as Yoshitsuné. 'You didn't accept? All those honours, and from Go-Shirakawa? Yoritomo will be enraged. No samurai accepts anything from the Court unless he wishes it. You know that. He spoke of it repeatedly at Fuji and Kamakura. You didn't accept?' He stared at Yoshitsuné in disbelief.

'What could I do? Refuse the Cloistered Emperor?'

Noriyori shook his head. 'Better that than disobey Yoritomo. You're insane. Oh, I know you *deserve* the honours but...' He poured out saké for them both and called for more.

Yoshitsuné said earnestly, 'When we saw Go-Shirakawa after Uji, we were too tired to understand – at least I was – but this time, alone with him and at his mercy, I really felt that he was someone special, someone different, a descendant of the Goddess. I couldn't say no. My mouth wouldn't say the words!' His eyes pleaded with Noriyori to understand and agree.

Noriyori sat gazing at the floor for a few minutes. Finally he said, 'That explanation is not likely to appeal to Yoritomo.' He looked at his brother sadly. 'Yoshitsuné, you know what Yoritomo will expect you to do. Now that you've walked into this disaster, this disobedience?'

The brothers stared at each other; no sound broke the silence of the room.

Finally Yoshitsuné said shortly, 'Kill myself.'

Noriyori looked away. After another long silence Yoshitsuné asked, 'Would you?' Noriyori shrugged. Yoshitsuné could practically smell his brother's misery and to his surprise he found himself suddenly much cooler, much steadier. He knew his life was not in danger, at least not from his own hand. Yoritomo's voice pounded in his head, grinding in a message of complete loyalty and obedience to the samurai-dokoro, declaring that any lapse could only end in death and that the only true samurai expiation was to die honourably by one's own hand. Well, he wasn't going to do it. He had won battles at Ichinotani and Uji and he was needed to push the Taira into the sea. Noriyori could not do it and neither, probably, could the others. He was the natural commander for the task. It was his karma. Why should he die? It was ridiculous.

Noriyori said softly, 'You are not going to then?'

'No. Yoritomo is my lord and I have done my best for him. I do not believe I have been ... disloyal.'

Noriyori nodded and stood up. He walked over to the garden door and slid it back, letting in the balmy afternoon

air. A patch of sun spread across the floor. 'It would be a terrible waste if you died now. And the anger won't last.' But he kept his face turned away.

Yoshitsuné stared at the broad shoulders covered in brown silk and realised the terrible predicament in which he had placed his brother. Gently he said, 'Noriyori, I know what is bothering you.'

'Do you?'

'Yoritomo wouldn't hesitate to order you to kill me. He would quite enjoy it, I think.'

'Yes, I think he would. He's a cold bastard.' But Noriyori did not turn away from the garden.

Yoshitsuné walked over and clapped his brother on the shoulder. 'But I don't believe he will. He's ruthless, but he's practical too, and he might have some use for me yet. I will write a letter to the samurai-dokoro to explain. I will bow low, behave myself and the trouble may pass.' He smiled and his optimism reached Noriyori, who turned from the garden and dropped his arm around Yoshitsuné's shoulders.

'He's no fool, our elder brother. And you are the best general he has. We will think only of that. Let us finish the saké!'

*

Towards evening, utterly exhausted, Yoshitsuné walked through the complicated maze of corridors and courtyards in the Rokuhara Palace to his own quarters. Noriyori had taken the whole business far more seriously than he had expected. His easy-going brother obviously believed that Yoritomo was capable of demanding the highest penalty, even from his own family, for what he would regard as disobedience. Well, if that was to be his karma, so be it. He was too tired to care.

The light was waning, a grey-gold glow from the last of the sun lit his chamber. A letter had to be written but, for the moment, he could not think. Standing in the centre of the room, undecided, listless, his eyes caught a sudden gleam in the pale light. The Sanjo dagger, lying on its

stand, caught the dying sun – inert, evil, silent. The familiar shudder ran through him but stronger, sharper. He turned and strode out of the room, closing the door firmly behind him.

He called for his horse and rode through the lovely evening city to the Horikawa mansion.

The gatekeeper was expecting him and ceremoniously pushed open the great cypress gates for his new master. A servant was called to escort him over the compound but Yoshitsuné preferred to go alone. Despite his fatigue and depression he found himself wandering round his new home with voluptuous possessiveness. The beautiful mansion, the servants' and guards' quarters, the stables and courtyards, the gardens and water pavilion, even the kitchens and bath-house, thrilled him. Servants hurried around preparing for his household. Household? Benkei, Yataro, a few samurai, grooms and servants – something would have to be done!

In the stable yard he found a black cat, a tom with ragged ears, the champion of many battles, who could regard the victor of Ichinotani as an equal. Yoshitsuné dangled the cord of his fan invitingly but the cat chose to scratch its scruffy neck. The samurai and the tom studied each other: the tom's thoughts were a mystery but the samurai wondered who the cat had been in a previous existence, perhaps a proud warrior, riding the pinnacle of his success, praised, rewarded and admired. What unremembered foolish act had sent him tumbling? What unfilial gesture, disloyalty, unconscious mistake had caused him to return in another life as a cat?

Yoshitsuné looked around the luxurious compound but his possession of it now felt very precarious. It had come to him by chance and chance could blow it away like dust along a dry summer street. Until yesterday his karma had been lucky, but now events swirled round him, leaving him helpless.

He walked back to the water pavilion. Leaning on the railing watching the carp weave through the water plants, the letter he must write to Yoritomo weighed heavily on

him. The sun had dropped behind the city and the small lake was as dark and mysterious as the cat's eyes. If victories and loyal service had failed, he could think of no phrases to assuage his brother's suspicions. Yoritomo and Go-Shirakawa were men who understood phrases. Yoshitsuné did not. He did not like his older brother but his loyalty to him as chieftain was absolute. His loyalty to the Imperial House was absolute. And his loyalties were now irreconcilable.

*

Yoshitsuné sent his letter of explanation, but received no response from Kamakura. His new honours went unremarked. Kajiwara returned to the Rokuhara where he tried Noriyori's patience to breaking point with talk of strategies and complaints about the coming campaign. The prospect of possible naval warfare worried all the commanders and tension in the war councils, already high, was increased by Kajiwara, who claimed to represent Yoritomo's exact wishes and insisted on the final approval of all arrangements.

If the other Kamakura samurai disapproved of Yoshitsuné's acceptance of Go-Shirakawa's honours they remained silent. His exclusion from the list of commanders was so obviously ridiculous and provoking that most felt his actions, if unwise, were understandable. Miura said several times in Kajiwara's hearing that morale among the warriors might be weakened by his absence.

Noriyori, who frequently fled to the peace of the Horikawa mansion, came the day before they were due to march and sat, surrounded by empty saké jars, venting his frustration over the difficult campaign and his hatred of Kajiwara.

'When he is arrogant and overbearing I can just bear with him, but lately he has taken to being ingratiating and that I cannot tolerate. When he tries to charm it is like smearing honey over filth. Ugh!' Noriyori emptied his cup. 'Why does Yoritomo put so much faith in him? I wouldn't trust him through a gauze curtain. No, I won't drink more.

172

I have . . . an appointment in Muromachi and I am late.' He rose, stuck his sword through his sash and made his way towards the middle courtyard where his horse and escort waited. Before he mounted he punched his brother playfully.

'These are rather confused times, Yoshitsuné. If we defeat the Taira, Yoritomo will have one less thing to worry about and then no doubt he will be reasonable. But be careful while you are alone in the Capital. These politicians are wily. Give me a soldier any day!' He heaved himself into the saddle. 'We march at dawn. Take comfort. It's my belief that Yoritomo will see the truth and you will be following us very soon.' He grinned at his brother and rode off to Muromachi and his whore.

*

Yoshitsuné spent his days with the Imperial Guard and his nights with Shizuka Gozen. He no longer bothered with other mistresses and as she was much in demand as a dancer they prized their hours together. She continued to surprise him with her differences from other women he had known. Asuka had been utterly innocent and the others were harlots or ladies of the Court for whom lovers were the only variety in a monotonous existence. He had never known a woman who lived for a talent she believed more important than herself. And yet, Shizuka did just that. The daughter of Zenji, a famous shrine dancer, as soon as she walked she had been dedicated to the Inari Shrine. Yoshitsuné marvelled at her warmth and tenderness, but even more at her discipline and concentration, qualities he regarded as natural in a samurai but rare in a woman.

Often, when he arrived in the evening, she would still be preoccupied with a performance she had just given, and this he found provoking and yet exciting. Slowly her attention would turn towards him and she would become as passionate in her desire for him as in her desire for a perfect step sequence or hand gesture. The novelty of competing with an abstract rather than another man for a

woman's affection appealed to his sense of adventure and sharpened his appetite for her. As for Shizuka, she had always pursued her career with total dedication, but the growing intensity of her love began to rival that dedication. She watched the conflict between her two passions with fascination; a life without dancing was beyond her imagination but whether she could live without Yoshitsuné was a new conundrum.

The question was not resolved without compromise on both sides. Memories of the warm whispering sweetness of Hogen's women's quarters still lingered with Yoshitsuné: the fragrance, the sudden hushed giggles, the slither of silk came to him at night when he was alone in the dark Horikawa mansion. His own women's quarters were empty, silent rooms dusted by his one maidservant who chose to sleep in the rougher servants' outhouse rather than stay alone amid such soulless luxury. If Shizuka came she would bring maids and her mother, and there would be laughter and gossip and gaiety and perhaps even children. Unwisely Yoshitsuné mentioned this to Benkei who snorted in disgust. He had been reared in the women's quarters, he said – it was all tears and jealousy and malice. Yoshitsuné did not know how lucky he was to have been brought up among sensible men. But Yataro agreed with Yoshitsuné, not just because it would be pleasant to have pretty maids about the rooms but because women gave some heart to a house, as long as a man could escape to the guardroom when he needed peace.

When he proposed to Shizuka that she should move in with her household she reacted with consternation, explaining the position with her customary directness. 'A dancer needs musicians and privacy and quiet for contemplation before a performance. These I have at home. You know, Yoshitsuné, my house is almost like a nunnery. I have had few lovers; my dancing has always been more important. It is impossible.'

Offended, Yoshitsuné replied, 'Then your dancing is more important than I,' and was furious with himself for whining to a woman. When she would not change her mind

he returned to the bracing masculine familiarity of the Horikawa and ordered an expensive courtesan brought from Muromachi. But she quickly bored him.

Yoshitsuné threw himself into drilling with his company of guards and at night he drank with Benkei and womanised with Yataro, all with great bravado so that Shizuka would hear how busy and unconcerned he was. But life was too empty without either her or a campaign. If, he thought to himself twenty times a day, I were in the west with Noriyori I would not be bothering over a woman, and although this was true, he still fumed at her obstinacy, choosing to forget that it was partly her discipline and concentration that had attracted him.

Shizuka, even with her dancing to consume her energy, missed Yoshitsuné. She had no one to consult; her mother, Zenji, was ambitious and dedicated and did not approve of the affair with the samurai. But when Shizuka began to lose weight and sleep badly the older woman saw that something had to be done to conserve her daughter's looks, and she urged Shizuka to write to Yoshitsuné, sending a poem that might imply some compromise. One did not bargain with a lieutenant in the Imperial Guard but perhaps ... Zenji guessed shrewdly that the bored young man might be vulnerable enough to manipulate. And certainly it would be an honour to be the recognised mistress of Minamoto Yoshitsuné, the darling of the Cloister Court.

Shizuka hesitated; living with Yoshitsuné was bound to restrict her dancing, the one steady consuming passion of her life. If she compromised would not her talent lose its purity; would not the inner, heaven-given fire that made her that much finer a dancer, be lost? Distracted, she worried over the problem. She had been graced with a special gift – would this gift be snatched back by the gods if she dissipated it? And yet, she was dissipating it now; her hand lying on her grey silk lap was thin and white and her hollow, sallow cheeks were no longer enhanced by the chalky make-up. Sadly she picked up a brush and composed a poem:

> Almond blossom falls
> on the path in the garden
> but a few petals
> fluttering beyond the wall
> dance a moment in the breeze.

Well, she had danced a moment in the breeze. Now it was up to Yoshitsuné.

Courtesy demanded an immediate reply but he waited a day, knowing it was churlish. Then, on fine Chinese paper in his best brush strokes, he wrote his response:

> In the mists of late spring
> the pine tree casts no shadow
> and then the sunlight
> brings noon along the branches
> when a few drops fall like tears.

Zenji did the negotiating: musicians would be made available and Shizuka's days would be devoted exclusively to practice and performance. Before an important appearance she would be left in complete peace for several days. The rest of her time would be Yoshitsuné's.

Shizuka, Zenji and her maids moved in and during the day the women's quarters of the Horikawa mansion had the austere atmosphere of a shrine in which a ceremony is about to take place. Only at night when chatter and female intrigue took over were they like the women's quarters of other mansions. If Shizuka's fire diminished, she was at least very happy most of the time. Yoshitsuné relished the raised eyebrows and scandalised murmurs behind drooping sleeves that greeted his arrival anywhere. He was the unconventional samurai-courtier who tolerated a shrine dancer as a mistress and he, and eventually Shizuka, enjoyed the notoriety.

Benkei was furious. He muttered for days about women bringing bad luck and distraction from important things.

*

By the beginning of the year the bulk of the Minamoto

army was wedged between Tomomori, who had returned to the main island, and Munemori, who with the child Emperor and the Regalia was on the island of Shikoku. Both had large armies and fleets of war junks. Although Noriyori was not trapped, if he struck at Tomomori he risked a rear attack from Munemori and the inevitable sea battle he could not yet fight. He was not a brilliant commander and he knew when he needed help. At first Yoritomo offered encouragement and sympathy but not much in the way of aid. Finally, on his own, Noriyori was able to acquire a few dozen pirate ships and some unwieldy junks. However, the Taira remained unthreatened.

Yoritomo sat in Kamakura and deliberated. Kajiwara was with a smaller force at Watanabe so he had only Tokimasa to consult and the older man vigorously urged reconciliation with Yoshitsuné who undoubtedly had a flair that Noriyori and Kajiwara lacked. Yoritomo, knowing Tokimasa was right, gritted his teeth and sent a courier to the Capital with a letter reinstating his younger brother as joint Commander-in-Chief, ordering him to join up with Kajiwara's army and lead a sea attack on Munemori at the fortress of Yashima on Shikoku immediately.

The letter was received at the Horikawa mansion with jubilation. A lieutenancy in the Imperial Guard had proved no consolation when Yoshitsuné's peers were on the brink of battle. His retainers resented their inactivity as much as he did and the atmosphere in the mansion was explosive. Only Benkei, although longing for a campaign, managed to keep calm.

Yoshitsuné handed in his commission to an unhappy Go-Shirakawa, who wanted his Imperial lieutenant under his thumb. Shizuka was hastily kissed farewell and the band galloped out of the city the next day.

They reached the port of Watanabe in a week. Kajiwara sat in sullen command of a stationary army, staring unhappily at the Minamoto pirate ships and war junks riding in the harbour. Noriyori had sent them to Watanabe when, to his great relief, he had learned that he was to tackle Tomomori's army on solid ground once the result of

Yoshitsuné's sea campaign was known. To Yoshitsuné fell the task of attacking Shikoku by ship, and although Noriyori was fond of his brother, he was delighted to relinquish the naval campaign to someone else.

The fortress of Yashima stood on a spit of land two days' sail across the Inland Sea. Yoshitsuné had studied the plans from Oni-ichi Hogen's files. Asuka's ebony desk, the sweet scent of her room came back to him for the first time in months as he strove to remember the detailed descriptions in a noisome tent in Watanabe. He was fairly convinced that the spit was fortified against sea attack only, therefore the fortress would not be difficult for a land army to take. But Yoshitsuné would have to reach the island first, and the Minamoto were horsemen not sailors.

On the night of Yoshitsuné's arrival, a war council was held and he presented his plan based, as before, on a surprise attack led by himself. He proposed to take a group of a hundred and fifty picked men, cross the sea to Awa on Shikoku and by a quick march across the island attack Yashima on its undefended land side. By the time they could reach the fortress, the bulk of the army under Kajiwara should be in position around the spit and prevent a Taira escape by sea. Yoshitsuné would use the speedier pirate ships, leaving the heavy war junks to Kajiwara. Reluctantly Kajiwara agreed, if only because he knew the horsebound eastern army could not launch a successful naval offensive directly on the fortress, but there was one point he was determined to make.

'These war junks must be equipped with reverse oars before we embark. It will take only a day and the sailors say a storm is coming, so we must wait in any case.'

Yoshitsuné replied impatiently, 'On the contrary, the storm will help us surprise them. Munemori won't expect any action during bad weather. But what are these reverse oars you speak of?'

'A reverse oar is fixed in the bow and directed at the stern. It allows the ship to reverse direction. It makes it more manoeuvrable and it is easier to retreat if necessary.'

'Retreat!'

'You know nothing of naval warfare,' snapped Kajiwara. 'It may be necessary to regroup at some time during the fighting. Horsemen do it all the time, why should a sea battle be different?'

'I never retreat and I never pull back – only a coward or an incompetent leader does either. How can you expect the men to have the will to win if you have already created an atmosphere of defeat?'

Kajiwara's lips curled. 'And you, Yoshitsuné, risk men's lives for your own glory. They die to make you a hero. What do you know of fighting when you have only seen two battles?'

The jeers made Yoshitsuné's face colour. 'While I am Commander-in-Chief, Kajiwara, there will be no idiotic reverse oars on my vessels. After I am dead, killed on the offensive, you can put on your reverse oars. Have only reverse oars and then you can back into battle!'

Several of the captains sniggered and the ridicule pushed Kajiwara, never the calmest of men, to the edge of anger. He drew his sword and faced Yoshitsuné.

'You may be the Commander-in-Chief now but I am the official deputy of the Lord of Kamakura. How dare you speak to me thus! You only hold your position because of your father, you insolent scab. Draw your sword. I don't want to kill a man armed only with vanity.'

'You cannot kill me. You are incapable! You can only malign me to my brother Yoritomo!' Yoshitsuné's voice rose sharp and cold to cut through the silence like a blade.

Benkei grabbed Yoshitsuné's shoulder just as he pulled out his sword. 'Don't be a fool. We are here to fight the Taira, not each other. You, Kajiwara, you talk of vanity. What sort of example do you set, for all your years of well-practised modesty. Put up your swords! Both of you!'

The two men glared at each other a few seconds longer then Yoshitsuné snapped at Benkei, 'Organise the men. We sail for Shikoku tonight, storm or no storm. The sooner the wind takes us away from this contaminated company the better.' He turned contemptuously to Kajiwara. 'As for you, Lord Kajiwara, when you have arranged for your

orderly retreat, please be so kind as to join the rest of us in battle.' Grimly he strode past the silent warriors, his face set, hard lines deepening around his nose and mouth.

A few hours later the storm blew up and the unhappy samurai embarked on the rocking pirate junks, clutching the rails as the boats lurched out of the harbour. But the gale favoured them, whisking the lightly built ships before it, making the two-day crossing in ten hours. Just before dawn, one hundred and fifty pale, sea-soaked samurai landed on the beach at Awa.

Yoshitsuné let the men rest for an hour before beginning the march to Yashima, a day's hard walking across the island. In order to avoid farms and villages they stayed away from the coast, making their way through the deep green forests of camellia and oak. By dusk they were struggling up the steep slope to the fortress built on the end of the promontory jutting out over the sea. Several paths went down through the woods towards the water, and Yoshitsuné calculated that they led to beaches under the promontory. The men paused while Benkei and Rokuro went ahead to scout, reporting back that the fortress was indeed vulnerable – no moat, two gates carelessly guarded and all the towers facing the sea. The only problem was two hundred yards or so of open field that would have to be crossed in any approach, but even that should not be too difficult in the dark. Obviously no attack was expected.

'We will rest here and attack before dawn,' murmured Yoshitsuné.

'Even if Kajiwara's ships have not arrived?' Benkei asked.

'Especially if Kajiwara has not arrived. Once his ships are spotted the Taira will be alert and put more men on that gate. We want to attack them while they're unsuspecting. Yataro, take ten men and spread out to watch the gates tonight in case some loyal peasant has seen us, and wishes to slip in and warn them we are here. Don't let anybody get through alive. No fires – dried fish and salt vegetables.'

An hour before dawn the hundred and fifty men crept through the scrub, past the field to the palisades. The

sentries were swiftly dispatched and the gates easily breached. Just inside was a small guardhouse where a dozen soldiers played dice by the light of torches. Yelling fiercely, the Minamoto stormed the guardhouse and cut down the men, then splitting into groups they ran screaming through the fortress, killing or firing everything in their path. The hardest battle was at the barracks, but Yoshitsuné had been right once again about the element of surprise. The Taira were utterly unprepared and the easterners managed to compound their confusion by making enough noise for a force of a thousand. Once the barracks were ignited Yoshitsuné found Yataro and a few other men.

'Now we must reach Munemori's quarters and capture Antoku before they recover.' The dawn light showed one building finer than the rest towards which the Taira were running.

'That must be the place,' Yataro bellowed over the clamour. 'And it has no fortifications!' Taira soldiers had re-grouped in the courtyard and on the veranda of the mansion, swords drawn ready for the last fight. Among Yoshitsuné's men were two fine archers who climbed on to carts and from there thudded fire arrows into the thatch, which kindled immediately. Flaming arrows hissed quivering in the wooden structure, forcing the Taira away from the veranda. Yoshitsuné, fighting near Yataro, called out, 'Kill your man and follow me into the building.' Two swift strokes and they were able to leap across the burning veranda through the unprotected door into a large hall lined with weapon racks and standing suits of armour. Despite the gloom and billowing smoke they could see the hall was empty. The opposite wall was composed of sliding panels leading to another dim room where crumpled sleeping pallets littered the floor. The door here was broken, jerked off its runners by someone in a hurry. A long corridor stretched before them.

Yataro looked quickly around. 'There's another door, a side one to the veranda.'

'You take it. I'll take this one – be careful.' Yoshitsuné raced along the narrow corridor, away from the shouts of

battle and the smoke, into the silent house. Curtained doorways concealed a line of rooms – armouries, offices, sleeping quarters, women's and children's rooms – all deserted. At the end was another large armoury opening on to a vast porch surrounded by thick railings. Yataro, panting, joined him. 'Nothing,' he grunted. Yoshitsuné peered over the railing. Three hundred feet below the Taira fleet sheltered in the curved horns of scrub-covered rock that formed the natural harbour of Yashima. The blurred horizon was empty – no sign of Kajiwara's ships. Below them on a narrow strip of beach surged a mass of crimsons and ochres, blues and mauves, glowing satin and dull steel, as the Taira and their women and children struggled into dinghies. A few small boats were already on the water, making their way to the harbour entrance where the war junks waited, red pennants limp in the still, grey air.

Yoshitsuné crashed his fist on the railing. 'There, in that first boat, two women and a child – you can see their kimono! And in the next one, Munemori. He's still in robes so they didn't even have time for armour.' He pointed down. 'They even have the Regalia. It's sure to be in the big black box in Munemori's boat. They're getting away and we can't stop them!' He pounded the railing in fury.

Yataro looked away; angry at their failure but embarrassed by his master's anger as well. In a corner he saw a gap in the railing and grabbed Yoshitsuné's arm, stiff and unyielding in its sheath of lacquer plates. 'Stairs!' he barked and ran towards them.

Three bedraggled Minamoto burst on to the porch followed by Benkei, smeared with soot and blood. He grasped the situation immediately. 'It can't be the only way down. What else do you see?'

Yataro peered out. 'There's a path in the woods. It must come from the bluff.'

Yoshitsuné said quickly, 'We passed it in the forest on the way up. Benkei, get as many men as you can and find that path to the beach. Yataro, you and I will take the stairs. They can hold us off easily but at least we'll distract them.

Rokuro, get some men and join us. Quickly!'

It took the easterners six hours to win the beach. The Taira samurai, although often inadequately armed, fought desperately to keep them back while their nobles escaped with the fleet. Nearly all of the Taira defenders perished and many of their women and children, but when the evening tide lapped over the hacked corpses, sweeping the gory sand salt-clean, Munemori, Antoku and the Regalia were safely on the open sea bound for Tomomori's camp on the Straits of Shimonoseki.

Kajiwara sailed in the next day to find the dead cremated and the few prisoners listed. The red banners of the Taira had flown over a supposedly impregnable fort, now the Minamoto white flapped over the charred remains. The samurai congratulated Yoshitsuné in public, but in private most agreed with Kajiwara that the young commander's premature attack had cost them the prize of the child Emperor Antoku and the Regalia. If he had waited hidden in the forest until the rest of the fleet had arrived the Taira would not have escaped so easily. As it was, Tomomori and Munemori, the Emperor and the Regalia, and the remains of the Taira clan had successfully re-grouped at the fortress on the Straits of Shimonoseki.

*

A temporary camp was established at Yashima and messengers sent to Kamakura and to Noriyori. But Yoshitsuné could not wait for instructions; the acquisition of a fleet large and efficient enough to attack the Taira on their own chosen site became an obsession with him. Dressed in his battered primrose-yellow corselet, mounted on a fine black stallion rescued from the stables to replace his beloved mare left in Watanabe, he galloped around the island of Shikoku, bullying and cajoling the remaining warlords into supporting the Minamoto. And indeed, most proved willing to throw in their lot with a commander who had destroyed an impregnable fort. Furthermore the Taira had not been generous overlords and Yoshitsuné promised great rewards in the name of the samurai-dokoro. Word

spread: within two weeks Yoshitsuné had attracted ten warlords, some merchants and one hundred and fifty ships – fishing boats, war junks and traders. They gathered in Yashima harbour and small brown sailors from Kyushu, incomprehensible and savage, mingled with the languid Shikoku noblemen and their tough crews. Miura arrived from Noriyori's camp, bringing with him his cousin from the Aki coast, suddenly converted to the Kamakura cause and proving his new loyalty with fifty ships, manned by sailors experienced in the tricky Inland Sea currents.

Yoshitsuné took Miura aside. 'What is Noriyori doing?'

'He will do as Yoritomo tells him!' Miura had heard of Yoshitsuné's rash attack and, while understanding, he also disapproved.

'Well, where is he? How can Yoritomo tell him what to do if he's isolated in the east, in Kamakura, and Noriyori is down here in the west?'

Miura shrugged and scratched his beard, now much whiter after two years of campaigning. 'Be careful, Yoshitsuné. I know you sometimes regard Noriyori as lazy and unimaginative but if you are thought to be taking too much on yourself . . .'

'Then don't let them think that. Support me,' replied Yoshitsuné curtly.

Miura, smiling, punched his fist into Yoshitsuné's shoulder. 'I probably will. I probably will.'

He did. Kajiwara's one bid to be Commander-in-Chief was squashed by Yoshitsuné and Miura, augmented by the local warlords who refused to serve under anyone but Yoritomo's brother. Kajiwara, with no choice but to accept the decision, muttered to the few who would listen about Yoshitsuné's high-handed behaviour. A few days later when the Abbot of Kumano Temple sailed into Yashima harbour with two hundred assorted junks and a detailed set of charts of the Straits of Shimonoseki, Yoshitsuné sent a messenger to Noriyori, ordering him to move into position behind the Taira camp in order to block any attempt by Tomomori to escape by land. Two days afterwards Takeda of Kai arrived with twenty-five heavy,

broad Chinese war junks and the news that Lord Wada had joined Noriyori. The fleet and the army were now at their best and primed to fight. After one month in Yashima the Minamoto were ready for their sea battle, and on a fine spring morning Yoshitsuné and his armada set off for the Straits of Shimonoseki.

*

Tomomori was angry but not surprised when he heard of the defections of the Kyushu and Shikoku warlords. Capital politics did not matter much in these parts and in instances where no personal oaths had been sworn to the Taira, provincial samurai might be expected to join with whichever clan actually held power. In fact, as he explained to Munemori, he suspected that not all their allies in Shimonoseki were completely reliable.

'But they will stay with the winning side and that will be us,' he said grimly.

Antoku, a pale thin child of five, watched his two uncles apprehensively. They had come to his quarters – very bleak quarters – ostensibly to inform him of the battle plans, but the boy knew that they were barely conscious of his existence. He sat on his pile of cushions wrapped in silk gowns that only just held off the dank spring chill and day-dreamed about his palace in the Imperial Enclosure. This drifting unsettled life was frightening and he missed his cats and his puppies and his quiet beautiful gardens; the cherries would soon be out, their branches filled with singing birds. These coastal fortresses were damp and dreary and at each one Munemori had promised they would be safe, but always there had been more fighting and another frenzied flight.

His uncle played nervously with the fringe on his sash and shot worried glances at Tomomori who was gruff, short-tempered and forever ordering the boy to act like a man because he had samurai blood. But Antoku knew, even if Tomomori forgot, that Emperors are not men but gods. He just wished the Minamoto would remember he was a god. He could hear Munemori speaking about

Minamoto Yoshitsuné now.

'Who would have imagined he would become such a general?' he said wonderingly. 'Do you remember how Hogen claimed the Minamoto had no leaders unless they won over Miura? Now, not only Miura and Kajiwara but scores of warlords rally to that boy – and to Yoritomo.'

'Father was mad not to kill them off after the rebellion. I told him so then, but when he finally realised it, it was too late,' muttered Tomomori.

'Yes, but at the time there had been enough bloodshed.'

Tomomori suddenly remembered Antoku and said to him, 'Your Highness and the Dowager Empress Tokuko, your mother, will be on a special junk – no markings and well-manned. You will be safe, but remember that you are the grandson of a samurai. Your grandmother will be there and she has the courage of a hundred men.' Antoku blinked and gave his uncle an Imperial nod; his mother wept a great deal but he was fond of his grandmother.

'As for you, Munemori,' Tomomori barked, 'you had better sail on the same junk.'

Munemori opened his mouth and closed it, the long narrow fingers on his sash twitching. He said hoarsely, 'Shouldn't I have command of a squadron? Perhaps I could march against Noriyori?'

Tomomori's choleric face grew redder. 'We will not attack Noriyori until Yoshitsuné is beaten at sea. They'll have to come to us and they will have to fight a naval battle – here! Yoshitsuné is full of luck but his luck will run out. He made clever guesses at Ichinotani and Yashima and he outwitted me, but he can't do that here.' He was shouting now. 'I know these straits and the currents. I've sailed the whole coastline a thousand times since I was his age –' he gestured rudely at the Emperor – 'and my captains know the currents and the tide-rip. Yoshitsuné can't get enough help. We have five hundred ships – five hundred! He had two hundred at the last report. He may have a few more by now and his Kyushu men know these waters but he's never fought a sea battle and he is too arrogant to listen to advice. I've seen him and I know. He is beaten. His karma has

186

turned and so has mine.' When he subsided suddenly the room fell strangely silent.

Munemori smiled kindly at Antoku who had listened intently to the explosion. 'We have one thing they can never have,' he said. 'We have the Emperor and the Regalia.'

Tomomori laughed abruptly. 'So we have. So we have. We cannot fail.'

Antoku gave his practised Imperial nod.

'There is one problem.' Munemori chewed his lips and looked unhappily out at the salt-blasted garden.

'What's that?' asked Antoku, nudged into rare speech by curiosity.

'Whoever wins this time – and I'm sure it will be us – will have to fight at least one more battle.'

'Against who?'

'Yoritomo. He's the dangerous one.'

*

Tomomori's determination to fight entirely at sea decided all his plans. When his scouts reported the positioning of Noriyori and Wada on the land side of the spit of Dan no Ura, the vast population of the fortress, swollen by the refugees from Ichinotani and Yashima, was transferred to the ships, leaving only a small contingent of soldiers in the Taira stronghold. If Noriyori stormed it he would find nothing – no Emperor, no Regalia, no high-ranking Taira or their women or their heirs. All these were distributed among the fleet. The captains grumbled at the number of non-combatants cluttering their decks but Tomomori was adamant – there must be nothing and no one for Noriyori to seize. The Minamoto would have to fight at sea or give up their pursuit.

Antoku, his mother and his grandmother, Munemori and the Regalia were placed in the main cabin of a large unmarked three-masted junk. Court attendants, a few of the men in corselets but most in cumbersome formal robes, were relegated to the smaller cabins or sent amidships. Wandering children and whimpering women were a

constant hindrance to the warriors on the crowded deck. Antoku peeped occasionally round the leather curtain at the furious activity, but he was not really very interested and soon returned to a desultory game of chess with a courtier. Dowager Empress Tokuko, his mother, sat quietly in a corner, staring at nothing and moving only to cover her face with a veil if a stranger came in. All her life she had been a puppet in the hands of her father or her brothers, marrying, breeding, breathing because it was expected of her, and now she was incapable of any thought or action unless instructed. She only wept or smiled when it seemed the appropriate thing to do. However, Kiyomori's widow, Lady Nii, was a woman with a sense of duty to her clan and her family, which gave her considerable courage for this ordeal. Tomomori was her favourite son and she, unlike her daughter or grandson, was vividly aware that he must win this encounter if the clan was to survive. She paced the cabin and watched the preparations on deck with the clear eye of a samurai's woman. Several times she ordered out Munemori, wringing his hands and muttering, to give instructions to the soldiers – to correct a line of shields or change the position of some archers. The badgered Munemori finally took permanent refuge from her on the deck, pretending with his corselet and sword that he was in command. The bluster fooled no one but himself; even Antoku had only an absent-minded cynical smile for his strutting uncle.

The Straits of Shimonoseki, three miles wide at the most narrow point where Kyushu jutted toward the main island, ran for ten miles between steep, ribbed, holed cliffs. Centuries of rock falls had littered the shallows with submerged heaps of limestone, grey and ominous under the turbulent water. The tide-rip, swift and unpredictable, was Tomomori's chosen ally. He stretched his fleet across the straits, just east of the narrow neck, by a line of crags known as Dan no Ura and waited confidently for Yoshitsuné.

The Minamoto fleet came into sight in the late afternoon, did not press an attack and dropped anchor.

Tomomori climbed on to the roof of the flagship's cabin; the sun behind him illumined the enemy ships, glowing on their furling sails and the shields lining the gunwales. His eyes were sharp and could be trusted – what he saw appalled him. At least four hundred ships rode at anchor – well over half were fishing smacks and small traders but the pennants of the Abbot of Kumano and Takeda of Kai flew over junks as strong as any of his own. Takeda had been expected to join Yoshitsuné, but the Abbot of Kumano's pennant was a shock. His expertise in these waters made him a dangerous adversary and it could be a bitter fight, thought Tomomori. But that boy would not take advice – he was too arrogant, too sure of his generalship. The tide was in his favour now and he was not taking proper advantage of it, although no doubt the Abbot had told him he should. Tomomori smiled, a smile that split his square, brick-red face. The boy was planning one of his tricks, no doubt, but there was no trick he could pull. As he clambered down from the roof Tomomori chuckled to himself, his confidence renewed. Yoshitsuné had made his first mistake.

*

Yoshitsuné, standing in the prow of the Abbot's flagship, a flat-bottomed boat with a high bow and stern, looked back at the Taira. The water pulled rapidly into the straits, luring him to Tomomori, but the Abbot had been definite. No attack tonight. It was too late and the tide would turn. Well, Yoshitsuné had to accept that he was right, but he was unhappy. On land he would have known immediately what to do – send someone behind Tomomori to smoke him out into open ground for a proper fight – but here, between claustrophobic cliffs on this unpredictable battleground with such unwieldy weapons, he knew that he had to trust the Abbot's judgement. It was an uncomfortable feeling for a man who had made his own rules for past battles. But he was sure that as long as the Abbot read the tides properly he could deal with the rest. All the warriors had undergone extensive archery practice in

Yashima because Yoshitsuné had realised that the initial stages of battle would be duels between the ships and the bowmen. Only at the end when the fleets met and grappled could the sword play its part. He wore a black lacquer quiver filled with arrows, long shafts with forked points that could take off a man's head at fifty paces. The decks were piled with arrows, hundreds of them wrapped in tar-daubed cloth ready to be dipped in the smouldering braziers and fired into the Taira sails of matting. The real problem would be to reach the Regalia and Tomomori, and he had no idea of how to accomplish that. But, looking out over the high carved prow of the flagship into the sunset, he was confident. After the first moments at Uji battle nerves had never been a problem. Death held no fear for him and once the battle had begun he always felt an innate certainty of what action to take. The subtle machinations of Yori-tomo or Go-Shirakawa might unnerve him but the mind of another warrior he could understand. With a sword in his hand, he had never needed to ask questions for he controlled all the answers. The sea battle to come was something new and he relished the challenge.

Behind him, the Abbot cleared his throat. He was a tall thin priest in saffron and steel, severe and unimaginative. His augurers predicted a Minamoto victory so he had abandoned his intended neutrality in order to put himself in a strong position with the new authorities. Kumano's considerable wealth had declined under the Taira and the Abbot wanted it restored.

His austere face revealed nothing. Yoshitsuné asked impatiently, 'Well?'

'Well, we wait. Tomomori must be surprised we have not attacked, and it may make him a little rash. The dawn tide will be in his favour and I predict that he will use it.' Slowly he swept an arm out toward the Taira fleet. 'I did not expect to find him here in the straits, but we are in a good position to breast the tide and we should hold him.' He looked coolly at Yoshitsuné. 'If, of course, we do not hold him, which is possible, the cross-currents will carry us on to the rocks – one fleet is going to go on to those rocks

tomorrow. The only alternative is to turn now and run –
against the tide.'

'No,' Yoshitsuné said.

'So I thought. It is time for prayers. Good night.'

*

The Abbot guessed correctly. Tomomori did not like
Yoshitsuné's unpredictable behaviour, but he did like the
dawn tide combined with a westerly wind. The Taira line
sailed down on the anchored Minamoto to be met by a
barrage of arrows. From behind their shields the eastern
archers pounded any Taira ship within bow range, paying
special attention to the helmsmen – no vessel could beat the
treacherous currents without a skilled man at the rudder
and the number of these men must be limited. The Taira
returned the fire, but Yoshitsuné had devised shelters over
his steersmen to protect them. The archers and sailors,
however, took heavy losses and soon the decks were
covered with the dead and dying. Benkei with his great
height could see farthest from the cabin roof and reported
that the Taira archers were also being cut down in great
numbers. Peering out over the fleet he could see no sign of
an Imperial pennant but he did locate the flagship opposite
Miura's squadron.

The Abbot shrugged at the news. 'It would be foolish to
risk the currents now. Look how close Kajiwara is to those
reefs.'

Tomomori, frustrated at the efficient Minamoto resistance but determined to use the tide to his advantage, tried a
new tactic. He ordered his smaller boats, light fishing
smacks, to attack the heavy war junks, using fire arrows.
The nimble little craft, flitting in and out like mosquitoes,
managed to isolate several of the junks on the exposed flank
and to pepper them with flaming arrows, driving the
blazing ships out into the open sea. There was no way to
help them. Kajiwara, on the port flank, suffered badly; two
of his junks floundered in the swirling currents and were
dashed on the rocks.

Realising how unmanoeuvrable the junks were, Yosh-

itsuné, after brief consultation with the Abbot, ordered them not to engage with the enemy but let the smaller boats fight defensive actions to protect them. The heavier ships were to be preserved for an attack on the afternoon tide. Although the Taira still managed to do a lot of damage, Yoshitsuné's plan saved most of the war junks from the currents and the rocky shallows.

Throughout the morning Tomomori sent wave after wave of ships, large and small, against the Minamoto line to break it. Although many Minamoto vessels lost control in the fast tide-rip and smashed or sank, Tomomori's losses were also great and the Minamoto line held. The sea, dotted with flaming ships and debris from the wrecks, was a perilous battlefield for both sides. Smoke drifted in the misty spring air, sweeping news of destruction westward down the channel in the changing wind.

The Abbot found Yoshitsuné with his tired archers on the starboard side of the flagship. 'The wind has come round and favours us. The tide is turning and in another half hour we will be in the middle of them. They will never hold against us now.'

Yoshitsuné accepted this news as impassively as it was delivered, wearily resting his bow against a shield and taking a long draught from the saké jug proffered by Benkei who had climbed down from his perch on the cabin roof.

'How are the other squadrons holding?'

'Quite well. Kajiwara and Takeda, on the flanks, took the heaviest casualties. Kajiwara lost six ships by the spit. Unfortunately he wasn't in one of them,' the monk snorted.

The Abbot regarded Benkei disapprovingly; the renegade monk did not flinch but held out his jug saying, 'Have a drink.' The Abbot turned away to his chart, his long thin back registering cold disgust.

Suddenly Benkei seized Yoshitsuné's arm. 'Look over there – at those ships! They've struck their red pennants!' The men crowded against their shields, peering through the chinks at a group of five ships, each one slowly running up a new flag of pure white.

'Taguchi,' the Abbot muttered, 'a Shikoku man and an opportunist. Tomomori's failed and I think Taguchi will soon be joined by others. Deserters.'

'He should know where the Emperor and the Regalia are hidden,' said Yoshitsuné.

Benkei pointed to a dinghy making for them. 'We'll soon learn if he does. I'd judge that's him coming over now.'

Yoshitsuné turned to the Abbot. 'Now is the time to attack. The sign should be passed to Kajiwara and Miura and Takeda, but we will wait until we have talked to Taguchi.' The Abbot nodded and went to give his captains their orders.

A small wiry man with a flat face and a heavy pendulous lower lip clambered up the side and jumped on to the deck. 'Taguchi of Shikoku, my lord. Accept my humble services.' Yoshitsuné replied to his deep bow with a curt nod. Traitors, although useful, were not men he admired. Taguchi ignored the cold response and continued in his sibilant Shikoku drawl, 'It was a perfect defence, my lord. Tomomori counted on the tide-rip to push you in the shallows but he's finished now and I, for one, am not going down with him.'

'Where is the Emperor and the Regalia? Do you know?'

'On one of the bigger junks, unmarked. Important Taira are distributed around the fleet. You have the whole clan in your power, men, women and children.' Taguchi bowed low again.

'All right. Get back to your ships while you can. And good luck against your former allies,' Yoshitsuné added drily.

*

Tomomori watched helplessly as the Minamoto ships smashed through his already chaotic line. The helmsman was dead, so was his replacement, victims of Miura's archers, and the flagship wallowed dangerously close to another junk, also without a helmsman. Yoshitsuné had thought of everything, and now the gods had sent the wind and the tide to help him – already half the Taira fleet was

ablaze or foundering in the shallows; of the survivors several had been already grappled and boarded by the eastern warriors. Those, thought Tomomori bitterly, were the lucky ones; at least the samurai on them would have the chance of a fight. How many ships were smashed to pieces around that cursed spit with the swords aboard them still innocent of Minamoto blood? But for him there was no luck; his karma was fixed. Wearily he signed to a sailor to prepare a dinghy.

The scene on the junk was chaotic: arrows, red-hot wood, blazing sheets of sail fell on to the samurai, tense and exhausted, waiting for their last battle, jostled by terrified courtiers and wailing children, all begrimed with soot and stinking of fear. The wounded had been put together amidships but no one had time to tend them or carry water for the dry, dying throats. The dead had already gone overboard to make way for the living.

Tomomori was greeted grimly as he pushed through to the cabin where his mother, sister and nephew huddled together, surrounded by weeping women. Munemori was nowhere to be seen. Kneeling stiffly before his mother, Tomomori removed his helmet, a wide-winged one with horns of brass of which he was very proud, and said, 'The battle is over; most of the fleet is lost; Taguchi and others have joined the Minamoto and Yoshitsuné is sighted off the port bow. It's only a matter of minutes before the eastern samurai are here.' He looked at the pale, calm, waiting woman. 'The clan is finished, smashed on the rocks off Dan no Ura.'

She smiled sadly into her son's deeply marked face. 'Your father will know that you have done your best. Farewell, my son.'

He bowed to his sister who held a sooty sleeve over her face and steadily sobbed. She seemed very little like the plump, pretty Empress Tokuko, daughter of a samurai and consort of an Emperor. Beside her stood Antoku, silent and anxious, for once fully conscious of the turmoil surrounding him. Tomomori had nothing to say to either of them. A gilt ebony box lay before the boy and seeing it, Tomomori

194

turned again to his mother. She nodded and opened the box. As he left the cabin she carefully lifted out the Sacred Sword.

His attendant, covered in blood oozing from a head wound, waited on deck and together they walked to the stern where one of the stone anchors lay. Tomomori leant against the railing and hurled his helmet out into the churning, filthy water and watched it sink. The Minamoto flagship, white banners snapping, was coming up so rapidly that he could clearly make out the faces of the men on deck, illumined by the lowering sun. The commander stood slightly aloof in the prow, his helmet removed for better vision, a long sword in his hand. Tomomori could distinguish in the hardened adult features the memory of a soft, boyish face on a brave youth who had fought with his fine sword in Hogen's courtyard long years before. Because Kiyomori had permitted that boy to survive, Tomomori was now to die, but his only regret as he stared across the short stretch of water was that he and Yoshitsuné had never fought hand to hand as samurai should.

The servant diffidently cleared his throat. 'There is not much time, my lord.' Tomomori nodded and together they lifted the iron anchor chain and wound it round Tomomori's body; the links caught and held on the steel plates of his corselet. They heaved the anchor on to the lurching railing; it teetered and then balanced, one chiselled prong piercing the wood. The Minamoto ship pulled close to the junk's bow – men stood poised with grappling irons facing a barrage of Taira arrows. In the prow, oblivious to the arrows, Yoshitsuné, unsmiling, lifted the Hachiman sword in salute to his vanquished enemy. Tomomori did not reply but hauled himself on to the railing. The anchor tilted, swayed and then fell, jerking him sharply over the side into the sea, his childhood playmate and unfaithful ally.

*

Kiyomori's widow gathered up Antoku and the Sacred Sword in her arms and made her way unsteadily across the

crowded, swaying deck. The boy, a sadly frail load, white with fear, snuggled into his grandmother's silky bosom. Holding him close against her with one hand, she slipped the Sacred Sword into her sash – the Jewel and the Mirror would have to be taken by others; she was too burdened with the child. She stroked his narrow face and spoke gently, her voice audible only to him among the screams of the dying and the roar and crash of shattering wood. 'Look to the East, Your Majesty, to your ancestors who watch you now. We must bid them farewell.' She pressed his hands together in prayer. 'We shall pray to the Lord Amida to accept us in his paradise.' Holding the sobbing, praying Emperor tight in her arms she stepped to the place where Tomomori's weight had smashed the railing. The Minamoto had closed with the Imperial junk and the warriors were already boarding, but they would not reach her in time. She whispered, 'Lord Amida,' and hugging her grandson to her, hurled herself through the railing into the cold green foam.

Empress Tokuko, no longer sobbing, placed the Sacred Mirror in her kimono and left the cabin. As she approached, her mother and son disappeared over the side, but no cry came from her grey lips. Her luck, too, was finished. Clutching at the edge of the snapped rail, her small hand white and delicate against the splintered wood, eyes closed, she murmured the chant to Amida and pitched herself into space. She fell forward with a terrible jolt; her heavy robes, caught on the jagged rail, held her suspended. Tokuko struggled to follow her son into the sea but a hand seized her long hair and roughly dragged her back on the deck.

'Too late, Your Majesty. You will go back to the Capital in chains with your brother.' A huge Minamoto soldier picked her up and plucked the Sacred Mirror of the Sun Goddess out of her bosom. 'The Sword is lost but at least this is saved.' He pushed her back to her cabin. Munemori was slumped in a corner: he too had not reached the side in time. The final rays of the setting sun filtered through the window, falling on the heirs of Kiyomori, to pick out the

196

gold embroidery on the gown of the Empress and the
unbattered steel of Munemori's corselet.

8. The Provocation

'I think, Yoritomo, that you are being unreasonable.'

Conversation in the samurai-dokoro stopped. The councillors, cross-legged on reed mats, swords lying by their sides, turned in a body to stare at Lord Miura. The drumming of heavy spring rain in the thatch and against the rough pine walls filled the startled silence.

'What did you say, Miura?' Yoritomo's voice was harsh.

Miura replied evenly, 'I said, I think you are behaving unreasonably. Kajiwara and I have both reported on Yashima and Dan no Ura. I was not myself at Yashima until after the battle, but I accept that Yoshitsuné acted rashly. He should have waited for Lord Kajiwara.' He bowed to the scowling general. 'But I was at Yashima during the preparations for Dan no Ura and I was at that battle, and Yoshitsuné acted as a commander should. He consulted all those who could help him with control of the fleet.' Several samurai grunted in agreement. 'He deferred to those with naval experience and the battle was executed according to the information in the charts brought by the Abbot of Kumano. Lord Kajiwara's account implies the boy was arrogant, which I suppose he was up to a point, but also that he ignored the other commanders. Lord Wada and Lord Takeda of Kai agree with me that this is not true. And yet, you completely discount our opinions.' Miura was flushed with anger but his voice remained soft and reasonable. 'There are three of us and our combined importance *should* equal that of the solitary Lord Kajiwara.' Only in these last words did sarcasm ripple through his mild tone. The others watched the protagonists covertly.

'May I remind you, Lord Miura, that this is not the only instance of my brother's insubordination. His behaviour before the attack on Kiso and at Ichinotani showed a greed

for self-glory, as does his basking in the admiration of the Court and Go-Shirakawa. Furthermore, he accepted posts and a mansion from the Cloister Court despite my strict instructions to the contrary. He curries favour with Go-Shirakawa. Why? We all know that Go-Shirakawa enjoys pitting one faction against another; remember how he used us against Kiso and now he may try to use Yoshitsuné against us. Go-Shirakawa still cannot be trusted.'

'Yoshitsuné feels he has been neglected,' Miura said. 'Noriyori was promoted to Court rank and received lands and titles. Yoshitsuné was hurt and he is only young . . .'

Kajiwara interrupted him with a short bark of laughter. 'He is *hurt*? Is he a warrior or a woman? He should accept the instructions of his lord without question, not whine like an infant to the Cloistered Emperor. Compare his actions throughout the campaign to Noriyori's. *He* never made a move without consulting the samurai-dokoro. He always obeyed orders and never seized the initiative; and he fought like a samurai, face to face after offering a challenge – not stealing up on his enemy and attacking him unprepared.'

Lord Wada remarked, 'If Yoshitsuné had not seized the initiative at Ichinotani and Yashima Noriyori might still be looking for someone to offer a challenge to. You exaggerate the boy's motives. He only wants to be a hero.'

Yoritomo snapped, 'We don't need heroes any more.'

Impatiently Tokimasa broke in. 'There are many things to discuss. Now that Antoku's younger brother is Emperor, we must find a regent to suit us and the Court. There are still uncooperative warlords to deal with, and the fate of the Taira prisoners. Yoshitsuné has served his purpose. Must we waste time on him?'

'As it happens, my honoured father-in-law,' Yoritomo said, turning away from Wada whom he disliked, 'the cloistered Emperor wants the prisoners decapitated immediately in the Capital, but of course we cannot allow that. Munemori and Shigehira are prisoners of the samurai-dokoro and must be dealt with by their peers. The woman, Tokuko, goes to a convent. But Yoshitsuné will be

instructed to bring the others to Kamakura and then he can talk to the samurai-dokoro and defend himself. Is that sufficiently reasonable, Lord Miura?'

Miura gave a brief nod. 'It would appear to be.'

As the warlords left the building Kajiwara moved closer to Yoritomo. 'May I speak with you? I think it would be a mistake to let your brother actually reach Kamakura. First teach him his place.'

Yoritomo glanced at his colleague. 'I tried to teach him his place some time ago on these very steps, and that certainly did not work. But I will try again.'

*

Yoritomo's terse command to bring the prisoners to Kamakura came as a relief to Yoshitsuné. His return to the Capital after the victory at Dan no Ura had been tumultuous – the temples, the city and the Court vied to fête him: blossom viewings, processions, festivals, parties: his presence was an essential ingredient for success. Even the courtiers, usually so aloof from military affairs, fawned over the young general who was the fashion of the moment. He enjoyed it all. That is, he enjoyed it all until Noriyori was made Governor of Kyushu, the still unsubdued southern island, and given all the confiscated Taira estates there. Miura, Wada, Kajiwara, Takeda of Kai, Doi and the Abbot of Kumano – all received land and titles, suggested and confirmed by the Lord of Kamakura. Nothing came for Yoshitsuné. Reluctantly he resumed his lieutenancy in the Imperial Guard and lived in splendour at the Horikawa mansion, but with no estates, no rice lands to fill his storehouses, to feed his retainers or to pay his debts the splendour was precarious. Celebrations and parties quickly palled. He said nothing except to Benkei, but as the days passed, the more he thought of Yoritomo's neglect the more his anger and frustration grew. Another letter to the samurai-dokoro was obviously of little use, and he was contemplating a lightning trip to Kamakura when Yoritomo's orders came. Yoshitsuné relaxed. Once in Kamakura he was sure he could assuage his brother's

suspicions and reason with the samurai-dokoro. His conscience was clear, he told himself. He only wanted his share of the spoils.

Journeying along the Eastern Highway was enjoyable. The rice terraces, tender and promising, reflected blue sky and an occasional jagged peak spotted with stunted, wind-twisted cypress. In the mountains, fresh with early summer vegetation, they were serenaded at night by warblers and nightingales; monkeys chattered and howled, flinging pine cones down on the procession of men and horses winding their way along the narrow, sun-dappled road through the pines. Munemori and Shigehira were no trouble; in fact, they proved to be pleasant companions. Even Yataro enjoyed the trip to the dreaded eastern stronghold – the food there might be appalling but he had found that what the girls lacked in quality they made up in enthusiasm. Only Benkei remained glum and pessimistic, muttering ominously about the evils Kajiwara could perpetrate.

When Fuji's cone soared above them, a serene cinnamon red in the summer sun, Kamakura was only two days' ride away. Yoshitsuné, eager for the meeting with his brother, urged his men on, but at the last post station they found Hojo Tokimasa and a large party of soldiers. Yoshitsuné and his retainers were ordered to remain at the station while the prisoners were taken on to the samurai-dokoro by Tokimasa. No explanation was offered.

Benkei indulged in an irritating string of gloomy prognostications and the Oshu samurai drank; in an argument over a saké house whore Rokuro throttled one of Tokimasa's men, an incident immediately reported to the samurai-dokoro. The others waited: confused, sullen and bored.

After several days of frustrated inactivity Yoshitsuné decided he could wait passively no longer. By-passing his brother, he composed a long letter to the samurai-dokoro. He wrote that he had dedicated his life to Yoritomo and the Minamoto clan, enumerating the hardships of his childhood (an unwise inclusion as Yoritomo regarded hard

childhoods as his exclusive prerogative); the victories against Imperial enemies were modestly brushed aside but the cruelties of false accusations and gossip were themes well embroidered. Finally he begged to be allowed to refute any charges laid against him and to pledge his loyalty in person.

It was a good letter, and when read aloud in the samurai-dokoro genuinely moved many of the warriors who had despised Yoritomo's and Kajiwara's persecution of Yoshitsuné. After the younger man's service, the continuous criticism seemed shabby and petty. But more important to the hard-headed warlords, there seemed no question of treachery and for Yoritomo to call his alliance with the Cloister Court treason seemed a ridiculous fabrication. Admittedly he had unwisely accepted the Cloistered Emperor's favours, but if he were really plotting against Yoritomo he would be in contact with Hidehira in Oshu or with Taira refugees, and the samurai-dokoro would hear about it.

Yoritomo, however, was not moved. Jealous of the letter's effect on his colleagues, he decided it proved to him that his distrust of his brother's ambitions was justified. Yoshitsuné was using his wiles to gain sympathy, to turn the samurai against Yoritomo. He went to his wife's room to take his plain meal of millet and vegetables; Lady Masako knelt nearby, listening attentively to her husband.

'Leaving him at the post station was a mistake. Kajiwara misjudged his cleverness. It gave him the chance to write that letter!' He looked at his wife and said plaintively, 'Everything comes too easily to him! Look at them – Takeda, Miura, Wada. They are won by his youth, his charm. So is that old fool, Go-Shirakawa. But if Go-Shirakawa is a fool he is a dangerous fool. The Oshu Fujiwara, the Kyushu warlords, the Taira's former allies in the west? I am not secure yet. Yoshitsuné is much too popular, a lode-stone to all those groups, and together they could bring trouble upon me.'

Lady Masako murmured, 'I understand, my lord. Kiso thought he was safe but he underestimated our strength.'

'I don't underestimate my enemies, but I would like the problem of Go-Shirakawa and Yoshitsuné solved. The Court won't be any trouble. We have appointed Lord Kanezane, a nobleman belonging to no faction, as Regent: he's acceptable to the Court and the samurai-dokoro, but it is the influence of the Cloister Court that must be crushed. There cannot be any real progress until it is.'

Yoritomo put down his eating sticks and smiled at his wife who smiled back and said, 'My lord, if we continue to frustrate Yoshitsuné he will turn to the Cloistered Emperor, and the warlords will not tolerate that. Yoshitsuné is a good general but he is proud, my lord. Let us bring him to Kamakura for a ... talk ... but give him nothing. Then we shall see what happens.' She smiled slyly at her husband who was struck, not for the first time, by her shrewd mind and her ruthlessness. And not for the first time, he was relieved that she was his wife and not his enemy.

He smiled back. 'Yes, perhaps neglecting him was not the right course. I will talk with him, but not before the warlords. There is one thing that worries me ...' He paused and then shrugged. 'Lord Hachiman forbids bloodshed between brothers. My father killed his own brother, Kiso's father. And within a year my father was dead himself.'

Lady Masako smiled again, extending her small hand and laying it on her husband's arm. 'Kiso is dead too, my lord. We all die. It signifies nothing.'

*

Summoned curtly to Kamakura, Yoshitsuné rode directly to the samurai-dokoro, expecting an audience with his peers, only to find that his appointment was with Yoritomo. The lords had been dismissed and his brother alone awaited him in the dim hall.

They bowed formally and then stood, a few feet apart, each waiting for the other to speak. Finally Yoshitsuné broke the tense silence.

'It is good to see you again, elder brother. It seemed

when I was waiting at the post station as though we would not meet.' He could not keep the edge from his voice.

Yoritomo laughed. 'Oh, your letter was very winning.' He gestured to Yoshitsuné's well-worn corselet of primrose lacquer. 'Is this the famous armour described in song and story? Did you wear it to do battle with me today or,' the sarcasm was unmistakable, 'to impress the old war horses of the samurai-dokoro? Ah, you flush! That *was* the reason!'

Furious, Yoshitsuné felt his face burn. As always, Yoritomo had taken control, reducing him to an inexperienced youth. But it would not do to let this feeling show, and to cover it he slapped his palm on the hilt of the Hachiman sword, forcing himself to look straight into Yoritomo's lined oval face. Yoritomo looked older and plumper, a little soft for a samurai, and this encouraged him.

'You told me several years ago that I had not proved my right to the Hachiman sword. Now I have used it on Kiso and I have used it on the Taira. Do you accept my right now?' His accomplishments were genuine; there was no need to beg from this man.

Yoritomo raised an eyebrow. 'On Kiso? I heard that you never fought Kiso. You missed him at Uji and it was one of Miura's men who took his head. Tomomori killed himself, as a warrior should.' He stepped closer and said harshly, 'No, I don't accept that you deserve the sword. I am chieftain and it should be mine, but this is all unimportant now. The fighting is over.'

Yoshitsuné stared at him. 'Over? What of Kyushu, the Taira who escaped? I thought I was here to discuss the campaigns.'

'Noriyori will deal with Kyushu. I have made him governor. The western lords will stamp out the Taira. You are a general with no army and a hero with no more heroics to perform. The glory is finished. What will you do? What are you fit for?' He paused. 'Do you want some saké? You must be thirsty after your journey here. It is rough wine, of course, compared with what you drink in the Capital, but

here life is simple.' He poured two cups from an earthenware jug.

Yoshitsuné drank. 'I'll take some men west and chase the Taira who fled there. They could be dangerous.'

'And who will pay? Where will you get horses and supplies?' asked Yoritomo coldly.

Incredulous, Yoshitsuné watched his brother walk towards him and carefully refill the saké cup. Their eyes met; Yoshitsuné had never encountered such blank hatred before, never, even on the battlefield. But it was hatred mixed with something he could not immediately identify: guilt, fear, envy, it might be all or any of these things.

'I defeated the Taira for you,' he whispered.

'Anyone would have done that – eventually. The famine and Kiso weakened them.'

'No!' Yoshitsuné shouted. 'No! Noriyori couldn't do it and neither could Kajiwara. You know that! They tried. *I* did it!' He pounded his primrose lacquered chest, shouting with frustration and rage, '*I* did it when no one else could.'

'We don't need generals any more. And you did not obey orders. You were arrogant and overrode my representatives.' Yoritomo turned on his heel and strode away. 'You defied the samurai-dokoro and you are not needed any more. Go back to your women and your courtiers and tell them of your exploits. Earn your rice that way. There is no honour for you here.'

Yoshitsuné strode after him and caught Yoritomo's shoulder. 'Why? When I came to the Fuji camp I wanted to prove myself, to serve you and the clan. Why has this happened?'

'You wanted to be a hero,' barked Yoritomo. 'We all saw it at Fuji. Heroes can be useful so I let you be a hero, but you abused it. And now you are finished.'

'No, I'm not finished! I won't let you destroy me. You want me dead. I don't know why, but you do.' Yoshitsuné laughed. 'Well, I won't die to please you. My death will be an honourable one in battle or at a time of my own choosing. Not a death of your choosing – so that you can sleep safely at night.'

'Is that a threat?' asked Yoritomo quietly.

'You hate me. Why? I only did what needed to be done.'
Yoritomo turned away again.

'Why?' Yoshitsuné was no longer angry but genuinely
puzzled. What had he done but win battles that had to be
won? Warnings from Miura, Wada, Benkei, mutterings of
Noriyori came back to him in confusion. He should have
known this would happen. He had been warned. He said,
'You trust no one, not me, not Noriyori, but we are your
brothers and have proved our faith.' Yoritomo's back was
stiff, straight and unyielding. 'I think you fear us *because*
we are your brothers. Is that why Kajiwara and Tokimasa
are trusted and we are not?' Suddenly he remembered
Yoritomo on the beach at Kamakura, baiting him over the
sword. 'You said test the sword on Kiso, a cousin, and on
Noriyori, a brother, but if I did that only Yoshitsuné and
Yoritomo would be left and Yoshitsuné would be guilty of
fratricide, a sin to Hachiman, so only Yoritomo would be
left. Only one Minamoto left.' He burst into laughter,
nervous but released. 'You fear me as a rival.'

Yoritomo wheeled again. 'Nonsense! You will never
challenge me!'

'If you leave me no choice, perhaps I shall have to ...'

'By what authority?' snapped Yoritomo.

'By the authority of Hachiman and his sword. *I* am his
chosen warrior. A samurai. You are getting fat, brother,' he
added maliciously, for the first time completely confident
in Yoritomo's presence. Then depression swept over him.
He looked at his brother.

'I am not a politician and I don't want to be one. Leave
me alone to do my job, subdue the Taira and the Kyushu
lords, and we will live in harmony.'

'Don't be a fool. You are dangerous!'

'A samurai serves his lord. Yoritomo, I am a samurai and
so are you. We have the same father, the same blood, the
same beliefs. Let that bring peace between us. Give me
some land so that I can live and feed my men and then I
won't need the Cloister Court. Trust me and I will trust
you.' His voice was steady and strong. It was not a plea but

a bargain he offered.

'Get out!' barked Yoritomo.

After a long pause Yoshitsuné shrugged and said, 'Very well. But you chose this way.'

*

Since this was no doubt his last visit to Kamakura, there was something Yoshitsuné had to know. He mounted his horse and rode through the pines to the beach and the old Hachiman shrine. The torii, the gateway, still stood proudly before the home of the god but the little hut was a ruin, thatch sagging on tumbled walls. Gulls screeched and argued, the sand was warm and bright under a friendly sun. Yoshitsuné clapped twice and stood by the broken porch, breathing in the sweet summer air, waiting for the presence of the god. But he felt nothing: no communion, no power. Kneeling, he gathered a handful of sand and let it run through his fingers. Nothing. Slowly he rose and walked away. The god had departed.

Yoritomo's shrine to Hachiman lay through the trees, a vast building still raw in its newness. Yoshitsuné left his horse by the gate and reluctantly walked up the long avenue through a series of red torii towards his brother's monument to the War God. He had once sworn to himself he would never set foot in this monstrous extravagance, but now he must know whether the god had deserted his old shrine for the new one – or whether the god had deserted Yoshitsuné.

The building stood in a ring of bare earth studded with the stumps of pines murdered to make room for construction. Only the Hall of Sanctuary had been completed, but Yoshitsuné knew there were plans for a huge compound eventually. He stood glaring around him, his face hard and grim from the tension that held him in an iron grip. His head pounded and his neck and shoulders ached with knotted muscles and nerves. Children played in the woods and their shrieks and cries pierced his weary brain like a hundred steel-tipped arrows.

He forced himself to relax a little, and then rinsing his

mouth and hands, went purified up the steps of the shrine. The god could not be here, not in all this sliced, oozing wood, not in these splinters and tiles that were too new. He walked across the floor, not yet polished smooth, to the closed sanctuary and drew his sword from the scabbard. Closing his eyes he held the blade out towards the small shuttered doors and waited. His arms tensed, ached and the pain moved up to his shoulders, a steady, exhausting pain. He forced his arms up, offering the blade closer to the god. Sweat stood out on his forehead, his back, his shoulders. No answer came. Slowly, stiffly, he lowered the blade and opened his eyes. He bowed to the empty sanctuary and went down the steps of Yoritomo's shrine into the warm sunlight.

The children had left the woods and gathered in the unfinished courtyard. Several older men, carpenters and woodcutters, had joined them and silently the group watched him approach, studying his sunburnt drained face as if it were a sacred text. As he came up to them, one small boy stretched out a grubby hand and brushed the tips of his fingers very lightly on the battered primrose corselet. His small round face glowed, his black eyes fastened on Yoshitsuné's. 'Ichinotani, Yashima, Dan no Ura,' the boy whispered.

One of the carpenters dropped to his knees and touched his forehead to the ravaged earth of Hachiman's compound. He spoke in a hoarse, muffled voice, 'Bow to Lord Yoshituné, the heir of Hachiman Taro. Bow to the chosen of the War God.'

Numbly, Yoshitsuné watched them as they knelt, one after the other, murmuring his name. Then he too bowed from the waist, and silently, his mind empty, washed clean, he walked past them, alone, down the avenue to his waiting horse.

*

He returned to the post station to learn that Rokuro had been seized by Tokimasa's men and summarily executed for his murder of the Kamakura samurai. He mourned his

208

retainer's death in six jars of saké. Even Benkei dared not approach him.

After a few days, Munemori and Shigehira, interrogated by Yoritomo, were returned to Yoshitsuné who was ordered to escort them back to the Capital for punishment.

They left the station immediately and rode hard, glad to leave the chill eastern mountains for the sunny plains of the west. A few miles north of the Seta bridge the rearguard spotted horsemen coming at a gallop. Yoshitsuné halted and ordered the prisoners to dismount and wait, encircled by his samurai who had drawn their swords; a Taira raid to free their leaders had always been expected. The horsemen carried no recognisable pennant but as they approached, the large form of Kajiwara was unmistakable, even through a cloud of dust.

He reined in his horse in front of Yoshitsuné and, with no preliminaries, shouted, 'Give me Munemori. Stand back. You there, let the prisoner come through. Here.' He rode his horse through the men and seizing Munemori by the shoulder, he pushed him in front of his horse to some of his retainers. 'Get him ready.'

'Stop! What are you doing? This man goes to the Capital.' Yoshitsuné glared at Kajiwara.

'His head goes to the Capital. His corpse stays here. Shigehira, however, goes to Nara. He has an appointment with the monks whose temples he so unwisely burned when they sympathised with Minamoto Yorimasa. Remount, Lord Shigehira, the monks will see to your future.'

Shigehira climbed grimly on to his horse. One of Kajiwara's men tied his wrists – Yoshitsuné had not felt such an indignity necessary – and taking up the reins of the Taira's horse started to lead him away. Yoshitsuné drew his sword and severed the taut reins. As he leant over to grab the bridle of Shigehira's horse he commanded Benkei, 'See what those men are doing to Munemori and stop them.' He glared at Kajiwara. 'I have instructions. The Emperor disposes of prisoners, not the Lord of Kamakura.'

'The Lord of Kamakura decides that, not you.' Kajiwara nodded to his samurai who drew their swords and sur-

rounded Yoshitsuné and his men. Benkei, his face purple with rage, was forced back into the jostling group. Shigehira's horse was roped and at Kajiwara's command, led off toward Uji and the road to Nara. Shigehira turned in the saddle and, looking straight at Yoshitsuné, made a clumsy bow.

'I want to see your orders,' Yoshitsuné snapped.

'Your wants are of no interest to me or the Lord of Kamakura,' Kajiwara hurled over his shoulder as he rode across to Munemori who now knelt in the field, in the midst of pale green spears of millet. Beside him stood a samurai with a naked blade. Yoshitsuné heard Kajiwara tell Munemori to commend himself to Amida Buddha; he would be given a few seconds to pray.

Yoritomo's intentions were all too obvious: he had given Yoshitsuné one set of orders and then insulted him by ignoring them. Made him appear foolish in front of his men. It had all been carefully planned, both at the post station and now here. He knew that if he drew his sword Kajiwara's men would cut him down with pleasure. Kajiwara would call him a rebel, killed for insubordination and his name would be disgraced. As if reading his thoughts Benkei caught his eye and his lips mouthed the word, 'Wait.'

Munemori died with commendable courage, humbly offering his bared neck to his executioner. The severed head was wrapped and placed in a box especially designed for the purpose; his corpse was left in the young millet, a feast for the crows who had gathered in anticipation.

Kajiwara and Yoshitsuné rode on to the Capital together, not a word or a glance exchanged between them. By the Rashomon Gate they parted; Yoshitsuné went to the Horikawa and Kajiwara to the Rokuhara where he had further duties to perform. Yoritomo had not forgotten that it was Kiyomori's indulgence that had spared the sons of Yoshitomo to avenge their father's death. Kajiwara's task was to ensure that no Taira offspring imprisoned in that grim fortress would survive to avenge in their turn. Two hours after his arrival, at sunset, Kiyomori's elder grand-

sons were beheaded, the granddaughters drowned and the infants buried alive. The Rokuhara was a big place and such things could be accomplished quietly and efficiently within its high walls.

The Court was informed at midnight. Lord Kanezane, the new Regent, was shocked by Yoritomo's high-handed behaviour. He called Kajiwara to the Imperial Enclosure to demand an explanation. The samurai replied coolly that Taira raids were anticipated or perhaps even a last desperate attack on the Capital, led by the scattered survivors of Dan no Ura, yet to be captured. Kanezane accepted that as reason for the deaths of Munemori and Shigehira, but the children ...? If the children had lived they might become a focus of a future rebellion. Surely Lord Kanezane wanted to preserve peace? What were the lives of a few children compared with the horrors of civil war? Lord Kanezane could but unhappily agree.

*

He peered up sleepily at the familiar bulk, 'I can tell it's bad news. What is it?'

Benkei's voice came from the gloom, 'The Taira children have been executed, all of them, and Shigehira has been hacked to death by the Nara monks. A messenger just came from the Cloister Court. Go-Shirakawa expresses his displeasure and asks what you are going to do.' He added irritably, 'He can hardly imagine you will bring them back from the dead.'

Yoshitsuné climbed over Shizuka, asleep, and arranged his clothing. He walked out into the warm summer dawn, alive with birdsong and insects' cries. He splashed cool water from a vast stone bowl on his face, rinsed his mouth and spat. 'Yoritomo's work. All of it?' he asked.

Benkei rubbed his pock-marked cheeks and yawned. 'Whose else? Kajiwara wouldn't dare act without Yoritomo's orders. My informant says he has been to the Enclosure already to hear the displeasure of the Emperor via the Regent. You were lucky not to be called.'

'It's a deliberate insult that I was not!' He kicked fiercely

at the gravel path and glared at Benkei. 'Yoritomo and Kajiwara should have told me of their plans. They all treat me the way they do Yukiiye.' He scooped up some of the gravel and hurled it at the big black tom prowling sedately among the peonies. The cat growled and spat at him. 'That cat may fight back when it is insulted but I am expected to remain calm. I have fought Yoritomo's battles for him and he serves me with contempt.'

Benkei let out a deep breath. 'I don't know what happened in Kamakura between your brother and you, but don't do anything foolish. The samurai know which side is the winning one and they won't desert Yoritomo easily.

'Now, you'd better put on your Court dress and see what Go-Shirakawa has to say.'

*

Go-Shirakawa had a great deal to say. The children's deaths were disgusting and illegal; Yoritomo was as barbarous a samurai as his father; bloodshed in the Capital was a sacrilege and the fault of the clans – it had not occurred until the Minamoto and Taira had brought their personal rivalry into the city.

Yoshitsuné received the tirade impassively. Invited to speak, he informed the Cloistered Emperor that he was appalled by his brother's orders and would not have obeyed them himself. Yoritomo had insulted the Court and Yoshitsuné was shocked. Furthermore, had he known his brother was capable of such bloodthirsty revenge he would have hesitated before joining his cause. How could he and Yukiiye, who would no doubt also be appalled, make amends for the clan's behaviour?

Go-Shirakawa smiled and replied softly, 'Yukiiye can do nothing yet – but you can. I want you to set aside your wife and marry the daughter of Taira Tokida.'

*

The Koga mansion was on the Imedagawa River which flowed through the north-western corner of the city, an enclave of prosperous houses in the decayed and ab-

andoned suburb. Several important Taira, high officials in Kiyomori's government, had chosen to live there, preferring the river and quiet hilly avenues to the bustle of the more affluent districts. In the aftermath of Dan no Ura most of these Taira families were forced into exile or hiding and the houses had become deserted. Once proudly kept gardens slowly crept into the empty rooms, and wild animals and vagrants spread themselves over polished floors that had known only silken-clad and dainty feet. Imedagawa crumbled like the neighbouring western wards.

But the Koga mansion maintained its elegance. Taira Tokida had always served his Imperial masters well, showing sympathy to the Cloistered Emperor during the latter's struggles with Kiyomori. Although Tokida had appeared (but not fought) with the Taira forces at Dan no Ura, Go-Shirakawa had managed to reprieve his supporter from banishment. Summoned to the Hojoji Palace soon afterwards, Tokida had learned the reason why he had been spared.

'The young Minamoto general is very personable, Lord Tokida. We find him most charming and agreeable, a respectable servant of the Cloister Court. We feel that a marriage between a Taira family and the Minamoto would be a symbol of the peace we wish to see in the nation.' Go-Shirakawa, plump on a satin cushion, purred his little speech at the top of the kneeling samurai's headdress. Tokida knew what was coming. '*You* have an unmarried daughter, have you not, Lord Tokida? She would make the perfect wife for Yoshitsuné, don't you agree?'

Tokida murmured that he did indeed agree and backed from the Imperial presence. In the palanquin on the long, jolting journey back to Imedagawa he reflected that Yoshitsuné was landless and held low rank at Court but that these oversights might be remedied. The boy could have no more powerful friend in the Capital than the Cloistered Emperor. Still, Tokida felt a certain unease at this sudden honour thrust upon him.

Tamako was a pretty girl of fourteen. Her existence was

213

secluded as was that of all young noble women: the languid days filled with music lessons, clothes, flowers and calligraphy. But Tokida valued education – he believed his own learning had saved him from an undesirable career as a warrior and had propelled him to a high Court rank – therefore, all of his children, even daughters, were given a solid grounding in classical literature. Tamako displayed a feminine lack of enthusiasm for the rigours of the Chinese classics, but she devoured the romances of her own language, especially Lady Murasaki's *Tale of Genji*. Many peaceful hours were spent isolated behind her screens, imagining a lover as beautiful, as sensitive, as perfect as Prince Genji. The only men she knew were her father and brothers and as they were infrequent visitors to the women's quarters she was able to indulge in her dreams, undisturbed by any knowledge of the brutality or selfishness that real men, outside the confines of ladies' fiction, so often possess.

Rumours about her future husband reinforced her romantic vision. Her maids delighted in describing the handsome face and proud physique, which of course they had never seen. It was said he had defended himself from six enemies at once at Ichinotani, and it never occurred to her or her ladies that the slain enemies were perhaps her own Taira kinsmen. His skill with a flute and his grace as a dancer were exaggerated and regarded with admiration. Furthermore, in the amorous tradition of Prince Genji, that most energetic of womanisers, Yoshitsuné's liaison with Shizuka Gozen was tantalising – any man who could make the celebrated dancer his mistress must be a worthy hero.

Yoshitsuné's first night visit to Tokida's mansion was arranged. On the third visit, if both parties agreed, there would be an exchange of rice cakes and presents and the marriage would be made public. He was now sufficiently experienced with aristocratic young women to realise that tact and delicacy would probably be necessary to woo his bride. She was pretty enough, he found, but with Shizuka to satisfy his physical wants, her innocence roused no great passion in him. He amused her with gossip and encouraged

214

her to match poems with him. Tamako showed off her accomplishments with a gaiety that was touching, but she was less responsive to his caresses and it was more with a sense of obligation than anything else that he took her virginity.

Tamako could not hide her shock and consternation. Yoshitsuné's gentleness and charm had rivalled Genji's, and had so entranced her that she had forgotten the main business of the evening. The tearing pain confused as well as hurt her; however, more poems and caresses proved sweet consolation and by the third visit she had begun to reconcile sexual realities with feminine dreams.

Shizuka accepted the marriage with equanimity. She knew that she could never be principal wife and was pleased to have a little more time to herself. Her affair with the brilliant general had enhanced her appeal in the Capital and any of her performances evoked a great deal of public interest. As long as the new first wife remained at her father's house and did not make life difficult at the Horikawa mansion and as long as Yoshitsuné spent two or three nights a week with her she was perfectly happy.

Yoshitsuné found the situation most satisfactory. His wife's unconcealed adoration was a pleasant balm when Shizuka was absorbed in her dancing, and Shizuka's greater experience was a welcome antidote to Tamako's cloying worship. In fact, he reflected one hot afternoon as he sat with Shizuka in the water pavilion, if only his problems with Yoritomo could be solved, the words spoken in the white heat of anger forgotten, if only he had some land and some troops and a campaign to fight, life would really be very pleasant.

*

Yoritomo had no intention of making life pleasant for his brother. A few weeks after the marriage had been made public Hojo Tokimasa arrived at the Rokuhara Palace to serve as political liaison between Kamakura and the Court, joining Kajiwara who represented the military side. Yoshitsuné was immediately summoned to the vast compound

for an audience with the two samurai.

Yoritomo's distaste for luxury and courtly decadence was reflected in the new arrangements for the Rokuhara. The screens, hangings and warm braziers favoured by Kiyomori in the former Taira stronghold had been swept away, replaced by racks of weapons lining the plain wooden walls. Even on this hot late summer day the rooms seemed bleak and cold to Yoshitsuné, accustomed to the airy charm of the Horikawa mansion.

Tokimasa greeted him shortly; Kajiwara kept contemptuous silence.

Yoshitsuné bowed. 'Why have I been called here? Does my brother finally intend to make use of me?'

Tokimasa stuck out his long jaw and replied ponderously, 'The Lord of Kamakura understands that you have taken the daughter of Taira Tokida as principal wife. You have disobeyed explicit orders and insulted your father-in-law, Lord Kawagoe, a valuable participant in the samurai-dokoro. Your brother is very angry.'

This was what Yoshitsuné had expected and his answer was carefully rehearsed. 'The marriage was desired by the Cloistered Emperor. Naturally the wishes of the Imperial Court and the Cloister Court are paramount and I had no choice but to put Lord Kawagoe's daughter aside. Surely Yoritomo, as the servant of the Court, appreciates this.'

He spoke only to Tokimasa but Kajiwara stepped forward and snapped, 'Your obligation is to Kamakura, as Go-Shirakawa well knows. This is a deliberate challenge. It can be no accident that this woman is a Taira. Her father was at Dan no Ura.' Kajiwara's voice was shrill with indignation.

'Taira Tokida did not participate in the battle. One of the sons, it is true, fought and was killed, but Tokida was a non-combatant and was pardoned by the Cloistered Emperor,' Yoshitsuné recited patiently.

Tokimasa nodded. 'That is true. Yoritomo was not pleased by the pardon but he accepts it – for Tokida alone.' He took a letter from his sleeve and unrolled it. Yoshitsuné could make out his brother's cypher. Tokimasa began to

read in a grim voice. 'Minamoto Yoshitsuné has disobeyed the instructions of the samurai-dokoro whose authority he is sworn to uphold. He is commanded to terminate his treasonous marriage and to reinstate the daughter of Lord Kawagoe as his principal wife. Taira Tamako, daughter of Taira Tokida, is to be decapitated. Minamoto Yoshitsuné is to carry her head to Kamakura for inspection by the samurai-dokoro. Such are the just deserts of the families of the Taira rebels against the Imperial throne and its servant, the Lord of Kamakura.'

Yoshitsuné strode up to Tokimasa, snatched the letter, tore it into pieces and threw it on the floor.

'You can send that back to the Lord of Kamakura.'

He left the room.

*

Soon after dark a monk knocked at a small gate in the south wall of Yoritomo's mansion in Kamakura. The gate opened narrowly, the dim gold of a shaded lantern wavered briefly and he disappeared inside. An hour or so later he re-emerged, observed by two samurai passing by, who wondered why Tosabo, a notorious leader of a band of renegade monks in the hills, was paying a late night visit to the Lord of Kamakura.

*

In times of peace, however fragile that peace, fifty armed bandits could not ride through the streets of the Capital without attracting questions and a response from the Rokuhara. Tosabo, therefore, ordered his men to dress in the white garb of pilgrims visiting famous temples and, as most of the gang were renegade monks, they made a reasonably convincing sight, provided one saw only their shaved skulls and white robes. Few had the gentle features usually associated with holy travellers. Large wickerwork chests were packed with arms and armour and these were wrapped around with sacred plaited straw ropes and marked clearly as rice to offer to the Kumano Shrine. They entered the city after sunset and lodged at a once prosper-

ous temple, now gutted by fire and poorly rebuilt, used as a resting place for pilgrims of the lower kind. The temple was less than two hundred yards from the Horikawa mansion.

*

A full moon glittered over the roof and spilled into the gardens of the Horikawa mansion. From the house strains of music drifted into the clear, chill, autumn night. Servants scurried along the corridors carrying food and steaming jugs of saké to the main hall, from which laughter spilled out into the midnight silence.

Shizuka knelt by Yoshitsuné and poured saké into his cup, as she had for many nights recently. He told no one but Benkei and Yataro about destroying Yoritomo's letter; he lived in a condition of uneasy suspense, waiting for something, anything to happen. Convinced that his marriage was no fault of his own and that the Cloistered Emperor had to be obeyed, it was now up to Yoritomo to agree or disagree. Until then, saké and his women were the easiest way to pass the time. Saké was especially consoling, even if his drunkenness irritated Shizuka.

Yataro had noticed the large group of pilgrims arriving at the temple. He had mentioned it to Benkei because he thought he recognised the leader as Tosabo, an unlikely candidate for a pilgrimage. Yoshitsuné was too drunk to be interested, but it puzzled Benkei. Tosabo was not a pious man and his party was an unusually large one – all Kamakura men as well – but as the drinking progressed even Benkei could not remember what it was that had seemed so strange.

An hour or so after midnight the gathering broke up. Yataro and a few friends left for the pleasure houses of Muromachi and the others weaved off to sodden slumber. Benkei, bellowing in a lusty baritone and now and then executing a dance movement with unsteady grace, wandered off to find his own comfort in the dark city.

Yoshitsuné tumbled Shizuka over on to the cushions but fell asleep fumbling with her numerous under kimono.

She pushed him off and arranging the cushions more to her comfort than his, settled down beside him. The house was silent.

Shizuka was the first to hear the commotion. Shouts oddly like war cries drifted through the closed shutters, the din increased by pounding and crashing and splintering wood. She tugged at Yoshitsuné's sleeve. No response. Quiet as a cat, she crept across to the shutters and, forcing a crack, peered out. Light from torches flickered in the street outside the main gate. Over the pounding she heard men yelling for Yoshitsuné. 'Come and fight! Come and fight, Sama Kuro Yoshitsuné! Face the penalty for disloyalty!'

Shizuka knew where some of the armour was kept. As she passed her lover she kicked him sharply several times to bring him to consciousness and then ran on to the armour chests, calling the retainers to arms. Her voice echoed through an empty house – there were only her women and a few servants. She dragged the armour back to the main hall and found Yoshitsuné stirring stupidly, not fully awake. She grabbed a full jug of saké and threw the sticky liquid in his face. 'Quick. There must be at least fifty men at the gate. They are shouting for you to fight.' Hauling him to his feet she shook him hard, saké flying off him like water off a dog. He shuddered and then snapped into focus.

'Tosabo and those pilgrims! Benkei warned me. He felt something was unusual. Where is my armour? Call the men.'

'There is no one here. The house is empty but for the women.'

He stumbled into the pile of armour and began to tie the pieces on. 'Go and look again. Someone must be here – Benkei, Yataro – they're just drunk. First help me with these cords. Whose corselet is this – a child's?'

As she ran from the room he called after her, 'Ring the bell over the inner gate to bring help. The halberds are in the armoury. Get one for yourself and each of your women – we all fight tonight.'

The corridor was stippled with moonlight. Horrified, she saw a shadow crossing the streaks of light; someone was

creeping towards her, hugging close to the wall. It must be one of the household but just in case she groped for the cloisonné dagger in her sash – it was not there. It must have fallen out as she ran.

A strange voice murmured urgently, 'My lady, it is no one to be afraid of. This humble person is Kisanda, one of the grooms. The house is under attack. Can you hear them pounding at the main gate? There are no samurai here and this humble person is the only male servant. The others were permitted to visit the pleasure houses after the party.'

'Go to Lord Yoshitsuné. Servant or not, you will have to fight.' She ran past the youth to the women's quarters.

Kisanda hurried to the main hall, pausing respectfully on the step leading to the room. Yoshitsuné, his armour on, barked at him, 'Come in here – this is no time to act like a groom. There's a corselet here. Put it on. Can you fight?'

'I can shoot a straight arrow, my lord, and swing a halberd, but I have never used a samurai's weapon.'

'There's a bow in the ante-room – hold them off as long as you can while I fetch my horse and the women are arming themselves. If you can prop the gate open a little the bastards will have to enter one by one and you can kill them as they come. Can you manage that?'

'Yes, my lord.'

Kisanda tied on the breastplate, gathered a bow, a few dozen plain arrows and a halberd. The gate was beginning to splinter under Tosabo's log rams, but between blows he eased the bolts and, using the heavy poles as buttresses, propped the gate narrowly open so that a man would have to squeeze slowly through, making a superb target. He stood back in the shadows, bow strung, tensed, waiting. The metal crest of a helmet glinted in the moonlight, then another. Kisanda let fly, fitted a second arrow and shot again. There was a shrill scream. In the moonlight he could see a hand pinned to the gate, transfixed by his arrow. There was more flashing metal. Kisanda shot again and again, and two men toppled into the courtyard. A gruff voice shouted from the road. 'This is Tosabo. Who is the disloyal warrior who defends a traitor's gateway? Declare

yourself and prepare to die!'

Kisanda dared not answer. If this Tosabo learned the gate was held by a lowly groom he would realise that Yoshitsuné was alone, without his retainers. Under no other circumstances would a mere servant shoot at a warrior monk.

Yoshitsuné, mounted, galloped into the courtyard. 'Answer him, Kisanda. You should be proud of your marksmanship, servant or not.'

Kisanda raised his head and cried in a clear voice, 'This is Kisanda, groom of Yoshitsuné. Come through the gate and let me show you how to die!'

The battered weakened gate suddenly smashed and a dozen mounted men forced their squealing horses over the bodies of their comrades. Kisanda finished his arrows and ran among the horses, slashing at their bellies with his halberd, a miserable thing for a groom to have to do, whose life was horses. His master charged down, sword flashing, and between them they dispatched five men. The others backed on to the road as the alarm bell began to toll over the still city.

Shizuka and her attendants appeared on the veranda, in corselets with their skirts tied up, brandishing halberds with unconvincing ferocity. Kisanda found that his arm was bleeding and he sank down on the step. Shizuka herself bound up the groom's wound with a silk scarf.

*

By the time Benkei had danced a mile or so through the chill morning he was sober. The desire for adventure considerably reduced, he wandered into a saké stall and settled down to sleep. Something worried at the back of his consciousness but eventually he dozed, only to dream he was fighting back to back with Yoshitsuné against a vastly superior force of pilgrims, about a hundred shouting monks in white. The noise was terrific: horses screaming, men yelling challenges and shrieking in pain, the metallic clang as steel clashed on steel. He woke with a start. Men were shouting and horses *were* screaming. Somewhere in

the Capital an alarm bell was booming. Pilgrims!

Benkei leapt up, buckling on his corselet, and ran out of the stall. Back at the Horikawa, he slipped through a concealed side gate and crept towards the main buildings. Suddenly the clamour ceased. He climbed quickly up to the top of the middle gate where he found a frightened maidservant standing by the still quivering alarm bell. She pointed a shaking finger toward the front courtyard where, in the greying light, he could just make out a horseman and a single foot soldier. The straight back and proud tilt of the horseman's head were unmistakable – Yoshitsuné and one other man against how many? Benkei clattered down the narrow stairs and hurried along the veranda.

Yoshitsuné saw the obscure figure and whispered to Kisanda, 'They have broken through one of the side gates. My men will get here too late to help us but in time for some revenge.' He slid off his horse and strode towards the veranda. 'Who is this coward approaching by stealth? Name yourself!'

A voice bellowed, 'Saito Masashibo Benkei is my name and I serve Yoshitsuné. Whoever considers my approach stealthy must be hard of hearing.'

'You're lucky I don't cut you down. Tosabo has attacked, and he has a small army in the avenue outside. There is only you, me and a groom to fight but the groom is fierce with a halberd. Shizuka and her women are armed, but I don't know how much use they'll be.'

With a sudden crash a host of Tosabo's monks rushed over the splintered gate and charged on foot into the courtyard, followed by mounted men picking their way carefully over the debris. The defenders surged into the mêleé, cutting down the men on foot and dragging likely opponents from their horses. Shizuka darted from the veranda to slice at an unguarded arm or flank, her attendants poking and pricking but with less enthusiasm. One girl was snatched by her long hair and hauled from the porch by a snarling pilgrim who struck off her head and tossed it back among the terrified women. Shizuka, nearly sick with fright herself, rallied them with threats, pleas and

vivid reminders of their fate if Tosabo were victorious. The weaker fled, but most stayed and defended their honour like she-demons.

Tosabo fought hard for the reward promised by Yoritomo, but as Yoshitsuné's men rallied quickly to the alarm bell and poured into the Horikawa he knew that it was time to retreat. He fled out of the sundered gate and urged his horse through the strange streets of the Capital, riding in his confusion on to the flat expanse of the Kamo beach where Yoshitsuné's men easily caught him, dragged him from his horse and forced him to kneel before his vanquisher.

Yoshitsuné looked down at the tonsured man in blood-stained white, sprawled on the sand before him. 'What shall I do with you, Tosabo? Cut your head off, or beat you and send you back to Kamakura so my brother can do it?' he asked with interest.

'I have failed to carry out my commission. Cut off my head and let it be finished.' The defeated renegade touched his forehead to the ground.

'There are a few things to find out before we send you to hell. Are you the deputy of the Lord of Kamakura? Did he order you to kill me or was it by the command of the samurai-dokoro?'

The monk sat back on his heels. His face and voice held no expression. It was as though he were already dead. 'No, it was by his command. He called me to his residence at night and I saw him alone. Wait, I am wrong. There was another man. Lord Kajiwara. They promised me rice fields and gold if I brought your head back and the head of your uncle, Yukiiye, another traitor. But they said no one was to know who I served.'

'My head and Yukiiye's? That is very interesting.' Yoshitsuné glanced at Benkei. 'Do you think my uncle knows how precarious his position is? Yoritomo obviously means to destroy us.'

Benkei grunted. 'He seems to find his family an embarrassment.'

Yoshitsuné looked down at Tosabo. 'Face the Western

Paradise and repeat the name of Lord Amida. You are, after all, a monk.' He motioned to one of his men to behead the man and watched impassively as it was done. Then he remounted and rode home, his face set in a frown. Tomorrow, with Yukiiye, he would visit Go-Shirakawa. If it was to be open warfare with Yoritomo, the Cloistered Emperor would have to decide finally which brother would have his Imperial support.

News of Tosabo's raid spread through the Capital. By noon the wildest rumours were circulating and it was commonly accepted that Yoritomo and an army of two hundred thousand were camped at Seta bridge. The population, remembering the looting, burning and suffering that accompanied the struggle between Yoritomo and Kiso, dug itself in for a period of disaster. Overnight it became no longer fashionable to sing the praises of the gallant young hero Yoshitsuné.

9. The Flight

Go-Shirakawa put out one plump, slightly unsteady hand, plucked a sugared loquat from a dish, popped it ostentatiously into his mouth and then held his quivering fingers out to be wiped, keeping an eye on his visitors as he did so. To his disappointment, Yoritomo and his samurai remained apparently unmoved by this display of rudeness, sitting stolidly in their semi-circle, impassively watching the proceedings. Well, what could be expected from men who wore armour in the presence of the Cloistered Emperor, plain leather armour at that? They should never have been permitted admittance looking as they did, he thought irritably, clinging blindly to the fiction that their admittance could have been prevented.

'It was outrageous, gentlemen,' he protested uneasily. 'Yoshitsuné and Yukiiye stood in this very room, swords drawn, and threatened us, the Cloistered Emperor, with violence unless we issued them an Imperial order to raise troops against you in Kyushu.' Go-Shirakawa's voice and chins shook with dishonest self-righteousness as he looked from Yoritomo to Tokimasa to Kajiwara and back to Yoritomo, who nodded with cold sympathy. 'He said he had the assistance of the monks on Mount Hiei, and we had no way of knowing if this were true or not but of course the monasteries ... But we had to agree so that they would leave the city. We could not allow the Capital to suffer again as it had under Kiso. You understand that? There can be no more fighting on sacred ground. Of course, we shall not acknowledge any rebellion started by your brother in the Imperial name. We were forced ... under duress. Shocking!'

'Of course, Your Highness,' said Yoritomo, his hard voice loud and brusque in the luxurious room. 'The samurai-dokoro is sworn to stop my brother's treasonable

activities. His victories have corrupted him and in his naïvety he believes that he can defy his clan and his Emperor.' He pointedly did not mention the Cloister Court or Go-Shirakawa. 'But he will be captured before he can organise those few warlords who are disloyal to his Imperial Majesty. To reach the coast to sail for Kyushu he must pass through land belonging to members of the samurai-dokoro, and he and Yukiiye will certainly be taken.' Yoritomo bowed politely. If he found Go-Shirakawa's story of threats ridiculous he gave no indication of it. The important thing was that Yoshitsuné and Yukiiye had been granted an Imperial mandate – it did not matter if they had threatened Go-Shirakawa for it or if, as Yoritomo suspected, Go-Shirakawa had forced it on them in order to push such dangerous plotters out of the city.

Go-Shirakawa sipped a little saké, looked at his cup and said suddenly to Tametoki, 'Bring some wine for our guests.' Covering his surprise, the servant hurried off to give the orders.

A change of subject seemed a good idea. 'We have heard that the army arriving at the Rokuhara Palace is very large ...' Go-Shirakawa began.

Yoritomo broke in quickly. 'The members of the samurai-dokoro wish to pay homage to their Emperor and of course they always travel with retainers.'

Go-Shirakawa ignored this and continued with a sly smile, 'We have already met Lord Miura and Lord Wada, but they are not with you it seems?'

'No,' replied Yoritomo coldly.

'But they may follow later,' added Tokimasa. After a brief bow he lifted his wine cup from its lacquer tray.

Later, as the three commanders strode through the exquisite rooms of the Hojoji Palace, Tokimasa chuckled to himself. 'He knows his power is finished and he knows we know he tricked Yoshitsuné into believing the Cloister Court was supporting him. Drawn swords! How would they get past the guards?'

'The boy is a fool,' Kajiwara said shortly.

'But what a useful fool!' Yoritomo brought his hand

down on Tokimasa's leather-covered back. The two men grinned at each other and Yoritomo said, 'Go-Shirakawa has been trapped by his own plot and there is nothing he can do. We have him tighter than Kiyomori ever dared dream of, and with his own permission. Emergency powers to catch the rebels! Rebels! An arrogant boy, an idiotic old courtier and a few samurai from the north who don't even know where they are going! But what we have gained from this 'emergency', eh? We have Imperial authority to run the country now! Finance, local administration, trade, military, everything comes to Kamakura.' He gave an uncharacteristic chuckle and slapped Tokimasa playfully again. The older man made him a deep ironic bow.

Kajiwara caught Yoritomo's arm. 'But Yoshitsuné must die. As long as there are warlords who might support him, as long as there is confusion in the country, he is too dangerous alive. Remember how Miura and Wada defied the samurai-dokoro rather than fight against him – and Go-Shirakawa knew about that. And what is this about Mount Hiei – it may or may not be true? He might actually raise an army and use the Cloister Court's mandate against us. We can't trust Go-Shirakawa. Yoshitsuné must be caught and killed!'

Yoritomo laughed again. 'He will be – when the right time comes. After we have used the threat of his rebellion to secure our grip on the Court – and to put members of the samurai-dokoro in control of every province in the country. Rule by the samurai has begun!'

*

The rain thundered down on the small port of Daimotsu, bouncing off the wooden jetty on to the two men; the samurai in a sodden fur cloak and the seaman covered by a thick cape of straw, his horny feet and legs bare in the winter rain.

'What are you going to give me to take them, then? It will have to be a fair price for the lot of you. I don't like women on boats.' The seaman spat into the rain.

227

Wet, tired and depressed, Yataro said impatiently, 'I told you, all the horses and the three carts and two bales of silk. You can't complain.'

The sailor looked at him shrewdly. 'Ain't complainin', but in this rain ...and women ... How're they travellin'? On foot?'

'Palanquins,' Yataro answered, resigned to the inevitable.

'Right! I'll have them too, and the horses' saddles. Sail at dawn. Go and tell your party.'

Yataro glared at him and splashed back up the track to the squalid inn where horses, palanquins and carts waited for their new master. He shouted to Kisanda who sheltered from the rain under the ragged thatch overhang. 'Take everything down to the jetty and unload the carts. Only the armour chests come in the boat with us and don't let the old bastard see those. They drive hard bargains in Daimotsu.'

Yataro pushed aside a leather curtain, left his boots in the vestibule and stepped up into the dim, smoky room, filled with the stench of steaming fur, dirt and dried blood. Men slumped against the walls or sprawled on frayed straw mats; a few slept but most were cleaning their weapons or eating, grumbling among themselves. In a corner by the smoking fire, behind a low paper screen, sat Tamako and her two maidservants, snuffling and miserable as they had been since Taira Tokida had stuffed them into a palanquin and hurried the grunting bearers out of his gate into Yoshitsuné's convoy. Poor girl, thought Yataro, wait until she heard she had lost her palanquin! Even Shizuka, splendid as she has been, might despair this time. This was no place for women; that bastard of a captain was right. Yoshitsuné must be mad.

He walked through the sullen men to his commander, who stood with Benkei by the meagre fire. Benkei looked tired, the massive shoulders sagged and his voice had lost some of its boom. Yoshitsuné, his face etched with deep fatigue lines and stained with blood from an arrow graze, studied Yataro with red-rimmed eyes. 'Well?'

'He'll take us, all of us, but it will cost horses, saddles,

carts and palanquins. He doesn't like women, it seems. Frankly, Yoshitsuné, I think he has a point.'

'They stay with us,' the other replied brusquely. 'He is taking us to Kyushu tonight?'

'He'll try to take us to Kyushu.' Yataro squatted beside the dull fire glowing weakly in a deep fire pit, and held out his hands, numb with cold. 'Not tonight. There is not much wind and the rain is worse than ever. It's foul out there. The dawn tide is the best he'll do.'

Benkei ran his hands over his stubbly head and down over his broad pock-marked face. 'I'll put some men on guard duty. We're still in Kanja's territory and he may attack tonight. I'd fight better with something besides burdock and bonito in my belly.' He shuffled off and stirred up several warriors who, complaining bitterly, went to stand by the doors. The two sliding windows were shuttered and barred safely on the inside.

Yukiiye stood slightly apart with his manservant in attendance; his whining voice carried across to Yoshitsuné. 'That man is right, nephew, the women should go back and take their chances with Yoritomo. They are a terrible burden.' Without his usual thick layer of powder and with the blacking flaking off his small teeth he looked old and shabby; the swansdown straggled from his satin jacket and his badger-skin coat steamed sadly. He had grumbled and complained all the way from the Capital, blaming his nephew volubly for allowing Go-Shirakawa to manoeuvre them out of the city, and by now everyone was immune to his complaints. Yoshitsuné bowed sardonically to him and turned to Benkei again.

'Are all entrances guarded?' Benkei nodded. 'Lady Tamako is crying again – so are her maids.' Yoshitsuné shrugged and walked deliberately over to Shizuka who sat a few feet away from Tamako in the makeshift women's quarters set off by the torn paper screen. Very pale and obviously exhausted, Shizuka's eyes were swollen and deep lines marked her mouth and cheeks, but she smiled and made room for him beside her. He laid the Hachiman sword on the floor and leaned his head against the wall, his

229

black hair escaping untidily from his top knot. Shizuka had used a woman's resources and had combed and dressed her hair very carefully in an attempt to cheer herself. 'When do we leave here, my lord? We must be dangerously exposed in this village with Yoritomo's retainers in the area.'

'Hm,' he answered without opening his eyes. 'We have a boat for the morning but I don't think there will be trouble after the raid this afternoon. At least six of them were killed and five or more wounded so they'll think again before attacking, especially as we have some cover now.' He tapped the crumbling plaster wall. 'Were you afraid?'

'I had my dagger, but Lady Tamako's screams were alarming and of course there is always ...' She patted her belly.

'The baby. You should have told me before we left the Capital and stayed there in safety,' he said wearily.

'In safety?' she asked with the merest touch of irony. 'At the Horikawa mansion? My lord, I would rather be with you. If Lady Tamako was to come then so should I.' She did not add that no one wished to see a performance by a dancer defiled by pregnancy. Her part in the compromise between Yoshitsuné and herself had culminated in total surrender. Her reputation and career were utterly lost when she followed her lover into exile. She had indeed danced her moment in the breeze, but as long as she had Yoshitsuné and the baby she could survive.

Yoshitsuné said, 'There was no choice – for either of you. Poor little Tamako. She does not have your courage.'

'She may develop it,' said Shizuka drily.

Kisanda came into the room, water draining from his stiff straw cloak. Seeing Yoshitsuné he approached diffidently as befitted a servant, but Yoshitsuné and Shizuka both smiled at their comrade-in-arms from the Horikawa raid.

'Everything is at the jetty, my lord. Yataro said the sea captain was taking everything: carts, horses, palanquins.'

'Palanquins?' asked Shizuka. Involuntarily her hands went to her belly. 'How will we travel in Kyushu, my lord?'

Yoshitsuné looked at her sadly. 'I don't know, but we have Go-Shirakawa's blessing and the warlords will have

to help us.' He smiled. 'Anyway, Noriyori will be there and he won't abandon us.' He hoped that she was reassured and wished that he could be, but he knew that Noriyori would be mad to help him now. What sort of brother would he be to ask Noriyori to endanger himself? And yet, thought Yoshitsuné, how much choice does Yoritomo leave me?

It was a quiet night. The rain and the reputation of Yoshitsuné's excellent bowmen warned off marauding samurai and in the morning the bedraggled party embarked for Kyushu, relieved to escape from Yoritomo's long arm.

An hour out of the harbour the rain suddenly increased and wild winds blew, howling and rocking the vessel as though it were a toy. The women shrieked and even Shizuka lost spirit and wept. For the passengers, crouched in the low-ceilinged cabin stinking of vomit and fear, claustrophobia added to their miseries. Tamako wept; Shizuka lay back, tangled in a hunting-cloak; Yukiiye, all dignity lost, puked alone in a corner.

Yoshitsuné could not bear it. He plucked Benkei's sleeve and motioned the monk to follow him on deck. Rain was driving across the ship, making it impossible to stand. The two men clung to each other and, sliding and crawling, struggled past the sailors battling to control the wildly flapping sails. They found protection between lashed barrels and the wall of the cabin, pulled a soaked reed mat around them and hunched down in their wet, unsteady nest. The camphor-wood wall of the cabin gave off a sharp, refreshing scent that helped to clear their aching heads.

Suddenly a gnarled hand groped around the matting and tugged at Benkei, who looked out and scowled at a sailor hanging on to the wall.

'What do you want? Speak up, you son of a shark!'

'We need you, big man; need your weight over by the mast. The gale is a freak. We weren't ready. Come. Lend a hand if you want to see another day!'

The monk hauled himself to his feet. 'I'll go and give this useless crew a hand.' He lumbered off into the rain.

Yoshitsuné pulled the matting close to him; he was cold,

wet and his guts heaved with every lurch of the boat, but he closed his eyes and leant against the rough comfort of the wall and dozed. Gradually a sound, a voice, began to penetrate the dense roar of the storm – a deep hollow voice calling his name.

'Sama Kuro Yoshitsuné, listen to me.'

He strained to distinguish who the disembodied voice belonged to; it was not Benkei or Yukiiye or any of his retainers.

'Sama Kuro Yoshitsuné, listen to me.' It was very close now, dominating the storm. 'You have come back, Yoshitsuné. I could not come to you, so you have come to me. We did not meet in hand-to-hand combat as warriors should. You won the battle but where has your victory gone, Yoshitsuné? Come, make your death as noble as mine was. Take up your Hachiman sword and come to fight me. You are called a hero. Are you a hero, Yoshitsuné? Prove to me that you are.'

'What is this? A joke?' He threw the matting aside and glared out into blackness and rain. There was no one there.

'You know who I am, Yoshitsuné. My father spared your life. Where are my children? Did you spare them? Their blood seeps into the soil of the Rokuhara and it cries out for revenge. Come and meet me. Bring your sword and fight.'

'Who are you? Tell me who you are; I cannot fight a man I do not know.'

The voice whispered in his head, 'You know who I am. Taira Tomomori, son of Taira Kiyomori and general to the Imperial Court. I was a great warrior and you were my equal. But I died a warrior's death. Will you, Yoshitsuné? You won a great victory, but do you understand? I understand victory as only the vanquished can. Take up your great Hachiman sword and meet me!'

The wet matting suddenly whipped in the wind and curled itself around Yoshitsuné's arm. A quick pitch of the boat sent him sliding along the deck towards the railing, dragged by the reed mat that smelled of the sea. He wrenched the Hachiman sword free.

'I'll fight. Sama Kuro Yoshitsuné challenges Taira Tomomori. Where are you?'

The whisper continued in his ear, reverberating through his skull. 'Here, come to the railing. Over here. Over the railing.' Yoshitsuné struggled against the wind. He found a foothold and tried to climb but something held him back. Another voice, loud and sharp with panic, cut across the murmuring voice in his head.

'Yoshitsuné, are you mad? That is the side – you'll go over! What's the matter with you? What's happening?' Benkei encircled his master's waist with one huge arm, tugging hard, and Yoshitsuné let go of the rail, his sword clattering to the deck. As he sank down Benkei, with a monumental effort, swept him up over his shoulder and carried the unconscious man to the cabin wall.

'He's dead. No, he's breathing. He would have been into the sea if I hadn't come.'

Yoshitsuné's eyelids fluttered. He groaned and rolling on one side, vomited violently. Weakly he said, 'Tomomori. Must fight. Fetch my sword, Benkei. Fetch my sword.' Retching, he pulled himself to one elbow.

'Tomomori?' Benkei pulled a little-used rosary out of his sleeve and shook the beads. He whispered, 'Yoshitsuné, can you understand me? Listen. Take this rosary. Close your fingers over it. That's right. Now, pray with me. The old monk is good for something.' He chanted hoarsely, holding his master's cold hands on the rosary, forcing his palms back and forth over the beads. Again and again, Benkei chanted the charms. Haltingly Yoshitsuné murmured with him as the powerful rhythm of the invocation caught him up.

The wind screamed around the crouching men, rain drove across the deck and then suddenly the storm died away; the rain ceased, the wind dropped, the seas calmed. When Benkei, drained and exhausted, staggered to his feet obscurity was giving way to silvery grey. He dragged himself to the rail. A full moon filtered through the dispersing clouds, weakly illuminating the sharp black shapes of jagged hills. The ship, battered and broken, was

only a few hundred yards away from land.

Yoshitsuné lay against the cabin wall in a deep sleep. A few sailors began to clear the debris while others sat at the oars. As the ship limped along the coast the forlorn members of the party came out on to the dawn deck.

Benkei dealt with the sullen captain – both Yoshitsuné and Yukiiye were too weak to resume command. The avaricious seaman wanted to dump his passengers and struggle back to Daimotsu, but, with Benkei's mighty hand kneading his shoulder, he agreed to drop anchor while Kisanda and Yataro went ashore to assess the local situation. The ship had been blown down the coastline rather than across to Kyushu: whose territory they were in no one knew, but it was not likely to be hospitable.

While Yataro and Kisanda were scouting, Yoshitsuné spent his idle shipbound day deep in thought. At this distance from the Capital, away from the machinations and enticements of the Cloistered Emperor, he saw his situation in a rather different perspective. There had been moments of glory and he had served his brother to the best of his ability, but nothing was permanent. His karma had turned, brought him down and there was nothing to do but accept this change in fate.

Rocking in the comforting winter sunlight, the cold politics of the Court and Kamakura seemed particularly futile – a rebellion against Yoritomo could only cause more bloodshed and sorrow. Although he had no family left in the Capital to suffer, why should he pull down disaster on the parents, wives and children of those who served him?

Revenge seemed a paltry, empty emotion. What had he felt at Dan no Ura? Elation and bloodlust, the challenge of competing against the enemy, yes; but he had not once thought about redeeming the spirit of his father. He did not want to remember Tomomori and his voice in the storm, but the hollow sound came back to him, unbidden, unavoidable, 'I understand victory as only the vanquished can.' Perhaps he *was* beginning to understand victory. The victor of Dan no Ura had fallen lower than the vanquished,

hounded into flight by his own brother. Yorimasa, Kiso, Munemori, Tomomori, Shigehira, all dead; Yoshitsuné and Yukiiye fugitives; Noriyori in Kyushu and likely to stay there. Who had won? Yoritomo. In the sunshine Yoshitsuné felt no bitterness, only sadness for the deaths and an immense desire to be free of the whole business.

And so, should he die? Was death the only alternative if his life no longer held any purpose? And if he should die, where? Here, on the deck? Or in Kyushu? Should he ask Noriyori to be his second, to slice off his head after he had slashed open his own belly with Hidehira's dagger?

The sea glittered, blue and green and gold under the sun, stretching out to Kyushu – to death? No! He sat up. He must die facing Yoritomo, not running from him. He would land somewhere on this coast and make his way to Yoritomo's enemies; the big monasteries or Oshu – not the Taira, never the Taira – and march on Kamakura to demand his rights. Not rebellion, not treason. He only wanted his rights. Perhaps it was possible, perhaps not, but he could not die running away, with his back to his brother.

Tamako's high whine drifted across the cluttered deck as she fretted with exhaustion and fright. It would be better to risk sending her back now to the Capital and then, when everything was quiet again, he could fetch her and they would produce the son he wanted. He was reluctantly pondering the problem of Shizuka when Yataro and Kisanda returned with the news that landing was not safe, the countryside was patrolled by Kanja's samurai.

Yukiiye joined them. The older man had finally lost his taste for intrigue, the once quick sly eyes were bloodshot and dull with fatigue. Yoshitsuné said, 'My men report this coast is controlled by Kanja and his samurai. We seem to have little choice, uncle.'

Yukiiye shivered as he stared out over the wide expanse of sea. 'No, nephew, we do not have any choice. Call the captain and listen to what he has to say.'

The captain was summoned and sullenly explained that the storm damage was too great, that the ship could not travel far. 'I'll take you away from here down the coast to

Izumi on the tide. My boat will have to make that journey anyway, even in this condition.' The man looked stubbornly at Yoshitsuné. 'I won't do more, my lord. You might find another ship somewhere on the Izumi coast. But they are independent-minded folk with no love for Capital politics or rebel samurai.' He nodded and turned away.

Yukiiye said in a soft voice, 'We shall part at Izumi, nephew. I have a friend, an old friend from the good times long ago. He is the Abbot of Sakai Temple and he will hide me if it is necessary. I have done him favours in the past.' A long sigh whistled up in the old man's breast. 'I cannot return to the Capital, not against the will of the Cloister Court. I shall take holy orders, perhaps. Yes, that might be a good idea. To pray for release from this unjust world, from this tired body.' His small teeth gleamed through a thin smile.

The sun was losing its heat and the winter afternoon would be very cold. Suddenly Benkei's form blocked the sun, casting the two seated men in shadow.

'I'll put those women below. There may be trouble and we don't want them screaming under foot.' His deep voice, resonant with disgust, roused Yoshitsuné to action.

'Send them below. Tell the men to arm and stand prepared.' The sailors shouted cryptic instructions to each other as they weighed anchor. Yoshitsuné glanced at his shrivelled uncle and took pity. 'You go below as well. I'll send for you if there is any trouble.' Yukiiye scuttled towards the hold.

'Benkei, I've been thinking – even if we did get to Kyushu we would put Noriyori in an awkward position. He will have to choose between brothers.'

'It is against all Hachiman's teaching,' agreed Benkei. 'And a bad thing for the clan. And so, what do we do?'

Yoshitsuné squinted up at him, against the setting sun. 'Surrender or fight . . . We have the Cloistered Emperor's mandate.'

'That should be worth something, even if Yoritomo is in the Capital. Look, Izumi means the Yoshino Mountains and that means Zao Gongen, a big monastery with no love

of outside interference. Yoritomo may not have reached them yet. It's worth a chance.'

'And there is still Hidehira in Oshu,' Yoshitsuné muttered. He looked up at Benkei again. 'This afternoon I wanted to die. It is all so pointless.'

Benkei's reply was low and firm. 'You cannot die. Why give him what he wants?'

'There are men in the samurai-dokoro who will say I'm a coward.'

'Do you care?'

'No.' He stood up. 'When the captain puts us ashore I shall send Tamako and her women back to the Capital. Two men will accompany them.'

Benkei grinned, relieved. 'This is no place for a woman.' A frown crossed his face. 'Lady Tamako, her women – and Shizuka? You didn't mention Shizuka.'

'Yes,' he said with resignation, 'she must go too, dressed as a page though. She is too easily recognised as she is. Do not tell her. I will speak with her later,' he added miserably.

With a great sigh of relief the monk turned on his heel and strode to the group of women, 'Everybody go below. Down to that nice safe little cabin.' He drove the women before him like so many chickens.

*

Some time after dark the captain informed Benkei that the ship stood off Izumi, a fierce unfriendly district dominated by the Yoshino Mountains. The party were ferried to a narrow desolate beach gleaming dully against dark pines and looming crags. A fire would be too dangerous so women and samurai alike huddled shivering in salt-stiff cloaks under the inadequate shelter of the towering trees. At dawn they withdrew into the protective gloom of the wood to eat the last of their food. Yoshitsuné singled out several of his Oshu retainers and told them of his decision to send the women back to the Capital, giving the samurai instructions to deposit Tamako at her father's villa, and then disappear into the city, keeping a watch on the house in case Yoritomo's spies found her there. They

were to visit the Horikawa mansion from time to time, as Yoshitsuné hoped to return there eventually. The men agreed to the assignment with enthusiasm – none of the northerners had looked forward to the hot, sticky climate of Kyushu.

Tamako received the news impassively. The flight from the Capital, harried by raiding parties, the storm and the buffeting had numbed her. She no longer noticed her torn robes, stiff with sea spray and vomit. Her attendants had washed her filthy hands and face with sea water but she was barely aware of it, surviving only in a small quiet centre of her consciousness, isolated from her physical surroundings. The ruined clothes and itchy roughened skin were those of a stranger who bore no relation to the perfumed soft creature who luxuriated in comfortable idleness. More dirt, more pain, went unheeded. It would be some time before she would respond to anything.

Her ladies, although fearful of the return journey and their possible reception at Imedagawa, were glad to be rid of this frightening adventure. Older and somewhat tougher than their mistress, they grumbled as they endured the trek northward on the dirty, rickety cart their escort had provided. An irritable but invigorating relationship was struck with their samurai protectors and, propelled by necessity, all but Tamako derived a passable enjoyment from the journey through the barbarous winter landscape.

*

After Tamako had left, Yoshitsuné walked to the small clearing spotted with glowing winter gentian where Shizuka sat preparing clothes for her page's disguise. She greeted her lover warmly. The departure of the other women had left her feeling rather forlorn and lonely and as conditions deteriorated she was beginning to fear for her baby. Yoshitsuné had not had the courage to tell her she too would be sent back to the Capital and she displayed the boy's clothes cheerfully, believing they were a disguise to accompany him to Kyushu. To her irritation her voice faltered when it came to the matter of her hair.

238

'It will have to be cut, my lord. Who will believe in a page trailing hair along the ground.' A strand drooped from her limp fingers. 'It need only be waist length.' She looked shyly at Yoshitsuné. 'Would you cut it yourself, my lord? It is presumptuous of me to ask but the loss of it would be much easier to bear if it were your sword that took it.'

He lifted a heavy handful. Shizuka was justifiably proud of her magnificent hair, a black river flowing down her back to her feet. He would miss it.

'Shizuka, I have been thinking that maybe you should return to the Capital too, just until things are better. Then I can send for you.'

She sat very still, her thoughts in confusion. Part of her longed to return to an organised life, a peaceful existence while she waited for her child – but where could she find a normal life? The best that could be hoped for was months of idleness and seclusion in her mother's house, listening to her mother bewailing her lost opportunities and glories.

Tears trailed down her cheeks. Despising herself for showing such weakness, she asked, 'Are you tired of me, my lord?'

Exasperated, he replied, 'You know how I love you. I kept you here this morning because I could not bear the idea of parting from you. But we are not going to Kyushu. We are fugitives, outlaws, rebels, fleeing my brother's retainers, and few men, if any, will dare help us. I don't want you to suffer. A quiet time in the Capital should see you safe until this is over. Please, don't cry.' He turned away helplessly.

'And my baby?' she wept.

He turned back and looked down at her – why couldn't she understand? He tried once more. 'But that is the reason you must return; immediately, tonight; no, you must rest tonight, but in the morning I will send you back to your mother. The child may be the only good thing left in my life.' He spoke to her urgently, 'I am a samurai and there is no other life for a samurai. I wanted to be a great general to prove myself a hero to my brother – now I wonder how much it matters. No, that is not true. It does matter.

239

Shizuka, if it is a boy raise him as a samurai. Promise me that!'

Shizuka's head drooped gracefully, her slender neck arched in a movement from a dance. 'So, I am to bear your child and then what happens? Suppose Lord Yoritomo hears of it? Yoshitsuné's son will not be welcome even if the mother is a discarded mistress from the lower rank.' She was fighting, harder and surer now. 'Our karma is bound together – let me stay with you and share your future. I will die with you willingly but I am terrified of dying alone in the Rokuhara or Kamakura. Let this child be born in the forest or the mountains and serve his father.'

He knelt down beside her. 'No. I have decided, and when you are calm you will see that I am right.'

Sobbing, she knelt against his chest. Gently he rocked her and his child.

Later he slipped away long enough to appoint the warriors, men from the Capital, to escort Shizuka. They were good swordsmen and although he would have been happier to place her in Yataro's care, these men would be less likely to be recognised.

In the morning Shizuka dressed in page's clothes for the journey, her hair cut and tightly bound. Yoshitsuné gave her a warm fox cloak and bade her a muted farewell. The small resolute figure, flanked by four tall samurai, disappeared into the pines. Shizuka did not look back.

The next to leave was Yukiiye; he had aged a decade and his hands shook even when he grasped the hilt of his sword to still them. The whole scabbard vibrated like a palsied limb.

'I doubt, Yoshitsuné, if we will meet again. Yoritomo has proved a most unnatural nephew but he will pay for it in many lives to come. The Lord Hachiman frowns on bloodshed between relations and his displeasure will fall on Yoritomo, a child of his chosen clan.' The old man sighed. 'We have seen much since we first met in Kiso. Of those eager to carry the white banner of the Minamoto, only one survives unscathed. Your father and Kiso were brave, ruthless men, a little stupid perhaps, not very subtle, but

Yoritomo is ruthless, clever and subtle enough for ten men.'

For a few seconds his tired eyes burned with a fierce light. 'It is up to you to destroy him before he destroys you, Noriyori and me.' The light died and he shook his head. 'The old gods have not approved. They brought down the Taira and now, one by one, they consume the Minamoto. Have you noticed, nephew? We have interfered in their scheme of things. When our clans are a mere whisper of memory the gods will thrive and so will their earthly manifestations on the Throne of Heaven. Yoritomo hopes to control the throne, but he suffers from illusions. Only the gods, the old gods who built these islands in the sea, and their servants, the Imperial family, will endure. Farewell, nephew.'

The old courtier turned and followed by his retainer walked off through the forest. He, too, disappeared into the gloomy pines without a backward glance.

'My lord.'

Yoshitsuné turned to face two of his men, Kaga and Sato, samurai from Oshu, who had fought by his side for five years. Kaga had crossed the Uji river behind him and he had saved the life of Sato at Yashima by killing a Taira warrior as he raised his sword to decapitate the stricken northerner. Neither would meet his eyes now. Kaga, a fierce killer, spoke again in a voice gruff with embarrassment.

'My lord, we wish to speak to you about the future.'

Yoshitsuné looked around the clearing. The large party had dwindled: no chattering groups of women, no elder statesman. Squatting in the sunlight, cleaning their weapons, eyes carefully averted, were five warriors beside Benkei and Yataro who stood talking, and Kisanda, who remained a respectful distance from the samurai. Of the thirty warriors who had accompanied Yoshitsuné from the Capital, only ten stood on the beach of Izumi. Throughout the night men had drifted off into the woods to make their own way to the Capital or Oshu, none with the courage to face their master and tell him of their intention. It was

easier to leave the camp ostensibly to urinate and then hurry away. The two men before him had at least not taken the cowardly way and Yoshitsuné grudgingly respected them for showing more spirit than the others.

'You want your freedom to go? To find another . . .more successful . . .master? All right. Be on your way and take the others.'

Five men in the clearing, hearing his voice deliberately loud, with obvious relief turned away to gather up their weapons. Kaga and Sato remained, misery plain on their tired, battered faces.

'Well?'

Kaga muttered, 'We want you to know that we won't join with Yoritomo. We'll make our way back to Oshu and live on our farms again – if old Hidehira will have us.'

'It seems that peace has come, my lord. The civil war is over now; the Taira are defeated and there is no one else to fight.'

Yoshitsuné replied coldly, 'My cause you obviously regard as hopeless.'

Sato started, aware suddenly of his blunder. Kaga said in a gentle voice, 'Yoritomo has the warlords behind him – Taira and Minamoto. He is stronger than Kiyomori ever was.'

'You think my cause is hopeless?' Yoshitsuné repeated, staring hard at Kaga.

The samurai was a brave man and he looked Yoshitsuné in the eye. 'I think the wisest path is reconciliation with your brother. You are the same blood and you should work together.'

Yoshitsuné nodded. 'The wisest path is not always possible. Yoritomo attempted to have me murdered. Reconciliation is out of the question. I will not die to please my brother.'

Unable to make a satisfactory reply, the men bowed and walked away. Yoshitsuné called after them, 'Wait!' They turned. 'I hold no grudge for this. My fight is no longer yours but you were brave companions in battle. Good luck.'

They bowed and strode off.

Watching the seven men disappear into the woods, he reflected wryly how much Yoritomo would have enjoyed that scene. Where, he asked, was the authority, the charm so praised in the samurai-dokoro and by the poets and balladeers? Charm could not fill an empty stomach or buy horses and swords. How well Yoritomo understood that, and how efficiently he had kept his younger brother without rice lands or farms. 'Well,' he murmured, 'they fought like giants when life was good and they received precious little for it. They are right to ask what kind of lord it is who cannot even reward his followers. I just pray that those assigned to Tamako and Shizuka complete their task before they leave my service.'

Benkei spoke from behind him. 'It is karma. There was nothing more you could do.' Yoshitsuné shrugged and looked at his three retainers, Benkei, Yataro, and Kisanda, the groom.

'We don't make a large army.'

'A samurai sticks by his lord,' said Yataro gruffly, forgetting his own desertion of Hogen.

Yoshitsuné grinned at him. 'These samurai virtues do indeed seem easier to preach than practise. Well, perhaps we are better as we are, starting off all over again, the way we were before we met Yoritomo. Except, of course, now we have young Kisanda. What do you say?'

'If we try for Kyushu now, we're escaping, running. Before us are the Yoshino Mountains and the Zao Gongen monastery, full of monks who are not likely to love my brother and his taxes. Yesterday I would have settled for Kyushu but today I fancy myself at the head of an army of bonzes ready for a last battle with Yoritomo. I told him in Kamakura he would not defeat me and he will not. Shall we continue the fight?'

Benkei leant on his huge sword and grinned. 'A dirty lot, those Yoshino monks – fight like the very devil. With them we can march on Mount Hiei and collect more war-loving priests. Then to the Capital for a last good brawl.'

Yataro slung his sword around his slender waist. 'It

takes a dirty monk to know one. Benkei's word that they are fighting men is good enough for me. Let's go, my muscles ache for battle.'

By noon the men had turned their backs on the sea and Kyushu and were striding through the frozen forest to the snow-bound mountains of Yoshino.

*

Shizuka, huddled in her fox-fur cloak, leant against the door of a small mountain shrine. Through the sacred gate a few yards away she could see a steep path, its snowy surface just visible in the last of the light; soon the gate and the path would be obscured by darkness. Her only companions were the Fox God closed in the sanctuary behind her, and a large grey stone statue of a fox standing in the tiny courtyard before her. The statue had seemed friendly in the sunlight, some comfort against the bleak cold forest, but now, as lengthening shadows flickered around her, she wondered if its spirit were not an evil one – the snout was becoming sharper and the eyes wicked slits. Somewhere a stream dashed on its rocky bed, tempting her deep thirst, but she dared not wander too far from the shrine into the gloomy woods where the wind moaned and wolves prowled.

She had been there most of the afternoon waiting for her escort to return. After hours of wandering through the Yoshino Mountains the men had decided that they must risk the next village for food and horses. Shizuka begged to accompany them but it was felt her presence, even disguised as she was, might be dangerous so they gruffly bade her wait at the little shrine. Seated in the sun, she had been miserable but warm. But now the sun had dropped behind the trees, the wind whipped up the snow on the frozen ground and it was very cold. Shizuka stood and gathered her fox cloak around her. The statue loomed in the last light, seeming to lean forward with a malicious smile on its sharp stone face. Shizuka lurched through the gateway and on to the path. Once free of the shrine she picked her way in the direction the samurai had taken. The trees closed in above the uneven path to create a chill, dark

tunnel. Suddenly she dropped to one knee, a sharp pain shot through her foot and ankle – her straw sandal, the thong broken, rolled away into the rocks. Shizuka wept and any desire to move or help herself rolled away with the sandal.

She lay crumpled on the path until darkness engulfed her and snow began to fall. Finally panic forced her to inch forward, following the only possible route marked by the tall pines on either side. The cloak and her padded clothes, soaked with snow, dragged heavily around her and the sharp, stony ground hurt her unprotected foot.

The lights were at first so irregular that she thought she imagined them, the dull glow of lanterns came and went through the snowy trees like ghost fires, but soon she heard the unmistakable murmur of men's voices broken occasionally by a coarse laugh or a curse. Drawing as far back off the path as she dared she pressed her back against the trunk of a pine soaring into the sky.

A group of men approached, trudging unconcerned through the forest, swearing and grumbling. As they rounded a fall of rocks and bore down on her, the leader raised his lantern to survey the path, light gleaming on his bald head and glossy cape. He swung the lantern from left to right.

'Hurry, lads. Not much more of this miserable forest. Here! What's this? Bring your light up, Genda. Do you see what I see?'

Another lantern was thrust forward. Shizuka crouched in a pool of light.

'Well, well, by Amida. A boy, isn't it? Or is it a girl?'

'In these woods? At night? Hey, you. What are you and what are you doing alone after dark?' The men crowded around her; they gave off a sharp, unwashed stench, even in the cold crisp air. Here and there she caught glimpses of saffron tucked away under thick winter cloaks and all had shaven heads, but each monk was armed and many of the faces peering into hers were dissipated and cruel.

'Did a wolf eat your tongue?' A fist punched her shoulder. Another filthy hand jerked her chin up, holding her face in the light. 'Not bad, eh? Boy or girl, not bad at

all.' The hand drew a few inches away and then slapped her cheek smartly. 'Talk!'

'I ...my name is ...' Her voice faltered. Shizuka swallowed, took a deep breath and whispered, 'My name is Koman. I was on a pilgrimage to the Zao Gongen Temple but became separated from my companions. Please help me to find shelter or direct me to the temple, I beg of you. I am so tired and cold and lost.' Tears rolled down her cheeks.

The first monk looked her up and down. 'A pilgrim? What kind of nonsense is that? Why aren't you dressed like a pilgrim?' He pulled at her furs. 'A pilgrim dressed in the skin of an animal! Disgusting! Don't you know the Lord Buddha tells us not to take life?' He laughed and adjusted his own badger cape. 'No, I think we have a pretty little page here who is fleeing from something and is afraid to tell us what.' The dirty hands ran expertly over Shizuka's body missing nothing, even through the padded tunic. 'It's a girl!' He plunged into the neckline and groped for her breasts, full in pregnancy. Shizuka cowered against the tree, too paralysed with fright to fight back.

'Keep your hands off her, Kenzo. Her father may be rich and he won't pay if the goods are returned soiled. What shall we do? Take her with us?' asked Genda, the young monk with the lantern.

'Why not? It is only a short way. You may be right about a reward from her father.' Kenzo insolently rearranged Shizuka's clothes, grinning at her. 'You are lucky, my dear. My devout mates and I are on our way to the Zao Gongen. You must have missed the turning in the dark, a mile or so back. Can you walk with us?'

'Yes, sir,' she replied quietly.

She had indeed missed the turning; after twenty minutes' walking they came to an avenue of giant cryptomeria trees leading to the vast gateway of the Zao Gongen. The compound straggled over the mountain terrain, the various halls and outbuildings connected by stone paths and stairways weaving through the cryptomerias and rhododendron. Shizuka, exhausted and footsore, dragged herself

up step after step, along the uneven paving stones, badly lit by flickering torches, urged on by Genda at her elbow. Everywhere monks hurried, hundreds, thousands it seemed to the confused girl. She turned to Genda. 'Are all these pilgrims gathered for a festival? There are so many.'

'Pilgrims? Hardly! The word is that Yoshitsuné is in these mountains with his rebels and we plan to hunt him down. We were ordered by our abbot at Watanabe to collect here at Zao Gongen.'

Shizuka stopped, blood pounding in her ears. 'But why should the monks of Zao Gongen turn against Yoshitsuné? He has done nothing to offend your sect.'

'That is what I feel. Come now, hurry. I'll have to leave you in the rest house. No, I don't see why we should turn Yoshitsuné over to the Rokuhara, but Yoritomo is powerful and the local abbots are afraid of him. The Nara temples were razed and monks killed when there was just a rumour that they sympathised with Yorimasa's rebellion. This is an ancient foundation and they don't want it burnt down around their ears by the armies from the eastern plains.'

He pulled Shizuka along a dark narrow alley between thick rhododendron to a small thatched house, shuttered and closed. Sliding open the door he lit her way into a dim room. She could just make out pallets on the floor with several women and old men huddled on them.

'Stay here until morning. We'll see what to do with you then.' He closed the door, leaving the room in blackness. She groped her way to an empty pallet and collapsed, her mind unable to cope with the enormity of her problems. Plans to escape and find Yoshitsuné struggled with hunger until sleep finally came.

When Genda shook her awake daylight was pouring into the room. Three monks in stained and greasy robes stood round her. A fourth, dressed in clean saffron silk, said happily, 'There is no question at all. I saw her dance in the Capital many times. You have had great luck, Genda. This prize will be worth something to the representative of the Rokuhara.'

Shizuka struggled to her feet, looking wildly for a way

out, but her wrists were seized and she was dragged from the hut, along the alley deep with snow, past the rhododendrons hanging heavily under their white load, and into a vast courtyard filled with scurrying monks, most of them armed and wearing breast-plates. Before her was the main Buddha hall of the Zao Gongen – a huge building with colossal wooden pillars and a sweeping roof, the prominent eaves ornately carved and gilded. As she was pulled up the wide shallow steps the temple bell began to boom. Again and again a huge log struck the magnificent bronze cone, sending reverberations through the snow-covered hills. The hall smelt of incense and she could hear the click of rosaries and tapping of prayer drums, a sound once comforting, now sinister. In the holy area, behind richly lacquered altar rails, stood poised a superb gold Shaka triad under a canopy of ebony and gilt, but Shizuka barely saw them in her agony.

Somewhat away from the worshippers stood a tall samurai surrounded by soldiers. Genda pushed Shizuka in front of him. The monk in clean saffron spoke. 'Now, Lord Kajiwara. What do you say to this? The Lord of Kamakura could hardly question the loyalty of the Zao Gongen when the Abbot makes you a present of Shizuka Gozen, concubine to the rebel Yoshitsuné!'

*

Benkei was the first to hear the boom of the Zao Gongen's bell. He paused and held his hand up to halt the others trudging through the snow.

'Listen! We've been in the Yoshino district since dawn and only the Zao Gongen could have such a mighty bell.'

Yoshitsuné stood, head tilted attentively. 'I heard what could have been a bell before dawn but that would be for early prayers. Who are they calling at this time of morning?'

Benkei mused. 'I don't like it. That's no bell to remind farmers to chant a sutra. It's calling monks to arms. Who are they going to fight, I wonder?'

Yataro said, 'Either Yoritomo has sent men to attack the

248

monastery or the monks are looking for us?'

'Hm.' Benkei stared in the direction of the booming sound. 'Zao must be a little way further into the foothills – with the clamour for a guide I can find the compound quickly and look round. You wait here until I return.' Without waiting for an answer he strode off rapidly across the white countryside.

He located Zao easily but skirted the thick wall and climbed up into the hills behind the monastery, finding a good vantage point to look down on the complex of trees, paths and buildings set in the snow. His shrewd eyes located the Buddha hall and he concentrated on that. There was not long to wait. A tall, broad-shouldered samurai followed by monks and soldiers strode down the wide steps to where a palanquin and warhorses stood in the courtyard. Only one horse had a rider, a page bearing a tall standard. The flag snapped and curled in the fresh wind, the crest of cranes and plum branches barely visible. But Benkei did not need the crest; he had already recognised Kajiwara Kagetoki.

He turned and hurried back through the woods, unfortunately not waiting long enough to see a wretched, fainting figure, wrapped in a drooping fox cloak, bundled into the palanquin and carried through the north gate of the compound, towards the Capital.

*

'What an efficient man my brother is! I don't suppose a well-aimed arrow could have sent Kajiwara down the long slope to hell? I would hate to die knowing that creature still breathed.'

'Perhaps I could have killed him, but then I'd have brought the whole rabble down on me and it seemed wiser to warn you. But I too would like to see Kajiwara's life blood melting the snow.'

'How many men were there ...Benkei?' asked Kisanda, still slightly uneasy at addressing his erstwhile masters as peers.

'Eastern samurai, maybe twenty-five or thirty; monks,

about two thousand, not all armed of course, but most were. Yoshino is so sacred that it is riddled with temples full of pugnacious monks and the bell is obviously calling them in from the whole district.'

'Horses?'

'Kajiwara and his bandits are certainly mounted. There was a stable yard filled with horses – perhaps fifty. But I'd wager most of the monks would be on foot.'

'Twenty-five mounted and two thousand foot soldiers will scour the countryside pretty thoroughly,' Yataro said morosely, 'and if the mountains themselves are cut off by snow, that reduces the area they have to search. The passes will be impossible if there's another fall.'

As if to verify this prediction flakes were beginning to float thickly down.

'We will have to separate. There is practically no chance of fighting our way out of it. We will have to make our way separately back to . . . back to where?' Yoshitsuné looked around helplessly. 'Where can we meet safely? If the Yoshino monks have joined in with Kamakura who can I trust?'

Yataro said, 'The immediate problem is to get away from here. The Capital will be the safest place. We can meet at Horikawa – no, that will be watched. Somewhere neutral. A man alone can hide out in the Capital for weeks if he uses his head.'

'Yataro is right,' Benkei said. 'Men can hide easily as long as they are roughly dressed and keep to the west and south. After the rainy season, come each night to the Rashomon Gate. The beggars and rabble will provide a cover and by then we should all know more about the situation around the country. Yoshitsuné, we will make for Mount Hiei. That's our best chance now. Since you and I are the most notorious and noticeable of the band we might as well brazen it out together.'

'No, let us all stay together,' Yataro pleaded. 'Four men can fight better than two. If we split up, who knows what will happen?'

Yoshitsuné looked at Benkei. The big monk shrugged.

'We got to Oshu all right – how long ago was that? But it's different now, Yataro. They'll be looking for the tracks of a large party because it would never occur to them there would be only four of us left.' He snorted. 'Even then, four men are more noticeable than two. I think we must split up.'

Yoshitsuné nodded unhappily and Yataro sighed. 'Kisanda and I will go together – how about it, groom? – and then separate later.' He turned to Yoshitsuné. 'You've come a long way since Oni-ichi Hogen and we've all changed. I'll miss you.'

Yoshitsuné embraced him quickly. 'May your karma prosper better without me, my old friend.'

'I'll see you at the Rashomon Gate,' Yataro said, and hastily turned away. Kisanda bowed low but Yoshitsuné clapped him on the shoulder. 'Good luck, Kisanda the groom. You've served me better in hardship than many men did in glory.'

Benkei nudged him impatiently. 'Come. This is no time for speeches.' The others paused only long enough to watch the two men fade into the white flurries and then they too went their way through the winter afternoon.

The bell of Zao Gongen boomed on.

*

The Cloistered Emperor drew his robes closer about his shoulders, deep purple brocade accentuating the drawn pallor of his old man's face. He shivered and testily pushed a cloisonné dish of sweetmeats away. Glancing around the room at the decorously kneeling attendants, all samurai, he called out in a voice scratchy with irritation, 'Tametoki, where are you? Come here immediately!'

Around the room the heads of the waiting attendants snapped up, significant looks were exchanged. A rough-hewn man whose silk court robe sat uneasily on square shoulders rose and approached Go-Shirakawa.

'Your Highness, may I have the honour of serving you?'

'No, you may not! Where is Tametoki? He has been adequate for forty years. We do not need you.'

The man knelt and touched his forehead to the floor. 'We are here to serve Your Highness. It is our privilege to be seconded from Lord Yoritomo's household to the Cloister Court. May I fetch some wine for Your Highness?'

'No. Here is Tametoki at last. Go back to your corner.' With a curt bow the warrior moved away. Tametoki scurried across the floor and creaked to his old knees before his master.

'Where have you been? We have been calling for you.' Go-Shirakawa lowered his voice and continued querulously, 'We will not be attended by these uncouth samurai. Why doesn't Yoritomo take them away and let us have our own people? There is only you, Tametoki, and you must not desert your post.'

Tametoki murmured, 'My deepest apologies. I was called to the Reception Hall. Lord Kanezane, the Regent, requests an audience with Your Highness.'

'Well, we will not see him. We want to see our old friends. We want to exchange poems with courtiers, not sit alone, surrounded by samurai!'

Tametoki said patiently, speaking to the Cloistered Emperor as though to a child, 'Your Highness, the guard placed by Yoritomo will allow only certain visitors into the Palace. Everyone is kept out but the representatives of Kamakura and Lord Kanezane.' He peered nervously behind him at the kneeling attendants, all with sharp eyes and strained ears.

The Cloistered Emperor stared at his servant with wide, terrified eyes. A pale emaciated hand darted from the pile of purple brocade and clutched at Tametoki. 'What should we do? Oh, we are so vexed. It has all gone wrong. Get rid of these men! We will not talk to Kanezane. He is a nobleman, at least, but he represents that barbarian, Yoritomo, who will not even take a civilised title for himself. The Lord of Kamakura!'

Tametoki leant nearer to his master. 'Your Highness, may I be permitted to speak frankly?' He shuffled slightly closer to the Imperial cushions. Go-Shirakawa eyed him uneasily but nodded. 'Lord Kanezane is the only hope of

the Cloister Court. He alone has managed to disperse some of Yoritomo's anger against – against Your Highness.'

Go-Shirakawa interrupted. 'Yoritomo's behaviour was unforgivable. He inferred that we were responsible for that shocking attempt of Yoshitsuné to force an Imperial mandate from the Cloister Court. And Yoshitsuné was supposed to be captured and killed. Why was he not? Where is he? Because of him we have given Yoritomo authority to levy taxes on rice and to place his own appointees as military constables in all the provinces. His puppets are serving as ministers of the Court – incredible powers for a mere samurai – and all to capture his own brother who is supposed to be fomenting rebellion. We have heard of no rebellion! And then Yoritomo will not even call himself Lord Chancellor, or Minister of the Right, but he wants to be made Shogun! Well, we will not make that mistake again – no more Shoguns! Kiso was the last.' He shuddered at the memory.

Tametoki gently brought him back to the point. 'Your Highness, Lord Kanezane is a wise man of undisputed integrity and a loyal servant of the throne. He alone can ensure that the wishes and opinions of the Cloister Court are heard in Kamakura. Forgive me, Your Highness, for speaking so boldly.'

Go-Shirakawa shook his head. The sagging dewlaps of his once plump throat quivered. 'What you mean, our loyal old friend, is that by granting Yoritomo the right to collect taxes, appoint provincial officials and decide the most important ministers of the Court, we may be allowed to retire to a life of peace, of sutras and meagre meals. You believe Lord Kanezane can assure that peace.'

'I believe that Lord Kanezane is the key, my lord.'

'Oh, yes, yes. Very well, we will see him now. Call him in. But first bring that brazier closer. And we want some tea.' The shrivelled figure shrank further into the purple robes. 'We miss our old friends and we have lost our taste for rich food.'

*

The samurai and monks searching the mountains south of the Capital did not find Yoshitsuné – the fugitives vanished into the pines and snow-drifts – but the easterners did discover a prize almost as great in a lonely temple. Minamoto Yukiiye had only a few monks and one warrior with him who, nearly as ancient and tired as himself, gave no resistance. The burly minions of the Lord of Kamakura hustled the old men out into the snow, struck their heads from their shoulders and kicked the corpses into a ditch. Yukiiye's head, lips drawn back in a death grimace from tiny white teeth, was wrapped in strips of cloth for the long journey to Kamakura. Only the smoking ruins of the fired temple and the blood-streaked snow indicated where Yoritomo's uncle had spent the last weeks of his futile life.

*

The arrival of Shizuka Gozen in Kamakura brought Yoritomo an irritating problem. The dancer obviously knew nothing about her lover's whereabouts so whether she lived or died seemed unimportant to him, but the Lady Masako wanted her dead. 'The child she carries will be a rival to your sons. We cannot afford to let them live.'

Tokimasa, however, disagreed with his daughter; to murder a shrine dancer, a mere woman, would be unpopular and appear cowardly. Besides, her presence in a lonely convent might lure Yoshitsuné into a trap. Tokimasa pressed his arguments in the daytime, Masako insinuated hers all night, and Yoritomo was soon tired of the whole business.

His one interview with Shizuka, heavily pregnant, was unhelpful. Kneeling, head lowered, she refused to say a word. Disgusted, he stamped out of the room and would not discuss the problem for several weeks, despite the honeysweet hissings of Lady Masako in his ear. Finally Masako took matters in her own hands and sent one of her servants to Shizuka's room to dispatch her, but the man was discovered and Yoritomo, irritated with his wife, decided to let the dancer live, although he agreed that the

child, if a boy, should certainly die. Somewhat mollified, Masako subsided.

To await the birth Shizuka was placed in the Kamakura household of Lord Toji, an elderly samurai who remembered Yoshitsuné with a warmth that was not cancelled by rumours of his treason. The principal wing of his mansion was devoted to Shizuka, displacing his own wife and children, but when Lady Toji complained at this the old man muttered, 'Who knows? She is Yoshitsuné's favourite. He may not always be in disgrace and if he returns to power he will be pleased we helped her. Yoritomo doesn't seem to be anxious to hunt him down any more. Let us just wait and see what happens.'

The birth was easy. Months of hardship had toughened Shizuka and made pain an everyday affair. She enjoyed the warm sensuous explosion of pleasure as the baby rushed from security to a world inhabited by enemies, but when she opened her eyes and looked at Lady Toji, the old woman's face told her everything. Shizuka turned away. It was a son and he would have to die; why learn to love him?

Told the news, Yoritomo gave the expected orders. He too had no curiosity about a doomed infant.

The same evening a samurai arrived at Toji's house, received the small whimpering parcel of white silk without comment and rode off towards the beach. As the horse's hooves thudded away on the beaten earth of the courtyard Shizuka began to shriek. Lady Toji strove to comfort her, but she thrust the older woman aside and struggled up from the bed.

'If he must die, let me at least have his body. Prayers must be said. He must be buried properly. Yoritomo will not stop his pure soul from entering the Western Paradise.' She fought fiercely against the attendants.

Lady Toji was essentially a sympathetic woman. She had not wanted the responsibility for Shizuka but she had become fond of the unfortunate girl and besides, she had lost infants herself and understood the heartbreak of bearing a child to have it die. After soothing Shizuka as best she could, the samurai's wife put on a plain cotton

outer robe over her silk and drew a long scarf around her hair and face. Accompanied by two menservants she followed the tracks of the horse. The beach was deserted, except for children playing; the sea sparkled and the white sands stretched out in the late afternoon sun. It seemed much too peaceful a place for the murder of an innocent baby, but the children said yes, they had seen a mounted samurai toss something into the pines straggling along the beach.

They found the corpse still warm on a pile of dead pine boughs and carried it back to its mother. Shizuka, rage and passion exhausted, watched silently as Yoshitsuné's son was washed, placed in a tiny coffin, blessed and carried away to a corner of an adjoining temple to be buried under a paulownia tree in the velvety blackness of a summer night. The tree was in full bloom, a little past its best, and when the first streaks of dawn fell across the grave, the newly turned soil was covered with a blanket of fallen blossom, frail indigo bells.

*

Lake Biwa lay still and glassy in the hot sun, the reeds motionless in the heavy air. Hori Yataro waded into the shallows to splash his face with warm water. Pulling a pickled plum from his sleeve, he chewed it slowly, savouring the tartness. The lakeside was deserted except for fluttering dragonflies and cicadas humming relentlessly in the heat. The steady buzz of insects made him sleepy. Even when he served Oni-ichi Hogen he would take the time to stretch out and doze on a day like this, but now he was afraid to relax. Only an hour earlier he had stopped to beg food from a surly farmer's wife. The woman had stopped scratching among her vegetables to fetch him a bowl of cold aubergine stewed in bean paste, watching him suspiciously as he wolfed the food and grabbing the bowl from him before he had swallowed the last morsel.

'Now, get away from here, samurai. If you were in the service of Naganuma Goro you wouldn't be in rags as you are. Or begging food. So you must be one of the rebels.'

Her narrow black eyes glinted from her weathered face. 'Naganuma Goro is our lord and he is sworn to capture all Yoshitsuné's outlaws, so if he catches you, don't say who gave you food. I would never have given you a scrap if you hadn't had a sword and a mean face. Now, get out.' She called up a huge yellow dog that growled at Yataro's heels as he left the wretched farmyard.

Naganuma Goro was a fierce partisan of Kamakura, and Yatàro had not intended to pass through his district, but he frequently became lost among the trees and fields; the vegetable patches and paddies all looked alike. Kisanda had gone on to the Capital but he had stayed by Lake Biwa; he loved the water and the reeds and the thick clumps of bamboo rustling and whistling in the slightest snatch of breeze. The place reminded him of a happier, carefree time when he, Yoshitsuné and Benkei had fled the Capital for the north and a new life. Now he was tired and dusty but this evening, using the stars and the great bulk of Mount Hiei as a guide, he planned to circle the city and approach the Rashomon Gate. The rainy season had been unusually short and the summer heat had come quickly on the western plain. It must be time to meet the others.

But he wanted to rest before his journey. The bamboos were impossibly dense, but a little way back from the lakeside were thickets of bush clover, a sweet-smelling secluded bed to sleep in with only insects and lizards to worry about.

The first samurai appeared as he was walking back along the wide stream towards his chosen hiding place. First one, then two, three, four horsemen rode up to the opposite bank of the stream.

'There! That is the man the old woman was talking about. Stop, you! Explain yourself!'

Yataro quickly summed up his position. The samurai had the crest of Naganuma Goro on their corselets. They had only to ford the stream to be on him. The lake? Too far, and he could not outswim the horses. The thickets? A better chance. He was fast on his feet and once he was hidden in them a horse could not follow. The decision took

a split second and then he ran as fast as he could. The horses splashed through the stream and thundered down on him but Yataro managed to reach the thickets, draw his sword and with his back protected by the dense shrubs, face the first horseman. He struck the horse's chest, forcing the samurai to leap off his rearing mount.

Yataro's wide mouth twisted into a grim smile. 'This is Hori Yataro. I hope you are a worthy opponent to send to hell.' Before the man could answer, Yataro slashed out. The steel blades hissed in the still afternoon. Yataro brought the first man down quickly, driving his sword under the corselet into the soldier's belly.

Two more dismounted samurai faced him. One dying, two before him, where was the fourth? With no time to find out, he met the second warrior full on as the other jockeyed for an opening. Gradually Yataro was drawn away from his hedge, slashing and jabbing at the men. One staggered backward, blood spurting from his head, an ear cleanly sliced off. As Yataro wheeled to take on the third man he realised too late that his back was exposed. The horseman loomed up behind him, his sword sweeping down on Yataro's unprotected neck, severing the artery. Hori Yataro toppled forward, a fountain of blood, dead before he hit the ground.

The horseman wiped spattered blood from his face and looked down on his handiwork. 'It's sure to have been one of Yoshitsuné's men. Better take his head back to Naganuma. Is Kubo finished?' He gestured to the second samurai, moaning in a crimson pool and rocking his gushing head in his hands.

The third warrior said, 'That was no honourable way to kill a good swordsman. Were you afraid of him in a fair fight?'

The horseman spat on Yataro's corpse. 'What difference does it make? He was only a traitor. Take his head. I want to get back. Naganuma will be pleased with this. What does he care about fair fights?'

*

In late summer Shizuka returned to the Capital, to a convent in the eastern suburbs. Her head was shaved and her threadbare robes exchanged for the dull grey of a novice. Zenji, her mother, was summoned and they met briefly in Shizuka's tiny cell, but there was little to discuss. The old dancer bewailed her lonely life, scraping a meagre existence as a teacher of dance to those willing to be taught by the mother of a rebel's concubine. Shizuka had had nothing to say to anyone since the death of her son. She sat quietly, hands in her lap, naked head bowed, only waiting for Zenji to leave.

A few days later she lay down on her straw pallet and did not get up again. She was wracked by a high fever. For a while the hallucinations it produced excited some passion in her – distorted visions of the past left her weeping or screaming in futile rage. But the fever subsided, just as her dancing had ceased, her lover had deserted her and her son had died, and Shizuka turned her face to the crude pine wall of her cell, listlessly repeated the name of Amida Buddha and died.

She was nineteen.

10. The Return to the North

The vegetable seller looked tired and hot sitting on a stone by an unkempt hedge and wiping his sunburnt face on a greasy forearm. The mountain vegetables in his panniers were wilting in the heat. He eyed a foot-soldier squatting beside a gate in the hedge; the soldier carried a bow and a dirk, and a halberd rested against the hedge.

'What a lot of weapons you've got on you! What are you expecting? A war?' The pedlar chortled at his own wit but the soldier, unamused, yawned and drew patterns in the dust with his dirk. 'Here, you! Not very friendly are you? It was just a little joke. I heard tell the Capital was all quiet now – otherwise I'd have stayed in Kurama.' The pedlar scratched himself. 'I don't want to get mixed up in any fighting.'

'You won't,' said the soldier shortly.

'Oh, you *can* talk! Well, what are you carrying that armoury for then, eh?'

'I'm on guard duty, fool!'

'Guard duty? Here in Imedagawa? What are you guarding? A few rats and foxes?' The pedlar gestured at the derelict house behind them. The hedge, overgrown with creepers and briars, lay like a huge prickly caterpillar in the sun. Beyond, the mansion itself was crumbling. One wing was only a heap of wattle and thatch and the rest of the house was little better; veranda boards were broken and sliding doors tilted drunkenly off their runners, the sagging roof sprouted weeds and sprawling untrimmed shrubs drooped over a brackish pond in the garden.

'No one lives in there, do they?' asked the pedlar.

'Someone does. Taira Tokida lived here once but now he's dead and his daughter remains. Even where you come from you must have heard of *that* family?'

The vendor scratched his head and then an armpit.

'Can't say I have. Was he one of the Taira lords that used to rule in the Capital?'

'He was an official at Court, I think. Of course, he's dead now, but anyway it's his daughter that's important to us. She married the rebel, Yoshitsuné.' The soldier spat. 'But he sent her back here and so we keep watch in case he tries to visit her. Mind you, we don't watch all that hard any more. Been nine months or so since he's been seen.'

The pedlar smiled, his weathered face softening. 'I remember Yoshitsuné when he was just a boy at Kurama Temple. Used to sell my vegetables there when he was just a little lad; white skin, black hair, always wore silks.' He examined his own dirt-encrusted nails and hoisted up the stained loin cloth. 'Yes, dressed like a little prince and smelt lovely. Been on the run for a long time – guess he don't look nice or smell nice now. But he was quite a hero in his day.'

'Don't need heroes any more. We have peace.' Seeing the pedlar glance at his weapons, the soldier added irritably, 'Well, we'd have peace if this Yoshitsuné could be caught. Then I could go back to my farm.'

The pedlar scratched himself vigorously again. 'Well, listen, general, it's getting late and these greens have got to be sold. If there's gentry living in there – even poor gentry has to eat – let me go in and sell this lot off. Then I can get back to Kurama before dark, eh? Don't like the city after dark nor the roads neither, come to that. Dangerous.'

The soldier growled, 'Don't need heroes and the roads ain't dangerous. We cleaned the bandits out. There's samurai in charge now and things work better. Least, that's what they tell us at the Rokuhara.'

'What a dull world – no heroes, no bandits. Anyway, let me unload this lot and then I can get on my way.'

The soldier yawned. 'Yes, go ahead. But there's only her and a few maids. Everyone else is dead or gone off. Ghosts don't eat.'

The pedlar got up. 'Thanks. Don't want to take anything back to the mountains. Don't know what made me wander into this part of the Capital anyway.'

He pushed open the rickety gate and went into the garden, picking his way carefully over the roots and dead plants, and hailed the house. A maid rolled up a splintered reed blind and peered out. The pedlar was on the veranda now, a quick glance told him the soldier was dozing; he dropped his basket and whispered to the maid, 'Show me to your lady. It is her husband who wishes to speak to her.'

The girl gaped and then, pulling herself together, said loudly, 'Oh, bring the basket in. No doubt my mistress will want to look over the vegetables herself. A little tired, aren't they? They'll be cheap, I suppose.'

The empty house smelt of mould and decay but the girl led Yoshitsuné to a small sunny room looking on to an inner courtyard pretty with well-kept shrubs. Although Tamako was partly hidden by a pair of patched and ragged screens Yoshitsuné could see that she had kept her beauty. Naturally startled when her maid entered with a pedlar, a clear pink flushed her pale face and accentuated her exquisite colouring. Yoshitsuné noticed, however, that she was not as horrified by a strange man's intrusion as a girl would be whose life had been peaceful; it was clear that Tamako had recovered from her brief exile, and that the experience had toughened her.

'Who is this man, Oharu? Have you gone mad, bringing a vegetable seller into the house?' The sweet voice had a new firmness.

Oharu bowed. 'My lady, it is Lord Yoshitsuné.'

Tamako had not entirely changed. Her eyelids fluttered and her complexion drained. After a few moments, however, she recovered and dismissed the maid. Then she gazed at her husband in fascination. 'Is this what exile and flight have done to you, my lord? Your skin is so brown, almost black. And your beautiful silky hair! Where is it? How you have changed!'

Yoshitsuné laughed. 'The colour is from the sun and from staining and will wear away. My hair is all there, just bound up tight under the scarf, but even when you see me in fine clothes again it will be a shock, I fear. Gone forever is the man of powder and perfume. I am now a fugitive.

And you,' he stroked her pale cheeks, 'how have you fared? I see this mansion is nearly as decayed as the one at Horikawa.'

'Oh, my lord, my parents died, one after the other, and one of my sisters is also dead. The others and my brothers have gone elsewhere. I have disgraced my family and they will have nothing to do with me.' She grasped his brown hand in hers. 'Please do not leave me here. Whatever fate you ask me to share cannot be worse than this living death, watched day and night by Yoritomo's guard.'

He looked at her intently. 'Would you come to Oshu with me? On foot? Disguised as a boy? We would dress as yamabushi, nomadic monks, since they can go anywhere. Benkei, Kisanda, you and me.'

'Where . . .?'

'Dead or gone away. I don't blame the ones who deserted; being the retainers of Yoshitsuné made outlaws of them when they should have been treated as heroes. Yataro is dead, killed by one of Yoritomo's men near Biwa and his head stuck on the Rokuhara gate. Benkei saw it but I couldn't . . .' His voice broke and for a few seconds they sat in silence. Then he looked up. 'Shizuka is dead too. And her son. They captured her and took her to Kamakura.' He laughed bitterly. 'Oh, my brother runs a very efficient organisation; I found that out travelling around the country over the last few months. He has offered the samurai a chance to be respectable, to have some power, to become rich, and they love it. Even Miura and Wada, who hate Yoritomo, even Noriyori and the Taira lords won't disobey Yoritomo to help me. Not even Doi – for a good fight and the booty – would take on the samurai-dokoro.' He took Tamako's hand and turned it over in his own. 'Maybe the Oshu Fujiwara won't either. It's a risk that we are taking.'

'The Court, the Cloistered Emperor?' she asked.

'Go-Shirakawa is a sad, drivelling old man, exhausted by his intrigues. He eats, sleeps and dreams of death. His only passion is to keep Yoritomo from being Shogun while he lives. The Regent keeps the peace between the Court

and Kamakura, but no one would help a rebel.' He laughed again. 'Even Mount Hiei ... Benkei and I stayed there a few weeks but eventually ... Yoritomo threatened to revoke any temple's immunity from civil law if it sheltered us. You don't understand that, I know, but the point is it was time to move on. You see, it's a matter of risking Hidehira's charity, or having a stained face for the rest of my life. While there is one more chance I intend to try it. If that doesn't work ... we'll see.'

She remained silent, deep in thought. Finally she smiled at her husband. 'Life as a page to nomadic monks could not be more dreary than life in this collapsing house. I accompanied you to Kyushu when I was young and my parents suffered as a result, forced to bear slander and rejection by the Court, but now my brothers have cast me out of the family. Soon there will be nothing to eat and the maids will leave me as the menservants have already done – only Oharu remains faithful. But I am stronger, much stronger than a year ago. Although I may be a burden, let me come with you. In Hiraizumi we will make fine sons to avenge us both. Now, what preparations should I make?'

Yoshitsuné remembered another time, when this house was rich and safe. Birds sang in cages of gilded bamboo, silk-wrapped women giggled behind lacquered fans. When he had asked Tamako to forsake it all and go to Kyushu to provide him with a son, she had fluttered and wept and swooned and had needed her attendants to do her very breathing – a mere child bearing a woman's burden of exile. But then there had been a future. Now ... He marvelled at how much stronger she had become.

'Is the guard here at night?'

'Yes, but he sleeps, I am sure. Anyway the hedge is so broken at the back, by the stream, that you can easily come in after dark.' Her eyes glowed with excitement.

'Benkei and Kisanda have assembled yamabushi clothes at the Horikawa mansion. Well, we have played every other part in the last year or so,' he added grimly. 'We shall come for you very late. We can follow the Imeda River out of the

Capital; there are few people around at night in this isolated area.'

He stroked her glossy hair. 'You say you can trust Oharu. Get her to cut your hair – I'm sorry, but it must be done – and bind it up under a boy's cap. Have you suitable clothes for a page? And sandals for walking?'

She pondered. 'Of course, I have sold most of the fine clothes in the house but there are a few of my brothers' things. Oharu can stay in the house and that will deceive that fool of a soldier for a few days.'

'When you hear the call of a nightingale it will be me. Be ready, Tamako.'

He left his vegetables behind and went out through the gate. The guard was slumped against the hedge, mouth gaping, fast asleep. Yoshitsuné spat and, hoisting his empty basket on to his back, shuffled off through the city.

*

The huge cypress gate of the Horikawa mansion, smashed by Tosabo's rams, swung loose, and Rokuhara guards patrolled the broken-down walls, occasionally searching the grounds, but it was an easy matter to evade them. After the destruction and strife of the past few years, many of the great houses were occupied by beggars or wild animals, so the guards hardly noticed the three tramps in rags. The mansion itself was a charred ruin, only the stables and a few of the outbuildings had survived – and the water pavilion still rose gracefully over the lake, singed but beautiful, red lacquered railings elegant in the sun.

Avoiding the stables as the obvious place to hide, Yoshitsuné shared a small granary with a ferocious mother cat and her kittens. Otherwise it was empty – looters had efficiently removed anything saleable or edible.

Yoshitsuné met the others in an overgrown part of the garden. Benkei, much thinner, was already a convincing yamabushi; his grown hair was bound up under the black cap favoured by wandering ascetics and he wore a soiled white robe hitched up over blue leggings. For the moment Kisanda wore the tattered smock of a beggar while

Yoshitsuné passed as a rural pedlar. Kisanda, the former groom, and Benkei, the renegade monk, had been quite convincing in their roles as beggars, but Yoshitsuné found it a constant effort to disguise his samurai carriage, the unmistakable hauteur of a proud warrior. He slouched and scratched to make himself believable but now it would be a great relief to dress and act as a yamabushi, a man who at least had some dignity and who accepted no authority but that of the Lord Buddha.

There had been considerable tension over Yoshitsuné's decision to take Tamako; a woman was slow, a burden at the best of times, and her disintegration on the ship was well remembered. Benkei did understand, however, that his master had to have sons and that Yoshitsuné, after a year of wandering loneliness, craved the warm security of women around him. Just the same, the monk was relieved to hear that Tamako had matured and might make a reasonably sensible travelling companion.

They ate some rice balls and dried fish and after dark swam in the lake to wash themselves; then each man bound up his damp hair and tucked it under a black cap. There were simple but respectable robes and a dirk, prayer beads and a rolled copy of the Lotus Sutra for each; Benkei had a sword and a ceremonial conch shell since, as the only one with a plausible knowledge of doctrine, he was the official leader. But Kisanda carried a pannier on his back in which were not the paraphernalia of yamabushi but the swords of samurai – if discovered they could at least fight. Yoshitsuné had reluctantly turned the Hachiman sword, a far too famous weapon not to be dangerous if it were recognised, over to Kisanda's care. He did wear Hidehira's dagger but he had never used it and each time he touched it the slight frisson of fear shivered down his spine. But it must return to Oshu with him – that he understood.

He left the others for a few moments and wandered over to the water pavilion. The moon gleamed on the once polished floors where Shizuka had danced. Her death and that of Yataro depressed him deeply – his life had caused nothing but pain to those he loved. Abandoning Shizuka

had been a tragic experience and her death bore heavily on him. Benkei had claimed that she was only a female and not important, but he had loved her and like Tamako and Asuka, she had been his responsibility. If he deserted Tamako now, or encouraged her to kill herself, by what privilege did he continue his own existence? His lord and his family had rejected him. His only position in this life was as a master and friend to these men and protector of his wife. If he forsook these obligations he would continue to breathe, eat and sleep but his spirit, the whole essence of his existence, would be a vacuum. To cling to such a life was moral cowardice, rightly condemned in his world. But he did not wish to die yet. Even in his deepest depression in the last fruitless year he had believed that the wheel must turn again in his favour. Oshu and Hidehira were his last chance, and he could not abandon hope in the ever changing pattern of life. Death by his own hand, at this moment, was to admit to a defeat he still did not accept. Others – samurai – might call him a coward, but he was not afraid of death. He had been close to it many times, risked it so often in battle. He had never feared that kind of death at all. But to die alone, by his own hand – to give Yoritomo that victory – he shuddered. Was that the samurai way? Was that what Yorimasa would advise? Hidehira? But he was the chosen of Hachiman. The god had spoken to him. To die in dishonour would be a betrayal of the god. He stared at the water, listening to the last insects murmuring. No, not yet. But watching the moonlight play on the lake he knew he would never see the Horikawa mansion again.

*

A dull light showed through the broken shutters of the Imedagawa mansion. Yoshitsuné gave the fluted call of a nightingale, a door slid open, a shadow briefly blocked out the glow and then Tamako joined him.

'My lord, I am ready. There is only a small bundle, one I can carry myself. All the women but Oharu have left. She will keep the house looking occupied.'

She stood before him, a tiny figure in boy's clothes and straw sandals, her hair concealed under a black cap and wearing the make-up of a young page. She had cleverly placed a wooden sword and a flute in her sash; although Tamako could use neither a page would certainly carry both.

'You are ready, Tamako? You have thought it over carefully? The journey will be long and dangerous.' As he spoke he took her hand and pressed it, a gesture belying the generosity of his words.

'No, my lord. I have decided. I must come with you. No one will suspect a page of being the daughter of a disgraced noble and the wife of a rebel. For a little while there will be no past and no future, only existence, day by day, with you. I shall be slow, at least at first; I have seldom walked on anything but floors and garden paths, but if you have patience I shall become as strong as the boy I imitate.' She smiled at him. 'Wait and see. But if I cannot do it, leave me in a convent and I shall become a nun.'

'Then we must hurry, my love, if we are to join the others and clear the Capital by dawn.'

'I am ready, my lord. When I cast aside my woman's kimono tonight the sleeves were wet with tears, but now I am ready.'

Touched, Yoshitsuné embraced her, holding the small, slim body in his arms. Her hair tucked up under the cap gave off a sudden strong fragrance of almond blossom. For a second he forgot Tamako: she became Asuka and, shivering, he pushed the ghost away. Not another innocent death! Startled, Tamako gazed up at him, confusion and hurt in her eyes.

'Shall I go back to the house?' she asked quietly.

'No.' He stroked her smooth cheek. 'It is just that there you might be safe. If you go with me ...'

'My karma lies with yours,' she whispered.

Yoshitsuné looked down at her and knew she was right. Her life was already tied to his. It was too late to reconsider. 'Come,' he said. 'We must meet the others.'

They passed through the gap in the hedge and followed

the Imedagawa River to the city boundary. There were no walls – so much of the Capital's turmoil had been caused internally that it was considered pointless to maintain expensive defences to contain trouble; ditches, filled with rubble, made effective barriers, certainly for poor Tamako who cut herself badly scrambling over them in the dark. There were no guards and they speedily met Benkei and Kisanda who greeted Tamako politely, firmly ignoring her obvious fatigue.

'We have to reach Lake Biwa by dawn,' commanded Benkei, striding out. Yoshitsuné supported Tamako and urged her gently along the road. Her tender feet were swollen and bleeding already and from the weight on his arm he knew she was near collapse.

By sunrise they had reached only the eastern edge of the Capital and Tamako could go no further. The long miles to Lake Biwa and the ferry crossing were out of the question until she had rested. A young page, half carried by yamabushi, made a bizarre sight on the quickly filling highway. Reluctantly the men led their burden to a secluded grove and eased her to the ground. Kisanda bound up her bruised and battered feet while Benkei fumed.

'It's ridiculous. This will endanger us all. She'll die of exposure and exhaustion before we reach Kaga, let alone Hiraizumi.'

'There must be some way we can help her. Her feet have never been used to anything but a short walk on a smooth floor,' said Yoshitsuné.

'Please, gentlemen, I know that I am a nuisance, but let us rest for a while and we can continue on our way. Look, these bandages will protect my feet and help me bear the stones.'

Pleading, Tamako thrust out a pathetic pair of bound feet, blood already soaking the crude wrappings. 'Just a few minutes. Please, please do not send me back to the Capital. I cannot bear to be abandoned now. I have no one but my lord Yoshitsuné. Let me at least die with him. But if you will not take me then stab me quickly and leave me

here, under the trees.' Tears streamed down her face leaving two tracks through the grime-blurred powder.

Sheepishly, Benkei turned away. Yoshitsuné sat alone, his head in his hands, not wanting to be separated now from the men who had suffered so much, yet not able to desert the girl.

Benkei tapped him on the shoulder and nodded toward Tamako. 'All right, we walk slowly,' he said decisively. Yoshitsuné relaxed as the monk resumed control. 'While her ladyship rests we had better plan our journey and tell her what to do. Now obviously we cannot use our names, so I have chosen rather priestly ones.' He bowed to Tamako. 'I am at your service, madam. Arasanuki, formerly a priest in the Abbot's quarters of Haguro Temple, unless we meet monks from Haguro in which case I was in the Abbot's quarters at Kurama Temple. I am the leader of this little band because I can recite more of the Lotus Sutra than anyone else. Kisanda is our porter and his religious name is Kazuabo. Yoshitsuné is to be called Yamatobo. He will attract less attention if he is just an average wandering ascetic with no aristocratic blood. We are all Haguro monks returning north after a pilgrimage. Now what name shall we give to the Lady Tamako?'

Yoshitsuné, relieved that the crisis was over, volunteered, 'Perhaps something with a provincial touch – would Shimotsukebo do? Tamako, do you like it? Could you remember a name like Shimotsukebo?'

'With my family I once visited the Shimotsuke temple, but of course I could not talk about the province. I hardly know where it is.'

Benkei said briskly, 'It has lots of mountains and rivers and you were taken to Haguro when you were only three. That will do. We are going to travel the Hokuriku route because the road is frequented by yamabushi and because the other highways lie entirely in provinces controlled by Yoritomo. In the west we may find a little help and besides we can travel some of the way by sea. But never drop your disguise for a moment, even if you think we are safe with the enemies of Kamakura. No one can be completely

270

trusted. Now, how do you feel, Shimotsukebo? Could you travel a bit?'

Tamako tottered bravely to her feet and smiled. It was not a very convincing performance but the others chose to take it at face value and the party set off along the highway, Benkei in front, an impressive figure, Yoshitsuné and Kisanda trailing behind giving discreet assistance and encouragement to the small, frail page leaning heavily on a makeshift staff.

The highway from the Capital to Lake Biwa was filled with traffic of all sorts moving at varying speeds. Farmers in coarse-spun kimono and sedge hats with loaded baskets of produce to sell in the city hurried past country craftsmen pulling handcarts piled with clay pots, iron utensils or baskets and mats woven from the reeds of Lake Biwa. A fish merchant with his cart of lake trout, odorous in the early warmth of the sun, passed a group of monks chatting and laughing, ignoring a solemn party of pilgrims led by a lady of some importance in a closed palanquin and accompanied by servants barefooted and simply dressed. An ox-cart jolted along with several aristocrats screened from vulgar eyes by a hanging frame of curtains, presumably bent on viewing some of the beauty spots on Lake Biwa. A mounted samurai, bolt upright on his precious horse, contrasted with ragged foot soldiers straggling north in search of a bellicose master to serve in these times of temporary peace. The inevitable beggars, blind, crippled, diseased, wove relentlessly through the crowds, plaguing any likely travellers for alms.

Scattered along the broad roadway were small inns and tea houses where men could pause for a rest, refreshment, or a brief dalliance with a maid or country courtesan. Tamako gazed longingly at them sprawled in open rooms, drinking saké and resting their tired limbs and feet. Hers were numb and they left bloody tracks in the dust. The harsh straw of her sandals aggravated the tender soles and the hard sun hurt her eyes, used to the dim light of shuttered rooms. The sun beat down on her useless cap and she longed for a wide sedge brim to protect her head. They

passed a vendor hawking hats, sandals and rolled sleeping mats and she confided her need to Yoshitsuné.

'I don't know. Yamabushi don't carry any money but I'll consult Benkei and see what he says.'

Benkei grumbled that it would be very unorthodox for holy men to purchase something on the road but just this once they might try to get it free. He marched up to the vendor, a hard-eyed pot-bellied little man and boomed, 'My good tradesman, this is your chance to set out on the path of enlightenment. Our page, a pretty but somewhat silly boy, left his hat at last night's stopping place and he needs a new one. We will pray for you tonight at Sekidera Temple and your soul will, no doubt, feel instant peace. What an opportunity! That one there over your arm should be about the right size.'

'Here, what do you think you're playing at? I've got to feed myself in this life, never mind the next! You priests always have money hidden on you somewhere. Pay up like everyone else. I'm no believer.'

'What have we here? A blasphemer? And you expect these pious travellers, many of them pilgrims themselves, to buy the wares of an unholy ruffian like yourself?' Benkei's already stentorian bellow rose. Passers-by, cheered by a little free entertainment, began to gather around the towering priest and the cringing, furious huckster. The vendor yanked the hat from his arm and threw it viciously at Benkei.

'You'll give me a bad name, you fool. Here, take it. Priests!' and he spat over his left shoulder, barely missing a chortling farm boy.

Benkei bowed. 'Your soul will benefit from this, kind sir. Many thanks,' and he bore his prize off to Tamako, muttering to Yoshitsuné, 'Well, nobody can say we're not professional priests, begging for all our needs.'

'It was well done, Benkei. You were most convincing.'

'It is only the beginning. Just watch me say my prayers tonight.'

*

A damp sea mist wafted slowly inland through the pines; sounds were softened and obscure and even the sharp cry of a wild goose became ghostly and hollow as gradually trees and rocks dimmed and floated in the undulating haze. In the great new Hachiman shrine at Kamakura the sharp odours of cedar and cypress were muffled by the dank sea smell. The walls and railings seemed to melt away.

Yoritomo stood, spread-legged, arms crossed, in front of the sanctuary, feeling almost on equal terms with a god whose magnificent home he had himself built. He could think clearly here, sure that Hachiman would understand. He clapped briskly, twice, and began to whisper to the closed sanctuary.

'He is on his way to Hiraizumi, Lord Hachiman. The reports are coming in from the military posts at the barriers. Now that is a good thing. Hidehira is very old, but he is rich and too independent. We must control Oshu and the samurai-dokoro know it but they are hesitant, the warlords respect the old man and fear his reputation. But they will have to act if Hidehira threatens the peace. We'll let Yoshitsuné go, let him think he is safe, but he will help us break the Oshu Fujiwara the way he helped us break the Cloister Court.' He looked earnestly at the silent sanctuary. 'The success of the samurai-dokoro and the supremacy of the clan, your chosen clan, are the most important things there are. I know you understand that and that you understand that Yoshitsuné has placed himself above these and therefore . . . In my plans there are more important considerations for a samurai than just heroics.'

The sanctuary was finally obliterated by the sea mist. Yoritomo clapped his hands twice again and then stood, staring at the closed doors, awaiting some sign, some token of disapproval. Nothing. No sound, no light, no movement. Lord Hachiman understood and accepted.

Yoritomo turned and strode out of the shrine into the fog swirling and shifting on the mountain side.

*

Yoshitsuné pushed aside the skin curtain and stepped inside the hut. The small room was gloomy, with a stale human smell; dim light came through a tiny hole in the wattle wall and a smoke-hole in the roughly thatched roof. Tamako lay on heaped boughs and grasses, her face pale and wan although her smile was relaxed.

'The sickness has passed, my lord. I have recovered.'

'Tamako, this sickness is peculiar. It comes in bursts every day and then passes off again.'

She smiled again. 'It will pass away completely quite soon, I think, my lord. I have been lying here counting and I know what ails me.'

'Counting?' He looked down at her. She had survived the journey so well; as her feet had toughened and her legs grew strong she could walk many miles a day without complaint. Of course she slowed them a little but until these recent attacks of nausea and fatigue she had kept up a goodish pace. But now he was afraid her presence would become an irritant again.

'Yes, counting, my lord. It is very inconvenient in many ways, but you want a son and now it seems you may well have one. It was foolish of me not to know sooner for it seems, if my counting is accurate, that the child will be born in spring or early summer. But the walking has changed my body so much that only now do I realise how my breasts have ached and that my waist is thicker.'

'A child *now*?' He sank on the dirt floor in despair.

Tamako said anxiously, 'But my lord, you have said, Benkei has said so many times that a son is necessary. That is why you have all suffered my slow and stupid female ways. Now we know a child exists and you are sad.' Tears glistened in her eyes.

Yoshitsuné turned away, unable to face her tears. 'Tamako, this baby won't survive. You'll begin to get heavy and how will we disguise you? Where will we stay? A pregnant page? We will have to live through the winter in the mountains and where will the baby be born? Under a tree?' He gestured angrily towards the woods. 'Poor little soul, its karma has been determined by the father's sins.'

274

'But surely we shall be in Hiraizumi by spring, my lord? The child will be born in Fujiwara's palace and presented to the gods in the great temple there.'

'How can you walk across mountains and rivers if you are pregnant?' His voice, harsh with disappointment, resounded against the sturdy mud walls.

She touched his hand and replied quietly, 'Then I shall give birth in a hut like this and bear him in my arms to Hiraizumi. I am strong enough. The sickness has passed for today. Each day it is less. I am ready to start now.' She sat up and began to arrange her clothes.

'No, no, stay here.' He rose and moved to the doorway. 'I must talk to Benkei.'

The hut was in a forest clearing. Kisanda had built a fire and was skinning a rabbit while Benkei sprawled in the sun. He called, 'How is her ladyship?'

'She is better.'

'We have decided to stay here tonight. It is as good a place as any and we can't get much further now. We'll have to make for the coast tomorrow. She'll never get over those mountains.' He gestured to the huge blue and white peaks glittering around them.

Yoshitsuné ignored this information and said in a dead tone, 'Benkei, what are we going to do? She's pregnant.'

Kisanda let out an involuntary groan but Benkei took the news calmly. 'That could have waited until Hiraizumi. It will take a little thinking about. When should the child be born?'

'She says in the spring, late spring. She also says she is strong enough to continue, but soon her condition will be visible.' Yoshitsuné shrugged miserably. 'Do any of us know anything about this sort of thing? Even you, Benkei, must be beaten by this. I suppose we must leave her in a convent somewhere in Kaga.'

'Nonsense! What convent would protect the wife and child of Yoshitsuné against Yoritomo's agents? What happened to Shizuka's child, eh? Just the brat of a discarded concubine! Think what Yoritomo would do to your wife – and a Taira as well. No. She stays with us.'

Kisanda sighed. 'My lord, we must protect the lady and your child. It would be too great a victory for Kamakura.'

Yoshitsuné looked at Benkei who nodded. 'Kisanda speaks the truth. We'll try to get to Oshu, but if necessary we will hide until the child is born.'

Yoshitsuné turned away. 'It is only a matter of time. It must end in death – ours, hers, the child's.'

*

They managed to find a willing fisherman who sailed them across the bay to Echigo. They moved slowly along the coast from village to village, hunting or begging food and lodging as they went. In these isolated western districts cut off by vast mountain ranges, few representatives of Kamakura had penetrated and the local fishermen and farmers were secretive, primitive people who regarded the holy men without much interest. Priests at various small temples where they slept and begged food were accustomed to travelling pilgrims and if they were surprised by Tamako's unorthodox appearance, they apparently attributed her plump softness and impractical voluminous clothes to the cold weather or hitherto unguessed excesses of fashion in the south. If the page seemed unusually pampered he also was unusually pretty.

The real danger was at the barriers in the passes of those mountains they were forced to cross; the responsibility for those check-points lay with loyal members of the samurai-dokoro and their soldiers would be on the alert; Yoshitsuné might be recognised. The group had not yet been seriously challenged at a guard post which, for Tamako's sake, relieved Yoshitsuné but he, Benkei and Kisanda had discussed it and agreed that it was strange that there was not more suspicion. Benkei, speculating over their amazingly uncomplicated journey, began to feel that the lack of interest was more ominous than being followed by attacking bands of Kamakura ruffians led personally by Yoritomo himself. Therefore he was encouraged when they finally met some opposition.

They were struggling over a steep pass of sharp blue rock

in a steady drizzling rain. The path was wet and slippery and their progress slow as they pushed along the narrow gorge. Kisanda, slightly ahead, spotted the barrier unexpectedly blocking the path through the gorge. Several guards were sheltering under an overhang and he noticed a richly dressed samurai sitting in the makeshift pavilion.

Benkei accepted the news calmly. 'Obviously Yoritomo expected someone under suspicion to pass through here. We must take our chances. Keep Lady Tamako to the rear and I'll do the talking.'

A soldier hailed them as they approached the wooden structure and told them to identify themselves by the orders of the Lord of Kamakura and his loyal retainer Togashi no Suke.

'Identify! You can see for yourself, fool, that we are priests on a pilgrimage. What blasphemy is this? To challenge a holy man? If you don't want to view your next life through the eyes of a lizard, you had better let us pass on our way to Haguro Temple.'

Lord Togashi no Suke rose and peered out through the veil of drizzle at the yamabushi. His instructions from Kamakura had been obscure and he was not completely confident how to proceed. All clerics were to be challenged, as much information as possible gathered, and then allowed to continue. If Yoshitsuné was detected he was not to be stopped but his presence reported immediately to Kamakura.

Togashi was a soldier with a soldier's rigid mind and craving for precise orders; if Yoshitsuné was a dangerous rebel why should he wander up the Hokuriku highway undisturbed? A rebel should be dealt with and this greying of black and white issues irritated Togashi but, determined to do his best, he surveyed the motley group before him. There was the giant leader bellowing at the guards, an undistinguished priest, a porter and a rather plump page. In his service under Noriyori during the campaigns against the Taira, Togashi had seen Yoshitsuné several times and remembered the small delicate features and broad-shouldered slight body well. None of these men seemed

quite right, too sun-burnt, too old, too coarsened to be the attractive young general he recalled. And yet, that leader did seem familiar. Yoshitsuné had always been accompanied by his big lieutenant, a noisy bull of a man. But surely the general would be in command, not the lieutenant? Even in disguise the proper social order should be kept. Togashi sighed and signalled. His men brought the group to him, splashing through the puddles to the pavilion.

'I am Togashi no Suke, deputy of the Lord of Kamakura. We are looking for the traitor Minamoto Yoshitsuné and have reason to believe he is disguised as a monk. Therefore, every passerby must be questioned. I am sure you understand the necessity.'

'No one deplores the terrible behaviour of the upstart Yoshitsuné more than I do, but surely you can see we are genuine monks. Do we look like fugitives?' Benkei asked.

Togashi smiled but did not answer the question. 'There are two priests, I see, and a porter and a page. What temple do you come from and where are you going?' His eyes rapidly scanned the men's faces as he asked. One of the priests could be Yoshitsuné – tired and worn looking, but the fine eyebrows, the sensual mouth and, most of all, the oval face did seem familiar. Certainly disaster could bring terrible changes to a man.

'Yes, two of us are priests. I am Arasanuki of Kurama and this fellow here,' Benkei gestured to Yoshitsuné and lowered his voice to a hoarse whisper, 'this fellow is one, Yamatobo, who joined me on the way. He wants to make a pilgrimage to Haguro and although I don't know much about him he is certainly a devout lover of Buddha. Prays all day long. Sutras with morning, noon and evening rice.' Benkei gave a ludicrously exaggerated wink.

Togashi replied with stiff dignity, 'It is interesting that you do not know the man because there is something rather suspicious about him. Who are the other two? A page and a porter – both in holy orders, I assume?'

'Yes, yes. The porter is a good boy, strong as an ox and just as reverent. That pretty lad's name is Shimotsukebo.

But what is this nonsense about Yamatobo? I am not letting any bedraggled hanger-on slow us up. If you have any doubts about him – off 'he goes!' Benkei wheeled on Yoshitsuné, his thick staff gripped in a mammoth fist and shouted fiercely, 'You, you snivelling chanting miserable parasite, do you hear what the samurai says? You look like an outlaw. We don't want you travelling with us.' He twirled the staff over his head and brought it whistling down a fraction away from his master's ear. 'Get on with you.' He delivered several well-aimed blows to Yoshitsuné's back and shoulders, driving him deliberately along the gorge, away from the barrier, away from the guards and Togashi. As the blows pounded down, the victor of Dan no Ura covered his head with his arms, gave a cowardly howl and ran stumbling along the path.

Benkei returned to Togashi, panting and ignoring the stunned, horrified faces of his companions. 'There, that's the last we'll see of him. I didn't like him. Sanctimonious. We will proceed on our way now if we may, Lord Togashi.'

The two men stood facing each other, their gaze locked, two warriors holding the same values, the same deep belief in loyalty, duty and respect above all else. For the briefest instant their eyes reflected common knowledge of the terrible thing Benkei had forced himself to do. For that instant Benkei and Togashi understood each other as deeply and completely as it was possible for two separate individuals to do. Then Togashi no Suke nodded abruptly; Benkei bowed and turning on his heel marched off. Only the relentless drizzle on the rocks sounded in the still gorge.

Yoshitsuné joined them some hours later as they were resting under a scrubby pine where the gorge plunged towards a bleak valley. Before he could speak Benkei threw himself down before him.

'Forgive me, master, forgive me. I shall pay for this terrible crime in three lives to follow. The God Hachiman will take revenge on my soul but please, you, master, forgive me! I cannot die without knowing you understand.'

Yoshitsuné laughed. 'I forgive you, Benkei. That was

brilliant. I was good, too, I thought, although those blows hurt. Come on, get up. Hachiman is a forgiving god. He knows true service when he sees it.' He pulled Benkei to his feet and the two men embraced. His hands on the monk's shoulders, Yoshitsuné looked into his eyes and murmured, 'Besides, I have long wondered who is the master and who is the servant. We are not tied in conventional ways.'

*

Yoritomo received Togashi's messenger with a jubilant shout. He threw the letter to Kajiwara. 'He's going north, like a rat to a storehouse. Fujiwara Hidehira will commit himself, I'm sure of it. Send for Noriyori, bring him back from Kyushu and let him prove *his* loyalty to the samurai-dokoro. We have only to bide our time and the whole land will belong to us!'

Kajiwara frowned and tapped his thick fingers on the iron fan in his belt. 'If he were a true samurai he would have died by now, by his own hand. But he still hopes to steal a little glory for himself, still hopes to be a hero.'

Tokimasa looked up from his writing table and ignoring Kajiwara said curtly to Yoritomo, 'Bide your time, son-in-law. By all means bring Noriyori, but don't do anything yet . . .'

*

The episode at the barrier cheered Yoshitsuné considerably. The uneventful journey had bored him and paradoxically he was disgruntled that Yoritomo apparently had dropped his pursuit. Now he began to see even the baby as a positive sign that things were improving, that the wheel had turned and his karma was not all bad. His better spirits encouraged the others except Benkei, who still worried over the barrier incident. His initial relief at some antagonism from Yoritomo had faded as he thought things out. Togashi no Suke had most certainly suspected Yama-tobo of being Yoshitsuné and probably thought the leader was Benkei. Then why had he not objected when the suspect monk fled? Why had they not been followed?

280

Yoritomo was too skilful an organizer to have such inefficient vassals in important posts. Could it be, Benkei speculated, that Yoshitsuné was no longer a sufficient threat to worry about?

What worried Benkei most was the disturbing idea that kept returning to his mind that Yoritomo might want Yoshitsuné to go to Oshu. Perhaps because it was far enough away to keep him out of politics and because Yoritomo, who was known to be superstitious, did not really want his brother's blood on his hands? Lord Hachiman frowned on fratricide.

Or perhaps he had a more sinister reason? Benkei, no subtle politician, did not like it. As always, he felt Yoritomo's mind, his actions, to be too complicated for him to understand. Guile and cunning were one thing, respectable in a warrior, but Benkei knew that Yoritomo's plots pushed these simple virtues into a mysterious realm where few samurai could go. Kiyomori had tried but it had ended in disaster. How could a provincial, uneducated outcast hope to succeed where the sophisticated product of the Capital had so miserably failed? It all made Benkei tired and confused.

They stopped for a few days at an isolated temple in the mountains, a poor, primitive place run by filthy but pious monks who extended charity without questions. The fugitives slept in an outhouse of rough-cut pine, draughty and dirty, but with a protecting roof.

One afternoon as Tamako slept heavily on her pallet, Kisanda wandered off for a walk and Benkei catnapped, Yoshitsuné, taking advantage of the peace, sat on the veranda cleaning his weapons. The saffron sun glowed through the stark black boughs of an oak and a few late birds twittered and complained in the autumn chill.

Yoshitsuné hummed to himself as he carefully cleaned and oiled the Hachiman sword, squinting along it to check for any spot of rust. Gently he caressed the blade with the last of the paper preserved to serve the magnificent steel, and then reluctantly he slid the sword back into the scabbard and put it beside him on the floor. Then he drew

the Sanjo dagger from inside his ragged clothes. He stared at it.

'It's a beautiful dagger.' Benkei's gruff voice came from the corner.

'You're awake.'

The monk rose, stretched, scratched and wandered on to the veranda. Squatting next to Yoshitsuné, he held out his hand for the dagger. The narrow evil blade caught and distorted the sunlight.

'Perfect. Near perfect. The balance.' He glanced at Yoshitsuné. 'You never use it. Never. Why?'

No reply came.

'Hidehira gave it to you. There was trouble over it, you know, with those two sons of his. News of it even reached the barracks. Some of the men mentioned it to me later, after we'd left Hiraizumi. Several asked why you never used it. I often wondered. Needs cleaning as well. You neglect it.'

Yoshitsuné looked at the dagger and then at Benkei. 'I'd give it to you but ...'

'You can't do that! Hidehira gave it to you.' There was genuine horror in Benkei's voice, unusual in a man always so consciously cynical.

'No. No, you don't understand.' Yoshitsuné shook his head, striving, once and for all, to face and to state his hatred for the blade. A cold dull pain burrowed into the bones of his skull, into his teeth. 'I don't think I'm a superstitious man but I believe in the Hachiman sword. At Kurama, once in the shrine at Kamakura, and again sometimes in battle, at Ichinotani and at Yashima, I could feel the spirit of Hachiman in me. I knew, *knew*, I couldn't die in those battles. At Uji I was afraid at first and then forgot my fear. You know how it is.' Benkei nodded, watching him closely, the Sanjo dagger held loosely in his right hand. 'Dan no Ura was different, but I was holding the sword as I watched Tomomori jump and it came to me that I could never die that way as long as I had the sword.'

'The sword was made for you. I've often thought that,' said Benkei. 'I'm not a superstitious man either but the

Hachiman sword is a rare weapon. Only a great warrior could use it.'

'And the dagger? What do you think of the dagger?' asked Yoshitsuné quickly.

Benkei looked at it. 'It's beautiful.' He shrugged. 'Beautiful and perfect. And you don't use it. Why not?'

'I hate it. And what's more, I fear it. Laugh if you must. A twenty-seven-year-old man hating and fearing a piece of steel!'

'No. Every sword or dagger, every *good* sword or dagger, is more than just a piece of steel. But this is not necessarily the blade you must use if there was no choice but suicide. There is your short sword.' Benkei's voice became firm, resolutely prosaic.

'No, it will be that dagger,' Yoshitsuné said dully. 'I don't fear death. I have been close to it too many times, but I want a proper one, in battle, not a furtive death. I want to die like the hero I was. They said I would be like Hachiman Taro – a great hero – magnificent. I believed it and it has been the centre of my life. Oh, of course there have been other things: women, comrades, you. But the real thing was to be a hero. I thought it was my karma. So did everyone else but Yoritomo. He knew that heroes have only a limited use and then they become expensive luxuries, and he is an economical man. He knew that my karma was to serve him, and he wants to reward me with an outlaw's death.' He laughed bitterly. 'After we met that last time in Kamakura I went to the shrine, *his* shrine, and I couldn't find the god. Perhaps even Hachiman serves him now.'

Benkei listened, knowing that Yoshitsuné was calling on him for strength but knowing, too, that he could not help and that Yoshitsuné realised he could not help. Death was part of life, a release from worldly bonds, a step to paradise, but it was lonely. Benkei sat silently, refusing to give an answer that neither of them would believe, distressed by the despair of the man beside him, and his own ultimate failure in his chosen role.

Finally the monk said, 'There are already stories, songs

about Uji and Dan no Ura, Ichinotani and Yashima. You are already a hero. If it comes to suicide, we can make it grand, not furtive.'

Yoshitsuné stared out at the darkening sky. 'Not furtive, but will it be a hero's death, in battle?'

'No,' Benkei said, 'perhaps not in battle. But you are a hero and Yoritomo can never take that away from you.'

*

Tamako was becoming heavier now. She had recovered from her nausea and weakness but her belly was large and her legs and feet were often still swollen in the morning after a few hours' rest. However she plodded on over the stony paths and through the long grasses sparkling with hoar frost, ignoring the chill wind and the sad moan of the wild geese. Because of her bulk they began to avoid temples and shrines and to stop only at isolated villages where any stranger was unusual.

Winter set in, the pines became weird, rime-cloaked clumps scattered over the snow; the wind searched their clothes and they suffered from frozen hands and feet; Tamako had frostbitten toes and ears, an ailment shared by Benkei, much to his fury. Food was difficult to find and a kill had to last a long time. Occasionally there was nothing but bark to gnaw. Tamako never complained, but as the cold intensified it was obvious that she would have to stop.

The party halted at a forlorn farmhouse in a small, bleak valley; the men offered to pray for the souls of the household, to hunt and to help with any winter farm work in return for food and shelter. Priests were a revered novelty so they were accepted with few questions. The family consisted of an old man and woman and their sons, wives and grandchildren and a few serfs crowded into the large, low, dirt-floored house with pigs and chickens. Tamako was placed in a corner near the rough earthen hearth and secluded from the noise and activity of the rest of the house by a screen of split reeds. With the animal sense of those who live only a step from beasts, the peasants

never doubted her true sex or condition but never questioned why three priests should be travelling with a woman in the advanced stages of pregnancy.

They hoped to linger until the child was delivered, but one mild day the old farmer remarked that the passes were clear of snow and that the local constable would be around to assess their arable fields and livestock. 'He brings soldiers now,' said the old grandfather in disgust. 'Samurai to get our crops, but there's no reason for it. We pay up – always have.' The next day the fugitives began the last leg of their journey, after pleading with the family not to mention their stay. 'Won't say anything. Don't like these samurai coming round. We mind our own business,' said the grandfather, weighing the small bag of silver Benkei had handed him. He had never seen silver before and was not sure what to do with it, but he sensed it was valuable and might help with the taxes.

They forded the river into Fujiwara Hidehira's vast domain a week later. A few more days brought them into the Kamewari Mountains, the last natural barrier before the valley where the exotic teak palaces and gold temples of Hiraizumi spread in a northern sun.

The larches were sharp pale green and here and there witch hazel poked up its narrow little flowers, adding colour to the landscape. The days were bright but mists still rolled across the hills at night and their world was wrapped in a damp spring chill.

It was under one of the tall pines, in a swirling haze, that Yoshitsuné's son was born. Tamako shrieked and writhed in agony, encircled by the three terrified men; only Kisanda had seen birth before, but delivering a child was not like helping a mare to foal. Yet his experience was valuable and it was he who caught the infant in his hands and clumsily cut the cord and slapped the baby into squalling furious life. After they had cleaned it and wrapped it in a cotton under-kimono and a badger skin all three lay down under the tree, too exhausted to care about the unclean ground, contaminated by the blood and filth of a woman. They warmed Tamako and the child with their

285

bodies and incredibly found mother and son still alive in the morning.

Benkei held the boy high in the soft morning sunlight. 'Look at him, Lord Hachiman. A fine boy, one day a great warrior. We now have two masters. Bless him, Lord Hachiman. His karma may be blighted but bless him all the same.'

They named the child Kamesuru, taking the name from the hills that witnessed his birth. Tamako rested and nursed him while the others hunted badgers and rabbits. Her body rapidly recovered and within two weeks she was on her feet, marching toward Hiraizumi, her son carried in a pannier on Benkei's broad back. In the Capital she would have remained unclean and in bed for a month, unseen by men, but here she resumed her rough life immediately. Even a peasant woman would have been isolated for a set period, but Tamako and her samurai companions could not afford such luxury. She found that she did not regret her lying-in and her joy in the baby was boundless.

As for Yoshitsuné, this small red thing seemed an unconvincing bundle to carry forward his great hopes. As they approached Hiraizumi he worried that Hidehira was dead or would not accept them. What hope then for the child? Or for himself? Privately, he decided that if their presence was unwelcome, he would fight no more but make his death quickly, as honourably as possible. Then Tamako and the child might be allowed to live in peace. Benkei sensed the decision, knew it was the right one and that he himself would follow his master.

*

Although he was very frail, Hidehira's mind was still sound and active. He lay propped on a high wooden pillow, tears pouring down withered cheeks as he embraced Yoshitsuné, apparently unaware that the fresh beautiful boy he had watched depart seven years before was now a tired man whose once generous mouth had become a thin line.

'Your dear face is so welcome to my eyes, dim as they are

now. Tell me of everything later, when I am stronger and used to your being here, but now, very briefly, give an old general a summary of your tactics at Yashima.' He nodded to his eldest son, Yasuhira, who stood stiffly by. 'We have heard many stories but it is from you that I want the details.'

Yoshitsuné sat by the old man's good ear and related the crossing to Shikoku and the events at Yashima. When he had finished, Hidehira leant back, exhausted but pleased.

'How proud you make me. Would that my own sons had proved half so magnificent, but Yasuhira takes pleasure in bureaucracy and Tadahira thinks about his women, his horses and his dice. If only I had a son like you.'

Yasuhira, broad-hipped and sag-bellied from too little exercise, kept his features impassive, but what, he thought furiously, would have happened to Oshu if he, the eldest son, had gone risking his life in quarrels that could not possibly profit the Fujiwara, dissipating his intelligence with the crudities of a soldier's life? What had this man accomplished – arriving on foot in the rags of a yamabushi with two shabby retainers and a hard-bodied whore he claimed as his wife? What was there in this to be proud of? Better a shrewd brain to keep an eye on accounts and affairs at home than the worn-out shell of a hero for whom there was no longer any use.

Hidehira's eyes opened. 'Tell me, my son, do you have the dagger with you?' This was the moment Yoshitsuné had dreaded and his smile was tight as he drew the knife from his sash. He had never been able to bring himself to use it in combat on another man but Hidehira must not know that. He said brusquely, 'I carry it always next to my flesh and with the Hachiman sword it has served me through all my adventures. A superb blade.'

'It was made by the great Sanjo Kikaji,' muttered Yasuhira. 'How could it be other than superb? And it is worth a fortune.'

'Ah, Yasuhira, you have learned to appreciate good steel, I see.'

'Only its price, not its true value,' replied Hidehira

wearily. 'My son is no warrior. Now, you must excuse me. We shall talk again soon.'

Yoshitsuné and Yasuhira left the room, the former deeply moved by his old friend's affection. As a boy he had loved and respected Hidehira and had been accepted as his son, so it had not really seemed possible, even after seven years of contact with Yoritomo, that this bond could be rejected for political reasons. Although he had not fully faced up to the danger he presented to the Oshu dynasty, Yasuhira had, and now his antagonism puzzled Yoshitsuné. They had never been close but they should be brothers in sentiment, sharing a mutual honour for Hidehira. Yet Yasuhira had shown nothing but cold courtesy and even now he was reciting the arrangements made for their accommodation rather than reciprocating Yoshitsuné's deep emotion.

'And my father has instructed that a house be built for you and your family at Koromogawa, a good spot on an easily defensible bluff over the Koromo River. Of course,' he sniffed, 'we hope it will never need to be defended, but Hidehira has commanded the residence to be a fortress as well.'

'He is a splendid man. All through the last years he has been my model for a warrior, a truly great man,' Yoshitsuné exclaimed.

'Hmm. Now, your retainers will no doubt choose to stay with you but you will need more men and your lady will need attendants; I will have the constable look into the question of samurai to serve you, and my wife will deal with the women.'

Yoshitsuné stroked one of the teak pillars of the veranda. As a youth he had loved the strange smoothness of the wood, carried to Hiraizumi in ships from unimaginable rain forests over the seas. This is a beautiful city, he thought, really a more beautiful one than the Capital, but he said aloud, 'He is still in marvellous condition for a man of ninety. Obviously he tires but his brain is very clear. To have known him has been the one great pleasure of my life.'

Yasuhira sighed. Now the man was becoming maudlin,

no doubt part of his general disintegration. What mindless blockheads these soldiers were. 'Do the arrangements satisfy you, Yoshitsuné? I am sure it is important to my father that you are comfortable,' he asked sharply.

Yoshitsuné removed his hand from the pillar and looked at Yasuhira in surprise. 'What? Yes, yes, of course. I have had nothing for so long that a roof over my head will be undreamed-of luxury.'

Yasuhira cleared his throat. 'There is one small point I feel I must raise. My father is now too old to take one aspect of your arrival into consideration. However, my brother and I are strongly committed to the independence of Oshu. In our view the Lord of Kamakura will take what steps he can to curb Fujiwara authority and to take the provinces for himself.'

'I would be the last one to doubt Yoritomo's ambitions and his ruthless pursuit of them,' replied Yoshitsuné drily.

'Then you will also understand why we will not tolerate a campaign launched against the samurai-dokoro from Hiraizumi – in fact why we feel your presence here should be kept a secret. There are, I believe, rumours circulating of your suicide; these could be encouraged.' Yasuhira's round face quivered in his solemnity.

What a tedious man he is, thought Yoshitsuné. He obviously thinks that suicide is the answer and wishes I would comply.

Yasuhira smiled thinly as the two men parted, one to his writing table and coffers, the other to the guest quarters where his wife and friends awaited him to hear their fate.

*

Hidehira had commanded a large fortified mansion to be built on a defensive bluff over the Koromo River. It was simple, as a warrior's house should be, and if there was no exquisite water pavilion over an artificial lake, from its wide verandas Yoshitsuné and his household viewed the passing of the precise northern seasons. Tamako had pleasant quarters and attendants to care for young Kame-

suru. Gradually she softened and melted into a gentle lady of good birth again; silk gowns relaxed her hard little muscles and the polished floors smoothed her calloused feet. Soon she was happily pregnant once more and her agonising journey slipped further into the past.

Several young samurai drifted into Yoshitsuné's service and the old life of sword play, hunting and archery resumed. Yoshitsuné, out of respect for Hidehira, did not attempt to raise a force against Kamakura but occasionally visitors arrived from the Capital with ambiguous messages from certain courtiers, mentioning Go-Shirakawa's deteriorating health while emphasising that, as Yoritomo had not yet been created Shogun, the Cloistered Emperor might still be considered sympathetic to the Lord of Kamakura's enemies. But there was no sign that Kamakura even remembered Yoshitsuné's existence; perhaps the suicide story had been believed or perhaps, thought Yoshitsuné ruefully, he did not matter any more. He talked to the visitors, made non-committal responses to their hints and enquiries, and was mildly gratified that there were a few, if only a few, who believed he was still a man to be reckoned with. There might be time to consider their offers later, but he could not disturb the neutrality of Oshu yet.

*

Noriyori arrived in Kamakura a few months after Yoshitsuné's presence in Hiraizumi had been confirmed by spies. He was not sorry to leave Kyushu, a hot, sticky, mosquito-ridden island with too many typhoons and bellicose warlords, but he was afraid he knew what Yoritomo would want from him, and although he already knew what his answer to his brother would be, he dreaded a confrontation.

His orders were as he feared; with a force of three thousand soldiers he was to march to Hiraizumi, arrest and execute his younger brother and Fujiwara Hidehira and annex the province of Oshu for the samurai-dokoro. Both men, he was assured by Yoritomo, were traitors, plotting against the Imperial throne.

Noriyori stared into Yoritomo's narrow cold eyes. 'Where's the evidence of this plot? Where are the Imperial orders of execution? I will not commit fratricide unless my *Emperor* commands it.'

'Noriyori, I am your lord, your chieftain and your elder brother. Yoshitsuné has brought shame on the Minamoto. He started for Kyushu to raise an army against me, deceiving that old fool Go-Shirakawa into supporting him. Death is the only answer to Yoshitsuné.'

Kajiwara, seated at Yoritomo's right, snapped sharply at Noriyori, 'Your chieftain has given you an order. The samurai-dokoro wishes Yoshitsuné dead for excellent reasons.'

Noriyori looked from one man to the other – two hard, dedicated, ruthless administrators. Human life, whether that of thousands of foot soldiers or of a blood brother, was unimportant set against their ambitions. But this was not just ambition; it was mindless, petty jealousy. He took a deep breath. 'I will not do it. If you have an Imperial warrant for treason, which I do not believe you have, any competent member of the samurai-dokoro can lead an army on Hiraizumi. I am not going to murder my own brother. Tomorrow, I'm going back to Kyushu.'

Yoritomo stared hard at him. 'So your loyalty is also in doubt.' It was not a question.

*

The samurai-dokoro agreed with Noriyori; Yoshitsuné was quiet and his death seemed unnecessary – although several samurai felt he had no real excuse to go on living and should have killed himself. Hidehira was an old man with a weak, greedy son for whom an offer of gold or another rich rice province would be enough to make him co-operate with the desires of Kamakura after Hidehira died. So why commit men and horses to a private blood feud if the territorial gains could eventually be won peacefully? The arguments were led by Miura and Wada, Yoshitsuné's old supporters, but Tokimasa also showed little sign of enthusiasm for the campaign, although he did agree that

Lord Wada was uncooperative in his continual questioning of policy. Furthermore, young Wada was suspected of sympathy with Yoshitsuné, or at least there were rumours that he was in contact with the potential rebel even though the two men had not met since Dan no Ura. Tokimasa was not sure he believed the rumours, which were probably started in Kamakura, but he did want the obstructive Wadas out of the way.

*

Hidehira lived for two more years; his last instructions were precise and unequivocal, especially concerning the future of Yoshitsuné: any messengers from Kamakura bearing bribes or demands concerning the fugitive were to be beheaded. Looking directly in the eyes of his eldest son, the dying man repeated twice that the protection of Yoshitsuné was the ultimate obligation of his heirs and even if the rich rice fields of Hitachi province were offered, or the eastern hordes crossed the Shirakawa barrier burning harvests, no bargains were to be made. To betray this trust would result in three generations of bad karma.

Yoshitsuné, summoned from Koromogawa, arrived only a few minutes before Hidehira died. The old man bade him draw the dagger and hold it up one last time before his fading eyes.

'It is a good blade, my boy. I will bear the sight of that perfect steel to the next world. My sons have been instructed to shield you from Yoritomo, but they are poor things and if they fail you, that blade will not.'

Hidehira blessed his wives, sons, daughters and their children, and last of all he turned to his foster son. But before he could speak again a terrible shudder seized his wasted muscles. The limp body collapsed like a puppet for whom the puppeteer no longer had any use.

The women busied themselves around the corpse; no one spoke, no one looked at Yoshitsuné. The death room was laden with silent accusation at the heavy burden Hidehira had left to his family. Deep in grief, it was some minutes before Yoshitsuné intercepted the strong waves of

antagonism. He glanced at the first wife, now first widow; she averted her gaze as did the other women, but Tadahira, his eyes red-rimmed, dropped an arm around Yoshitsuné and gently urged him out into the winter-grey garden. As they passed Yasuhira, the new chieftain shot both men a look of pure venom.

Tadahira sighed, drawing the harsh cold air into his aching lungs. 'My father commanded that we continue to protect you from Kamakura, and that may prove a difficult – and expensive – responsibility after the samurai-dokoro learns Hidehira is dead. The warlords can only despise Yasuhira.' He turned to study his foster brother's pale face. 'What will you do? Stay here in peace or try somewhere else, Kyushu or the west, to raise an army?' He added apologetically, 'We do really need to know your plans.'

Yoshitsuné swept his hand over his eyes, brushing away tears. 'Hidehira's death ... you'll understand ... I can't quite grasp it ...'

'My father is at peace, free from earthly ties,' Tadahira said firmly. 'You must have given this matter some thought in the last two years; those visitors from the Capital, messages from the Cloister Court.'

Yoshitsuné shook his head to clear his mind. 'Oh, I have thought.' He glanced back into the room where Yasuhira's plump form could just be seen. 'With the wealth and the brave samurai of Oshu behind me, perhaps Yoritomo could be overthrown. Without Oshu's army, he is invincible.'

Softly Tadahira said, 'There will be no help from Oshu while Yasuhira is chieftain.'

'Yes, I understand that. Then my intention is to live here in peace, for as long as that is possible.'

'Then the might of Oshu will protect you, for as long as that is possible.'

The two men bowed and separated, each to indulge his own grief.

*

The day Hidehira's death was announced to the samurai-dokoro, Yoritomo also produced two letters: one purported to be from Yoshitsuné to a fractious member of the Court, and the other was supposedly from Yoshitsuné to Lord Wada's son. The notes indicated that Yoshitsuné was not only in contact with courtiers unsympathetic to Kamakura but also that he was plotting with young samurai.

Yoritomo demanded action from the warlords of the samurai-dokoro. Lord Wada declared the letters to be forgeries, protested his son's total innocence and withdrew from the assembly. Lord Miura was away on his estates, which left few to defend Yoshitsuné. Doi, anticipating a share in Hiraizumi's wealth, volunteered to lead an army, but Hojo Tokimasa intervened against an immediate attack on Oshu, saying that the southern provinces were restless and he was unhappy about deploying too many men for too long a time in so remote an area. To make things easier he suggested that an Imperial death warrant be wrested out of Go-Shirakawa and a bargain struck with Yasuhira to execute the rebel in return for Hitachi province. Once Yoshitsuné was out of the way, the samurai-dokoro could launch an army to mop up any resistance to the complete take-over of the administration of Oshu. Yasuhira would fall like a ripe plum. A fine general like Yoshitsuné could have led the Oshu samurai, but Yasuhira and Tadahira alone would provide no opposition to an efficient eastern force. The plan was agreed to be a sensible one – Oshu was a long way off and communications would be difficult; better not commit a larger army than necessary. Not one man in the samurai-dokoro doubted that Yasuhira would betray Yoshitsuné; the man's greed was too well known.

A few hours after the samurai dispersed, a retainer of Lord Wada's arrived in Yoritomo's compound; an old samurai too crippled with arthritis to mount a horse, he had long served the Wada family and now, tears streamed down his cheeks as he stood before Yoritomo with the news of the suicides of his master and his master's son.

Yoritomo received the news coolly and waved the old man from the room. Kajiwara, as always by Yoritomo's side, glanced at his commander. 'A pity,' he said, 'but Tokimasa will be pleased.'

'Neither will be much of a loss,' replied Yoritomo. 'They had served their purpose. Their suicides are an obvious admission of guilt, so send a party to their estates and seize them in the name of the samurai-dokoro. Let Doi lead it — he doesn't ask questions.'

*

Kajiwara made a quick visit to the Capital. Bearing Yoshitsuné's death warrant stamped with the Emperor's cypher, he strode into the Hojoji Palace to face Go-Shirakawa. The Cloistered Emperor sat in an airless, overheated room filled with smoking braziers; his scrawny body was piled with deep red satin robes, a skeletal head teetering on top. Yoshitsuné's name proved only a vague memory extracted with difficulty from a cobwebby network of failed intrigues. He signed the order for his protégé's execution without a sigh of regret.

But his wavering mind was perfectly clear on one point. As Kajiwara left the room the old man's weak but determined voice followed him. 'That man, Yoritomo, will never be Shogun while I live. Never. Never.'

*

Yasuhira received Yoritomo's envoy discreetly; Tadahira was summoned from his stables and the three men talked late into the night. The new Lord of Oshu accepted the Imperial death warrant and the offer of Hitachi province. He agreed solemnly that Yoshitsuné, one man, must not be allowed to disturb the peace of the nation and professed to be shocked and horrified to learn that Yoshitsuné had been communicating with potential rebels and plotting with young samurai while enjoying the protection of Oshu.

Tadahira watched his brother grovel to the Lord of Kamakura's retainer; he listened to the sweet promises and

the reasonable arguments in favour of Yoshitsuné's death. Although an unambitious man, his code of honour was that of a warrior and for years he had despised his brother's expedient mentality. Hidehira's instructions had been precise and Tadahira knew that Yoshitsuné had done nothing to warrant putting those instructions aside. His promise of peace had been sincere.

Although Tadahira had disappointed his father in many ways the old man commanded the son's respect and his memory would continue to demand it. Back in his silent mansion he went to the family altar and clapped twice to attract his father's spirit. Then, speaking in a low voice, he revealed the appalling situation to the presence hovering in the still grey light.

Before dawn Tadahira composed two letters; one, to Yasuhira, expressed disapproval and contempt for his unfilial behaviour; the other, to Yoshitsuné, told of the envoy's visit and the Cloistered Emperor's death warrant and included the plans for the attack on the Koromogawa mansion. His most trusted servant carried the letter through the early morning mists to the condemned man.

The afternoon of the same day Tadahira was discovered slumped before the family altar, dressed in white; he had disembowelled himself in the samurai way.

*

The letter was brought to Yoshitsuné as he ate his morning rice. He read it carefully several times and then without a word refolded the paper and placed it in the sleeve of his kimono. When the servant came to remove the bowls he found his master sitting cross-legged by the window, staring at the spring landscape.

Some time later Yoshitsuné went along the covered corridor that led to the women's quarters where Tamako and her son and daughter lived. Although he had several concubines his relationship with his wife was still affectionate. He was often wryly reminded of Yoritomo's respect and affection for the strong-willed Masako, and he wondered if it was a characteristic of Yoshitomo's sons to

rely on resolute women. Then he would remember Noriyori frolicking with his prostitutes and decided that no family was consistent.

He paused to watch Tamako, kneeling gracefully beside her zither; music was her chief escape from her dour northern life to the ordered civilised world she had once enjoyed. Since Hidehira's death they had both been living in an atmosphere of suspense and expectation, but now that he brought release he wondered how she would accept it.

The tune was a sweet love song of passion and separation and she finished it sadly. When she saw her husband waiting Tamako put down the plectrum and touched her head to the floor in formal greeting. He waved off her attendants and came to sit beside her.

'My lord, is the day not exquisite? The blossoms in the north are all the more precious for being so late.' Although the phrases were conventional a nervous quality in her voice gave piquancy to the peaceful words.

'They are indeed, Tamako.' He lowered his voice. 'There has been a warning.'

Even under the meticulously applied make-up her pallor was obvious, but she did not waver. 'The Lord of Kamakura ...?'

'The Cloistered Emperor has agreed to my execution and Yasuhira will disobey his father's orders and is co-operating with Yoritomo. Fortunately, Tadahira, my old hunting companion, has some of his father's blood in his veins and has sent a letter to warn me.'

'And now, my lord?' She looked down at her small hands folded in her lap.

'There is no alternative, Tamako. While Go-Shirakawa gave me his blessing I was the servant of the Court but his name and cypher are on the warrant as well as his grandson the Emperor's. Yoritomo can now claim to be the sole protector and agent of the Sacred Throne.'

'Who will seize you, Yasuhira or Yoritomo's men?'

'According to Tadahira the Oshu men will be joined by a group of eastern warriors. Noriyori refused to lead them so

Kajiwara has taken on the task. They'll have already reached the Shirakawa barrier.'

'But the barrier is defended. Lord Hidehira ordered it.'

'I suspect that Yasuhira's men are halfway there to call off the guard.' He took her hand. 'It is of no importance. You know I have no choice. Some would say I have taken too long to make the decision but . . . The only thing left to decide is where to send you and my children.'

Tamako stared at their joined hands. 'Do not send me away or give me to someone else. I die when you die. Our karma are linked and as yours has turned to misfortune so has mine.'

'And my son and daughter?'

Tamako looked into his face. 'What did Yoritomo have done to the children of the Taira?'

For an instant the pressure on her hand increased. Then he rose and left her to begin her preparations.

*

Benkei had established himself in the warriors' quarters, where he dominated the samurai in Yoshitsuné's service, terrifying the guards and foot soldiers. Kisanda, traditionally barred by his lowly origins from the samurai class, had learned to accept that he was considered the equal of any samurai and he too lived happily in the barracks but near the stables to be close to his beloved horses.

The peaceful conditions during Hidehira's lifetime had somewhat reduced Yoshitsuné's reliance on the monk but the uncertainties that had followed the old lord's death brought a renewed closeness. Neither had doubted that the final crisis would come after Hidehira died. Benkei, the Buddhist, educated to accept the futility of physical existence, was determined to fight. Yoshitsuné, the warrior, accepted that victory or death were ultimately unimportant, now only the quality of his death mattered. Consequently his meeting with Benkei on that spring morning was brief; each man knew and respected the other's inevitable choice. Indeed, in formulating his own

scheme of action Yoshitsuné had relied on Benkei's pugnacious nature.

They completely agreed on one point. Every effort must be made to cover up this abuse of Fujiwara Hidehira's last commands, and the Lord of Oshu's honour must survive the hideous treachery of Yasuhira. Yoshitsuné particularly was determined that his death would not be on the head of his benefactor's son.

*

Kajiwara Kagetoki rode into Hiraizumi after dark with a contingent of fifty men and went immediately to Yasuhira's compound. Throughout the night and following morning vassals, whose loyalty had deserted dead father for reigning son, discreetly slipped into the palace grounds and by noon there were two hundred samurai eagerly polishing their weapons and boasting as to who would take the rebel's head. One member of the household, however, kept his pact with Hidehira; Motonari, exiled from the Capital after the Minamoto risings thirty years before, accepted by Hidehira, and now an aged dependant of the Fujiwara, judged that his gratitude lay with his dead lord. During the night he crept from Yasuhira's mansion and made his way to Koromogawa. Yoshitsuné had gained one more man to die for him on the morrow.

*

Before dawn Yoshitsuné appeared in the barracks. He ordered one large group of samurai to ride towards the mountains to head off any western retainers on their way to join Yasuhira. Another large group was sent to Shirakawa to block the most direct route from the east to Hiraizumi. An hour later, when the dusty confusion of horses and men had cleared there were three warriors left in Koromogawa Fortress – Yoshitsuné, Benkei and Kisanda. The other occupants were Tamako, her son and daughter, and old Motonari, too old to fight and so left to look after the mistress of Koromogawa.

*

Kamesuru humped Akiko on to his back and crawled up and down the veranda acting 'horsie' for his tiny sister. One plump hand clutched his jacket in a tenacious grasp, the other pounded on his shoulder as she shouted her baby commands. Then she slid shrieking with laughter down his silky side to land with a thump on the floor.

Yoshitsuné and Tamako sat, hand in hand, watching their children's last games. Tamako's eyes were glazed with unshed tears and her throat ached with a misery that must not show. The children suspected nothing, not even now that the mansion was mysteriously empty of servants and samurai; everything seemed to be an adventure and she wanted them to remain unafraid to the very last. Yoshitsuné's hard hand gripped hers, his fingers pressed into the fine bones, hurting but with a pain that gave pleasure.

'We should not have done it. We should not have had children,' he muttered. 'This end was inevitable.'

'No, my lord.' The words came with difficulty from her tight throat. 'They are so pure, they will go straight to the Western Paradise to be reborn into a better life. Do not grieve for them.' But her voice broke.

Yoshitsuné gazed at her, loving her and yet almost hating her for bringing him this last agony. 'If only you had gone away and taken the children to safety,' he said bitterly. 'I look forward to my own death . . . but yours . . . and theirs. It is the hardest part to bear.'

The children's laughter tore Tamako's heart. She turned away, unable to watch them but she strengthened her clasp on Yoshitsuné's hand. 'We are samurai, my lord. It is our karma. I am not afraid.'

He looked down at her and said softly, 'I have never told you how happy you have made me, how important you have been.' Her strength flowed into him, giving peace. They had made love one last time but now he wanted her again, urgently. There was no time left. Dusk was already sliding over the mountains and there were still prepar-

300

ations to make. Better leave her now. Before his resolution could weaken he leant over and kissed her gently. With a sigh she rested her head on his shoulder. His hand slipped down her back, over delicate bones and soft flesh under silk. He pushed her away and, unable to look into her eyes, rose quickly and went to the children. He stroked their glossy black heads and then hurried, blind and deaf with sorrow, from the room. Tamako looked after him.

At the door he stopped and turned once more. Their gaze locked for a brief moment. Finally he walked through the failing sunlight to the great hall.

*

Tamako sat quietly by the open window. The spring night was exquisite, the sweet scent of blossoming trees and damp earth promised summer and a lone nightingale sang somewhere in the peaceful garden. She looked from the refreshing blackness to a rosary, glowing dimly on her white lap. The two children slept a few feet away, alone with their mother at night, a rare and exciting treat. They all wore the same special white kimono, soft silk wrapped in rich full folds around their small frail bodies.

The nightingale trilled out another invitation to life and love. Tamako sighed, took up her rosary again and continued her prayers.

*

Motonari knelt in the ante-chamber off the women's quarters. Before him lay three gleaming blades, the long sword for fighting, the short sword for self-defence and a sharp dagger. A rosary of well-worn paulownia wood drooped from his gnarled fingers on to the pure white of his kimono. He was calm and composed, as befitted an old samurai whose long life had been a preparation for this night.

*

Kisanda patrolled the walls of the fortress. He wore a samurai's lacquered corselet but no helmet, his vision

already restricted by darkness. He was tense, every sense strained for an alien sight, sound or smell; his eyes glittered with excitement and his muscles and nerves anticipated the next hours with exhilaration.

But another emotion that he barely recognised filled his dry mouth with a strange salty taste. He was afraid.

*

Benkei paced through the middle gate from the front to the inner courtyard and back again; torches, driven into the ground, threw the monk's giant shadow into distorted patterns on the stone walls. He wore a brilliant corselet of black and yellow steel plates over his saffron robe, and slung low on his back was a black lacquered quiver filled with eagle-flighted arrows. A huge bow rested on his shoulder and he grasped his Rock Cleaver sword in his right hand. The very atmosphere around him, his living space, throbbed with life and ferocity. He was committed to the inevitability of what must happen but he would not lay down his soul without one last bellow of defiance. Challenge had dominated his life and now the blood lust exploding in his head propelled him forward. Only the knowledge that his master waited inside the silent house, depending on him, kept him from tearing open the gates and charging out to seize the end by the throat.

*

The great hall was gloomy and still, not even the nightingale's beguiling song penetrated through the closed blinds, and one open lantern, squat and square on the floor, illuminated only a small part of the room. Yoshitsuné knelt just outside its light in the vast expanse of shadow. When he moved his right arm the white silk of his sleeve shimmered briefly in the pale orange glow. The Hachiman sword beside him caught the flame and gleamed, but the blade of the dagger, lying in an ornately carved rest before him, seemed to float in dim space.

*

Yoritomo's instructions were to fight and kill Yoshitsuné. Under no circumstances was he to be allowed the final dignity of suicide.

The Koromogawa fortress was reported to be virtually deserted, the garrison sent off to fight eastern hordes that had already arrived. Yasuhira, that methodical man, had preserved the building plans in his archives and these Kajiwara pored over until he found weaknesses that skilled men could penetrate. There would be no trouble with just a handful of defenders.

Kajiwara anticipated the attack with cold excitement; two hundred men to defeat half a dozen, and the only question was the death of Yoshitsuné. Kajiwara was resolved that he and he alone would bring an end to that existence.

*

Three men whisked like three black cats into the fortress soon after midnight, each opening a gate for the troops waiting on the wooded bluff. Two slipped back the bolts and opened their gates undeterred, but the third was discovered by Kisanda and slain. The groom managed to warn Benkei just as the first eastern warriors entered the fort, only to be brought up sharply when they found their two opponents standing at the inner gate to the house itself. Yoshitsuné, nowhere in sight, must be in the mansion and the gate was the only way to approach it, isolated on the spur of the bluff.

Kajiwara stood in his stirrups and shouted, 'Lead us to the traitor, Minamoto Yoshitsuné! We come in the name of the Sacred Emperor and in the service of the Lord of Kamakura. In opposing us you blaspheme against the Throne of Heaven, the descendants of the Sun Goddess.'

Benkei bellowed back, 'Kajiwara Kagetoki has blasphemed against the Sacred Throne and the laws of Buddha and the will of the God Hachiman. We have nothing to fear from you. Come and fight Saito Masashibo Benkei if you are not afraid.'

303

'I will only fight Minamoto Yoshitsuné. Send the coward out!'

'First Kajiwara Kagetoki must pass Benkei.'

'Never!' Kajiwara turned to his lieutenant. 'Clear them out of the way!'

Benkei swiftly put an arrow to his bow and fired into the menacing samurai. The exceptionally long shaft, shot at such close range, skewered two men one behind the other. Kisanda also fired into the mob, killing another man, and then threw his bow away, useless as the advancing army narrowed the empty space. Benkei hissed, 'Hold them while I fire the gate.' He grabbed a torch and swung it over the wooden inner gateway, smeared with pine resin and bristling with dry brush. The brush caught immediately and in a second the gate was a flaming smoking rectangle.

'We will meet in heaven or hell, Kisanda. Occupy them while I warn the master.' He raced across the small garden into the house, running his torch over neat piles of brush and tinder as he went, leaving a wall of fire to protect the house.

The groom's sword flashed in the light, the fine lacquer of his new corselet glittered brilliantly and his voice, fierce with pride, rang out over the babble of the eastern warriors. 'This is Kisanda the groom, retainer of Minamoto Yoshitsuné, who challenges you, Kajiwara! Come and fight!'

'Samurai do not fight grooms.' Kajiwara gestured to his archers, who had moved up through the nervous horses, shuddering and prancing at the firelight. Bracing themselves in front of the uneasy animals, they drew their bows taut and released them with a shout. Kisanda, his proud corselet pierced with a score of arrows, threw up his arms and staggered back into the flames. Even in his terrible agony he knew that he must block the gate to his master's death room. Sinking slowly to his knees, the arrows alight, he blazed as a human torch, barring the only way into the mansion. His new sword, white hot, fell back beside him, unused.

*

Benkei found Yoshitsuné sitting in shadow. Hidehira's dagger in his right hand caught and held the lantern light, glowing from his palm like a shaft of molten gold. His left hand was opening the white kimono.

Their eyes met across the void; Yoshitsuné spoke in a soft hoarse voice, 'Motonari must know the time has come. He will bring them here. Farewell, my most loyal friend. I wish we could die together back to back, in battle, but Yoritomo has deprived me of that along with everything else.'

'You have only a short time, my lord, but the fire will hold them until I get back. Farewell. Until the next world.'

They stared at each other for a few seconds longer and then Benkei turned and left the room.

*

Motonari, hearing the fighting, seized the short sword and pushed open the sliding doors. Tamako stood before him holding a small limp body. Slowly she took the lifeless form of the baby Akiko away from her blood-stained bosom and held it out to the old man. She went to the pallet where her son lay. A harsh sob tore her throat as she turned the sleeping child over and closed his relaxed fingers over the rosary. She touched the beads of the rosary and then with one swift slash of her dagger she cut his soft exposed throat and slumped back on the floor half-fainting. Motonari lifted the second small corpse and hurried towards the main hall.

The sharp stench of burning cedar brought Tamako to her senses. Motonari and her children had gone and the hilt of the dagger lay on her palm, cool, smooth, comforting. Slowly she curled her fingers around the beautiful cylinder so that only the thin, stained, crimson blade showed. She placed her left hand on her throat, feeling for the place where the blood pulsed. Throwing her head back, she drove the blade into her throat as the cry of 'Amida' burst into the silent room. When Motonari came to bear her to her husband she was dead.

*

305

Yoshitsuné stared after Benkei's large form as it was swallowed up in the gloom, his left hand automatically resuming the unbinding and opening of his kimono. His fingers rested on the smooth hard flesh of his belly, warm and vibrating with life. But he was ready now. For a few minutes the shouts of the samurai, the clash of steel on steel had distracted him, broken into his long concentration on death. The temptation for a last battle was strong, to die crowded and jostled in action rather than seated alone on a straw mat in a dim room. But the desire was brief. His karma was set and he must be swept away to his next life; the irrevocable end of a samurai comforted him.

Suddenly he realised he was stroking the superb dagger – so light, clean and sharp. The perfect balance between the hilt and the blade gave him, for the first time, a pleasure almost sensual. His revulsion and fear vanished and he was overwhelmed by love for Hidehira and his present. Already warmth from the fire caressed his bare skin, the scent of cedar burning and the soft lantern glow reassured his senses. This world was good. And the next one?

With his index finger he ran down his ribs from his left breast to the place where the cage of bone stopped and the vitals were unprotected. The dagger point rested against his flesh. He slammed the heel of his right hand against the pommel. The blade slid in – a moment of wonder at such agony – and then – hurling himself into the pain – he dragged the dagger slowly across his belly. It was hard work and took what seemed to be a very long time. The resistance of muscle and intestine surprised him. His nerves shrieked with the torment and an attack of nausea seized him, throwing him off balance. He reached out with his hand and clutched at the Hachiman sword swimming dizzily just within reach. The sword, shaken from its cradle, clattered on to the polished wood but he managed to steady himself by grasping the stand. He rested a few minutes and then gripping the hilt of the dagger he drove it further into the slash in his abdomen, into a more hideous agony. The dagger fell from his fingers into a deep pit of darkness.

Yoshitsuné slumped after Hidehira's beautiful blade.

A sudden movement, the slither of moving silk and the brush of a hand against his. From a nebula of pain he accepted the presence of Tamako and the children, motionless, unresponsive, uncomforting.

Disembodied hands straightened his heavy limbs. Motonari's voice, from a thousand aeons away, drifted past his dreams. 'Amida Buddha, Amida Buddha.'

The bottom of the pit fell away and he slipped into an endless frozen universe.

*

By the time Benkei returned to the gateway the thatch of the mansion was ablaze and the gate was a huge column of flame and smoke, Kisanda a heap of lacquer and steel in the centre. Beyond the gate Benkei could hear the terrified cries of horses and the shouts of the samurai as they struggled to control them. Benkei grinned—the fire had been a good idea.

With a scream, raised from his very bowels, he leapt through the blazing gateway into the courtyard, a giant facing the milling crowd of horses and men. He stood with his mighty legs spread wide, a towering bull of a man, swinging his sword with both hands over his head. 'Come, you Kamakura lackeys! Scum of scum! Grovelling worms! Fight Saito Masashibo Benkei and when you are dead perhaps your cowardly leader will step forward and dare to take his turn.'

With a great whoop he charged into the struggling mass of warriors, slashing, jabbing, bellowing. Mounted on his warhorse, Kajiwara watched with awe and anticipation for the huge man to fall, but the brilliant blade cut a garish path through flesh and gristle and bone, driving back the startled swordsmen. Behind them, the mansion exploded into a fierce inferno.

Now Benkei stood alone before the gate, blood oozing from a hundred wounds, facing a semi-circle of samurai who glared from just beyond the reach of the Rock Cleaver sword. Illuminated by the leaping flames, Benkei drove the

hilt of his sword into the earth. In a voice hoarse with pain, dust and triumph he roared, 'Now Kajiwara Kagetoki, come and take Minamoto Yoshitsuné! Benkei is waiting to lead you to him.'

As he finished speaking he fell forward on to his sword blade, and his soul joined with his master's.

Benkei's huge form, supported by the solid strength of the Rock Cleaver, still stood in the gateway. The jagged fierce light of the blazing house threw his shadow unsteadily across the samurai faces. His corpse remained a ferocious barrier between the warriors and the house.

Kajiwara forced his skittering horse through the uneasy crowd. He drew his sword and rode towards the guardian monk. The horse, unhappy in the flickering firelight, pawed the ground nervously, side-stepped and suddenly reared up with a mighty whinny and thundered its hooves down on the hard earth. Benkei's form jerked violently and pitched sideways. The Rock Cleaver sword clanged down beside the corpse.

The men from Kamakura charged through the gateway and into the flaming house. The first across the veranda stumbled over the lifeless bundle that had been Motonari, a loyal, well-trained samurai and faithful retainer.

EPILOGUE

Yoshitsuné's was the only body recovered from the fire; his head was cut off and carried to Kamakura in a makeshift preservative of sweet saké, but when Yoritomo opened the black lacquer box he could not recognise the features of his younger brother. The spring had been unseasonably hot and the Lord of Kamakura's long-awaited prize had decomposed.

In the early summer of 1189 a large Kamakura army marched on Hiraizumi, and Yasuhira, as predicted, crumbled before the strength of the eastern samurai. Within ninety days Yoritomo controlled the rich, once invincible province of Oshu. Yasuhira paid for his misjudgement with his life; he was assassinated by one of his own household, a spy in the pay of the samurai-dokoro.

The Cloistered Emperor lived on for another two years, but immediately after he succumbed to disease and old age Go-Toba, the young Emperor, gave Yoritomo the title of Shogun. This honour did not decrease Yoritomo's jealousy and suspicion. He chose to accept accusations of treason made against Noriyori by Lord Kajiwara and although the charges remained unsubstantiated Noriyori was exiled to Izu where in 1193 he was forced to commit suicide.

In 1199, riding home from a religious ceremony, Yoritomo suffered a bad fall from his horse and died a few days later at the age of fifty-two. Kajiwara Kagetoki did not survive him long. Detested by the members of the samurai-dokoro, he was hunted down and murdered by a group of unidentified warriors. The chronicles note, however, that his old enemy, Lord Miura, was in the district.

Although the samurai-dokoro retained power over the land, the Shogunate itself fell on confused times. Hojo Tokimasa was appointed regent for Yoritomo's two young

sons, but a struggle for power developed between To-kimasa and his strong-willed daughter, Lady Masako. The two sons were assassinated, perhaps by Masako, their mother, or perhaps by Masako's step-mother. The succeeding Shoguns were children, puppets of the ambitious and efficient Hojo family, repeating the pattern of the young Emperors and the Fujiwara regents.

But even without a strong Shogun, samurai government, as established by Yoritomo, continued to flourish away from the influence of the effete Court. The samurai chieftains were now the major landowners and overseas traders, and from the samurai-dokoro they controlled Japan in the name of weak Shoguns and weaker emperors until 1873 when, after protracted civil war, the Emperor Meiji abolished the samurai class. But the philosophy and standards of the samurai were firmly entrenched as spiritual and ascetic ideals. Duty and loyalty, the virtues Yoritomo preached and demanded that others practise, were the basis of Japanese society, and the vigour of the samurai code, supplemented in the thirteenth century by the Zen school of Buddhism, affected every aspect of life – moral, cultural, artistic, military and religious, from Yoritomo's time until the end of the Second World War.